# Command the Raven

M.J. LOGUE

ISBN: 1519145691
ISBN-13: 978-1519145697

# DEDICATION

My thanks go to my boys, both the big one and the little one, for plot development, artillery titbits, and reading "The Furie of the Ordinance" when I really couldn't bring myself to. And for practising duelling in the garden all summer, not to mention seventeenth-century drill.

To my technical advisers (who know who they are) without whom this book would not, in a very real and practical sense, exist.

To my friends in the Wardour Garrison, who know what I am, and don't protest too much when I channel my inner Ironside over the embroidery.

Tam, Pixie and Geoff, Alan, and Antonia, for random canine company, clothing inspiration, friendship, silliness, and generally kicking me up the bum periodically. See? I do listen!

And last but not least, this book is for my dad and the Wascally Woyalist, both of whom died before it was completed, and both of whom would have been so very proud to see it in print.

# ACKNOWLEDGMENTS

…And other random stuff, on a need-to-know basis. The Battle of Edgehill, in October 1642, was the first major engagement of the English Civil War. And nobody won the day, which sort of set the bar for the general confusion of the next few months. After a few minor skirmishes, the Army of Parliament withdrew to their winter quarters in Windsor, and the King and his troops scuttled back to Oxford.

As you may have deduced, I am no Royalist supporter. In fact, I started writing the Babbitt novels some years ago because I was fascinated by the English Civil War and bored with the stereotype of dashing Cavaliers and dour Roundheads. The arrival of Oliver Cromwell towards the *end* of this tale is not due to any oversight on my part. At the beginning of the wars, the Royalist Army's commander-in-chief was, predictably enough, the King, and the Army of Parliament was commanded by the Earl of Essex, Robert Devereux. A man who possibly doesn't feature in my books as much as he ought to - a rather tragic figure, I think, whose personal life was something of a train wreck, and who history has almost completely passed over in favour of the much more charismatic Cromwell. Popular history also seems to have overlooked the lovely Black Tom Fairfax, too: a decent, honourable, somewhat sombre individual and far too modest for his own good. Essex - who, to be fair, was not blessed with a great deal of success during his period in charge of the Army - was succeeded in command by Thomas Fairfax, but people only ever seem to remember Cromwell! In fact the real significance of the very minor battle at Winceby, around which campaign this book is based, is that Black Tom Fairfax and Noll Cromwell fought together for the first time - a marriage made, you might say, in a very hot place indeed….

The Yorkshire campaign sounds like it might have

been enormous - and unprofessional - fun. Black Tom did in fact have his wife and his young daughter accompanying him on campaign, and Lady Anne really was briefly taken prisoner of war by the Earl of Newcastle. (Little Moll, if you were wondering, grew up happy, healthy and so far as anyone can tell unscarred by her wartime experiences, to marry the Duke of Buckingham.) Fairfax's troops did also engage in what are tactfully described as "raiding parties" from their forward post at Beverley. It's not an enormous leap of imagination to think that a group of like-minded young men with time on their hands and a long hot summer to fill, might have had a high old time tweaking the tail of the Earl of Newcastle for the sheer joyous mischief of it.

Finally, there are a number of appalling misconceptions about the Parliamentarians. They didn't all have short hair. Some of them even went for the elegant pointy moustache and Van Dyke beard look, and are indistinguishable in portraits from what we think of as "Cavaliers". They were almost as prone to writing poetry as the Royalists. Cromwell and his "Lovely Company" had a collective sense of humour apparently bordering on the slapstick, if contemporary reports involving Old Noll and a bucket of cream are to be believed. (I'd have paid money to see that.) There was also sufficient swearing in the ranks for it to be punishable by a fine under Cromwell's later command. Many of the surviving letters from the field show loving and devoted husbands, sons and friends - not miserable psalm-singing Cropheads, or poetic Cavaliers, but warm, human men, concerned with the little wenches at home and being told off by their wives for not writing often enough.

I hope you enjoy reading the Babbitt books as much as I enjoy writing them – and I hope they inspire you, a little bit, to think about the history of this period 'by the sword divided'.

And, I hope, to form your own opinions....

# 1 WINTER QUARTERS

*Windsor, March 1643*

The King and his Parliament had been at each other's throats for the best part of six months now with neither side having gained much advantage over the other, and Captain Holofernes Babbitt, commander of one somewhat ragged troop of Parliamentarian cavalry, still wasn't much the wiser as to what the hell it was all about.

It was different for Hollie, mind. He'd run off to be a soldier aged fifteen, anything being better than stopping at home in Lancashire being battered to within an inch of his life by his ever-loving father. Being big, somewhat unpredictable, and having had reflexes like a damn' cat beaten into him, it had turned out to be the best thing he could have done. He'd made a name for himself over a twenty-year mercenary career in Europe as either a daring, inventive and independent commander in the field - or as an ungovernable rebel: you paid your money, you took your choice. In his case, the Army of Parliament had been sufficiently impressed by his reputation to have offered him riches beyond avarice to cross the Channel again last year and fight for a cause he knew nothing and cared less about. (They'd lied about the wealth beyond the dreams of avarice bit, but then as he'd somewhat exaggerated his interest in their Cause at the time, that probably made them about equal.)

No, he'd been in this since the beginning, since the first engagement at Powick Bridge in Worcestershire last September, which he'd cocked up, having been working on the naïve principle that this was England and they didn't know how to have proper wars in England. Well, they did. Maybe not as grim and devastating as his own training-ground, the Thirty Years' War in Europe - he'd fought on both sides there and he'd rather put a pistol ball in his head than go through that again – but war it was. And it hadn't stopped bloody raining since he'd set foot back on English soil. When they'd approached him to fight for Parliament they'd made it sound so damnably civilised. A picture of a lush and placid England, where the sun always shone, and a virgin could walk the length of the country naked carrying a bag of gold and remain unmolested, all being threatened by the evil, grasping, rapacious figure of King Charles and his midget French queen. Looking out at the wet, grey, shabby back street in Windsor where the troop were presently quartered, it was difficult to think he'd actually been daft enough to fall for that one.

He had a forlorn hope that one of these days one of the more idealistic young men who swarmed round the Parliamentarian cause like flies round – well, anyway – were going to ask him what attracted him to their cause. Depending how pissed off he was feeling with the whole enterprise, he might just tell them, too. If you asked Hollie's most junior officer what he fought for, the chances were that Luce – as was short for Lucifer, poor bugger – would put a hand to his well-polished breastplate and roll his eyes to heaven and declare that in all conscience he could not allow the King to ride roughshod over the legitimate claims of democracy for a second longer. Luce was handsome, well-bred, well-educated, comfortably placed, romantic, earnest, and an absolute bloody pain in the arse at times. Hollie was very fond of the lad, when he wasn't being tempted to throttle him.

Calthorpe, the regimental Dissenter, would tell you that he fought in defence of the Church of England against the threat of Papist idolatry, as represented by the evil King and his distinctly dodgy French wife – Catholics, the whole boiling lot of 'em, as well as French, and therefore the next step removed from AntiChrist. Calthorpe's beliefs were independent, to say the least, that most upright and godly of men being a member of an obscure religious sect known as the Grindletonians. Hollie had known the man twenty years and he still wasn't sure of the finer points of Grindletonian theology, except that it originated in an even more benighted backwater of Lancashire than his own home turf and seemed to hinge around the typically Lancastrian thinking that preachers were nowt special and anyone who had a mind to could stand up and have a crack at it.

And as far as Hollie was concerned, this war was something to do with money, and something to do with liberty, and a lot to do with two lots of privileged buggers wanting their own way and both determined not to give an inch. It happened to be Parliament who paid him, but he wasn't ruling anything out - it was early days, yet. Hollie might have a reputation for intemperacy, but he wasn't anywhere near as daft as he let on to being. Nor was he as ignorant as he liked to make out. He might have given up any pretence at aping his father's dour Puritan ways when the old bastard had finally beat him senseless for the last time, but he liked to do the odd bit of reading here and there, just to see what people were saying. His father would be taken quite aback to know that Hollie was currently working his way through a pamphlet of Bridge's Puritan sermons – and less taken aback to know that that dog-eared copy of "Babylon's Downfall" was rubbing pages in the bottom of his scapegrace son's snapsack with a copy of radical John Lilburne's writings, published only the other year whilst that most radical of political activists was languishing in the Fleet jail.

Not that Hollie's tastes in subversive literature were much comfort to him, on yet another grey and miserable drizzling day in the Parliamentarian Army's winter quarters at Windsor. Most of the troop cooped up indoors getting under each other's feet – horses patched and tetchy with rain-scald, troopers curt and perpetually damp, too cold and too wet to drill, too mild to snow. Their quarters grew progressively more squalid, with a perpetual aroma of stale sweat and wet leather and Sergeant Cullis's socks, and Hollie had had furious words with his troop sergeant on his habit of hogging the kitchen fire with his rotten stockinged feet on the hearthstone, which had culminated in Cullis threatening to clip his commanding officer round the earhole and Hollie tipping his sergeant's chair over backwards with the sergeant still in it, to the detriment of the dignity of both. They still weren't on proper speaking terms.

He thought he would have been happier with the planning and decisions of the commander-in-chief of the Army of Parliament, if he'd ever had a clue what was going on in the bugger's head. A man he cordially despised, incidentally – but that was fine, because despite having gone to great pains to recruit Hollie from a successful mercenary career in the Low Countries, the Earl of Essex had rapidly come to the conclusion that Hollie was a surly Northern gobshite and not worth passing the time of day with. Doubtless Essex had some long-term strategic point of view for the war, but whatever it was, he wasn't sharing. As far as Hollie was concerned, he'd spent most of his time to date sat about various benighted backwaters for weeks on end staring into space, until some squeaking overbred whelp came bounding in expecting him to have eighty men and a hundred-ish horses tacked up and ready by this time yesterday.

Disillusioned, Captain Babbitt? Never illusioned much in the bloody first place. Sick of days of silence and inactivity, while Essex left his officers racketing round Windsor, bumping about like bees in a bottle, even though Luce Pettitt was Essex's nephew by marriage, and might thus be expected to get a sniff of the gossip. Gossip said Essex was a slow, deliberate, dilatory, over-cautious son of a bitch and for once gossip wasn't wrong. It was not best calculated to soothe the recently-ruffled nerves of this particular officer, and it wasn't doing his temper any good at all to see smug, shiny messengers careering in and out of the town all full of dispatches and self-importance, with nary a word of import shared with them as did the actual fighting.

And, if he was being honest with himself, the lack of word from the county of Essex, from whence he was most recently returned, wasn't improving his temper any. He'd spent six weeks convalescing on a farm in rural White Notley, near Colchester, at the turn of the year, half-mad and slightly broken after that first great battle at Edgehill. It had mended more of him than he'd imagined stood in want of mending, too. There had been a Mistress Babbitt, a long time ago. He'd been seventeen, and she'd been more than twice that. She'd died - after ten years of unlikely happiness - and he'd not looked at a girl since till now. Six weeks of the wholesome company of Mistress Henrietta Sutcliffe, plump and comfortable and freckled as an egg, and now he couldn't think of anything else. And the chances were that Mistress Sutcliffe looked on him as nothing other than some chance-met scruffy acquaintance of her beloved baby nephew, who just happened to be Lucifer bloody Pettitt. (Luce wasn't related to everyone in Essex, although it did seem that way at times.) He'd written to her. Once, to thank her for her care. She'd never replied.

He'd gone – ha! He'd been packed off – to White Notley because he was neither use nor bloody ornament after Edgehill. He'd lost the only friend he'd ever had in that bloody battle, killed in the cross-current of Prince Rupert's first wild cavalry charge. Hadn't cared for Rupert before that, and now it was an active loathing. He hadn't planned to come off the field alive, and he'd almost managed it. If it hadn't been for Luce flaming Pettitt he wouldn't still be here. It was easier to rejoin the world than have Luce prodding him from day's end to day's end. The brat's coup de resistance was to have him dispatched, like so much unwanted baggage – without his foreknowledge or consent, damn it - to be mollycoddled back to health on his aunt's farm. Hollie had thought, like a fool, that anyone known as Auntie Het had to be some plump, rosy, bustling goodwife, with a plump, jovial, plain-speaking husband. He'd braced himself accordingly.

What he'd got was probably wasn't pretty in the world's eyes but then Hollie had conspicuously odd tastes in women. A pretty face, fine eyes, golden curls – he could take or leave. Put him in the same place as a fine sturdy lass, a lass with some wit, especially if she had a backside like a draught horse and a generous hand with cake – oh, leave him there for more than a matter of days and he'd go down like an undermined wall. Spent probably some of the happiest weeks of his life at Fox Barton, just about the only man on the farm under the age of Methuselah since every other bugger had enlisted in the Army of Parliament, picking up all the dirty jobs. Being bloody useful, which was more than he'd felt like for some time as a commanding officer. She'd given him back a place in the world, and in giving him that, she'd given him back his ability to command a troop.

He wasn't on his own, mind, in this wretched state of romantic uncertainty, though he hoped he was keeping it better hid than Luce. The brat – and Hollie could never think of him as anything other than the brat, or Lucey, given that the lad was both regrettably pretty and depressingly youthful – had used his time immediately after Edgehill wisely, by losing his innocence to the widow they'd been quartered with while Hollie was too sick to travel. Luce was heading perilously close to a thorough-going pasting at the moment, being both sullen-mute and touchy at one and the same time. He never got any letters either, other than the ones from his lady mother, and it was pitiful to see the lad's face light up when someone mentioned that he had some correspondence. And then absolute hell to live with him for the rest of the day when he realized it wasn't from his erstwhile girl up at Edgehill, if you could describe a widow who'd been forty if she was a day as anyone's girl. Luce was assuming, of course, that the widow could both read and write, which assumption was more than Hollie would have made in his place, and that she was still interested. Had been interested in the first place, in anything other than a bit of posh leg-over. He had every sympathy with the young cornet, but by God Hollie didn't think he was making people's lives a waking misery by skulking round Windsor with a face like a slapped backside.

Any more so than usual, anyway.

"Pettitt."

The brat's head came up, and he glowered at Hollie across the table. Hollie's hand itched to give him a slap on account, and he restrained himself with some effort.

"What?" Luce growled – caught the glint in his commanding officer's eye – "Sir."

"Pettitt, you're starting to bore me."

"Well, I apologise for being so dull, Captain Babbitt. I will relieve you of my presence with immediate effect." He stood up, nose in the air, and headed for the door.

"You're boring everybody else, too, Pettitt. Sit down. Me and you need to have words." Luce stiffened, bristling in all directions, and Hollie was that far from kicking the feet out from underneath him. "And straighten your bloody face, lad. You're trailing round like a wet weekend."

Luce gave him a dirty look and then glanced ostentatiously out of the window. "I feel like a wet weekend. Sir. It's been raining, so far as I can tell, since –"

"What you will feel, Lucifer, is my toe up your arse, shortly, if you don't stop maundering on and sit down. Now." Luce sat. The chair creaked in protest. Hollie nudged a teetering pile of papers with his elbow, pausing briefly to glare at the ones that fell on the floor, being, so far as he could tell, three requisition notes, a list of pay still outstanding, and half a poem, and glared at the lad instead. "Any chance you can poke your benighted uncle and find out if we're likely to shift in the not too distant?"

"No," Luce snapped back, without so much as a heartbeat's consideration. "I'm not your personal spy, sir."

"Fine. So you're happy for us to sit here twiddling our thumbs while he does all the politicking on our behalf, are you?"

"My uncle is the Army's Commander, captain, and in him resides my sole trust."

"That's not what you said after Edgehill, brat. You reckoned he'd stitched us up properly. Providing Edgehill's not a dirty word in this house at the moment. Oh, for Christ's sake, Lucey! I'm not asking you to pass on state secrets. To be honest, I don't care if he's entering into negotiations with the Cham of bloody Cathay. I would like to get paid before the twelfth of never, which is something my lord seems to be remarkably remiss in, of late, and I would quite like to know if there's like to be a sniff of action any time soon, before the lot of us turn our swords into ploughshares."

"Well, I don't know!"

"Well, I suggest you might be better placed to find out than me!"

"And if you were any kind of an officer, Captain Babbitt –"

"If I was any kind of an officer, boy, I'd have had you bloody cashiered by now! He's not like to tell me owt, as well you know –"

"And whose fault is that?" Luce demanded haughtily, and Hollie couldn't help but grin, reluctantly.

"Me and your uncle have never hit it off, and you know it. He's up to summat, Luce. You know that. I know that. He's not just sat up Peascod Street in that draughty big house writing rhyming couplets to His Majesty's fine eyes –" Hollie rested his foot consideringly on Luce's half-finished poem. Rhyming couplets to the Widow Hadfield's fine eyes, and well he knew it. "You going to do it, brat, or am I going to have to do summat more than usually stupid?"

"Why don't you ask your particular friend Venning, given that he's on my uncle's staff? I'm sure he is better placed to answer than I –"

"Oh, use your brains, boy, provided your lusty widow didn't –"

The lad was quick, give him that. Hollie found himself eyeing the unwavering barrel of Luce's pistol without ever having registered the brat having drawn it.

"You will take that back, captain." The brat's voice was shaking, but his hand wasn't.

Hollie was equally quick, after that first initial heartbeat of shock, and Luce found his doublet sleeve skewered to the table top by a quivering left-hand dagger and a bloody livid commanding officer two inches from the end of his insubordinate patrician nose.

"Don't you ever pull a fucking stupid stunt like that again," Hollie roared, at full battle order volume, to disguise the fact that he was shaking with relief that the lad hadn't pulled the trigger, and to relieve his ruffled feelings further, gave Luce a flat-handed clip round the ear with the full weight of his arm behind it. If he hadn't had the brat pinned to the table at the time it would have knocked him sideways. As it was, it rocked the lad in his seat and Hollie's dagger came loose with a tearing sound, and he wasn't sure if Luce was meaning to knife him between the ribs or if he was just scrabbling out of reflex but even so he grabbed hold of his cornet's wrist and wrenched with desperate fury till the lad's hand went limp in his grasp, the bones in his narrow wrist grinding together. "Pettitt, what the hell do you think you're doing?"

Luce tore himself free, gasping. Hollie's dagger had nicked his wrist. Little droplets of blood now spattered the paperwork. "I am tired of you, sir – absolutely tired of you –" the lad was shaking, and Hollie had the uncomfortable suspicion he was on the edge of tears. "I am sick to death of your contempt, your rudeness, your – your vicious habits, sir –"

"Bloody hell, Luce, that's a bit –"

"I am tired of your treating me as your pet intelligencer in my uncle's household when it suits you, sir! Tired of it! You have no manners, no consideration, no thought, no –" And with one last despairing wrench, the lad dropped his head onto his folded arms and wept. Leaving Hollie somewhat at a loss.

"Brat." Not helpful. "Er, Lucey. Luce." Awkwardly, he put a tentative hand on the brat's shoulder. No reaction. He fished his handkerchief out of a pocket and laid it on the table in front of the young officer.

"Captain Babbitt, that – object – is disgusting," Luce said shakily, lifting his head slightly.

Hollie sniffed. "I've only cleaned my carbine with it, brat. It's not that bad. Luce. It's fine. It's nearly clean. Lucifer. Oh, for – Cornet Pettitt. Speaking as your commanding officer. I'm sorry. I don't mean to be an arse, but it appears that in spite of my best attempts –"

"You're an arse?" Luce said, with a shaky laugh. "I'm sorry, sir. I don't know what I was thinking."

"You weren't. And neither was I, which is what comes of never being out of each other's sight for God knows how many weeks. Just don't make a habit of it, lad, Having put our troop sergeant on his arse not that long ago, I have a degree of sympathy with your sentiments. I'm pretty bloody sick of the lot o'you myself. I'm just not fed up enough to do owt about it."

"I'm sorry," the lad said again, forlornly. "I just –"

"Luce, stop going on about it. I'll be straight with you, lad. I'm fed up with the whole bloody thing. Thoroughly pig-sick of your uncle dicking about, sick of not knowing what the hell's going on from one minute to the next –" he made a disgusted noise between his teeth. "For two penn'orth, brat, if any bugger'd have me, I'd be off like a shot. But. Lucifer. Look at me."

Reluctantly, the young cornet raised his head. He looked somewhat unlovely, to be fair. He also looked exhausted, ill, and scruffy, at least one of which was uncharacteristic enough of the debonair Cornet Pettitt to be of concern. Hollie sighed. "I've made my apology, and I'll take yours, and that's all you'll get out of me on this head. I'll not mention it more. D'you want a drink, lad?"

# 2 ALARUMS AND EXCURSIONS

Because Hollie, with his hands still shaking with relief, would have killed for one. He truly didn't bear the lad any malice, believe it or not. It always ailed men at winter quarters, mewed up inactive all on top of each other and getting more and more on each other's nerves, and there was damn-all point getting het up about it, or you'd have most of your troop on punishment duties before you could turn round. His best mate had broken his nose for him, in a very similar incident to this one, twenty years ago. You got like that, when you were all fired up to be on and fighting, and instead you were perpetually cold and damp and ill-fed and bored to tears while some dilatory bugger in authority pushed papers round his desk. "Lucey. Drink."

"Yes," Luce said, and blew his nose noisily. And then. "Captain, what is *that*?"

That, being Mistress Sutcliffe's tried and tested remedy for colds. She'd packed him off with assorted nostrums and medicaments, which he thought had to be a hopeful sign, in more optimistic moments. And it was effective stuff, in Hollie's experience -or at least, he thought it was, though his memory of the occasion was hazy. Her patent remedy was a smooth, spiced elderberry syrup, based on - "Mostly brandy," Hollie said, mostly truthfully.

Given that none of the Army had been paid since Candlemas, the nearest he had on hand to hard liquor was medicinal. Jesus, that was a sad state of affairs. There was one glass intact in the little cubbyhole they dignified as the troop's administrative quarters, and after he'd surreptitiously fished the remains of a dead spider out of the bottom of it, Hollie filled it and handed it to his cornet. The room was too dark to see the scum of dust on top of the deep red liquor. Luce sipped it, looking suspicious. Hollie, being as rough as rats in company, necked his out of the bottle without a shudder.

It was going dark. "Poke the fire up, there's a good lad."

"Rather poke Sarah Hadfield," Luce slurred mutinously, and Hollie groaned and poured him another glass. Some fool had been stupid enough to leave a bottle of wine in the kitchen, too, lying on its side under the settle by the fire. Lukewarm and tasted like horse piss, but slightly less medicinal than Het's – than Mistress Sutcliffe's - remedy. And it was more or less alcoholic, and further than that, who cared?

"Oh, give it a rest, brat!"

"'S all right for you!"

"Me? Hardly, lad - not all right for me. Never been all right for me, Luce. Never has, never will -"

"Got your feet well under Auntie Het's table, you have - "

"Hey! Thass - that'sh - that's not fair, Luce." Hollie straightened up with an effort. "'Not like that with me and Het. Mish- Mistress – ah, fuck it -" he gave it up, "- Het. By God I would, though, if she'd have me. Never looked at me twice, lad."

"Bollocks," Luce said firmly, and Hollie was startled into giggles. "Bollocks," the brat said again. "She fancies the arse off you."

"Lucifer, that's – that's enough!"

"Wha'? 'Nough of my aunt making a fool of herself over some, some –" some fuddled instinct for self-preservation was evidently beginning to filter through the alcoholic fumes, because Luce gave a sheepish grin and shut up.

"She's not interested in me, lad. What the hell would she do with some rag-arsed old veteran like me?" Hollie leaned his head back against the damp plaster of the wall with a thump, eyes closed. "Too old, no' pretty enough, too scruffy, got no manners –"

"Ah-ah. You're forgetting, captain. One, you're an oshifer."

"I'm a wha' – oh. I'm in charge."

"All the girls like an – well, 'cept mine. My girl don't like oshifers, Captain Babbitt. Or not this one, anyway. Not this one." He tapped himself, in the chest. "You think if I jack it in, she'll have me?"

Hollie shook his head mournfully, still with his eyes closed. "Don't reckon as she would, Luce. Better off without her, if you ask me. Don't know what she's missing. Nice lad like you. And – and - " he waved his hand vaguely, "- flat as a board, she was. Nowt to get hold of. Bloody skinny wench. What you want, young man – tell you what it is you want /"

"The thing with my Auntie Het," Luce changed the subject grimly. "She's a widow -"

"Like yours. How funny is that. Must have a thing about widows, me and you."

"Auntie Het's always been a widow. Can't 'member her ever having had a man. Poor old thing, she must be in want of a husband badly. Hey - you could be Auntie Het's man." He squinted warily at Hollie. "Everything works, don't it?"

"All in good order last time, owd lad, but that was a while back. Prob'ly before you was born, Lucey. Bloody hell. Must be – Christ, must be ten years since I had a girl. Thass a hell of a long time, Luce. I might be in want of practice."

"You ain't practising on my auntie unless you marry her, you drunken lecher," Luce said, wagging his finger in Hollie's vague direction. Hollie stood up.

"Then thass what I'll do. Right now. Right this minute. I'll go over t'White Notley and I'll say – what will I say, Luce – I have it, I'll say Mish – Mistress – ah, fuck it – Het, thass what I'll say, Het, it's a bloody long way from Windsor – now where you goin' to, brat?"

"Going to be sick," Luce said, and was, noisily - mercifully, Hollie got the window open in time, and left the lad slumped across the sill taking in great gulps of air, whimpering.

"Hollie," he said plaintively, "Hollie, I don't feel well."

"Gardy loo," Hollie said sardonically. Put his hat on. Turned to go out. Walked into the door, and collapsed against the wall rubbing the meat of his arm where he'd impaled himself on the latch, and swearing in several languages.

"Where you going, Hollie?"

"See if your Auntie Het wants to make an honest man of me."

The damp, chilly night air didn't clear his head in the slightest bit. A couple of Windsor's brave young bloods brayed and yapped down the cobbles towards him, spurs jingling on the slick cobbles, and he tipped his hat to them with his best bravo grin, and they were suddenly very quiet, scampering away like little mice. "Missish lil' bastards," he said, just loud enough for them to hear. "Not even man enough to – to – ah, fuck it. Let it go." Because without Rackhay, without his old sidekick, there wasn't anybody to tell him to leave quarrels alone. Luce wouldn't. Might drop some tactful hint, like – my lord Essex wouldn't like it, to which Hollie was likely at the moment to say, balls to my lord Essex and if he's hard enough he can come and tell me to my face. Het wouldn't like it. Now that'd work. Mustn't get sidetracked. Long old ride to White Notley, in the dark.

He found himself on Peascod Street, standing in the middle of the road and staring stupidly up at the elegant houses. "Thass how the other half live," he said aloud. Briefly tempted to go and knock up the Earl of Essex and tell that gormless, dilatory, overbred arse exactly what he thought of him. Before he had chance to do any such thing, Drew Venning ambled out of the shadows, relieved for the evening from his duties as the most disorderly orderly in the household of the Earl of Essex. Venning had been another unexpected ally, after Edgehill. Hollie wasn't sure if he'd call the freckled, square, unremarkable young man from Norfolk a friend, yet, but – an ally.

"Out late, bor? Just on my way round yours –" he held up a bottle of wine that he'd had tucked under his cloak, then sniffed, and a grin spread over his freckled face. "But I do reckon someone's beat me to it. Captain Babbitt, have you been drinking?"

"Oh, Christ, yes," Hollie said cheerfully. "You come to wish me happy, Drew?"

"You what?"

"On my way out to my girl. Going to ash – ask her to marry me, that's what I'm going to do. 'S not regular way of goin' about things, but she's got nobody else to ask – well, I asked Luce, and he said 'salright, and she's his auntie, so –"

"Whoa. Back up. You're going to – what girl? I didn't know you had a girl!"

"Neither did I," he said with dignity. "You know Het. Lucey's auntie Het. Lovely girl – " he considered this – "lovely arse on her. She's – she's just lovely. Bet she's nicer to share quarters with than her nephew, an' all. He bloody snores."

Drew blinked. Hollie drew himself up to his full height. "Bet you think it's funny, don't you? Me – right scruffy bastard, me. And she's all nice and lovely and – and - *nice*. You reckon she'd come back wi' me? Kick Luce out – *you* can put up with his bloody snoring –"

The big redhead looked so wistful, smiling up at the moon, that it was almost a shame to tell him to mind the missing cobble – so Drew didn't, and let him go staggering into the gutter. "And you're going to turn up on her doorstep tonight, like that –" unshaven, uncombed, stinking of spirits, and roaring drunk, though of course Drew was too polite to say so – "and, er, Hollie, you think this is a good idea?"

"Luce thinks so."

"And Luce is where?"

"Passed out on my bed, last I saw. 'S all right, though,

Drew, I'll move him before she gets in," Hollie said earnestly, and Drew snorted.

"Gets better, lad. Who says the age of romance is dead?" He gripped Hollie by the elbow and turned him about. "See, thing is, bor, wish I could let you go, but – you can't. That's what I was on my way round for. Give you a bit of a heads-up, see. All gone tits-up with His Majesty, and Essex is after his arse. We're marching on Reading – as fast as go can we. So no, you can't go hiving off to get your belly rubbed tonight, big lad. You've got to stop here and get them ruffians o' yours into fighting order."

"Fuck. Me," Hollie breathed, suddenly sober.

"She prob'ly will, bor, but not tonight."

# 3 KEEPING BAD COMPANY

Sometimes, when he'd been considerably younger, Hollie used to lie awake and imagine what his life would be like if things had been different.

He'd never lost the habit, and for a while after Edgehill he'd sit by the window upstairs staring at the street and obsessively trying to imagine what it was like to be Luce Pettitt. Born pretty and spoiled rotten – that would be a good start. Pampered and beloved, with a full set of normal parents, and a rat's nest of sisters and assorted friends and relations. Trying to hate the lad for being what he was, which was just about everything Hollie wasn't, and failing miserably because the little bugger was impossible to dislike. He liked the brat considerably better lately, since the Widow Hadfield had singularly failed to fall into his elegant patrician arms. Luce claimed he'd never look at another woman. Which was funny, because Hollie had caught him looking quite a lot, at several. Was too polite to mention, of course, but would occasionally raise a sardonic eyebrow when the brat's poetic sighing got too distracting.

And then last night the little bugger had blindsided him with that casual remark about whether or not Mistress Sutcliffe – see, sober he was perfectly capable of thinking about her in a cool and respectful manner – whether or not she -. Well, the lad had implied that she did. Would. And now Hollie had to stand here in this benighted hole in Peascod Street, listening to Essex banging on about breakdowns in negotiations and the Lord's will, at excruciating length. He must have been looking glazed because Henry Ireton was giving him a very odd look from across the room, the only one of Essex's personal lifeguard not to be paying rapt attention to their commander. Hollie wasn't thinking much about his orders, although he really was trying to concentrate his wandering attention on the serious task of laying siege to the innocent town of

Reading – he gave a shiver at the thought, and one of the older officers at his elbow glanced up. "Cold, young man?"

"Bit of a draught from the window," he said.

Essex gave him a narrow stare. Evidently the mutterings from the back of the room were distracting. "We march on the King's headquarters at Oxford," he said grimly. "Prepare your men to march with immediate despatch, for the garrison at Reading is all that stands between us."

There was a grim, martial muttering of agreement and approval, the officers nodding and scowling and stroking moustaches as everyone tried to look as if they'd thought of nothing since Christmas but smiting the heathen hip and thigh.

"Cake," Drew Venning announced into the muttering, and Hollie snorted rather louder than he'd meant to – lad was all bloody class – and Essex glared at them both in turn. "My lords," Venning amended hastily. "And some o' you lot might have to share glasses, but it be all right if you give 'en a wipe with your sleeve –"

"Master Venning, kindly comport yourself with the dignity of an officer, and –"

"Let the lad be, sir," Ireton said. "For myself, I should rather have a plain-spoken man who knows his business, than –"

"And you've been knocking about with that bloody Noll Cromwell again, haven't you?" his colleague, the blunt Yorkshireman Matthew Tomlinson, said fondly. "By, lad, you don't want to start picking up his bad habits."

"For myself, I've got a troop to ready, so with your leave, gentlemen," Hollie said into the good-humoured hubbub, and one or two people groaned and there was even a sarcastic cheer from some wag by the fireplace. There was a sudden air of holiday in the room, an air of relief and of half a hundred hounds slipped the leash to be about their hunting.

Essex's expression was priceless. "Your dedication to

your duty is commendable, Captain Babbitt." And wholly unbelievable, the twitch of his eyebrows said silently.

Hollie bowed. "Ever your obedient, my lord," he said, without specifying what nature of obedient he might be, and with as much sincerity as his commander. Venning materialised at his elbow. "You're up to suffen, bor," he said without moving his lips.

"Getting out of here before I punch him in the head," Hollie said out of the corner of his mouth, smiling brightly at the assemblage and backing towards the door.

"That be why you've had a silly grin on your face all morning, then?"

"Tell you later." Essex finally gave him a curt nod of dismissal and that was it, he was free to go. Free, thank God, to drop the cool, polite, clipped officer's accents that were bloody hard work for a North Countryman by birth - aye, and he knew broad Fenland Venning struggled the same way, to mind his tongue in company. Hollie only talked broad with them as he liked. So, he reckoned, did Venning.

Venning looked blank, and then comprehension dawned. "You are, ent you?"

"Don't know what you mean," Hollie said; blushed, scarlet, to the ears, felt himself doing it, and fled – routed, foot and horse.

He found himself whistling, on his way through the echoing rain-washed streets. Buying a pie for breakfast from the bakehouse two streets away from his quarters. Standing like a moonstruck idiot in the middle of the cobbles licking savoury crumbs from his fingers and thinking it wasn't a bad world, to have him and a hot mutton pie and Het Sutcliffe in it, all at one and the same time. If not in the same place. And passing by the baker's, going home with a loaf of new-baked bread under his arm thinking there was worse ways to wake up a hung-over cornet than bread and honey and possibly a hair of the dog what bit you

To his astonishment, the brat was up and about, pale and unsteady but with all his clothes on in the right order, collar straight, hair combed. He'd even shaved without cutting his throat, which, considering the amount of drink he'd put by last night, was an achievement. "Fresh air, breakfast, and warning orders," he said cheerfully to the lad, who gave him a bleary sidelong glance and swallowed.

"Without breakfast," Luce whispered, and Hollie laid the fresh bread on the table.

"Still warm, brat. You're missing a treat. Dip it in a bit o' honey, and –" He tore off a piece of crust and demonstrated. Luce turned even paler. "All right, all right, let's go and sit in t'yard, and see how you feel after you've got a few cobwebs blown off."

"I think my *head* might blow off."

Hollie held the kitchen door open. "Out." After Luce had puked – and Hollie hadn't laughed, much – the lad was sufficiently recovered to eye his commanding officer's breakfast, and since it was Hollie's second of the day he didn't mind sharing.

"So, then. What news?" the brat said, nibbling warily.

"All gone to rat-shit, brat. Whether due to the diplomatic skills of your Uncle Essex – sorry, Luce – or whether it's just because His Royal Majesty is a stiff-necked bastard who don't like being told what to do by the likes of us – anyway." Hollie sucked honey off his thumb with relish. Looked up to find the brat's eyes on him with an expression of horror. "What?"

"Nothing."

"Glad to hear it. Anyway. Uncle Essex, bless him, has got bored wi' talking – rest of us have been bored with him since December – so we're off to give his Majesty a kick up the arse."

"Indeed, captain. Is that quite how you received your orders?"

"Not in as many words, Lucifer, no, but that's what he meant."

“When?”

“Now."

“Now.” Luce raised his eyebrows. “Now as in this minute now, next week now, what?”

“Sort of between the two. You going to finish that last bit of honey or what?”

“Captain Babbitt, I am astonished you’re not as fat as a pig. Kindly be specific as to my direction.”

"Hollow legs, lad,” Hollie said indistinctly, and gave Luce a sticky and unexpectedly boyish grin. “Fill your boots, brat, for despite what your uncle seems to think, I’ve yet to come across a decently fortified garrison town that’s willing to just hand over the keys when we come knocking. No telling when we might next see a decent breakfast.”

# 4 A SMACK IN THE HEAD OFTEN OFFENDS

*Reading, April 1643*

The sky was just beginning to lighten in the east, from slate grey to pale fish-belly cream. Another cold one, he suspected, with further blustery rain. Another few inches of mud for the Army of Parliament, currently sat outside the benighted town of Reading like a cat at a mousehole. The first siege of the Civil War in England, and he hoped they had joy of it in there. All its citizens cosily snuggled up under their solid rooftops with their parasitic Cavalier garrison, damn them, whilst Hollie and his troop floundered about up to the arseholes in freezing mud eating undercooked salt beef and succumbing in their dozens to a regrettably un-terminal but bloody vexatious inflammation of the lungs. Half the troop were coughing their guts up, and the other half were heavy-eyed and tetchy after being kept awake most of the night by the phlegmy wheezings of their comrades. Well, God bless King Charles and his blessed Army, and the first representative of same that Hollie got his hands on he was going to skin, slowly, carefully, and with deep feeling. He flexed his right hand thoughtfully. Stiff, this morning, but not painful. A crowning mercy. Of sorts.

*My dearest Het,*

There was precedent for daily letters to your loved ones. Colonel Cromwell wrote to his wife every day, Hollie knew that for a fact, he'd passed the time of day with his courier on more than one occasion. (And the lad didn't mind at all, Mistress Cromwell being the kind of lass who was generous with the cake, and the Fen country being no more than a couple of hours' out of the way.) It wasn't that such correspondence was unusual, or frowned on, or a source of amusement.

No, he just was no bloody use at this kind of letter. Lacked the practice, lacked the words, lacked, he suspected, the sort of thinking that made it easy. Of course, he could ask Luce, but he suspected the lad wasn't in the mood for helping other people do their wooing these days. Not that the lass in question was ever going to read it.

*Dear Mistress Sutcliffe*

Still wrong. He looked up, hoping for inspiration. There was a drop of water collecting on the ridgepole of the tent. He sat and watched it for a while with his hand over the letter. None the wiser, really. His little finger still stuck up and out at the oddest angle, even with his hand flat – all things considered he'd done fairly well to come away from Edgehill with just a few small broken bones. They healed. The inability to flatten your fingers, and an ache in your wrist in bad weather, was probably a small price to pay for an otherwise whole skin.

"Someone's after you, sir." Percey pulled the tent flap open a few inches – which was about as far as he ever got from Hollie's side, sat outside the tent flap guarding him like some sort of benighted guard dog - and Hollie moved his hand casually over the letter to disguise the salutation: and the handwriting, which hadn't been the best since Edgehill.

"Oh?"

Well, Percey was useful, not only as a messenger, but because the lad was freakishly invisible. People spoke as freely in front of Percey as if he didn't exist. It would have driven Hollie mental, being ignored to that degree, but Percey just smiled and ducked his head ingratiatingly and reported every damned word back to his commanding officer, grinning like a gap-toothed fiend the while.

"Thass right," a familiar voice behind Percey said. "Old Robin's got hisself a new orderly, bor. I do reckon I ent orderly enough."

"Well, I'm not keeping you, you web-footed bugger." Hollie gave up his correspondence. Time enough to deal with that later, such as there was to deal with. Stood up – ducked, he was getting good at not cracking his head on the ridgepole, after a week's practice – and stopped in front of Master Andrew Venning, formerly of the Earl of Essex's staff.

Venning grinned at him. "Din't ask you to, Rosie. Come to take over my troop." The grin widened, and he slapped Hollie on the shoulder, most familiarly. "And thass *Captain* Venning to you, bor. I'm relieving you of the late Captain Rackhay's men. By orders of the Earl of Essex, see."

Hollie rubbed his shoulder and favoured Venning with a thoughtful look, and the lad flushed under his freckles.

"You don't mind, do you?" he said.

Now that needed consideration. For the best part of twenty years Hollie had fought shoulder to shoulder with Nat Rackhay; Nat had curbed Hollie's red-headed temper, and Hollie had provided a degree of subversive initiative sufficient for them both. Never apologise, never explain, and never wait for an order. But for his place to be taken by Drew Venning – broad-faced, square, dependable Drew Venning, who couldn't disobey a direct order to save his life, and who didn't have room for more than one idea at once in his head – he was a good lad, was Drew, a good man to have at your back in a fight, a reliable soldier. Just that Hollie couldn't imagine Venning sparking him to wild fire the way Nat had.

Nat had used to call Hollie Red, and it had stuck, and Hollie didn't mind that. (Anything being better than the common knowledge that his given name was Holofernes - hardly the most propitious name for a commanding officer, even if it hadn't screamed good Puritan origins, and God knows he'd rather not admit to that.) Bloody Venning, mind, had took to calling him Rosie about two hours into their acquaintance, saying Red didn't even come close to the distinctive dark-cinnamon of Hollie's hair. And the bugger of it was that now just about everybody called him Rosie. Knowing how much it wound him up, and knowing that looking at the unremarkable, mousy, freckled Venning there wasn't a damn' thing he could pick on in return about the web-footed frog-fucker's appearance.

On the other hand, Drew wasn't likely to disappear into the bed of his latest tart for days on end, or to spend all his pay on buying wildly unsuitable blood horses that broke down within weeks. And the lad was looking at him with a certain mute appeal, like a chained puppy. "No," Hollie said, and almost meant it. "No, I don't mind. You're welcome to the lot of 'em."

"Thass good, " Venning said, with audible relief. "I brought us orders, see."

# 5 BEARDING THE LION

Luce straightened his collar, brushing his collar strings straight ostentatiously. "Got a girl waiting, brat?" Hollie said, grinning.

"I have not."

"There's you told, Rosie." Drew Venning settled his back more comfortably against the stonework of the bridge, squinted thoughtfully up the river, and took his pipe out. "I do reckon as we might be sat here a bit, bor. Might as well get us comfy."

Hollie gave him an amiable kick. "Get up, you idle bugger. We're in exalted company, here. T'lad's on a diplomatic mission – going to beard the lion in his den, right, Lucey?"

"That is correct, captain. The Earl is sending a small party to discuss terms of surrender with the Governor of Reading, of which I am honoured to be a part."

The big redhead closed one eye and looked at him thoughtfully. "Are you going to talk to him like that, lad? In which case, we'll see you some time next week. When you've finished chewing on your dictionary."

"Ha ha, very funny. You know damn' well why he's sending me."

Venning sniggered. "Cos he's your loving uncle, Lucey, and he wants to see you right."

"No - because I'm one of the few officers left in this camp who is both dispensable and doesn't look like something the cat –" He broke off, blushing fiercely. It was true, though. The best part of a fortnight in the field hadn't improved the personal grooming of either of his commanding officers. Hollie always looked as if he'd spent the night in a ditch, even when he hadn't; ten days on campaign had given the redhead a distinctly piratical appearance. Venning didn't look disreputable – he just looked like a big, shaggy, brown-haired farm boy.

Hollie scratched at his patchy red-brown stubble, looked amused, and said nothing.

"Best crack on, then, lad, 'fore you catch something offen us two," Venning sniffed. "What wi' us being lousy and that."

"I didn't say that!"

"Din't have to, Lucifer. Can see how it is, Rosie, can't you? Too good for the likes o' we, now. "

"He's having you on," Hollie said gruffly. "Bugger off, brat, and get us home in time for supper."

Luce brushed some invisible fluff from his hat and placed it squarely on his head. The redhead surveyed him with some consideration, then reached across and adjusted it fractionally. "What d'you reckon, Drew? Is he going to show us up?"

Venning stood up and walked round Luce, sucking his teeth noisily. "Nah. Neat as ninepence. I don't know how he manages it."

"Oh, will the pair of you just stop it!"

And still blushing furiously, with Hollie's maniacal cackle ringing in his ears, Luce stalked back to Essex's quarters at the old moated manor house at Southcote, three miles up the river from the town.

Not for the first time, he was enormously relieved to be free of the unpredictable presence of Captain Babbitt. And now he had two of them to contend with, he thought ruefully, breaking off a sprig of rosemary from the hedge lining the knot garden behind the lovely old house. Venning was enormous fun to be around, but you wouldn't want him in a delicate situation like this – something like expecting a carthorse to walk on eggshells. He tucked the rosemary into his buttonhole – here's rosemary, that's for remembrance, as Master Shakespeare would have it – and straightened his shoulders.

The long parlour at Southcote was cool, in the early spring sunlight, reflections of pale light on the moat dancing on the high white ceiling. A calm, old-fashioned room, with a bowl of pale lilies of the valley in a Venetian glass vase set on the table scenting the air with honey. Essex's most recent aide – Drew Venning's replacement – brought in a jug of wine, with a faint sidelong smile at Luce. A much more elegant figure than the untidy young man from Norfolk, Luce thought approvingly. Definitely much more in keeping with the expectations of the commander of the Army of Parliament. There was even a narrow edging of fine lace to his impeccable linen. He set the jug down carefully on the table beside the lilies of the valley, and turned to Luce with a smile.

A good-looking young man, with smooth silver-fair hair to his shoulders and strikingly dark eyes – until you realised that he had a long puckered scar that ran from jaw to cheekbone, twisting the corner of his mouth into a permanent smile that didn't reach his eyes. Another one of Essex's deceptively smooth finds, then, because that scar was not something you came by cutting yourself shaving. "My lord?" he said enquiringly, and Luce shook his head.

Essex came stalking in, and it took Luce a moment to work out what looked strange about him. He was dressed civilian-wise, in a sombre doublet of figured black satin, with a collar of fine lace. He gave Luce an approving smile. "You look very smart, lad."

"I thank you, uncle."

"I see you've made the acquaintance of the newest recruit to my staff. Thankful Russell, late of Hampden's company –"

"Thankful?" Luce echoed faintly.

"Thankful not to have been named something worse. My sister is Fly-Fornication. But yes, my name is Thankful. How think you I came by this?" He tapped the scar lightly. "Taking exception to people making mock of my given name, is how."

"Speaking as a Lucifer, I can only commend your forbearance," Luce said wryly. "And as I guess you're aware, my commanding officer is Holofernes. So not much mockery from our quarter, you'll find."

"A puritanical little gathering, are we not? Mercifully, we are expecting to be joined by the somewhat plainer-named Colonel Fielding, shortly. I think I see him crossing the moat – if you will excuse me, my lords -" Thankful bowed graciously and left the parlour.

"Did Venning not suit, then, sir?" Luce said mildly. His uncle raised one dark brow. "I didn't suit Venning, Lucifer. A charming young man, but not the greatest asset to a well-ordered household. He's been champing at the bit to cross swords with a Cavalier for some weeks. I believe he was initially made surplus to Colonel Cromwell's requirements due to his well-meaning enthusiasm."

"What, Drew Venning was in the Lovely Company?" He didn't mean it to sound quite so disbelieving as it had – but the idea of stolid, secular Drew in the company of that crew of the devout was mildly comic, to say the least.

"For about a month, lad, yes. I believe he found that the company did not, perhaps, suit, and that he was – possibly, ah, better fitted to a less sober and godly troop."

"And so you put him in company with Hollie Babbitt? Inspired, my lord."

The Earl of Essex poured himself a glass of wine, admiring the delicate twisted stem of the glass, holding it up to the light. "Well, I thought so," he said thoughtfully. "Thought it might buck Babbitt's ideas up somewhat. The captain has been somewhat uncharacteristically quiet since his return from White Notley."

"Ah," Luce said. Not a subject he wished to get into, all things considered. Fortunately at that point Thankful Russell returned, the very picture of a discreet orderly – if you disregarded the furious flush on his face. "The Governor of Reading, my lord, Sir Arthur Aston," he said curtly. "And Colonel Richard Fielding."

Fielding was short, dark, and intended by Nature to be of a cheerful countenance. He bowed politely. Sir Arthur glowered with less civility. "Take thy marred Friday-face out of my sight, man," he said irritably. "I'll have no dealings with your master in the hearing of servants."

Behind Sir Arthur's burly buff-coated shoulder Fielding winced. The Governor, it had to be noted, was the only man who had failed to offer the courtesy of civilian dress. "Master Russell is my secretary, sir, not a household servant," Essex pointed out, mildly enough, and Aston's florid face flushed at the reproach.

"Cornet Lucifer Pettitt, my lord –" Luce bowed with a finely-calculated degree of condescension – "and Colonel John Hampden."

Hampden glanced up, looking faintly harassed, untidy brown hair falling in disarray in his eyes. Smiling a deceptively sweet, vague smile at the company, managing to look wholly disorganised and like a man who could scarce be trusted to find his own front door without assistance. Which was odd, because Hampden and his Buckinghamshire Greencoats were beginning to make a name for themselves for both ferocity and godly resolution. Any commander of that particular unit was not to be as mild as he looked. "My lord," he said civilly.

Aston's eyes flicked contemptuously over them. "And so this is the best the rebel Army has to offer, is it, my lords? A shopkeeper, two Puritan whelps, and an aged cuckold?"

`"Would you take a glass of wine, my lord?" Thankful said, somewhat white about the lips. "Colonel Fielding, sir? May I help you to refreshment?"

"Thank you," Fielding said, looking mortally embarrassed. "Kind. Most, ah, kind."

"I expect it would be most welcome," Luce said sweetly. "You must be starved." Near literally, from what he heard from Matt Percey, the eyes and ears of the troop. Three thousand men quartered on slightly less than twice that number of townspeople, and the wool trade that was the town's bread and butter all but at a standstill in the keeping of the King's army in clothes. Sir Arthur's bluster and stiff-rumped arrogance was not popular amongst the hard-pressed townsfolk, from what Percey heard. Not, of course, that a man like the Governor would care a snap of the fingers for the opinion of the townsfolk – was, again from Percey's first-hand sources of information, only barely aware of their existence other than as a source of revenue and unwilling hospitality.

Essex was pretending not to have heard the insult, though there was a scarlet flush high on his cheekbones that was a warning to anyone who knew Old Robin that his temper was running high. "Pray be seated, gentlemen, if you wish to tend straight to business without the civilities."

"Civilities?" Aston scoffed, with a sneering laugh. "I'll not accept the hospitality of a pack of traitorous Cropheads –"

"More fool you," Thankful murmured almost out of hearing, passing a plate of hot, fresh-baked, fragrant sweet cakes to Fielding. The colonel's mouth twitched with stifled laughter, and Aston glared at him.

"Something amiss, Colonel?"

"To business, then. My lord, I would request your agreement to surrender the town of Reading to my superior forces, by the authority vested in me by Parliament. I would ask that your men lay down their arms and surrender at such places as –"

"I should rather die," Aston said curtly. Thankful Russell turned his head and looked long and thoughtfully at the Governor.

"Should you choose otherwise, Sir Arthur, Reading would be subject to my orders as soon as any terms of surrender are signed –"

Aston pushed his chair back with a clatter. "I'll not listen further to this. You have my final answer, you and your pretty catamites. I should rather die, or be starved, in the service of my King, than to tamely surrender to the likes of you. I give you good day."

His abrupt departure was somewhat spoiled by the heaviness of the parlour door, which refused to slam. Colonel Fielding got to his feet, with a look of resignation. "My apologies, my lord. The Governor can be somewhat – intemperate – betimes – with thought and consideration he may reconsider – " he shrugged, clearly indicating without words that he personally doubted it very much. "The Lord's will be done, gentlemen, but I pray you remember that 'twas not Richard Fielding who refused your courtesy, and bear me no malice."

Thankful's scarred face was expressionless as he folded the untasted cakes into a clean napkin. Then he handed the parcel over to Fielding. "Pray tell the Governor, sir, that my lord Essex's, er, catamite sends these with his compliments."

Fielding flushed. "I thank you for your kindness, Master Russell, but –"

"But 'twere a shame to waste them," Essex said mildly.

# 6 IN WHICH LUCE CONSIDERS UNLIKELY ROMANCE

"He said *what*?" Hollie said, through a mouthful of cake. "And you didn't kill him?"

The rest of the cakes had found an appreciative audience with the troop, unsurprisingly. Luce shrugged. "He was discourteous enough to come in plate."

"You could've shot him in the head," the big redhead grumbled. Propped his elbows on his knees and sat there, peering through his hair at Luce. "Well? Is it true, d'you reckon?" "

"What, am I bedding my Uncle Robert? I am not, you vile-minded – "

"Not you, you soft-headed lad. *Him*. Laddie with the scar. I did hear as he got kicked out o'Hampden's for suffen shady - reckon as playing stretch the leather with Old Robin be enough to get him into a whole heap o'trouble with Hampden's lads. Proper righteous lot. Wouldn't want nawthen to do wi' that kind o' doings - "

"Captain Venning, you have an even more degenerate mind than he does, and that's something of an achievement," Luce said haughtily. "I have no idea whether Thankful Russell is bedding my uncle, and nor do I care."

Venning licked his finger, dabbed the last few crumbs from his sleeve and neatly ate them. "I do," he said mildly. "I'd like to think at least one of us is having his bed warmed of a night, because I'm bloody sure it's not me."

The redhead inhaled a crumb and choked, turning a most unflattering scarlet until Luce pounded him on the back.

"And I don't know what ails you, bor, 'cause you told me yourself you was getting your belly rubbed somewhere – now what did I say?"

"Sore subject," Luce said ruefully, as Hollie sulked off into the gathering dusk.

Venning shrugged. "Prob'ly gone to write more of his interminable bloody letter to that poor maid. What he thinks nobody's noticed, gret lollopin' mawkin. You reckon he's ever going to finish 'un?"

"At least he has someone to write to." Luce was thinking of his little widow in Edgehill – lovely, gentle Sarah, with the first frost in her dark hair. He still woke up thinking he was back there, in her arms. He'd written to her – twice, three times, since the battle. He lived in hope that when this war was over he'd ride back to her. He'd given Sarah his heart and his innocence all at once. Without the warmth of her bed and her open arms and her kindness, he didn't think he'd have been able to bear the whole nightmare that had been Edgehill. And it was only the thought of her waiting for him that made it possible to carry on, betimes. If only they'd had more time. She'd never had chance to tell him her feelings. Despite the difference in their estates, he meant to go back there and make her his bride. The world's opinion meant nothing to a man in love.

# 7 THE UNCOMPLICATED COMPANY OF HORSES

It might be April, but the nights were still cold, and a thin, perpetually damp blanket between Hollie and the night air did little to keep off the chill. Not that he'd slept much anyway, sharing quarters with Luce Pettitt – who snored, in a genteel and irritating manner, and periodically stopped breathing, so you spent half the night in a state of wakefulness, on pins to see if the little bastard was going to start up again. And now stuck with Drew Venning, who didn't snore, but who talked in his sleep, even less comprehensibly than he did awake, and farted like a dray horse. Hollie had given up, shortly before dawn: sat up, shivering, and gone to walk the horse lines till the sun came up, hoping to cadge a hot breakfast from one of the sentry pickets. At which venture he'd been predictably out of luck.

And now the bloody guns had started up again, taking the town of Reading to pieces brick by brick, and he had a thumping headache already, what with the lack of sleep. Gritty-eyed and irritable and distinctly disenchanted with life.

He wandered up and down the picketed horses, absently rubbing enquiring velvet muzzles and wondering how come every bloody horse in his troop seemed to think he carried the world's apple mountain about his person. Spoiled, the whole boiling lot of them, petted like as if they were children's ponies. He patted flanks and shaggy necks absently, running a practised hand down a foreleg here and there, checking for galls and sores. Most of the horses knew him, stood still at his touch – Cal Thorpe's old piebald Delilah offering him a massive forefoot out of habit, like a dog giving a paw, though he could no more imagine Calthorpe letting his mare go round with a loose shoe than he could imagine the trooper letting his children go to school with no shirt on.

Swore at some length at one of the men, some poor benighted sod who was both young and stupid enough not to pay attention to his horse's keeping in this continual mud – he had it in his head the lad was called Wilder, Wilding, something like that, and a less wild specimen you'd go a long way to imagine, but what he lacked entirely was common sense and Hollie told him so, in graphic terms. None of which was much use to the unfortunate brown gelding, patched raw and miserable with rain scald, and looking so sorry for itself that Hollie was bloody furious with Wilding, Wilder, whatever, all over again and went back and told him so. Even Tyburn was uncharacteristically subdued in the hock-deep slurry.

It almost relieved Hollie's feelings somewhat when Trooper Wilding slipped in the mud on his way back from the horse lines and fell on his arse, but then both trooper and mount were looking so draggled and forlorn that he sent the pair of them on some spurious errand to Essex's quarters up at Southcote, just so they'd get to spend a couple of hours under cover while Essex tried to work out what the hell they wanted. He doubted very much if Essex did have any messages for him. He thought Old Robin might be too busy for the time being slowly dismantling Reading a stone at a time, which caution and deliberation was infuriatingly typical.

Arrived at one picket cold and wet and grimly miserable just in time to see the last of the bacon he'd been scenting, like some benighted hound, half across Berkshire, disappearing down Muggy Davies' ravenous maw. Davies being ever so apologetic and if he'd known Hollie was planning to break his fast with the lads he'd have put a bit by, see, but the captain was welcome to a bite of bread and cheese – which Hollie had been quite hungry enough to consider, even knowing what he knew about the inedible properties of the local cheese. Watching Davies surreptitiously dusting the weevils off the stale bread he thought perhaps he wasn't that hungry after all.

Pettitt was usually good for an apple or two. Or there might still be cakes left from two days ago, from the abortive meeting with the Governor. Stale cake was better than no cake, and certainly better than Davies's maggoty cheese. A lifetime ago, when he was young and mostly even more starving than he was now, in the time-honoured manner of growing lads, he'd not been a bad fisherman – competent enough to catch his own supper on occasion, at least. He wasn't sure he'd fancy eating anything out of this river, nourished on dead Malignant and siege refuse, though.

He sat down in the long grass at the side of the bridge, propping his back against the wet stones. Christ, was it only two days ago they'd sat here and teased the brat about his spotless appearance on his way to meet with Aston? Seemed a hundred years ago. The guns had started up the morning after, and they'd not stopped since. The usual vicious rumours doing the rounds of the camp – the Malignant were surrendering. The Malignant weren't surrendering. The Malignant were slaughtering the good burghers of Reading, spiking babies on pikes, roasting virgins, and buggering aldermen. Prince Rupert was planning an assault on the bridge, and funny enough, Hollie had heard that one from the unimpeachable source of Matt Percey too, so he had an eye out for that bridge.

So far the most exciting thing he'd seen in the river was what was possibly a trout, and more likely a Royalist turf, spinning downstream. And after half a lifetime rattling about Europe either besieging, or being besieged, he was pig-sick of the Earl of Essex's favourite type of warfare. Hollie had it on the best authority – to wit, the man's favourite nephew – that the Earl thought he was a moody bastard at best; he wasn't likely to win himself any battle honours in this campaign, either, up to the backside in clotted spring mud.

He was just about weary enough to think about falling asleep, in the first coy rays of the April dawn, when he heard voices and splashing, up-river. Peered over the bridge parapet, cautiously, expecting to see some silly buggers watering their horses at the ford. Some of his own silly buggers, mind.

Instead, coming out of the river-mist, there was a boatload of bloody Cavaliers. More than one boatload of bloody Cavaliers. He swore, under his breath. Precisely sod-all he could do about it, except sit tight, try and count heads, work out what the hell they were about, and then go hell for leather back to the Earl of Essex and dump the problem in his lap. Wishing, not for the first time, that he wasn't quite so conspicuously tall and bright-haired – that, in fact, he was, oh, about Drew Venning's shape and size and colouring, and could get away with lurking unnoticed.

# 8 EXIT STAGE LEFT, PURSUED BY A BEAR

Thankful Russell was bored. It was raining – again – a thin drizzle that obscured the lush Oxfordshire hills. It had been good of my lord Essex to take him in – get him out of trouble, more likely, given some of the scrapes he'd been in of late – but he grew surfeited with soft living. And, to be fair, he was quite well aware that at some point in the next few weeks it would all change and he'd be back in a ditch with nothing but his wits and a sharp blade to rely on, but in the meantime there was nothing to do but tend to Essex, keep his gaze modestly downcast the better not to see the pity and the disgust in men's eyes when they looked on his scarred face, and keep his ears open.

The guns had started up again. There was no real strategy to the firing, just a ragged, relentless barrage intended to take the town apart a stone at a time if need be. Late yesterday afternoon there'd been a great roar of cheering from the artillery lines and oh, he'd hoped they'd broken through, just to relieve the tedium, but they hadn't, it had just been the steeple at Faversham Church going down, taking one of Aston's cannon with it. There'd been some wild carousing in the Parliamentarian gun crews last night. Thankful wondered if that explained the somewhat lacklustre firing this morning – any number of headaches, likely as not.

He was still staring out at the rain, moodily drumming his fingers on the windowsill, when that scruffy russet-haired cavalry captain came flying across the courtyard at a dead run. Thankful's first thought was that there'd been an assault – had the door open in a heartbeat, rudely pushing the dignified butler who'd come with the house, aside.

"Get – Essex," the redhead panted, leaning heavily

against the smooth white plaster and leaving a great smear of mud in his wake.

"Is there news, sir? Has there been an attack?"

The redhead shook his head, too winded to say anything further, whooping for breath and clutching his side under his unlaced buff coat.

"No news," Thankful said dryly, "but it would seem to be a somewhat urgent piece of no news, then? Be seated in the library and I'll fetch the Earl –"

"Don't. Piss. About."

"I will endeavour not to do so, sir. If you would be so good as to sit down – before you expire altogether, captain – and await my lord's pleasure –"

There was the sound of footsteps on the stairs. "I would hardly describe the captain's company as a pleasure, Thankful," Essex said, pausing part way down the staircase. "I should say rather that his current state of presentation is both discourteous and lamentably neglectful of his duties as a commanding officer. I trust there is some excuse for this, Babbitt, rather than your customary –"

"Shut. Up," the redhead wheezed. Looked up, his face as scarlet as his hair. "*Sir*. I haven't the breath – to – say this. Twice."

Essex caught his breath in shock, and "Sir, this incivility will benefit you naught," Thankful said sternly, and the redhead gave him a sideways grin.

"Six hundred bloody Malignant aren't like to do me much good either, lad, but there they are. Come in up-river at Sunning. The bastards. Three boat loads. With powder. And shot. I've run all twain back."

"At Sunning? But what -? Are you sure?"

The captain almost had his breath back – certainly enough in command of himself to do no more than click his tongue against his teeth in an irritated manner. "Sat and watched 'em coming in. Sir. For the best part of an hour. Sat in a bloody ditch by the bridge like a spare – er – "

"And what, pray, were you doing out at Sunning bridge just after dawn, sir?"

The redhead pushed his loose hair out of his eyes. If such an act hadn't been gross insubordination, Thankful would have suspected him of smirking. "You *seen* the officers I'm quartered with? Your nephew snores, and your late orderly farts like the Devil. And if you're trying to hint at me taking up sides with the Malignant, my lord, then you can take that insinuation and –"

"You're sure of the numbers?" Thankful said quickly.

"I had bugger-all else to do for an hour than hide in a ditch counting heads, lad, what wi' not being the least conspicuous officer in the Army of Parliament. And yes, I'm sure about the powder and shot. Two lads with *very* nice shiny new flintlock muskets stood about on a barge full of barrels? Wouldn't mind one o' them myself." He scratched his chin thoughtfully. "Come to think on it, if I happen to run across one of them same lads in town when we finally get in, be ever so wrong of me to leave the enemy with superior arms and equipment, wouldn't it?"

"Reinforcements and ammunition," Essex mused.

"Saw us coming good and proper, didn't they? Mind, they'll still be sorting their shi – er, apportioning the shot. They didn't see me, or I wouldn't be stood here – so if you ask me, we stand a better than average chance of catching them on the hop. There's arses want kicking, gentlemen." The captain was bouncing, very slightly, on his toes. He probably didn't even know he was doing it.

"Keen, sir?" Thankful prompted with gentle malevolence.

"Oh, hell, yes. With your permission, my lord?"

And to Thankful's astonishment, Essex nodded. "Indeed, captain. Let us carry the war into the enemy's camp. Thankful – would you be so good as to take orders to the artillery lines for me?"

"Orders, sir?"

"Throw everything we've got at the bastards," the

captain prompted. "'S what I'd do, were I in command. Worked for Wallenstein at Nuremberg – I should know, I was there."

Essex looked, long and thoughtfully, at the redhead. And then, eventually. "Even as Captain Babbitt says. Pray tell the battery commanders to increase their rate of fire. Let's make the town too hot to hold 'em."

Thankful bowed politely. "Indeed. After you, then, captain."

# 9 NOTHING WORSE THAN A SULKY DONKEY-WALLOPER

"Brought your own horse, did you, or d'you want to throw a leg over one of our remounts?"

Hollie was in tearing high spirits, and Thankful found himself – reluctantly – responding to the captain's wild good humour. Also found himself mounted on a big grey gelding with a mouth like an iron bar –

"Don't worry, lad, he won't put you on your arse and show you up when the guns start firing. I doubt the Rabbit's moved out of a trot in the last ten year. Unless you belt him hard enough."

"Yours, I assume?" Thankful said dryly, looking at the height of the fleabitten grey standing alongside black Tyburn.

"Mine. Got half the lads out on patrol most mornings –" he tapped his long nose – "acting on information received, you might say. What with them buggers sneaking in the back way, and folk in there writing love letters out to His Majesty requesting royal assistance any minute, might start to get a bit warm hereabouts shortly. So no offence, but I'm keeping the good stuff in reserve." Yanking the black's head up, he set the big horse splashing through the puddles at a thumping trot. Thankful set the grey ambling after – Hollie was right, you'd need a sharp stick to get the horse out of a sedate jog, though brisk application of spurs and a stick from the hedgerow soon communicated the idea that speed was of the essence.

"Have you some experience of this kind of work, sir?"

"Clearing out nests of rats? Oh, aye, plenty. Not my favourite task, but –" Hollie shrugged. "The death of young wolves is never to be pitied."

"Now I'd never have had you marked down as a

literary man."

"What, John Webster? My kind of man, Russell. By the end of one of his plays there's hardly a bastard left standing. Blood, lechery, and random acts of malice. What's not to like?"

The gun captain was a particularly villainous looking specimen with no front teeth and no fingernails to speak of, wearing an equally villainous leather jerkin with oily handprints where he'd clearly stood surveying his domain with his hands on his hips. He was presently perched on the gun limber bawling orders at a mute and embarrassed crew, as unlikely a shower of lads as you'd come across in a long day's march. As he was mid-roar Hollie leaned from the saddle and poked him in the shoulder.

The gunner spun round, linstock poised to poke his assailant.

"Shut it, big gob," Hollie said amiably. "I could hear thee in bloody Windsor."

"Fuck me, it's Rosie Babbitt. I see thee hasn't had a haircut since the Flood. Want to be careful you don't get mistook for a girl one of these nights, lad. Some o' my lot ain't choosy."

"They'd need to be *extremely* not choosy to mistake that for a girl," Russell said, and the gun captain squinted at him.

"Oh Christ, another long-haired bloody fairy. I worry about you, Rosie. Thee is always knocking about wi' the pretty ones."

"Someone has to protect 'em from thy villainous crew, Shuck. Russell – this is Black Shuck, who is a gobshite from Preston and a gunner of some renown. Possibly in that order. He used to follow me round Germany like a fucking lapdog - couldn't turn round without seeing his bloody ugly mug leering at me over a bloody gun. I reckon they only surrendered at Nuremberg 'cos you were camped that close to the walls they couldn't stand the stench."

"Aye, and I was still upwind o' *you*, ginger minge,"

Shuck said, and Hollie grinned.

"Thee is a filthy bastard, sir. This lad is one o' Essex's boys and he don't want his ears sullying wi' your coarse talk."

"Kettle calling the pot brunt-arse, that. What brings you down here? Come to see the grown-ups working, has thee? Bloody donkey-gallopers - always the bloody same, you, Rosie, poncing about on that bloody mental horse , too good to get your hands dirty - "

The big redhead scratched under his ponytail thoughtfully. "Aye, well. It's a bit like this. See, me and the lads are getting a bit bored wi' sitting round Reading scratching us arses, waiting for summat to happen. So we was just wondering if you'd be in the market for, er, jollying things along a bit."

Shuck grinned. "You ain't changed, Red. Still got no fucking patience. Shurrup, you lot. Ginger minge here got a proposition for us, hasn't thee, lad?"

"I do? Oh… Aye, I do. First man to have the top off of that tower –"

"That's St Giles' Church, you fucking heathen –"

"Whatever. I want it off."

"What for?" Russell said curiously.

"It'll piss 'em off," Shuck suggested cheerfully. "Anyways, nobody likes having great chunks o' masonry dropping on they heads, do they? And it be about time this bunch of bloody wet ladies got their eye in. This fucking idiot – yes, you, Butterworth – nearly put a fucking charge down the gun before it been cleaned, what with being half asleep, what with being out on the piss last night –"

"Does that matter?" Russell said, and Hollie rolled his eyes.

"Christ, lad, don't start him off."

"You tell him, Buttie. What'd have happened, if that charge'd gone off?"

"I'd have been wiping my arse left handed, sir," Butterworth said gloomily.

"And watching your hand disappear over the horizon," Shuck said, with the air of a man repeating a lesson he'd repeated many times before. "So you won't do it again, will you, Buttie?"

"No, sir, I won't."

"Or in addition to wiping your arse left-handed, Buttie, you won't be sitting on it for about a month, cos I'll bastard well skin it. So. There thee goes, girls. Ginger minge wants his steeple down –"

"Will you *stop* calling me that!"

"And what ginger minge wants, he gets," Shuck said, with malevolent relish. "Or he sulks, don't thee, lad? And there's nowt worse than a sulky donkey-walloper –"

"Oh, there is. A smart-arsed gunner."

Shuck surveyed his shifty crew balefully. "Well then, you lot. Best get to work, hadn't thee? Lad's give us a challenge –"

"Orders from the Commander of the Army of Parliament, sir, actually," Thankful said briskly. "My lord Essex instructs –"

"Pile it on, owd lad," Hollie cut in, leaning from his horse and peering consideringly at the gun's touchhole. "We are in the realms of heaping coals of fire. Fast as you can get that thing going, start chucking lead at the Malignant bastards."

There was a ragged cheer from the crew. The redhead looked at Thankful – winked – and folded his hands on the black horse's neck. "See that steeple, over yonder? Reckon you can have it down before teatime?"

"Captain Babbitt, sir, this is not a matter for levity -!"

"Stand clear," Shuck said, grinning. "And brace yourself, laddie. You ever stood behind a field gun, Little Miss Sunshine?"

It took Thankful a moment to realise that the gun captain was referring to him. He shook his head warily.

"It's going to sound like the end of the world, sweetheart. So if you've got duties elsewhere, I suggest the pair of you – "he jerked his thumb – "bugger off and haunt somebody else?"

"I mean it," Hollie said, and there was a glint in his eye that assuredly did mean it. "There's a drink in it for the man who takes me the top off that church."

Shuck took his disreputable hat off and scratched consideringly at his grey hair. "Too easy, big lad. You do know as we already had the steeple down off of Caversham Church last night, and took the cannon out with it? So you want to take that 'un down as well – easy money, boy."

# 10 SEEING ACTION

After the steeple of St Giles' Church had gone down, leaving Hollie somewhat the lighter in both pockets and spirits, Shuck's horrible crew and their associates developed a new lease of life, and the guns didn't stop from day's end to day's end.

Hollie was staring into space, in one of the few minutes he had to himself these days, idly wondering what Het was doing right now, when Ward burst into the tent.

"Percey's on his way in, Rosie – clocked 'em coming down the hill." The disreputable trooper closed one eye in an appalling leer. "Guess who he's brought with him."

"If that's intended as a formal report, trooper, I suggest you go out, come back in and start from the beginning - in good plain English?"

Ward gave him a snaggly grin. "You can wait for Percey, sir, if you don't like me manners?"

"I can always have you on shit-shovelling detail, if I don't like 'em, Trooper Ward. Stop arsing about and make your report."

Ward straightened up reluctantly,. "Sir. Enemy coming up the Oxford road, sir. Percey seen 'em from the bridge, about ten miles hence –"

"*Christ,* that lad's got sharp eyes," Hollie said admiringly, and Ward nodded.

"There's *a lot* of 'em. Enough of 'em to have brung the King out of hiding, by the look of the flag-waggers. Better than that, though –"

The contrast between the scruffy, perpetually-grubby Ward and Matt Percey was remarkable. Percey had spent most of his childhood years ragged and grubby by necessity and once given a decent suit of clothes the lad was rather touchingly determined he'd stay decent. Even after most of the morning on horseback or sliding about on his belly in the undergrowth, he still managed to look tidy.

"Morning, Matthew," Hollie greeted Percey as the lad pushed past Ward, and gave a breathless salute. "I hear the buggers are stirring?"

Percey was still too breathless to speak and he nodded enthusiastically.

"Ward tells me about ten miles off?"

Ward's expression had gone sulky again at having his thunder stolen, and Hollie couldn't be bothered to nurse him out of his sullens. "If you've got nowt further to add, Ward, I'm sure you've got duties elsewhere – dismissed."

Percey straightened up and ducked his head respectfully as Ward slouched past, and once again Hollie was impressed by just how bloody *nice* the lad was. Despite being dragged up in an alehouse stable-yard – despite the fact that the lad had managed to grow three inches in as many months on Army rations, which told you a lot about his previous care –Ward, God help us. In return, not one of the troop had taken the piss when the lad's voice had finally broken.

Although in moments of high emotion, Percey still had a tendency to go from a growl to a squeak. "And Rupert's with him!"

The troop didn't take the piss – it didn't mean they didn't find it funny, including their commanding officer, who kept a straight face with difficulty till the words sank in. Hollie paused, half in his armour. "You *sure*?"

Percey nodded enthusiastically, mousy fringe bobbing on his forehead. "I was stood looking up the hill from Caversham Bridge when I just saw the sun off something between the hills coming down from Watlington way – caught my eye, like – and the more I looked the more I thought, bloody hell fires. They're on the march, captain. Hundreds of 'em – foot and horse –"

A thought crossed Hollie's mind. "Essex knows this, right? You've not just come and told *me*?" Given the lad's perverse habit of assuming the sun rose and set at his commanding officer's whim, it wouldn't have surprised him. Most of the lads thought Hollie was one of their own. Percey thought Hollie was at the right hand of God Almighty. It was a sobering reflection.

Percey grinned. "Now, sir, as if I would. No, there was a dozen sentries stood alongside me, and we all seen 'em. Last I saw of the lads at the bridge they was running like rabbits, scurrying back here. Nice of Luce – er, Cornet Pettitt – to lend me his mare, mind, or I'd have still been down there trying to get old Windhover out of a walk. Want me to catch that up for you, captain?" And the lad caught the loose buckle on Hollie's breastplate and yanked it tight.

"Where the hell *is* the brat, anyway?"

Percey shrugged. "Not seen him since yesterday - probably gone off on some secret mission for Uncle Essex, like. Shall I whistle up the lads?"

"That'd be helpful, lad." Luce would turn up. Russell was a sound lad, if starchy - he wouldn't have left the cornet dead in a ditch. Hollie tucked his sword under his arm. "Bridge, you reckon?"

"Shouldn't we wait for orders, sir –"

"Got my orders up here, Matthew." Hollie tapped the side of his head, grinning. "Which is, intercept and kick the arse of, Prince Rupert and his lovely ladies. I owe that bastard one for Edgehill."

# 11 CAVERSHAM BRIDGE

Routed Drew Venning out of bed on his way down to the horse lines – he hadn't seen Luce either, which was beginning to ring alarm bells in the very back of Hollie's mind, but the lad would turn up – Venning had been out on patrol most of last night and was barely capable of agreeing with everything Hollie suggested. Which was precisely how Hollie liked it.

Christ, he hoped the King didn't decide to bring the whole bloody army by way of Caversham bridge. "Matthew –"

Percey hadn't left his side, which, in the absence of his bloody junior officer, was oddly reassuring. (Where the hell *was* the brat?) He gave the lad a rueful sidelong grin. "Thanks, Mattie. You've been right helpful this morning. Now if you want to get back wi't' lads, you're free to go."

Percey shook his head. "Not till Luce fetches up, sir, I'll not leave you," he said proudly, drawing himself up to his full height – all of five inches shorter than Hollie, and most of those since he'd joined the army, bless him. "You might need me?" the lad went on, hopefully, and Hollie coughed and hid a smile.

"Aye, well, I might that, yes."

There was a roar of excitement from the men coming up behind them. Such a sound, from thousands of throats – right put the hairs up on the back of your neck, it did. "What the –"

"Fielding's surrendered," Cullis said grimly, barging his old cob up next to Hollie. "Town's ours, Rosie."

"Fielding? But what the bloody hell's it got to do with – "

"Heh, keep up at the back, laddie. Word is that Sir Arthur got knocked on the head about a week since –"

"By Colonel Fielding, if the bugger had any sense," Hollie said, grinning. "From what Lucey said, Aston was a right stiff-rumped old bastard."

"Aye, well, not much to do with him at the moment, is it? So either Colonel Fielding has seen sense, or some bugger in there's doing the laundry, because for sure there is a large white flag hanging over the wall."

Drew Venning threw back his head with a whoop of glee. "All ours, Rosie-boy, and not a shot fired!"

"Want to tell them buggers that?" Black Tyburn bounced with excitement, and despite his carefully blank expression Hollie felt much the same as his horse. Reading was theirs. And as Venning pointed out, not a shot fired. Christ, it was the first engagement of this war where they'd actually succeeded. Not a deadlock – not a paper victory, to be claimed by one side or the other depending who was writing the reports at the time – but an actual, honest-to-God, victory. Aye, well, maybe the King and his army were coming down the hill towards the bridge, but balls to 'em. On a day like this, with the sun coming and going from behind the ragged clouds, and the first green shoots of spring starting to poke through the mud, the Army of Parliament was unstoppable. Even the Earl of Essex couldn't cock this one up. He swung the black round, one hand on the reins and the other on his sword. "Well, lads, here they come."

"Take it slow," Venning called, grinning." Let 'em wear 'emselves out and then we'll whip in and have us way with 'em while they're out o'breath!"

"You want to have your way with Rupert, lad, I ent going to stop you, but I don't think I'd like to watch," Cullis said, sniggering.

And then the first of Prince Rupert's cavalry was at the bridge, and some of the silly sods were trying to ford the river, which was in Hollie's opinion a God-damned stupid thing to do in a river running high after four weeks of solid rain, and that was before he nudged Brockis with his elbow and encouraged his regimental crack shot to start picking the stupid buggers off as they went flailing about belly-deep in the water.

Venning came up alongside, shaking his head at the sight of Rupert struggling in the press of men trying to get across the bridge. "Like trying to get a quart into a pint pot, bor. Had that trouble meself many a time."

"You're a filthy bastard, Venning, " Hollie said, laughing in spite of himself. "Fettled him, though, hasn't it? Here, you reckon I can hit him from here?"

"Not with your aim the way it is, Rosie-boy!"

And then the first of Rupert's elite was across, and Hollie was having none of that, thank you very much. Tyburn was a big horse, sixteen hands or more, and heavy-set with it, and Rupert liked his cavalry built for speed, not weight. Which was fine when you were coming on at a gallop but in a tight space Hollie backed his own horse to take out the terrified bay thoroughbred, hooves skidding wildly on the cobbles of the bridge. He looked at the wild-eyed bay horse on the bridge and the wild-eyed Malignant sod with his hand on the bridle, and he didn't spare it a second thought before he drew one of his pistols left-handed, and shot the horse in the head.

The bay went down without a sound and the Cavalier went down yelling, but as by that time the swine was under the hooves of his own oncoming comrades, it wasn't something Hollie was going to waste further powder on. He was too busy trying not to get himself killed. Next one through was a vicious little bastard, cutting backhand at Hollie's face with a fancy rapier and he threw himself backwards in the saddle, bringing up his own plain blade with a clash. Quite taken aback to be being so sworn at by a Cavalier man, too – the bugger was barely pausing for breath between curses.

Tyburn was backing and snorting, steady as a mule although not in the least bit happy about it, and Hollie's right wrist was beginning to ache as he kept blocking blow after blow from the persistent little sod.

"*Will* you piss off and pick on somebody else!" – that

being the right wrist that he'd broken at Edgehill and it wasn't really up to close work, and there was a creeping numbness up his arm. Sooner or later his wrist was just going to seize altogether. If he could have swapped hands he would have but by the time he got his sword into his left hand the rat-faced bastard would have run him through.

He yanked Tyburn up onto his hind legs, and the black squealed and lashed out bravely but this bugger had decided that Hollie was his mark for the duration and he kept on coming. His hand cramped suddenly, so agonisingly that for a fraction of a second he thought the bastard had had him, and he shook his head, trying to stay about as calm as you could expect to be with your horse's arse up against a bridge parapet and your sword hand near useless. Telling himself that he'd been in worse scrapes, and he'd got out of 'em mostly whole. And then Tyburn squealing as the Malignant's sword point whipped across the meat of the black's muzzle - and it was very clever, getting Hollie so tangled up in managing a stallion gone wild with pain and fury that he couldn't guard himself. The black reared again, those lethal steel-shod forefeet hammering the air wildly - but Hollie and his black had been fighting together these ten years and more and ten years of relentless cavalry drill steadied the big horse something marvellous. Tib was a weapon in his own right - even if it was a loose cannon.

The Malignant had darted off a stride, out of the range of Tyburn's lashing hooves, but as the horse came dancing back to all fours, snorting and tossing his head wildly, he came on again - same trick, slashing backhand for Hollie's face, and even if you had the balls enough to put your whole trust in the bars of a Birmingham steel lobster-pot helmet to shield your eyes, you couldn't but help flinch backwards, it was nature. And if, like Hollie, your plate and helmet were plain munitions-quality, like every other bugger in your troop, the flinching laid your throat bare.

And usually it never even crossed his mind but this one was tricksy, and if Hollie offered him a chance the sod would take it without blinking – and that put a thought into his head.

Only the one, mind; he used to say to Rackhay it's a poor mouse that has but one hole – and if it didn't work he was shafted, and praise be he'd made his peace with God and set eyes on Het, though possibly not in that order. His sudden stillness gave the Malignant pause. He flexed his wrist. Hopefully it was the plates of his bridle-gauntlet making that appalling crunching noise, though from the feel of it he suspected not. "Make it quick, you bugger, because I'm not standing here all day," he said aloud.

And then, out of nowhere, there was a sudden gust of freezing hail, blowing straight into the faces of Rupert's crack cavalry, stinging and blinding. The rat-faced Malignant's chestnut horse jerked its head and started to back nervously up, and with the last strength in his right hand Hollie lunged straight for the cavalier's unguarded face.

Would have been a good trick if he'd pulled it off. The cavalier swore – his horse reared, hooves scrabbling on the cobbles, as Tib's full weight smashed into it – and then that fancy gentleman's pin of a sword skated shrieking across Hollie's breastplate and slid into the meat of his shoulder like a hot needle into butter.

It hurt. He hadn't expected it to hurt quite so much, and it suddenly seemed like not such a good idea to disarm your assailant by getting yourself skewered good and proper. Little black spots danced briefly in the corners of his vision. For the first time, the Cavalier looked scared – seriously scared, given that his sword was effectively useless stuck through Hollie's shoulder, and he was about four inches from the prominent nose of a most underwhelmed cavalry officer. "You," Hollie said, suddenly and unreasonably happy, "have pissed me *right off.*"

And before he could think any better of it, he caught hold of the cavalier left-handed by the collar, dragged him partly out of the saddle, and punched him full in the face with the full weight of his bridle-gauntleted armoured right hand. Hollie had dropped his sword, but since his right hand was effectively useless anyway it didn't matter much. Then he dropped the bloody-mouthed and stunned cavalier at Tyburn's feet. Still feeling quite ridiculously pleased with life, he turned the black's head into the bitter hail, and trotted blithely out of the press. Venning was doing sterling service, hacking his way through Malignants like they was standing corn. The Weston brothers shoulder to shoulder, as ever – one of them grinned and nodded to him, then nudged his sibling and the pair of them peeled out and cut in behind him like some kind of benighted honour guard.

"No need for that, lads," he said, and the worst thing about lobster pot helmets was how they made your voice sound proper peculiar, and that was more or less the last thought he had before he passed out.

## 12 FIRST IN, LAST OUT

He could usually work out where he was before he opened his eyes but this one had him at a loss. The sour smell of horse sweat and unwashed linen and woodsmoke - could be anywhere in the bloody Army, really. Mildewed canvas. A sudden waft of someone cooking outside – bacon, gone over, and the greasy, overripe smell made him retch. Which brought it to mind that he was back in the tent he shared with Venning and Luce Pettitt, and that some Malignant arsehole had rammed a sword through his shoulder and it hurt like buggery.

Well, at least someone had pulled the damn' sword out in one piece, and that was something. He did have to put up with Matt Percey being reproachful and anxious and all over him like a rash, though. Which made a change from it being Lucey Pettitt.

"Where *is* the brat?" Hollie demanded, propping himself up on one elbow. Percey scowled and pressed a pad of linen against Hollie's shoulder. He glanced down. "Christ, lad, there's nowt there, give over. Where's Lucey?"

"Nawthen there cos Percey has sat there for an hour making you tidy while you was dead to the world. Sews a neat hand, does Matthew. I got shirts worse mended than that." Venning sniffed disapprovingly. "By hell, bor, you're an ungretful lout. All you're bothered about is Lucey. Thank you, Matthew, that'd be nice."

He sat up with Percey's arm at his back, which was humiliating and reassuring at the same time. "What are you blethering on about, Venning?"

"You, you lollopin' gret mawkin – thought you was dead, till you started cussin' at Percey. I'll tell you for what, Hollie Babbitt, you ever pull a trick like that again and if'n they Malignants don't finish you off *I* bloody will –"

If it had been Luce – where *was* the brat? – he wouldn't

have minded the weakness. He'd spent the last six months being picked out of ditches by Lucey Pettitt, and he was getting used to the brat seeing him at his most useless. Percey looked terrified, and Venning's accent was outrageous - and Drew only sounded like that when he was either drunk or emotional. Worse than Hollie had guessed, then. "What'd I miss?"

"Oh, bloody typical. Not, what's the butcher's bill, but what'd I miss. You didn't miss much, bor, what with them trying to charge the bridge and a certain person what will remain nameless cluttering up the place with dead 'uns."

"They couldn't get across, like," Percey added, peering at Hollie's shoulder again. "You start that bleeding up again, sir, and I'll ask Captain Venning to have you knocked on the head." He exchanged a glance with Venning that Hollie evidently wasn't supposed to see, then slopped something into a cup and shoved it into Hollie's hand. Hollie sniffed suspiciously.

"What are you lot up to - that's enough, Matthew, I'm dizzy enough without you trying to get me pissed as well. What the hell's going on?"

Venning grinned. "We done it, bor. There was such a bugger's muddle at the bridge, what with you giving it hell on, and half Rupert's lot thinking it be a lark to try and ford the river – *not* a good idea – it was just a holy lash-up, and after your mate Shuck trained the guns on 'em they thought it weren't such a good idea to come by Caversham Bridge. And, course, they was expecting Colonel Fielding to come running out to help, and wasn't they disappointed, given that he's been waving truce flags at us since sun-up? Mind, we let 'em use the bridge to go home, poor sods. Gone back off to Oxford with their tails between their legs, and bad luck to 'em."

"Christ," Hollie said. "Have I been out that long, then?"

"Westons carried you in about four hours back, lad, and you been flat out since." Drew leaned forward and tapped Hollie between his eyebrows. "You want to use more o' this, my friend, and a bit less of what the dog been licking. You want to make that gal a widow before you even made it official?"

His shoulder hurt. "All right, I consider myself told," he muttered, hoping it wasn't apparent to either of them that most of what blood he had left in him was flooding his cheeks.

"Bloody cross with you I am, Captain Babbitt," Drew went on. "*And* you never even come back with your sword, unless they Westons left it somewheres when pair of 'em brought you in. Told you, we all thought you was a dead 'un. And now, if you'll excuse me, I'm going to have to go and tell your lot that you ent done for after all, poor buggers is a-wandering round not knowing if they're coming, going or been."

"All right, Drew, I heard you. I'll mind out, next time. Now, where the *hell* is Pettitt?"

"Around and about, lad, 's all you need to know for now. Bonesetter's had a look at you and he reckons you need plenty rest and plenty decent food to make up for all that bleeding you done. So –" Venning shrugged, unconvincingly casual. "Don't you worry about Lucey. Shut up and get that down your neck. Sent special, that was. You're getting a bit of a reputation for – now what was it the lad Russell said, the one with the marred face – first in and last out, usually feet-first, is what they're saying."

"Drew, *stop* changing the subject!"

"The boy's fine! He *will* be fine. When he sobers up. Bad news from home, lad, thass all. Between me, you and the gatepost. What I hear, is the lad's girl has gone off and got herself wed to somebody else whilst he was off fighting. But you didn't hear that from me."

"But the lad hasn't – oh, Christ, he's not *still* hankering after that widow wench, is he?"

"No idea, Rosie. All I know is some letter come in for

him with the dispatches and off he took. He's all right, bor. Lad's what, twenty, he'll not be short of lasses willing to kiss it better –"

With a stifled yelp, Hollie stood up. Venning was right, Matthew's sewing was stout. The stitches in his shoulder pulled like hell, but held. Just as well he was right-handed, and after the brief enforced rest his wrist was serviceable. Matthew scowled at him. "Sir, I don't think –"

"Apparently neither do I, lad, or so Captain Venning tells me. I'm off to find our Luce, and don't take it personal." Automatically he went to find his sword harness – didn't stifle the yelp that time, and didn't find his sword. Matthew grimly handed over the pin-sticker that had come out of Hollie's shoulder. "If that's supposed to be funny, Matt, it's not –"

And he forgot how young Percey was, at times. Under that shaggy mouse-brown fringe the lad's dark eyes suddenly brimmed over with tears. "You're right, sir, it's not," he said furiously, shoved the elaborate hilt into Hollie's good hand, and flung out of the tent.

"Bloody hell," Hollie said mildly, turning to Venning. Who was looking at him in disgust. "What did I say?"

"Don't be any more of a cock than the Lord made you, Babbitt," Drew said furiously, and followed Percey out into the rain.

# 13 TO ABSENT FRIENDS

Leaving Hollie utterly bemused. The one thing he could rely on, thank Christ, was that his horse wouldn't have taken offence at some imagined slight, so at least Tib might be good for some uncomplicated conversation. And he had no idea what he'd done, other than, apparently, not being dead. There was just no pleasing some folk. He left the spindly blade across the bed, because he surely didn't want it, and pushed the tent flap open.

Lucas Weston, standing sentry just outside, wasn't talking to him, either. A gust of wind blew stinging hail into Hollie's face and he gave serious consideration to turning straight round and going back to the tent, claiming incapacity. He was starting to be intrigued, though. Everything that was anything in a cavalry troop ended up at the horse lines, and so that was where he headed. When he got his own sword back – if he got it back, or if he just quietly acquired himself a new one, from some suitably plain Cavalier type who wasn't using it any more – he might have to do a bit more left-handed practice. Probably on either Matt Percey or Drew Venning, for a start.

Tyburn was tethered at a tactful distance from the lines, ungroomed, his coat shiny with rain and his saddle stained with blood. There was a scratch across the horse's muzzle, but that was the only mark on him. "Looks as if somebody'd slaughtered a pig across thy back," he said ruefully, scratching the black's whiskery jaw as the horse investigated his pockets. "Mind my shoulder, owd lad." Not surprised he felt quite as shaky as he did, if all that blood was his.

And there was hardly a soul around – gone chasing Royalists, if the distant noises in the hills were anything to go by. He recognised about half a dozen of his remounts – The Rabbit, for a one – and the brat's red mare, standing disconsolately with her nose to the Rabbit's draggled tail.

"Now where the hell is the lad?" he said aloud – again – and the mare lifted her head and pricked her ears at him. She was wet, but she hadn't been tacked up, this day. As immaculately groomed as ever she was, her white stockings splashed with mud but not stained, her tail free from tangles. Wherever the brat was, he wasn't neglecting his horse. Which made matters somewhat more peculiar. Well, Hollie was in no state to ponder too many mysteries. He leaned his good arm over Tyburn's neck and pretended to be lost in thought.

"Captain Babbitt, sir."

Gruff. Midlands. Not friendly. Not Ireton, then, and that meant – he opened one eye.

"Oh, Christ, not you."

Sariel Chedglow, that upright scourge of the ungodly and eschewer of soap and water as a dangerous vanity, eyed him with equal disfavour. "There is no discipline in your troop, sir!"

"Well, there you go." He really wasn't in the mood for Captain bloody Chedglow, who could take his righteous indignation and shog off, as far as Hollie was concerned.

"Well, sir, what are you going to do about it?"

"I'm going to wait for you to bugger off, Chedglow, and then I'm going to go back to my quarters and lie down. Will that suffice?"

"Kindly do not take that tone with me, Captain Babbitt! I am reporting the – the insubordination and licentious behaviour of one of your officers, sir, I expect this complaint to be dealt with through the formal channels!"

See, some of the troops, when they were wounded, cursed and swore. Some of them – not many, in Hollie's raff and scaff lot – prayed. Some were unnaturally quiet. Hollie had a tendency to throw up. It wasn't one he was proud of, hanging onto his horse's mane with one hand and hoping to God he wasn't going to disgrace himself in front of Sariel Chedglow. The plain russet-coated captain glowered . "You hurt?" he said grudgingly, and Hollie started to laugh and then stopped because it pulled his stitches.

He meant to shake his head in a sort of devil-may-care, nonchalant way, and then thought better of it. "Absolutely not," he said instead, looking at Tyburn's rain-soaked mane and hoping Chedglow didn't come over all ministering angel. He didn't think he could stand it, at close range.

"Thee should not be abroad." He took Hollie's arm – the bad one – and attempted to steer him away from the horse lines. Hollie was incapable of protest, with his shoulder streaming blood again and his teeth sunk in his bottom lip so as not to scream with the unexpected pain of it.

It wasn't a long walk back, although drooping against Sariel Chedglow was humiliating enough. Percey was sitting on the ground outside his tent, parked on his coat cleaning his carbine. He looked up, squinting into the light, with an expression that could only be described as smug. "Told you you wasn't fit to be up," he said, and his air of self-righteousness was so bloody irritating that it gave Hollie a degree of relish to direct the young trooper to find him a bowl, and be quick about it.

# 14 MISSING, PRESUMED DRUNK

One of the great things about Drew Venning was that despite being built like the side of a barn he managed to give an impression of meekness and docility that soothed all but the most savage. Quarter of an hour of being hectored by Sariel Chedglow with no reply but "yes, sir" and "no, sir" and occasionally, "certainly not, sir" and Chedglow stomped away satisfied. Venning, on the other hand, looked unrepentant as he stuck his head through the tent flap.

"You need me, bor, just shout up."

Percey looked up and grinned. "Nah, mate, we'll be fine. Rosie is asleep –"

"Not surprised," Venning grunted, "the way you was pouring that wine into him."

"Medicinal," Percey said primly.

"Bloody wasted, is what I call it, bor. Right. Be back in a bit, I will. Looks like we cornered the market in bloody incapacitated officers." And leaving Percey with the unenviable task of minding Hollie in a somewhat unlovely tent, Venning headed back to the horse lines.

Most of the lecture had been the lamentable lack of discipline amongst the younger generation of Hollie's troop. And that meant Luce Pettitt.

"Leave me alone," the muffled voice came from under one of the baggage wagons.

"Get out from under there, will 'ee? I'll not have half the army thinking I'm stood here talking to a bloody wagon."

"Oh, go away!"

"No." Venning leaned casually against the wagon, whistling, until a couple of troopers from Skippon's troop had passed out of earshot. "I ent going nowhere, Lucifer. Not till 'ee comes out and talks to my face, and not my boots. Thass enough, now, lad."

"I don't care!"

"Don't care? Well, 'ee should care, sir. Got poor ol' Rosie worried sick, so 'ee has – "

"What, Hollie? Talk sense, Drew, he doesn't worry about me –"

"Oh, he do, Lucey. What with half the bloody army telling him what a bloody state you're in, and what's he going to do about it – first thing he said, it was, after they pulled him off the bridge – where's the brat, he said – " looking innocently skywards, Venning shook his head. "Poor ol' Rosie."

"What?" Luce slithered out from under the wagon and faced his friend squarely. "He's hurt? How badly? Why did nobody –"

"Cos you was sulking under a wagon, bor? I knew where you was, but I ent telling." Venning sniffed. "Luce, you stink wuss than a four-ale bar, and if you was one o' my boys I'd have 'ee on a charge. Which is what Captain Chedglow's angling for. Ent no gal worth that, you ask me."

Luce straightened his shoulders and lifted his head proudly. "I'm sure I don't know what you mean, Captain Venning."

Venning shrugged. "Fair enough, I'll not mention it more. All I'm saying is, it ent fair to the lads, it ent fair to Rosie, it ent fair to – well, if 'ee thinks that lil' mawther up in wherever the hell it was, if 'ee thinks that lass is worth losing your commission over then – well then 'ee's a sawny fule, Lucey Pettitt, an' I never had 'ee pegged for hully gatless."

There was a long pause. "Missed a good fight, 'ee did," he added reflectively. "Should have seen our Rosie goin' at it on Caversham Bridge. Silly bugger. Don't reckon he'll be doing that twice. Luce."

Luce rubbed a grimy sleeve across his eyes.

"It is that lil' gal up Worcester way - not had no bad news from home, nawthen like that?"

Silently, Luce handed over a creased, dirty piece of much-worn paper. Venning squinted at it – held it closer, then further away, frowning. "Owd gal can't hardly write, bor. Thass no kind o' lass for a – I'll shut up, shall I?"

"That would be kind," Luce said wryly. He knew what the words said without looking. A letter he'd waited almost six months to receive, then this.

*Dere Lus,*

*I hope you will wish mee happie for I was marryed to Tomass Waytonn the carterr from Pillertun two wekes past.*

*I hope you are stil well and serveing yr Cawse as faythfullie as whenn I knew you. Ples give my kind rememmbrances to Capten Babett allso and I hope his arme is nowe better.*

*Yr frend alwaies,*

*Mistrss Sarah Waytonn*

"Well," Venning said, after a while. Shook his head. "Well."

"I thought she loved me, you see," Luce said blankly. "I – she – she said she – I don't understand, Drew, I just don't see – I mean, we – how could she – I thought she loved me."

There was another long silence. The returning troops were beginning to celebrate their victory, noisily. "I don't reckon as she could of, bor," Venning said uncomfortably.

"But I don't understand," he said forlornly, and the freckled captain gave him a rueful grin.

"If 'ee ever gets to the bottom of how women think, lad, be sure an' tell me, for I've been wed to our Alice for ten year and I still can't fathom her betimes. Luce, 'ee ent be the first to be led by the balls, and 'ee won't be the last. There's times it just don't work out, and thass all there is to it. We all been there, bor. I remember, when I was fifteen, had my eye to a girl out Bury way. Threw me over for some bloody jumped-up little prick in a satin doublet. Best thing she ever did, botty lil' bugger. I went after our Alice just to spite her." He scratched his bristly jaw, smiling reminiscently at nothing. "By God, she give me the runaround, that gal. Took me best part o' three years to bring her round. Thass not helping, is it?"

Luce shook his head, tangled fair hair falling in his eyes, and he winced and pushed it back. "I just feel such a fool, Drew. Hollie knew she didn't care for me. He tried to tell me, and I wouldn't listen."

Venning sniffed. "Hollie bloody Babbitt got less knowledge o'girls than *you* have, lad, so I wouldn't pay him no mind. Comes to us all, Luce. Show me a man says he's never been put on his arse by a lass and I'll call him a bloody liar. To his face." He put his arm round Luce's shoulders. "I ent going to buy you a drink, cos I reckon 'ee's had enough of that, by the smell of 'ee. What I *will* do is cover your arse, cos our Rosie's going to be spitting tacks. So I want 'ee washed, shaved, and in clean linen – head in a bucket o' cold water if need be, bor, but I want 'ee sober and back at the horse lines in an hour. Not a minute more. And we'll face our Rosie together."

Luce thought about it. It was a kind offer. Then he shook his head. "I'll get cleaned up. But I'll not lie to him."

# 15 COALS OF FIRE

In the end it took him less than half that time to make himself decent. Feeling about three inches high every minute of it, and wanting to get his lecture over and done with – and he was furious with the widow, who could at least have done him the courtesy of telling him she wasn't interested. Like a man who'd been well and truly taken advantage of, basically. If all she'd wanted was a bit of posh leg-over, as Hollie Babbitt had so crudely put it, she could have said so, and not let him humiliate himself. The idea that he'd gone round for the last six months bleating about his love for the bloody woman - that he'd written to her, not once but three times, mewling on about honour and chivalry and - oh, God, it made his stomach shrivel with shame. (And no small quantity of strong ale, as well, but he was trying not to think about that.)

And the idea that half the troop knew, and were quietly laughing up their sleeve at his naïveté – or felt sorry for him, like Venning – or had kept telling him, like Hollie, and when would he listen? He was hurt – he was hurt all right, in the pride as well as heart-sore – but he'd learnt his lesson well.

And then for an officer to actually miss a battle – oh, the humiliation of that. To be so unmanned by – by a silly girl, no better than she ought to be – and no, that wasn't fair, because she'd never said she cared for him – she'd never been other than decent to him, and it was his own stupid fault, and Luce scrubbed at his stinging eyes again with a cuff that was both stained and damp.

"Thass better," Venning said, as he arrived damp as a frog, but fit for civilised company. "Almost know 'ee as our Lucey again."

The freckled captain's gaze was appraising, but perfectly friendly. "Change your linen soon as may be, mind. Don't want all the bloody officers for your ruffianly lot laid up."

Luce winced. "Were you serious about Hollie – about Captain Babbitt, that is?"

"Oh aye, Rosie's like to be off the field for a bit. Nawthen that won't mend, bor, so 'ee needn't look so. Big lad ent got the sense of a day-old chick, and 'ee can tell him I said so. Now come on, and take your lumps."

Venning draped an arm across Luce's shoulders, burbling away about what he'd had for breakfast and what was likely to be on the menu for supper. It almost worked, and Luce almost forgot he was a spineless, shameful object of pity and derision. Right until he pushed open the tent flap.

"Look what I found, then," Venning said cheerfully, and Hollie – sitting up on the edge of the bed eating bread and cheese one-handed and looking distinctly wan and gory – looked up. If he'd scowled fiercely, or even glared, Luce would have been happier about the whole thing. Instead, he just looked like a man trying very hard not to laugh, and that piled coals of fire on Luce 's head.

"I am so sorry," he mumbled. "You must be so disappointed – I've let you down, I've let the troop down, I've –"

"Made a bit of a tit of yourself," Hollie said, giving in to the grin. "Chedglow's after your arse, did you know that?"

"And I deserve it."

"Not sure any bugger deserves Sariel Chedglow, Luce. Well. I've had cause to speak sharply to my lads before, brat, but I don't reckon I've ever had to discipline one for being drunk under a baggage wagon. So, er, you got any, er, excuse, or -" he coughed, and hid the grin behind his hand, "- is the hangover sufficient punishment?"

Silently, Luce handed over the crumpled note. Hollie read it in silence, apart from a brief snort at his own mention. Then he handed it back. "Well, you knew *that* was coming, didn't you?" he said.

"I had - had hoped not, Captain Babbitt."

"Don't even reckon you deserve to call me by my given name now, then, brat?" Very gingerly, the big redhead tucked his loose hair behind one ear. "If I had a penny for all the half-arsed stunts I've pulled in my time, lad, I wouldn't - no, all right, maybe more than a penny. We've all dropped a bollock on occasions, Lucifer. The point is not that you decided to get pissed for two days and go sulking in the baggage train, but what you're going to do about it."

"Apologise," Luce said glumly.

"Don't want your apologies, brat. Can't run a troop on apologies. I've had to cover your arse - Drew's had to cover your arse - pair of us have had to lie to fellow officers - it's not the first time I've made myself look bloody stupid for a mate but - for Christ's sake, Luce! Don't you ever bloody show me up like that again, or I won't just have you subject to military discipline, I'll take you out and bloody wallop you!"

"I only hope you think I'm worth it, captain," Luce muttered, and Hollie scrabbled around the bed - unavailingly - for something to throw at him.

"You're lucky Percey's took that bloody sick-bowl out, brat, or I'd be tempted to chuck it at you. Consider thisself on a warning, Pettitt. Tha's got a choice. Either grow a backbone, or fuck off out of my troop. I've got no bloody room for whiny brats - and less patience with 'em."

"It's my fault, isn't it? If I'd been there-"

Hollie blinked. Looked at the stained linen wadded against his shoulder - back up at Luce with an expression of mild astonishment. "Don't flatter your bloody self, brat. If you'd been there you'd have just got underfoot. You ain't that good with a pistol."

"I could have -"

"Well, you could, but you didn't, so let's leave it, shall we? You cocked up. End of. I could have done with you, but you made a bad call, and you won't do it again. Will you, Lucifer?"

There was a long silence. There was a bee, bumping, against the tent canvas. Luce looked at it resolutely. Hollie poked him, not very gently, with his foot. "Will you, brat? - and don't, for God's sake, cry. I'm in the doghouse enough already without that lot out there thinking I've reduced you to tears as well. Get summat to eat - get out of that bloody wet shirt - and get some sleep. And *no whining*."

Luce took a deep breath. "Thank you, sir."

"Hollie. I ent doing it as your commanding officer, brat. Consider it a favour to a friend, and one which will not be repeated. Now bugger off and leave me alone. Bloody shoulder's killing me."

"Can I get you anything?"

"Oh, you could, Luce. But sending you over White Notley to come back with our Het, might not go down too well wi't' lads. Thee is supposed to be in disgrace. As am I," he added thoughtfully.

"You? What for?"

"A blinding inability to recognise what's under my bloody great big nose. Now get lost."

# 16 NOTHING PERSONAL

For the first time that day, Hollie was left alone. Not even having his pockets raided by one of the horses. Just him and the bee, alone in the tent. And for the first time in probably ten years, Hollie wished to God it wasn't so.

He wasn't particularly quick off the mark at recognising friendship when it was offered. Didn't know what to do with it when he had it, either, most of the time. He'd had most of that kind of confidence knocked out of him back in Lancashire thirty years ago, on the buckle-end of his loving father's belt. It was only now, lay in a tent with his shoulder aching like fire and the beginning of a sick headache behind his eyes, that the penny dropped. That Percey, and Venning, and all the rest of them, actually liked Hollie. Worried about him. Had a care for him. He'd always been solitary, by inclination and by necessity. He envied Luce his easy popularity, but knew it wasn't for him. Hollie wasn't a man who could give his affections that lightly.

He wasn't a good officer. Truth be told he was a bloody terrible officer. He lost his head in battle, he had no idea how to delegate, he was ungracious, sweary, rag-mannered and disrespectful. And that had been fine, and while Rackhay had been alive he'd usually been stood next to his big blonde sidekick – who'd been a gentleman by birth, if not necessarily by inclination – taking his lead from Nat, keeping his head down, and saying nowt, and he'd muddled through, and most people thought he was more competent than what he was. And now he had Luce stood next to him, taking his lead from Hollie, and that was an unsettling feeling.

And he wasn't badly hurt. He'd had worse. Felt a bit limp, the shoulder was sore but he'd tried hefting that flashy Spanish steel left-handed and the stitches held, so it'd serve, with a day or two's rest. (And his new sword might look like the fashion statement of a Dago pimp, but it was worth a few bob, and that he would swear to.) Twenty years ago they'd have had to knock him on the head to get him off the field, even with a sword stuck through the muscle of his shoulder. Ten years ago he'd have just fell back and latched on to Rackhay and carried on fighting, and holed up with Rackhay and got medicinally rat-arsed for a week afterwards. Now – well, now he just didn't want to be here. Had nowt personal against Charles Stuart. He hadn't even been back in the country long enough to take any grievance against the King. Mercenaries couldn't be too nice over their principles. He was little better than a well-armed whore, and he knew it. No, he was just tired, and lonely, and utterly bloody miserable, because he wanted to be where Het was. That was all there was to it, he wanted to be in his own place, with his own girl, he wanted to be exclaimed over and petted and fussed. Instead he was flat on his back in a tent that smelt of blood, mildew, and, faintly, of sick: being hectored by his subordinates for something he didn't even know he'd done. Christ, he hadn't asked for Percey's terrier-like dedication. If he hadn't been so tired he thought he could have cried. He could hear Percey, just outside the tent flap, still scrubbing balefully at his carbine.

"Matthew."

The sound of scrubbing stopped. Outside, Hollie could hear the camp beginning to get riotous. The frivolity hadn't, thank God, spread as far as his troop yet. "What?" Percey said sulkily. And then, a sniff, as if the boy had remembered his duty. "Sir."

"Get in here, Percey."

There was another long pause. Someone outside the tent – a number of someones, with drink taken, by the sound of it shouted an invitation to Percey. "Shut up, you bloody rabble," he called back, crossly. "Got the bloody guv'nor in here trying to sleep. I'll come down in a bit, all right?"

The guv'nor felt lonelier than ever. "Percey!"

"What?" The lad's scowling face appeared through the tent flap. "D'you need something?"

"Get in. And sit down. And yes, when I've finished with you, I do need summat. Now. Park your backside – Lucey won't mind if you sit on his bed." Now, if only Hollie could get through this without either moving or opening his eyes, because moving would hurt, and he thought if he looked at Percey's furious, hurt face he might not be able to say it.

"Matthew, I – uh –" Never apologise, never explain, never take a direct order. That was how him and Rackhay had operated. And now Rackhay was gone, and – He took a deep breath. "Sorry, Matthew. I never thanked thee for thy care. Which was – better than I deserved. I was rude, and ungracious, and – ah, the hell with it, Mattie, I didn't realise either you or the Westons or indeed any other bugger in this troop had such a care for me. I will try and remember next time."

"Aye, well," Percey muttered, sounding embarrassed.

"Well, speaking as an officer, I would like to commend your actions." He rolled over, carefully, and sat up. "Speaking as a friend," he said ruefully, "I leave a lot to be desired. I won't suggest that thee kicks thy commanding officer up the arse, but if thee wants to take plain Hollie Babbitt behind the horse lines and give him the hiding of his life, I won't blame thee."

Percey's face remained impassive. "Sir. You said you needed something?"

"Apart from a kick up the arse, Percey – give us a hand up, will you? I could do with a drink."

"I believe the invitation to join Okie's lads for a few drinks was not extended to officers," Percey said stiffly. Then he turned his head and looked straight at Hollie. "Plain Hollie Babbitt might be welcome, though."

# 17 DAMNED WITH FAINT PRAISE

Hollie thought that if he lay very still and kept his head buried in the pillow he might not die. Whichever benighted bastard kept shaking him didn't seem to agree.

Eventually the shaking resolved itself into a thoroughgoing poking, somewhere in the region of his lower ribs.

"Captain - Hollie - will you wake up, sir!"

"No. Go away," he muttered, opening one eye in spite of his better judgment. "Oh God, it's you, Luce. I'd have thought you might have some fellow feeling. Them buggers in Okie's can't half put it back. We didn't get in till dawn -"

"So I heard," the young cornet said, with deep feeling. "But."

Admitting defeat, Hollie sat up. "I hope this is important, brat."

"Russell's outside."

"Good for Russell. Get the lad some breakfast, if he's been stood there long." He was about to roll himself up in his blankets again, when he realised the urgent semaphore Luce was trying to send him. "Russell? What, - " he ran a finger down his cheek, trying to ask Luce without actually saying out loud in earshot - what, Russell with the thumping big scar? Essex's Russell?"

Sober, Luce was a quick lad. He nodded.

"What's he after?"

"You. At Southcote. As a matter of some urgency. Full dress," Luce said drily, looking at Hollie's crumpled and bloody linen. "Well, maybe not full dress, but at least dressed."

"He'll get me upright with breeches on, and put up wi' it."

Russell - impeccable, uncrumpled, clean, Russell - looked Hollie up and down with some disfavour. "You took your time," he said.

"Ah, well, doing it one-handed." He eased his shoulder ostentatiously. "It doesn't half hurt."

"Really? From what I understand, it was perfectly serviceable last night," Essex's prim orderly said coldly. And then he looked directly at Hollie, those odd dark eyes cool and level on the big redhead's face. And winked. "Which has nothing to do with my lord Essex, does it?"

The ride back to Southcote was unexpectedly pleasant. After almost a month of rain, the hills around Reading were green, and the hedges scattered with almond-scented may-blossom. The sun was shining, the birds were singing, and best of all, they weren't sat in a ditch outside Reading twiddling their thumbs. Life was good. Even Tyburn was ponderously skittish, about as playful as a sixteen-hand warhorse got, cavorting sideways across the road with his nose in the air barging rather rudely into Russell's neat bay gelding. Hollie expected a ticking-off for this evidence of high spirits, and was astonished not to get one. "Russell," he said, cautiously, "am I in trouble, or summat?"

"You? Indeed not. Though -" he raised an eyebrow -"I shouldn't look for evidence of favour, were I you. Not my lord Essex's favourite. Though I imagine you're used to that, by now."

"Any idea what I *have* done, then?"

The unmarred corner of Russell's mouth twitched, and Hollie looked hard at the lad. Bloody shame about that scar, poor sod. He must have been quite remarkable to look at, before that. "Couldn't possibly comment, captain. Here we are -" he dismounted, neatly, and stood waiting for someone to appear from the Southcote stables to take his horse. Which they did, post haste, as if they'd been lurking just out of sight expecting his return. The Essex household evidently ran on much more disciplined lines under the hand of Thankful Russell than it had done under

Drew Venning.

"Is that ungovernable beast feeling sufficiently temperate to be led, this morning?" Russell said, indicating Tyburn. Hollie dismounted - much less gracefully - and looked at the big black, whose ears were pricked, and who seemed to be fascinated by the wallflowers.

"Aye, I think he might be as full of the joys of spring as -" As I am, he'd been about to say, and then stopped because it was a stupid thing to say to this prim, self-contained orderly, who didn't look like he knew what joy was. Russell nodded, thoughtfully.

"Indeed. I shall bespeak breakfast, then. And Captain Babbitt?"

Hollie stopped - guiltily - in the act of breaking off a sprig of lavender. Not sentimental, oh no, not him. Tucked it defiantly in the top buttonhole of his doublet, as a reminder that there was somebody in the world on his side. "Master Russell?"

"Keep your mouth shut, and your demeanour civil, and you may find a much kinder side to my lord Essex." The lad gave him another of those unfathomable looks. "If you take my meaning."

A nod being as good as a wink to a blind man, as they said, and Hollie none the wiser as he slouched into Essex's presence in his full scruffy bloodstained glory. Essex glared at him, said nothing, rearranged the papers on his desk, still said nothing, and Hollie could only think - oh hell, here we go again. Stared out at the garden, watching a cock blackbird bouncing about the gravel in the sun, stabbing for grubs with his perky yellow beak. Lucky little bugger.

"Well, what have you to say for yourself?" Essex said eventually, and Hollie must have looked blank. "Yesterday – that display on Caversham Bridge!"

"Sorry?" Hollie said hopefully. Wrong answer. The commander of the Army of Parliament looked at him as if he'd finally lost his mind. Mentally scrabbling for something suitably heroic and martial to say, he finally latched on to, "I don't suppose anybody picked up my sword, did they? ... my lord?"

"I do wonder, Captain Babbitt, if you are truly insubordinate, or simply too stupid to know better," Essex said with icy contempt, and Hollie knew the answer to that one.

"Bit o' both, I reckon. Sir."

Well, for the first time in their acquaintance, the big boss was nodding in agreement with something he'd said. "Well, Babbitt. You are, I presume, aware of Lord Fairfax of Cameron?"

"I, er, I reckon. Probably." Tell him what Lord Fairfax of Cameron's horse looked like, and he'd be somewhat the wiser, but he nodded and tried to look intelligent, which was difficult with half a yard of unbrushed hair falling in his eyes and a hangover.

Essex glared at him. "Commander of the forces of Parliament in Yorkshire, Babbitt."

"Oh, well, *him*, aye."

"Well, you are Northern by birth. Lord Fairfax is requesting support for his forces. You will, I 'm sure, be delighted to return home."

It was, he thought, supposed to be a compliment. One Northerner was probably much like another, to Essex. Yorkshire, Lancashire, they were all practically bloody Scots anyway, what difference did it make? Apart from the difference of mortal offence to a Lancashire man by birth, to have God's own country mistaken for - the other place. "I see you are delighted with your recognition," Essex said smugly, and Hollie could have willingly gobbed him.

“You want me to go to –“ he tried not to make it sound like a curse - “Yorkshire?”

“Indeed, captain. No – there is no need to thank me – I can see for myself that you are quite overcome – you may return North with all possible dispatch.”

The stupid bastard even seemed quite affronted that Hollie wasn’t packing to leave straightaway. Staring rigidly out across the knot garden, he'd never been so relieved to see an approaching pack of Malignants in all his life: even if they were coming to discuss terms of surrender they let him off the hook because he was shaking with a most unreasonable desire to grab the Earl of Essex by his starched elegant collar and throttle him. And for all his failings, Hollie had quite a well-developed sense of self-preservation, and he suspected that giving the Army's commander-in-chief a bloody good pasting might count as court martialable.

He was just on his way out of Essex's quarters going like the wrath of God and about to give the door a good hard bang behind him when he found his way blocked by Russell.

"Get out of my bloody way –"

Russell looked up at him with that chilly, twisted smile, and braced his hand against the door so that Hollie couldn't slam it. And try as he might he bloody well couldn't, either. The lad looked like he'd snap in a high wind but he had muscles like steel wire, under that pretty black doublet. "Kitchen," Russell said coolly. "Now, captain, if you please."

Hollie must have looked mutinous, because Russell raised his eyebrows. "I can assure you, I did not put the cook to the trouble of preparing your breakfast for nothing. Now. Kitchen."

And sitting in a warm, dark, fragrant kitchen being plied with new-baked bread and bacon, by a terrified kitchen maid who gave every evidence of being more frightened of Russell than she did of Hollie, and with a mug of decent ale on the table in front of him, he felt slightly less murderous. But only very slightly. Russell said nothing, only sat at the kitchen table with his clean white hands steepled in front of him, picking daintily at a slice of bread.

"You going to eat that, or just reduce it to rubble?" Hollie said irritably.

Russell shrugged. "I've dined this morning already, captain. Not all of us were out till all hours carousing with the gentlemen of Okie's troop. I am merely being civil."

"Shame to waste it, then." Hollie snagged it neatly from Russell's plate. "I've got to ask, Russell. You're going to a lot of trouble on my behalf. You sweet on me, or something?"

Those cool dark eyes rested on his face for a moment, appraisingly. "Personally, captain, I prefer my companions to be –" the unscarred corner of his mouth lifted again. "Cleaner?"

"Don't push your luck, lad. I clean up as well as the next man."

"Doubtless. Now. I understood my lord Essex to be as much in your favour as he's likely to get, when he instructed me to bring you here . He spoke of recognition for your, ah, bravery –"

"Stupidity," Hollie muttered. "He never said bravery. He did say stupidity."

Russell flicked a hand. "I'm sure it's not what he meant. There was some mention of offering your services in a position of relatively independent command –"

"Yes, in bloody *Yorkshire*!" Hollie snarled, forgetting briefly that he was talking to Essex's dispassionate aide. Who looked at him as blankly as Essex had done.

"But you *are* a North Countryman –"

"Oh, for Christ's sake, not you as well! Being born in a stable does not make you a horse, Russell – I could spit out o't' bloody window and find you half a dozen bloody Yorkshiremen out of Essex's own lifeguard to toss out to Fairfax, if he wants a few more bodies. Matthew bloody Tomlinson, for a start – he wants to start handing out preferment, he could have started a bit closer to home, couldn't he?"

"I believe my lord would prefer to retain his own Lifeguard in its present form, captain," Russell said smoothly, and Hollie glared at him.

"Get rid o'me, more like. If me and thee are to reach any kind of understanding, get it into your thick head, I am not a bloody Yorkshireman. I am Bolton born, and Bolton bred, and I will live and die a Lancashire lad. Hast tha got that straight?"

"As far as I can comprehend your barbarous northern accent, I believe I may have grasped your meaning."

The lad was laughing at him. Unsmiling, prim, cool as ever, but he was laughing nonetheless. "Russell, I'll grasp thee shortly by the bloody throat, if thee doesn't stop taking the piss. It's not funny."

"There is a certain irony to the situation, Captain Babbitt, I think you'll agree. May I help you to more ale?"

Hollie buried his face in his hands. Smelt lavender, the bruised stalk he'd picked earlier on, still tucked in his buttonhole. Swore, at length, in several different languages, and didn't feel any better for it. Russell was looking at him inquiringly. "You married, Master Russell?"

And for the first time, he saw some unguarded human emotion on that pale, half-handsome face. Briefly. "I am not, sir," Russell said flatly, turning the scarred side of his face towards Hollie to look into the fire, as if the scars were the explanation.

"Aye. Me neither. Nor, thanks to my lord Essex's crack-brained ideas, am I likely to be. She's hardly likely to wait for me, is she? Christ, what a bloody lash-up. That's assuming I actually come back. They eat their own young in bloody Yorkshire, Russell. Ignorant bastards. What'm I supposed to do? Write to her? 'Wish me good speed, for I am going into a wilderness, where I shall find no path nor friendly clue to be my guide.' – aye, lad, that's Webster again. I bloody *feel* like I'm in a revenge play." He stood up, glared at the kitchen maid, who scampered out of his way like a startled rabbit as he started to pace the kitchen. "Oh, Christ, why am I telling you? You wouldn't understand – "

"Very true, captain. I have no conception of why you should leave your lady behind. Had *mine* been willing, I wouldn't have."

Hollie stopped pacing. Russell looked up at him blandly. "I haven't *always* looked like this. Now. Correct me if I'm wrong. You have been offered a – perhaps not a promotion, in as many words, but a step sideways – removing you and your men from the, ah, malign influence of my lord Essex. The issue with acceptance being twofold –"

"Russell."

"Hmm?"

"Do you already know my cornet, or were you two longwinded bastards just separated at birth?"

Russell gave him a faint, wintry smile. "I do know Cornet Pettitt. Now. One – your posting is in Yorkshire, a region to which you have some native antipathy – shall I stop, sir?"

"And the epitome of feminine pulchritude to which I made earlier reference is in Essex. I can play, too. I'm not so thick as you think I am, Russell." Hollie gave him a stern look. "And you're not half so up yourself as you like to let on. What are you thinking?"

"I am thinking, captain, that for a man so notoriously wilful in the heat of battle you have a remarkable lack of grasp of civilian tactical manoeuvres. Take the promotion, sir, and run like hell. You will not get it twice, from my lord Essex. He doesn't like you, Captain Babbitt. And I'm not sure, but I *think* I do." Suddenly, Russell grinned, and looked like a man, and not a marble statue. "If nothing else, you make things interesting."

# 18 WISH ME GODSPEED

Hollie had barely sat down – and he was determined to finish this letter to his girl, though Essex and Charles Stuart and the rest of both armies stood in the way – when Luce poked his head through the tent flap. "I think you're about to receive another summons, Hollie."

Russell gave the cornet a superior glance. "Not on official business, Cornet, you may be at ease. I am acting in the nature of a prompt. Before the summons, you might say." He inspected his immaculate fingernails casually. "Are you waiting for something particular, captain? Divine intervention?"

Hollie squinted up at him. "Oh, Christ, don't tell me Essex has gone sweet on me now. He can't keep away." Outside the tent, like a faithful dog, Percey snorted with laughter.

Even Russell cracked a smile. "Hardly, captain. My lord Essex is wondering why you're still here. *I'm* wondering why you're still here."

"We had this conversation about an hour ago, Russell. Want me to remind you my opinion of Yorkshiremen, or are your ears still burning?"

"I wasn't referring to Yorkshire, captain. I was referring to a certain – nettle, shall we say – of your acquaintance, in need of grasping."

It seemed to have gone very quiet in the tent all of a sudden. Hollie set his pen down and looked up at Essex's prim orderly. "I'm not feeling very quick this morning, Master Russell. Perhaps you'd like to explain what you're on about, in plain English?"

"Your horse is outside, Captain Babbitt. I took the liberty of having The Rabbit saddled for you. Less conspicuous, and, if you will forgive me, possibly easier to manage one-handed."

Hollie rubbed his nose, blissfully unaware of the great streak of ink he'd just transferred to that most prominent of features. "Are you suggesting, sir, that I should abandon my post –"

"I am *hinting*, captain, that were you *not* to abandon your post on a purely *temporary* basis, that the opportunity for a more *permanent* arrangement may be impossible to reach for some months to come." Russell was the only man Hollie knew who could talk in italics. "I believe *Essex* is most pleasant at this time of year, captain. Do we understand each other?"

"No," Hollie said honestly, and the orderly blew an impatient breath.

"Then I'll give it you plain, sir. The commander of the Army of Parliament is wondering why you're not whooping with glee at your promotion and packing your bags to be gone. The lady in the *county* of Essex of whom we spoke earlier is still there. She may *not* still be there if, and when, you come back from Yorkshire. *Now* are we clear?"

"I'm intrigued. What's it to do with you?" Said Hollie, standing up with his good arm through the sleeve of his buffcoat like he wasn't halfway out of the door already.

"Reasons many and various, captain." Russell lifted Hollie's tangled ponytail – wincing as he did so – from where it was trapped under the stiff oxhide. "Your temper is sweetened immeasurably by the good influences of that lady, so I am assured. Secondly, that your dithering is starting to vex me, and you stand in want of a kick in the seat of the breeches – in my humble opinion. And thirdly, because not a year ago I was a most respectable lieutenant of Colonel Hampden's Greencoats, before I came by *this* – " he tapped his scarred cheek and Hollie took an involuntary step back. Russell didn't look lively very often but by God when those dark eyes took fire he was a fearsome-looking bugger. "I dithered, Captain Babbitt. I *arsed about*, just like you're doing. And by the time I'd got up the nerve to speak to the lady in question, she'd decided her prospects were better elsewhere. And look where it got me. Now. You may consider me a soft-hearted fool, or consider me a meddlesome fool, but do your considering on horseback."

Hollie favoured him with a thoughtful stare. Then he did something he very rarely did, with anyone. He reached out and put a hand on Russell's shoulder in passing, and gave him an awkward pat. "I take thy point, then. And –" he glanced over his shoulder, just before the tent flap closed behind him –"sorry about your girl."

Russell took a deep breath, alone in the tent. "Yes," he said softly. "Yes, so was I."

# 19 MORE THAN A HANDFUL BEING A WASTE

Het Sutcliffe was elbow-deep in linen, turning out the contents of the big press in her chamber ready for the first wash of the spring and setting all the household linens into three piles. "Wash, mend, retire," she said, smiling up at her long-suffering housekeeper.

"Indeed, mistress. What d'you think to these sheets – pretty, but full of the moth."

Mary held up a heavy diapered linen sheet, then waggled a fingernail through one of the offending holes. "Get these mended and they'd be just right for the blue chamber. Be nice in there next time we have guests, now the window's fixed up."

And then mistress and housekeeper ostentatiously didn't look at each other by mutual agreement at the mention of guests. Het didn't think she'd made a total fool of herself over Cousin Luce's friend. She thought she'd struck a fine balance between being friendly, and being cool. Appropriately grateful, for the work he'd put in on the farm, and the company, and the conversation. But distant, at the same time, as befitted a respectable widowed matron of mature years. Not the sort of lady who'd stand behind a guest in her house, with her fingers itching to take the tie out of his tangled hair and comb it properly for once. Certainly not a lady who'd lose her concentration mid-sentence because her guest had remarkably fine tawny-green eyes. Absolutely not any kind of lady who would make it her business to fatten her guest like a Martinmas goose before sending him about his business, neat and definitely tidier. She'd had her way with the ponytail. She'd taken her embroidery scissors to it one afternoon in the parlour and trimmed the ragged ends off. To her shame and secret delight, she kept the trimmings, tied with a silk ribbon, in her embroidery bag. She took them out, sometimes, when she was alone, just to remind herself of the admirable and distinctive cinnamon-brown of his hair. Not the same colour as his eyelashes, though. They were a much darker brown, and as pretty as a girl's -

Well, there it was, and there was no point dwelling on his remarkably fine eyes. Captain Babbitt was a decent, shy man – and misunderstood, not at all the filthy-tempered ruffian of Luce's letter – she'd always found him to be gentle, and above all, rather forlorn. Life had not treated him kindly and Het had a soft spot for the wounded. She thought the Lord might turn a blind eye to her looking on Hollie Babbitt with a somewhat proprietorial eye, even if he never needed to know it. The poor man had no one else, after all – no other home to go to, and she allowed herself, briefly, to indulge in a whimsy where he came back to Fox Barton. Hurt, probably, and chased by a Malignant troop – or two – and she'd give him shelter, laughing in the face of the wicked Royalist, and he'd be smitten by her bravery and her daring, and -

Mary was giving her the sympathetic look again, and she smiled weakly and took the sheet from her housekeeper, folding it over her arm. "I think it may be time for dinner," Het said, feeling herself blush at being caught out once again in idle dreaming. "Shall we finish this afternoon?"

"Seems fair, mistress. I wouldn't want to waste that apple pasty that Williams has been slaving over all morning, either." Mary's dark eyes rested, with some sympathy, on Het's face. The same square, freckled face that faced her in the glass every morning, but somewhat more shadowed about the eyes than previous. "Wasting away, gal, so you are."

Which made her laugh, at least, and put a hand to her well-filled bodice. "Then God send more wasting away, Mary, for I'm still more than an ample handful!"

And so she ate in solitary splendour in the parlour,

looking out of the window – the stopped window, which now no longer leaked, another one of her gallant captain's endeavours – across the herb garden down to the river, and the rooks in the spinney on the edge of the water tossed like rags in a rising spring wind. Fresh bread, warm from the oven – creamy, salty, crumbly new cheese, still moist from the dairy – a wedge of ember tart. A handful of raisins. They were spoiling her – tempting her appetite, bless them, as if it were her appetite that pained her.

There was a tap at the door.

"Put it on the table, Catterall. I'm not yet done. I will ring when you can clear the dishes."

Her steward bowed. "Indeed, madam. I will do that very thing, when I have something to put on the table. You have a visitor, mistress. Captain Babbitt from Reading."

And Het had never fainted in her life but she felt the blood drain out of her face, and she put a hand to the mantelpiece, dizzy. "But – "

"I'll get some cordial," Catterall said briskly. "Stop where thee is, gal. Don't ee move."

As if she could. Standing like a mooncalf with her skirts brushing the embers of the fire staring at him, standing there in her neat, orderly parlour, and she thought for a moment he was a ghost, he was that wan and bloody. His left arm was strapped across his chest in a ragged-looking sling, most of his hair was loose from its bindings and tangled down his back, his linen was stiff with dried brown stains, he hadn't shaved in days, and there was a rather comical streak of ink down the bridge of his nose. "Oh love, what have you done to yourself?" she said without thinking, and he blinked at her as if he hadn't heard her properly and then flew across the parlour and took her in a fierce embrace.

Catterall cleared his throat disapprovingly, but neither of them paid him any mind. Tried again, louder. Still got nowhere. "I shall assume the captain will be staying for dinner, then," Catterall said grimly. "I'll let Williams know, madam."

The top of her head just about fitted under his chin. "Tha was meant to be there," he said contentedly, "see? Tha was fitted to held so –"

To which Het had no response but to hug him the tighter. "Oh Hollie look at you, you might have been killed."

He was shivering. She told him, in case he hadn't noticed, and he looked down at her with that silly grin on his face – it was a silly grin, she might be in love with the man but she knew a silly grin when she saw one – and said he wasn't shivering, he was shaking. "Thought thee might send me home with a flea in my ear, lass."

"You might have been *killed*," she said again, and then she burst into tears. Fetched him a hearty thump on his good shoulder and shouted at him, quite incoherently, until Catterall came back with a fowling-piece in his hands that must have last seen service when the old Queen died, adding some shouting of his own to the proceedings, and then Het started shouting at Catterall and Hollie thought the whole thing was getting out of hand so he waited till there was almost a lull in the cacophony and –

"Be quiet!" he yelled, full battlefield volume, and about the only sound for what felt like a hundred years afterwards was the soft burble of a wood pigeon half a mile away.

Het put her head against his shoulder – not the good one, but he didn't care – and sobbed like a baby. "The issue appears to be that I'm not dead," he explained to Catterall, man to man, over the lady's head. Catterall looked as confused as Hollie felt, but at least he wasn't pointing that antique weapon quite so threateningly any more.

"You are *stupid*," she said feelingly, into his armpit, with a watery hiccup. (A brave woman, given that this had been his last clean shirt, a week and a half ago.)

"Stupid, and not dead," he agreed. "I'm with you so far."

She straightened up and gave him a pink-eyed, disapproving glare. "Look at you. *Look* at you. You might have been –"

"Killed," he said, trying to be helpful, and set her off crying again.

They compromised, eventually. That Hollie might have been killed, but hadn't been, and that was a good thing. That Hollie was stupid, and he wouldn't argue with that either. That Het was the wisest, fairest, and best conditioned woman in the world; and that she was the fittest wife for him, that God hath allotted him, and therefore Hollie should rest himself contented in her and satisfied with her, and live with as much alacrity and cheerfulness with her as may be. He was impressed with that last, given that it was remembered wholesale from one of the Puritan marriage manuals – Gataker, he thought, from memory – that he'd read quite obsessively as a young lad. That and the dirty bits from the Song of Solomon were about the only religious texts that had stuck.

Het just looked at him with those pansy-brown eyes of hers on his face, and occasionally straying to his shoulder and brimming over with tears, and he looked at her and said, "Tha must get used to it, lass, if tha's to be a soldier's wife."

"I don't mind you getting yourself as full of holes as a sieve, as long as I'm there to mend you," she said woefully, and he'd been about to say something wise and comforting and –

"*Het.*" She blinked lovingly up at him. "Give over wi' that, lass, it's most distracting you sat there batting your eyelashes at me. How am I supposed to think straight?"

"You're not," she said demurely, and the thought crossed his mind that it was ridiculous, neither of them would see thirty again and here they were billing and cooing all over the damned parlour like a pair of elderly lovebirds. Shameful.

"*Henrietta*," he said sternly, and her lips twitched. "It will be Sunday tomorrow, lass."

"I know. Will you come to church?"

"No. I'll be in Reading." He thought about it. "I'll go to church in Reading, if tha likes? If we left any of 'em standing, that is… You attend service here, and I'll go in Reading, and we can each think of the other and – you're doing it again, Het. Distracting me. Lass, can we – would you – d'you reckon we can talk to the parson this afternoon? Get married before I have to go north?"

She stopped sweethearting him, just like that. It was one of the things about Henrietta soon-to-be-Babbitt that made him breathless, her ability to put her mind to business at a word. "North?" she echoed.

"Aye. Bloody Essex is sending me to Yorkshire. *And* I'm supposed to be grateful for it," he added bitterly. She opened her mouth and he gave her a stern look. "Don't you start. I'm not from Yorkshire. I've never been to Yorkshire, and I would happily go to my grave without going to Yorkshire."

"I was *going* to say," she said archly. "that if we are intending to call on the parson this afternoon, a change of linen may be in order. Would you come upstairs and see if any of my late husband's shirts are suitable?"

He didn't choke, or die, or do anything else unhelpful. He did stand up and she put her hand into his and squeezed his fingers very tight. "We decided earlier that I'm stupid," he said, and she smiled up at him indulgently.

"We did, love."

"That's *not* what you mean, then, is it? About the linen?"

She shook her head. "You're shaking again, Hollie."

"Lass, you scare me worse than the King's Army. All of 'em. Together."

"Then I suggest, my dear, that you yield with as much grace as may be."

And Hollie, recognising a superior force when he came up against it, surrendered.

# 20 CONCERNING THEM THAT REBEL

It was the third week where Het had sat in the cool, dusky church, quite alone in the midst of the congregation, listening to the stifled sniggers as her banns were read for the last time. Sitting with her hands neatly folded on her prayer book, her back straight, her eyes fixed on the shoulders of the man in front so intently that she could have told you to the day the last time he'd washed his hair.

Half the village thought she was besotted, and the other half thought she was an adventuress. She wasn't even sure that her own household were on her side. Holofernes Thomas Babbitt, widower of the parish of Bolton le Moors in Lancashire, sounded like a stranger. Come to think of it, Henrietta Sutcliffe, widow of the parish of White Notley, didn't sound like the person she saw in the mirror, either. Her future husband was also conspicuously absent. On her good days, the days when the sun was shining and a carpet of bluebells spread under the trees, she thought he'd come back. Was alive, and whole, with nothing worse than the whole of the Royalist Army between him and his wedding. Some days she thought he was probably dead: he was too conspicuous, with the height and that deep red hair, a prize for any sharpshooter. Reason told her that any Cavalier snipers would be more like to aim their guns at someone of more strategic importance than a plain provincial Captain of Horse, but even so. And then, on the long wet days when everything was grey and sodden, she thought he'd never meant to marry her at all. And she couldn't blame him – *he* hadn't suggested taking her to bed, that had been her own brazen suggestion, and now she was reaping the whirlwind.

Her eyes prickled, and she scowled down at her hands again. She'd shed enough tears. No point crying over spilt milk, what was done couldn't be undone. And at least she had that hour to remember him by. There was a scuffle at the back of the church – a stifled struggle, as of someone being physically removed from their place – someone purposefully striding up the aisle. Her traitorous heart leapt.

"Hutch up, lass," Captain Babbitt hissed, insinuating himself quite shamelessly between Het and stiffly disapproving Mistress Saltram from the village.

"Sir!" Mistress Saltram said, more loudly than perhaps she'd meant, and half of the congregation turned round, sniggering, to look at the pop-eyed goodwife struggling to free her skirts from underneath Het's intended. Hollie managed to look outrageously innocent as the plump matron wrestled with her trapped garments.

"Madam, kindly behave with more dignity in the Lord's dwelling-place," he said disapprovingly. "Be still, and pay attention."

Het refused to look at him. He settled himself more comfortably next to her – occasioning a further stifled yelp from Mistress Saltram – arms folded, in an attitude of fierce attention. She'd have almost believed him lost in godly thought if he hadn't poked her surreptitiously in the ribs. And then continued to poke her until she looked in his direction.

"Captain Babbitt, if you don't behave, I'll –" she glanced around for inspiration – "I'll fetch you such a whack with this prayer-book!"

"You wouldn't dare, lass." He said it without moving his lips, too, which spoke of unsuspected practice at such wickedness.

"Just try me and see, young man." She slipped her hand under the prayer-book and caught his fingers before he had chance to provoke her any further. And there they sat, hand in hand like a pair of naughty children, not paying the least bit of attention to a lengthy sermon against disobedience and wilful rebellion. "Well, that's me buggered then," Hollie whispered for her ears alone, and she choked with most irreverent laughter, receiving another scandalised look from Mistress Saltram.

Who laid in wait for them in the churchyard. "So this is your betrothed, Henrietta?" she gushed. "A amiable young man, I'm sure. What a delightful secret for you. How refreshing to find someone so charmingly - unconventional."

Hollie sighed with equal insincerity. "Ah, well, madam, an officer's duties must take priority over my own pleasure, you understand – hard work, rooting out the ungodly. Murmurous complainers, walking after their own lusts, and their mouths speaketh great swelling words, having men's persons in admiration because of advantage. The Book of Jude, madam, chapter one. Like my namesake Holofernes," he went on, looking heavenwards, "I am commanded by the Lord concerning them that rebel, let not mine eye spare them, but put them to the slaughter, and spoil them wherever I go."

The lady's jaw hung open unflatteringly. Whatever she'd been imagining of Het's intended, a straight-laced Puritan hadn't been amongst her imaginings. "Quite so," she said, backing away as politely as she could muster. "I – I wish you all joy of your marriage, Henrietta."

"That was unkind," Het said severely. "And she'll go halfway round the village telling everyone that you're possessed of an unnaturally godly zeal, and I'll never hear the last of it." She paused. There was, after all, a lot she didn't know about Captain Babbitt, after six weeks of acquaintance and something less than a day of formal courtship. "You're not, are you?"

He glanced at her sideways, thoughtfully, straight-faced, and she was filled with a sudden sense of foreboding - and then he grinned, and she was *sure* there was a lot she didn't know about him, including the possession of a dry as dust sense of humour. He shook his head. "Afraid not, owd lass. On the other hand, if she reckons I'm some maniac Dissenter, it explains why I'm not so fussy about a fancy ceremony, don't it?"

"I don't understand, Hollie."

"Ask your man there –" he nodded towards the parson, blinking hopefully in their direction – "us Independent types don't hold with all this ceremony, lass. As long as it's noted down, we could stand up in front of my *horse*. If the bugger was ordained."

"Holofernes, you are most thoroughly disrespectful!"

He caught her by the elbows and shook her, gently. "Essex is getting impatient wi' me, lass. I must have had every fever going, this last three weeks. He reckons I'm still a-bed with wound fever. I can't hold him off much longer, Het, he's starting to get arsy as it is. Come back to Reading wi' me, lass. Now. The hell with ceremony. I'll get one of Essex's Lifeguard to draw up the marriage contracts – buggers are all lawyers anyway, do 'em good to earn their keep - Philip Skippon's own chaplain is - *unconventional* in his beliefs, Master Erbery won't cavil if we stand up in front of him –"

"Stand up like this, Holofernes?" she said stiffly. "In my workaday clothes, without bridesmaids or ceremony? To celebrate my marriage hole-in-corner, as if it were shameful?"

He looked at his feet, and scuffled, awkwardly. "Tha looks fine to me, lass," he muttered. "But thee always does."

"I had hoped for at least another week, if only to finish my linen -"

"I'll be halfway to Fairfax in a week, Het. If I could marry thee now – aye, in all my soldier's dirt – I'd do it, and the hell with – beg your pardon, to perdition with clean linen. I'd have thee lawful before I go, love. Just in case."

She took a deep breath, and before the eyes of most of the population of White Notley brushed the loose hair off his face. "Come on, then. Let me bring my maid, for decency's sake."

"I am *not* marrying your Liza as well."

"No. But I imagine she has more expertise with lacing than you do, Holofernes." She gave him a sideways smile. "You blush most fetchingly, sir."

"And you, madam, are incorrigible."

He gave her his arm. She tucked her fingers in the crook of his elbow, astonished by the solid and reassuring feel of him under her hand. He was real, and alive, and whole. She had neither dreamed him nor been deceived in him. Every bird in White Notley was singing split to fit their throats in the trees.

She wasn't sure, but she was almost positive he winked at Mistress Saltram as they passed her.

# 21 ON A NEED-TO-KNOW BASIS

Luce was mildly astonished, to say the least, to walk into the damp kitchen of their quarters and find his Auntie Het frying eggs in a skillet over the fire. She inclined her head with admirable aplomb. "Good afternoon, Lucifer."

"Auntie Het – what – " he shook his head, blinking hard. "It is truly you, isn't it?"

"It is, Luce. Me and a dozen eggs fresh off the farm this morning, which I am presently endeavouring to make into something approaching a meal. That being, I believe, one of the primary functions of camp followers. Would you pass me the bread, dear?"

"Camp followers?" he yelped. "Auntie, have you lost your mind?" "

"Not as far as I'm aware, Luce, no. These eggs are catching, so if you would be so good as to hand me the bread before they stick to the bottom of this pan? Thank you. That's a good boy." She looked critically at the resulting platter. "It's hardly festive, is it? Mind you, this place could do with a clean –"

"Auntie Henrietta, will you kindly enlighten me as to what the –" he stopped himself in time from what he was about to say, which wasn't something you should say in front of a lady. "What you're doing, quite unchaperoned, in Reading. A city which was under siege until all of a month ago, madam, and do you have any idea of the wanton and licentious behaviour of the troops on their first entry into the streets?"

She straightened up. She was wearing her best pearl and pierced-gold ear-bobs, he noticed suspiciously. "Lucifer, if you cannot keep control over your own men, then you should leave the work to them as can. Anyway, I am not unchaperoned. Liza is here. She just happens to be at the market buying me a length of ribbon, presently." And she raised her chin and looked haughtily down her nose at him.

"Answer the question, madam."

"And I'm not your subordinate, young man, so you can speak to me with a bit of respect, or you're not too big to go over my knee. Now. My eggs are going cold, here. Dig in, dear, while they're still hot. I'll do the rest later. And sit down, you're making me nervous, standing about the kitchen like that."

"Well, thank God *something* is," he muttered, but didn't refuse the eggs. Fresh eggs were not something to turn down, in a town so recently relieved of occupation. Fancy Auntie Het knowing that.

"When you've finished, I imagine you've got time to change your linen. Do you think you could find time to shave as well?"

His hand automatically went to the minute amount of stubble on his jaw, and he found himself just as automatically checking his linen. Auntie Het never looked any different, always spotlessly clean and wholly unfashionable, whether you put her in workaday broadcloth or in festival silks. She was a terror for hunting out dirt and scouring, was Auntie Het. Not for the first time, Luce wondered exactly what she saw in the wilfully-scruffy Hollie. A challenge, probably.

Which thought put a dreadful suspicion into his mind. "Where *is* Captain Babbitt, auntie?"

"I hope he's not going to be long, Luce. Gone to hunt down a gentleman called – Herbery? Garden? – Sir Philip Skippon's chaplain, anyway. He will be most vexed, I'm sure, if he doesn't get an egg. He seemed very enthusiastic about the eggs earlier on."

"Erbery. William Erbery." Skippon's pet Ranter. A chaplain. A fellow Dissenter. Oh God.

Is something the matter, dear?" She put her head on one side, looking at him as she'd looked at him when he'd been a little boy grazing his knees falling out of trees in the orchard. Like he was making a great deal of fuss about nothing.

"Auntie Het –" he took a deep breath – "you and the captain aren't - you haven't been…. have you?"

And she looked at him blankly, and then threw back her head and laughed that gurgling bawdy chuckle of hers and he knew it was uncharitable in him but before God Auntie Het's laugh made him cringe. "Well, really, Lucifer, what do you *think*?"

What did he think? He thought it explained a lot. The light of maniac glee in the captain's eye, this last three weeks, and his sudden uncharacteristic dedication to matters of discipline and cleanliness. A most unlikely turn towards the virtuous, and clean shirts almost every other day. Luce gulped.

He had been perfectly well aware that his commanding officer had been – smitten, that was a good word, smitten – but the idea of Hollie as a relative by marriage hadn't seriously crossed his mind. "You are – going to *marry* him?"

"Well, I do hope so, dear, or poor Liza has had a long ride for nothing." She looked up from her eggs and smiled. "I could have asked your mother to attend me, but I didn't think it was really enough notice for Jane. I wouldn't like to shock the poor lamb. I don't believe she's met my Hollie. Close to." She tilted the pan consideringly. "Besides, dear, I don't think you'd have liked it if your mother had been one of the wedding party. I imagine she'd put a stop to any number of the interesting things that you young men get up to of an evening, wouldn't she?"

A pretty picture they must have made, Luce with his mouth unflatteringly agape and Auntie Het innocently tending to her cooking, facing each other across a plate of buttered eggs, as Hollie ducked under the lintel. "Hey up, am I missing summat? Ooh – buttered eggs. Put us one by, lass, I'm starved. Me and thee have got an appointment half an hour hence with Master Erbery, who disapproves mighty-wise of my hasty actions but reckons it's his duty to keep us from idle fornication –"

"At my age," Het murmured, straight-faced. "The opportunity would be a fine thing."

Equally straight-faced, Hollie looked ostentatiously towards the stairs. "We've got half an hour before it's legal, owd gal."

They'd both forgotten Luce was there. He might as well not have been. "Your eggs are burning," he said experimentally, to see what would happen. What would happen was that Het would put her pan down on the table, with a sizzle and a strong smell of burning, and that stout, sensible Auntie Het would stand on the tips of her sensible shoes and kiss lanky, scruffy Captain Babbitt with an alarming enthusiasm.

Her cap fell off. Luce thought it best not to point this out. Closing his eyes to blot out the image that he suspected might be burned into his unwilling brain for eternity, he left the kitchen at a fast lope.

# 22 HASTE TO THE WEDDING

Drew Venning appeared round the kitchen door when Luce was halfway down the third egg and munching grimly. "Did I, or did I not, just bump into His Highness on the way in?" he said, and then his eyes lit up. "Oh, Luce, don't let 'em go cold. You going to finish this lot up yourself or is one going spare?"

Uninvited, he sat down and helped himself to one of Auntie Het's lukewarm buttered eggs. Closing his eyes in bliss as the yolk dribbled down his chin. "Must have been months since I had an egg this fresh, bor," he sighed.

"Indeed," Luce said stiffly. "And yes, you did just pass the captain."

Venning scrubbed at his chin and then licked his fingers. "Can I have another one - d'you mind? Ah, Luce, bless you. You sure? Anyway. Rosie. That be, uh, that'd better be the future Mistress Babbitt with him, or there'll be hell to pay, and no pitch hot."

"What do you mean?"

"I mean, lad, I just nearly bumped into our Hollie and that nice respectable old date he was with halfway up Coldharbour Lane, and if he tells you he was trying to get a bit o' grit out of her eye I wouldn't believe a word of it. Mind, she had to stand on a step to reach –" he scratched his head, grinning, "- long mop and lil' bucket don't come close."

"That," Luce said through gritted teeth, "is my Aunt Henrietta. My father's sister."

"What, the one he –"

"*Yes*, Drew, the one he was staying with at the year's end, which makes you wonder which bed he was sleeping in, doesn't it?"

Venning looked mildly bemused, drawing a finger through the remaining egg yolk on his plate and sucking it with relish. "Well, what's the problem - is she married?"

Luce growled not quite under his breath. "She bloody well will be, in about an hour."

"What, to – *seriously*? Rosie's going to be your uncle by marriage?" He was trying hard not to laugh, and eventually gave it up. "Oh, that's her, then," he said, when he could finally speak. "Knew the lad had his eye on some poor – er, some lass or other, but I din't know she looked like that. Expected somebody a bit, well, uh - I'd of thought she was a bit above his touch, if you get me. She looked happy enough, mind –"

Luce shot him a venomous glare. "It's *disgusting*," he said irritably. "I mean, it's – it's – well, it's just – . They just shouldn't. It's undignified and – it's just *horrible*, Drew. The idea of Hollie Babbitt and my aged aunt at it like rabbits is just – " he pushed his plate away, wincing. "You know what, l think I've lost my appetite. Married, by all means – *eventually* - in a – a sober and dignified manner, as befits a mature lady and – and – and a middle-aged officer, but not – not – in Coldharbour Lane, Drew, of all places. Anyone could have seen them. I mean, it's just embarrassing. He must be almost forty, and she's not much younger," he finished, with withering contempt. "She must be nearly the same age as my *mother*!"

Venning closed one eye, and scrutinised Luce. "Antique," he agreed amiably. "*I'm* nearly thirty, Lucey. Trust me, I still kiss my wife, every chance I get. And you're what – rising twenty? Wait till you're my age, lad."

"That's *different* –"

Venning shrugged, reached over, and finished the last egg with relish. "Nice tits, mind, for an old date," he said indistinctly, and Luce gave him another filthy look. "She's not that old, lad, anyway," the freckled captain went on, wiping the back of his hand across his mouth. "Plenty life in the owd gal, by the look of her. And I wouldn't say Hollie's a beauty but she didn't look like she was complaining, so if she don't mind why should we?"

"Because – because –"

"Least he's marrying her, Lucey-lad: the way them two was going on I wouldn't be surprised if you don't get yourself a quiverfull of lil' red-headed nephews before long, bor. Here – you ent *jealous*, are you, our Luce?"

Luce stiffened. "Absolutely not. I would just prefer it if –"

Drew grinned suddenly, "- if you was gettin' a bit instead of Rosie, who's two yards high and plain as a pikestaff? Every old sock needs an old shoe, - if your auntie didn't take him off us hands some other poor female might have to. Anyway, lad, think how much nicer he's like to be when he's getting his belly rubbed reg'lar."

"Andrew," Luce said, with frigid dignity, "you are making me feel physically ill."

The Fenlander chuckled evilly. "Well, cheer up, then! We got an hour to see him turned off with a bit o' style. Tell you what – whistle up your lads and I'll round up mine, and let's see if we can't come up with suffen respectable."

And Luce had to hand it to Drew – reluctantly - the man was a born organiser. You didn't like to question Drew Venning's methods too closely, but if you wanted it, the chances were he could put a hand to it. He'd got Eliot and Ward clearing the barn, Wilder setting up a table down the length of the far wall.

Moggy Davies turned out to play the flageolet, of all people. Drew didn't seem surprised, as if it was commonplace to be able to lay your hand to musicians at a second's notice. "I do reckon if push comes to shove I can play the spoons. I ent danced at a wedding since my own and that was ten years back, so I ent hully missing much. Now then. Luce. You get the plum job, bor. Go see what Old Robin can rustle us up out o' the kitchens at Southcote. Best ask him if he wants to come as well, like."

# 23 PLENTY OF FISH

"Y'know what. It's main bloody miserable, fetching and carrying for Essex all day long," Venning said, lighting his pipe thoughtfully. "Go an' get Russell, Lucey."

"*Me*?" Luce yelped. "But I asked him - he said he didn't want -"

"Well don't bloody listen to him, bor! Ent no fun, sat there saying yes sir, no sir, whatever it was you said sir, from day end to day end. He wants to get down here and have a drink with some normal lads. I ent surprised the lad is strange, he spends all day with boring ol' farts like - er, sorry, Luce. But 'ee's got to admit, your Uncle Essex ent known for his lively conversation. Get him down here, lad." The freckled captain stretched his shoulders luxuriously and gave Luce that guileless, wide-eyed expression that had been fooling most of the young ladies of East Anglia since Andrew Venning was old enough to start shaving. "Lad's practically the guest of honour, Lucey. If it hadn't been for him kicking our Rosie up the backside, the lollopin' gret mawkin wouldn't of got up the nerve to go and fetch her back. It's only right he gets a proper invite."

At which Luce realised he was on a hiding to nothing - when Venning started looking five years old and innocent, you knew he'd dug his heels in and he wasn't for shifting - filled his pockets with what portable items there were from Hollie's wedding supper to keep him going on the journey, and set off to Southcote. Again. To be fair, the birds were singing fit to burst in the fragrant hedges, the air was warm, there was a balmy spring breeze blowing the scent of May blossoms into his face, and - it was a silly "but" but it was heartfelt - he was free of the confines of both buffcoat and plate, just a plain, fancy-free young man in his holiday clothes, riding idly along the lanes.

He hadn't thought of Sarah Hadfield all day. He

reminded himself briskly that he was supposed to be broken-hearted.

Well, he was being romantically brave and heroic, then, in his broken-heartedness. He felt faintly excited, too, as if some good thing was about to happen, though he didn't know what it was. The mare's head came up as though she felt his sudden excitement and she danced a few steps on the tips of her toes, tossing her head with a merry jingle of her bit. Half under his breath, Luce started to sing, and the mare kicked up her heels, full of frisk and frolic, and they arrived in a gallant spray of gravel at Southcote in a most alarming state of informality.

Walked up the front steps whistling - and hoping that neither Uncle Essex nor the very proper staff who'd come with the house knew all the words to that particular song - and found himself grinning appreciatively at one of the maids over the steward's shoulder as the heavy front door swung open.

"I was actually after Master Russell," he said , before anyone decided to helpfully direct him towards Uncle Essex. The steward looked disapproving - as well he might, Luce glancing briefly down at the drift of fallen petals on his shoulders where he'd gone careering heedlessly under the hawthorn branches - and raised an eyebrow almost imperceptibly. The little maid gave him a conspiratorial wink, and then whisked out of the hall, her heels tapping blithely on the polished floor. Luce felt heartened for being winked at. It went some way to restoring the warmth frozen out of him by the glacial steward.

"Master Russell is at supper in the kitchens," he said awfully, as if disclosing some grave indiscretion. "My lord Essex is dining privately this evening."

"Then I'm sure Russell won't mind if I join him, will he?" Luce gave his most charming smile. He was saved from having to fight his way past by the appearance of Russell himself, somehow shocking in his shirt sleeves.

"Is there a problem, sir - *Luce*?"

And just for a second, wide-eyed and slightly tousled and startled into emotion, Russell looked glad to see him, before that careful, blank mask slipped back into place.

"Put your coat on -" and Luce was suddenly sure that he could do this -"Thankful. I've been sent to come and get you, and they won't take no for an answer. Venning reckons you deserve a night off before you go stark staring mad with, er, present company - and he should know." Remembering Drew's words, he added, "And I'm sure Hollie would like to thank you for, er, prompting him into action."

Russell glanced up warily, tucking a wisp of loose hair behind his ear. (Luce had never seen him untidy before, either. It was really quite startling.) "You truly want me at this - celebration?"

"There's only me and you left flying the flag for bachelors, Thankful. Someone's got to show 'em what they're missing."

"Not a great deal, I fear." He smoothed his hair back, automatically feeling for the ribbon at the nape of his neck to confine it.

Luce was not the most observant of young men but even he couldn't help noticing that Russell's hands were shaking. "You all right?"

A stiff nod.

"I wouldn't bother getting dressed up. I think the bridegroom only just bout put a clean shirt on. Come on, before they eat all the pasties."

"You are most kind, Lucifer. If this is a sincere invitation, and not meant in humour –"

"I am pleased to say, I don't number anyone so unkind amongst my acquaintance."

"If you give me a moment I'll - I'll -" he took a deep breath, and then very deliberately pulled the ribbon out of his hair and shook it loose. "I'll get my fiddle, though I'm lamentably out of practice. It's been a while since I last had cause to play."

It was odd, and almost unsettling, to have Russell in informal clothes – not the elegant formal black, not the lace-edged linen, but a plain dark blue suit and a plain white collar - riding at his shoulder, making awkward conversation. He thought he might almost prefer the orderly as silent and formal, rather than nervously prattling. Luce knew nothing about the man - how old he was, what his family was - other than that he had been a lieutenant in Hampden's Greencoats and now wasn't. Russell wasn't anyone's particular friend, you rarely saw him in town, he seemed to spend all his waking hours at Southcote with Essex. He was possibly older than he looked, and possibly not. With a name like Thankful he had to be from a devout family, and he seemed to have been conspicuously absent from the debauch after the fall of Reading, although since Hollie's troop had also been conspicuously absent from same it was difficult to say for sure. No, the thing with Russell, there was just no gossip about him. Almost impossible to know what interested him, what vexed him, what made him a feeling being, in short, and not an administrative engine. That he played the fiddle was an astonishing disclosure of humanity.

"Lucifer." Russell reined his horse in abruptly, and Luce twisted in the saddle to look at him. "Luce, I - I'm sorry. I can't do this. Tell them I - tell them I'd gone out, or that I'm ill, or - no, tell them I'm dead," he said. "Or that I've left the country."

"What?"

"I can't do this -" Russell dropped his reins on the horse's neck. "I can't bear to go to another man's wedding, Luce. I can't. It should have been me."

"*You* should be marrying my Auntie Het?"

"Don't make me laugh," he said, muffled by both hands and his loose hair. "It's not funny. I should have been married to somebody else, Lucifer. Nobody you'd know. The most wonderful woman alive. And she left me, because I'm an ugly, marred- thing - and I can not go and wish another man happy when my own life is blighted -"

"Tell me about it," Luce said with feeling.

Russell dropped his hands. The scar stood out pale against his flushed cheek. "You, too?"

"Me, too. She managed to tell me the day before the siege ended. Which was a masterpiece of poor timing. So if you think you've had it hard - " he hoped he looked stern and like a man of the world. "Come on, Russell. Let's go and show them what real strength of character looks like. There's plenty more fish in the sea."

"I imagine marrying a fish could prove complicated, Lucifer." Russell picked up the reins with a sigh, and pulled his horse's head out of the long grass. "Well. I believe we have a wedding to celebrate, sir."

# 24 BEHOLD, THE BRIDEGROOM COMETH

The great doors of the barn stood wide open to the May dusk, the sound of laughter and noisy talk and the thin silvery notes of Davies's flageolet spilling out into the warm night.

Luce heard Russell stiffen again, catching his breath with a hiss as if something had stabbed him, and gripped him by the elbow, hard enough to hurt. "You've got this far," he said encouragingly, and went to smile at the fair-haired orderly. Who looked as if he were about to faint, white to the lips and unblinking.

"*Thankful.*"

"I c-can't," Russell said. He would have turned and bolted if he hadn't been abruptly deflected by Venning, sloping off into the yard to enjoy another quiet smoke. His freckled face lit with delight. "Found the lad, Lucey? We put a bit o' sluss by for 'ee – wasn't sure there'd be much left, the way them lot's going at it – I hope 'ee likes warm ale, Russell, cos Mistress Babbitt is perched on the barrel like a setting hen."

Luce's eyes accustomed to the gloom of the barn slowly – shadowy and noisy and somewhat inadequately lit by a few lanterns standing on the long trestle that ran the length of the building. He recognised a few of the ladies – women, rather, he suspected that ladylike behaviour might come at additional cost – present; he certainly recognised Auntie Het's sturdy right-hand woman Liza, standing by the supper table with a plate in her hand giving Sergeant Cullis a piece of her mind, by the way her head was wagging as she did it. Hollie was distinctive, being half a head taller than most and even in this light conspicuously coloured, with his arm casually round the shoulders of the new Mistress Babbitt. Most of the troop were clustered around the supper trestles, a few already comfortably settled on the straw piled against the walls, and the barn was filled with a homely, comfortable buzz of laughter and animated conversation.

Whatever it was, it was not a formal social occasion.

"Russell, 'ee looks like 'ee's seen a ghost, what's amiss?"

"Nothing, captain. I am unused to –"

"Off-duty, bor. The name's Drew. And I ent goin' to spend the night calling 'ee *Master Russell*, either. What's your friends call you?"

"Russell," he said coolly. And then –"No, that sounds as if I mean to be impolite, Captain – er, Drew – my friends do call me Russell."

Venning closed one eye and looked at him critically. "Aye. Aye, I can see that. Can see the logic there." He leaned his head against the rough limewashed wall with a sigh of satisfaction, and then hailed one of his troop as the man passed. "Bring us some ale out, will 'ee, lad? There's three of us sat here parched – and two of us not touched a drop yet, neither."

"I should prefer not –" Russell began, and the captain waved a freckled hand at him.

"'S a wedding, bor, don't be so mimsy. I ent going to snitch to Essex if you end up lay in the gutter singing dirty songs. Anyways, this was the only bloody troop to be in bed and lights out by teatime, on the day we entered the town. Essex owes us one. Good as gold, we was, thanks to our Rosie back along."

"You do speak Fen, don't you, Russell?" Luce said slyly, burying his nose in the proffered tankard of ale. "Or do you need a translator?"

"Shut up, Lucey, or I'll fetch 'ee a slap. Imperent lil' jasper. Where's 'ee from, Russell?"

"Buckinghamshire."

"Oh ah, might ha' guessed, Buckinghamshoire, thass it.

They dew talk roightly odd in Buckinghamshoire, don't they, Maaster Russell?"

"Kettle, calling t'pot brunt-arse," Hollie said amiably, looming up out of the darkness. "Take no notice of him, Russell. You two, get in there, get stuck in to supper, or there'll be nowt left. Very fond of my lads, I am, but they're like one of the bloody Plagues of Egypt, if you get 'em mob-handed." He took the tankard out of Luce's hand and drained it, with a defiant grin. "Missis has got her eye on me, gentlemen, so I'd best get back to headquarters."

"Bring us a pasty, Luce, there's a good sort," Venning called, stifling a dignified belch. "Them apple pasties is hell of a good."

# 25 AN EARLY THAW

Russell woke up early in the first grey light of dawn stiff, cold in patches, and thirsty. Luce Pettitt's tousled head lay on his shoulder, Venning the other side of him, and all three of them sprawled like puppies under a fur-lined cloak that smelt of lad's love, that must have seen service in the last century.

It had been his own idea to slip off unnoticed and try and make the garret where Hollie was quartered with these two, into something resembling a bridal bower. Whether the three of them managed it, in the dark, trying to stifle their giggles, and stumbling into each other at every turn, would remain a mystery. He remembered Luce staggering down the stairs – a crash and a deal of swearing as he missed the bottom stair in the dark – and returning with a quantity of bread purloined from supper and a jar of honey. It had been meant as a wedding breakfast.

He'd never known a troop like this one. Hampden's Greencoats – his mind swerved away from that regiment – stalwart, efficient soldiers, to a man. Apart from certain erstwhile lieutenants with a habit of seeking solace in the bottom of a wine jug when crossed. Stout men, the famous Greencoats, well-drilled and competent and – respectful. That little time he'd held his authority, he couldn't imagine for a moment that his men would ever, in a lifetime, have had the temerity to address him as anything other than Lieutenant Russell. Sir, maybe. But calling your captain Rosie? Or referring to a fellow officer as "the brat"? And what Hollie's troop called Venning was – descriptive, yes, best leave it at that. Luce might be a brat, but he was their own brat. And most of the men thought it was a joke that Hollie was one of the most disreputable-looking officers in the Army of Parliament, and that the whole troop had an unenviable reputation for wilfulness and intemperacy. They were unmannerly, and insolent, and -

- And affectionate, and honest, and they'd taken him in last night as if he belonged with them, as if he was one of them, as if he wasn't a disfigured Jonah, and it shocked him to realise just how much he craved even the meaningless kindness Hollie's troop had tossed his way. God knows his tastes didn't incline that way – life would have been easier if they had – and even if they did, they wouldn't take in Luce Pettitt, who was pretty enough and as green as grass, or sturdy and unromantic Venning –

Well, he was lonely. Missed being around people – people who weren't too high in the world to affectionately mock you, or to see that your plate was kept full, or to share a thirty-year-old fur-lined cloak with you in a cold barn overnight. (The late Master Sutcliffe's, apparently, and Mistress Babbitt had brought it thinking it might come in useful for her husband in bleak Yorkshire, and the dour Liza had thought it more suited to use by three half-drunk young officers sleeping rough.) It would hurt again for a while, just like being touched on any old scar, and he'd deal with it like he always dealt with it.

"Russell," Venning's muffled, drowsy voice came from the hay, "if 'ee needs a piss, get up and go, and stop squirming like a bloody toad in a lil' lad's pocket. 'Ee's letting a draught in."

The Earl of Essex's orderly would have taken exception to being spoken to in that uncouth manner. Thankful Russell jerked the big fur-lined cloak over his shoulder – causing Pettitt to wriggle and curse sleepily – and suggested that Venning should go forth and multiply. Venning called him something creatively obscene, and Luce Pettitt sat up with a handful of straw and jammed it down the freckled captain's shirt. "Go back to sleep, the pair of you," he said sternly, without opening his eyes, then fell backwards in the straw and took his own advice.

It was no use, though. He was starting to feel like the

Earl of Essex's orderly again. He slid out from under the cloak and made his way noiselessly across the barn, briefly cursed at when he opened the doors a shaft of sunlight fell across one of the more bleary of Venning's troop. He stood in the courtyard shaking the straw out of his hair and off his coat, to the enormous amusement of the whole of Hollie's troop, with the conspicuous exception of their cornet, dressed and readying their mounts on the cobbles.

And then Hollie himself appeared, and a silence fell over the courtyard at the sight of their commanding officer. Their notoriously wilful-scruffy, unkempt, insolent commanding officer, whose ungovernable judas-red hair had been confined in a neat braid, who'd shaved so recently his cheek was still bleeding, and whose faded doublet had been brushed and darned overnight. And was buttoned to the collar, the same tailoring fairies having replaced the missing buttons. His linen was irreproachable. His boots were, if not exactly polished, at least dusted.

"My God," the bolder of the troopers breathed, into the silence. "It's a bloody changeling, lads."

Hollie in his officer's black, clean, tidy, and correct, was an imposing figure. He turned on his heel and gave the speaker a level stare. Then he glanced, almost imperceptibly, up at the window over his shoulder – a blank window, with no sign of activity – and said, quietly and with deep feeling, "Another word out of you, Eliot, and I'm going to wring your bloody neck."

"Missis," Sergeant Cullis said behind him, as if that explained it all, and there was a general murmur of agreement and sympathy.

Hollie caught Russell's eye. "You coming with us, then, Hapless, or just seeing us off the premises?" The big redhead – braid already starting to unravel in the breeze – held up a hand to Cullis and mouthed, "Ten minutes," before pushing his way through the troop. "Oh and go and kick Pettitt out of bed, will you?"

"I'm up, I'm up," Luce was standing in the barn

doorway yawning and scrubbing his face with both hands, but awake, in a just about functioning kind of way. "Drew's not –"

"Drew's not going to bloody Yorkshire, is he? So he can stop in bed all day for me – now get on your bloody horse, brat, and catch up on your beauty sleep later, all right?"

"*Hapless*?" Russell said stiffly.

Hollie shrugged, grinning. "You don't have much luck, lad, do you?" He forgot himself sufficiently to run a hand through his hair and the braid finally gave up the ghost. "Do summat for me, Russell." His eyes were suddenly intent and more serious than Russell had ever seen. "Take care of her. See her back to White Notley for me."

"But my lord Essex –"

"Bollocks to my lord Essex, Hapless. Take Het home. Half a day, if that. Tell Essex you caught summat nasty off me. He'll probably believe you." He flung his head up, grinning. "Mount up, gentlemen. Let's go and show Yorkshire how the other half live."

# 26 WHISPERS IN THE DARK

They'd had a week of glorious sun, and the dust that the troop had kicked up on the roads, as Hollie had driven them up the length and breadth of the country like a furious sheepdog, lay thick and creamy on Luce's buffcoat, in his hair, on his boots, in his mare's harness.

Eliot – or Ward, he couldn't tell them apart, kick one and they both limped: the more vocal of those two complainers, at any rate – thought the captain had gone mad. (Again, Luce thought, but didn't say.) The sun had been high and warm, the morning they'd left Reading, and there'd been an unspoken feeling of joy and celebration amongst the men as they rode breast-nigh to the bluebells and the cow parsley, with the pollen gilding their horses' bellies and the birds singing in the fresh new green leaves. It had been a perfect, hopeful day in early summer, and they were – for the most part, at least – a troop of healthy, high-spirited young men, with not a care in the world, and a commanding officer so newly married that he was still tidy. It had come as something of a shock that Hollie had had them on the move so soon, the morning after his wedding. Someone had suggested, in an unguarded moment, that the sheets were barely dry when he'd left, and the big redhead had wheeled round without so much as a heartbeat's pause and punched the trooper in the head.

Which had somewhat set the bar for Captain Babbitt's temper. He'd had them riding at a killing pace, forty miles a day if he could get it, till both horses and men were parched and dripping with sweat in the heat, and even then the captain was vicious with temper that he couldn't force them any further. A week, they'd been on the road, and Luce had thought at one point it'd been touch and go that Hollie might suddenly turn the troop about for a single-handed assault on the King's person at Oxford as they skirted the surrounding countryside, the redhead's mood was that unpredictable. They'd taken a circuitous route, veering across the country towards Gloucester to avoid so much as the possibility of bumping into any of the King's patrols out of Oxford, and even though he'd kept his head down and his eyes demurely on his horse's mane.

Luce found it impossible to stay downcast at the sight of the great rolling hills of the Cotswolds laid out green and golden before him – the honey-gold stone of the houses, so strange to his Essex-bred eyes – the soft burr of the local accent, the foreign talk of dodmans and dew-ponds – it was all fascinating and adventurous and somehow wildly exciting to a boy who'd never been further than Colchester, this time last year. It was utterly unlike his own wide, flat skies, with the salt tang of the marshes when the wind was in the wrong direction. He'd bought a basket of early strawberries from a rosy-cheeked young maid in a village just outside Evesham. Strawberries, in late May, of all things, tiny and fragrant and with the gloss of freshness still on them. Had sat on a stile, in the violet dusk, heavy with the smell of elderflowers, and eaten every last one of them himself because he was so thoroughly pig-sick of Hollie Babbitt and his peevish tempers that he wouldn't have given Hollie so much as the discarded leaves, at the moment.

Which was fine, because the redhead was too busy trying to pick fights with the local militia to pay much attention to the dietary habits of his junior officers, when he wasn't picking fights with his own troop or drinking himself as insensible as you could get on Army pay. He seemed to have spent every waking hour since they'd left Reading at outs with someone, which Luce thought took a degree of commitment to unpleasantness that was really quite remarkable, even for Hollie at his worst. So much for the new leaf that seemed to have been turned, on his marriage. He was worse than ever.

And then, just north of Crewe, it had started to rain. Not heavily, nothing that would hinder their journey, just a grey lowering of the clouds and a constant light mizzle so fine that it was almost imperceptible.

And Hollie had flung his head up, looking keen for the first time since they'd left Reading three weeks ago, and snuffed the cool, damp air like the old warhorse he was. "Reckon we might as well go by Bolton, gentlemen," he said, wheeling his big horse so that Tyburn's solid hindquarters blocked the lane. "I got a bit of family business to see to,."

There'd been a degree of dark muttering from the usual suspects and the big redhead had grinned malevolently. "My troop, Master Ward, and that means I give the orders. Even if I have been conspicuously quiet this last couple of weeks. If I wish it so, you'll walk down t'bloody high street in a frock, lad. You with me?"

"Sir," Ward had muttered sullenly.

Hollie nodded. "Aye. Well." Took a deep breath, and scrubbed his hands through his hair. "Might as well make the best of it, lads. Reckon if we crack on we'll be there by dusk tomorrow. Welcome to my patch, gentlemen. See what thee reckons to the Babbitt family seat."

They'd ended up spending that night with the garrison at Nantwich, though, as the rain fell harder. Welcomed with open arms and an appraising eye by the commander of the Parliamentarian forces in Cheshire, a spaniel-eyed gentlemen with lank dark hair by the name of Sir William Brereton. He'd complained like hell about the unannounced arrival of eighty men on his patch, and then settled down for a comfortable and hospitable evening's idle banter with their officers in which Luce was convinced that more was meant than was being said. There was a deal of soldiers' boasting about the rout at nearby Middlewich, not three months past, in which the Royalists had been sent about their business in short order.

"Trust me," Brereton said grimly, pouring more wine

for his guests, "since the beginning of this unnatural war, God hath not given many more complete victories."

"Oh aye?" Hollie was being as abstemious as a novice nun with the wine, for the first time in about a month, but working his way through a hefty wedge of crumbly Cheshire cheese with blissful abandon. He looked up at Luce and gave him an almost imperceptible wink. "Who held command of the Malignants, at Middlewich?"

"Sir Thomas Aston," Brereton began, and Hollie nodded.

"Know him. Or at least my cornet here knows his uncle –"

"We've met," Luce said blandly, realising that Thomas Aston must be related to Arthur Aston, of the siege of Reading fame. "Dined together, on one or two occasions." If you could call having a plate of cakes practically thrown at you by a man who'd just accused you of sleeping with your own uncle, dining in company. However. It made Hollie's ruffianly troop sound that bit the better-connected, which was all to the good in this diplomatic thrust and parry.

"Nice snug quarters you have here," Hollie said, one less than impeccable finger circling the rim of his untouched wine glass.

"Nice part of the world, captain. Very comfortably placed. We had a fair bit of snow over the winter, but not as bad as some." Brereton looked up with an expression of mild concern. "They had it hard in Yorkshire, I'm told. Can get somewhat wild, up there in winter. Very bleak. Very lonely."

Hollie was nodding. "Aye, it is that."

Brereton cocked his head. "Mind, it promises to be a hot summer up there. If I were local to that area I should take care, myself. Much more of this kind of weather and the grass will be like tinder. The merest spark, and – whoosh!" he snapped his fingers. "And I imagine that any kind of fire in that locality might be difficult to contain, once set."

The conversation turned, idly, to events further afield – not to talk of the war, but to talk of expected harvests and books and marvels seen, of Hollie's marriage and Luce's sisters' accomplishments and Brereton's fascination with field sports. The fire was falling to ash, and Luce yawning over the last of the wine, when Hollie stood up.

"I've kept you up talking over-long, Sir William. I don't often get the chance to converse with a man so – well-informed," he said, with that peculiar emphasis. "I reckon we'll be for an early start in the morning, so we'll try not to disturb you. I'll bid you a good night, sir."

Brereton bowed slightly. "You would be welcome to make a longer stay, captain."

And Hollie bowed even more slightly. "Thank you for your consideration, sir. I will give the matter some thought."

As the door closed behind them, Luce opened his mouth to ask what all that had been about, and Hollie raised a hand for silence. Grabbed the young officer by the elbow and dragged him up the stairs at a fast and undignified scuttle.

"Captain Babbitt –"

"Gone back to titles, have we, brat?"

"I prefer you drunk and temperamental," Luce said sulkily. "You're easier company."

"*He* ain't. Which is why you will note I've been most temperate this evening." Hollie yanked the ribbon out of his hair and tossed it on the bed. "How d'you like your first acquaintance with your uncle's spymaster? Because he scares the hell out of me."

"Spy – what?"

"That nice, mild lad downstairs with the passion for duck shooting, brat, is the Commander-in-Chief of the Armies in Lancashire and Cheshire, and I doubt there's a mouse farts in those two counties without word gets back to Sir William. That man's got more eyes than bloody

Argus. He was sounding us out, Luce. Are we game for being added to the Parliamentarian forces of the Nantwich garrison – to which my answer is I'd rather cut off my own feet with a spoon, if that bugger's in charge, for I doubt he'd let me have my head as much as even your uncle does without having me up on a charge of insubordination – and more to the point, did I know matters in Yorkshire are getting somewhat desperate. The which I did not."

"I don't remember him saying any –"

"All that very polite conversation about the weather on the moors? You serious, lad? You honestly didn't wonder what he was alluding to, in a very nice and proper way, trying to warn us off fetching up wi' Fairfax? Oh no, Lucey, he's made me most hot to attend my lord Fairfax, and I doubt that was ever his intention. I'm off where the action is, brat, and I'm taking you lot wi' me."

He pulled the final button on his doublet loose with a savage jerk, and it rolled away under the wainscot. "Ah, Christ, Het had only just set that to rights," he muttered, and then looked up and met his junior officer's eye, blushing fiercely. "Aye, well, if I'm in Yorkshire up to the ears in Malignants, at least I'm not sat round like a dying duck in a thunderstorm pining for my wife, am I?"

# 27 A FURIOUS MAN ABOUNDETH IN TRANSGRESSION

Luce did not take to Bolton, and judging by the suspicious looks he was getting as he groomed his mare in the yard of the house where they were quartered, Bolton didn't take to him. The locals evidently thought he was dangerously effeminate, given that he'd shaved twice in three days and was wearing a clean shirt. That said, having seen the flower of local womanhood, he was likely to remain irreproachably chaste. A good half of the fair maidens he'd set eyes on had broader shoulders than he did, and one or two had a finer set of whiskers. He wasn't entirely surprised Hollie's tastes in women ran to the well-upholstered, if the captain's wild youth had been spent with the sturdy young maidens Luce had seen parading up and down the main road through the town, Bradshawgate – if that most old-fashioned thoroughfare could be described as civilisation. Luce suspected that if one of those maidens happened to cast her eye over a man, he'd be a brave sort indeed to say her nay.

Which made it somewhat disconcerting to see the captain turned out in what passed for finery. It had been a long while since Luce had seen Hollie Babbitt in his decent suit – it hadn't even made an appearance at his wedding - and being stuffed in the captain's saddlebags had not improved it. "Is there a – a – a festival occasion, sir?" he said tactfully, hoping to God it wasn't wearing stout clogs and a sensible shawl.

The indiscreet rose-pink silk ribbon tied halfway down the captain's ponytail was an interesting touch. Not a colour Luce would have chosen to go with that hair, himself. The big redhead glowered at him from under the brim of his disreputable felt hat, which, for reasons as yet unexplained, he'd adorned with a prominent handful of iridescent blue-green magpie tail feathers.

"Church," Hollie said flatly.

"You're going to church –" Luce thought, but didn't say, the words, "like that?"

"So're you, brat." He grinned balefully. "Get the lads formed up, there's a good lad. About time we paid attention to the state of our immortal souls. Bunch of bloody godless heathens."

"But – I hardly -"

" I'm not asking you, lad. I'm telling you. As you are, sir, no arsing about titivating. The Lord is not particular about your linen, Lucifer."

He gave Luce another narrow-eyed stare and then turned on his heel and stalked out of the stable-yard.

"He had a bang on the head or what?" Cullis said, emerging from behind his cob where he'd been lurking and eavesdropping since Hollie had arrived in the yard.

Luce shook his head. "God knows, sergeant. He's been behaving strangely –"

"Even for him," Cullis said, with a snaggly grin.

"Even for him," Luce agreed. "Since we got here."

"'S Bolton, innit. Home turf for him. Prob'ly showing off, like."

Luce cast a jaundiced eye at the clouds obscuring the horizon. They hadn't seen the sun in over a fortnight. The natives were barbarous – although having spent the last six months mentally translating Hollie's lapses into this heathen dialect, he flattered himself he almost spoke the language. He could see why any young man of spirit might have shaken the dust of this prim, godly, stifling town off his feet and run away to find adventure. There was no life in these bleak, wet cobbled streets, no joy, no liberty. The war was probably the most exciting thing that had happened since the old Queen died.

"Round up the usual suspects, then." Luce said with resignation. "Let's go and show our faces."

He doubted the damp little church at the bottom of the hill had ever been so full, what with the customary devout and a disgruntled troop of horse pulled untimely from their breakfast. And no sign of Hollie to impose some sense of order, because neither Cullis nor Luce was managing to offer any rational explanation to the men as to where this sudden abrupt turn for the godly had come from. There was a lot of disenchanted muttering from both sides, from squeezed parishioners and bemused troopes. There was also a fair amount of not particularly discreet criticism of the command structure of any unit left to its own devices in this slapdash manner, and Luce was sliding further and further inside his buff coat, scarlet to the ears, when the preacher made his appearance and although most of the parishioners continued to mutter and mumble amongst themselves Hollie Babbitt's troop were struck dumb, to a man.

Cullis swore, at some length, and with a degree of invention that was almost admirable. (Not sufficiently admirable  to avoid an outraged glare and a meaty elbow in the ribs from one particularly stout member of the Lord's Elect.)

Luce just blinked, looked away, shaking his head, and looked back again.

You wouldn't mistake them one for another. This man's hair was cut short, a rough and untidy sandy grey, and he must have had twenty years on the captain. Even so. "By, the old bugger's still alive, then." Calthorpe said admiringly, and Luce glanced at him with a quizzical look, and at that point, timing his arrival with a most uncharacteristic flair for the theatrical, Hollie came stalking into the church.

There was a long, a very long, silence. Hollie – hair brushed and astonishingly beribboned, scented like a backstreet bordello, and dripping with borrowed, if crumpled, lace – shoved his way through the mute and astonished congregation to take his place beside Luce.

Luce looked at him, then at the preacher, then back at Hollie. Hollie shrugged, looking elaborately unconcerned.

"If he starts on the subject of the Prodigal Son," he said, without moving his lips, "I am going to punch him in the head."

"That's – that's –"

"That," the preacher said, loudly and icily into the shocked stillness, "that overdressed bravo, is – was – my firstborn, though I hardly recognise him in his degenerate finery –"

Cullis snorted with laughter, and the man who was unmistakably Hollie Babbitt's father favoured him with a glare that would have taken the paint off wood.

Hollie sighed loudly. "Aye, well, as a dog returneth to his vomit, so a fool to his folly. Best get on with it, owd mon. I see you're as doting a father as you ever was."

Half an hour into a long, passionate, and mostly incomprehensible sermon on the matter of rebellion, revolution, and the duty of all devout men to resist the ungodly lures of Popery stretched out by His Majesty's evil advisers, Luce was stifling his yawns, Cullis was staring glassy-eyed at the back of the man in front, Calthorpe was nodding in stern agreement, and Hollie leaned over to Luce and announced, most indiscreetly, that he was bored, his father was a hypocrite and he was off out to see to the horses.

The sermon collapsed within minutes, and the King left to stew in his own juices, amidst a shocked muttering from the congregation.

"Explain yourself, boy!"

"I don't have to explain nowt to you!"

"To miscall me? In my own church? To arrive out of nowhere after twenty years without a word?"

"Well, thee *is* a hypocrite."

People were beginning to stare now, as father and son glared at each other in the churchyard in the rain. Hollie turned away and started to make minute adjustments to his big horse's bridle. "Tha's advocating rebellion, sir. Preaching sedition. Tha's arguing for the people to rise up against their lawful ruler, is thee not?"

Luce pushed his way to his commanding officer's side. "Sir, I don't think –"

"Thee has a lackey, Holofernes?"

"That was uncalled for, sir," Luce said severely. "Captain Babbitt is –"

"Is able to fight his own battles, brat," Hollie said, with a wild grin, and suddenly sounding like the man Luce knew once again and not a North Country savage like his father. "All right for you to encourage rebellion in your congregation, but by Christ you wouldn't take it from *me* when I was under your roof, would you?"

"I'll not listen to thy blasphemous talk," the preacher hissed, and without taking his eyes from Hollie raised his hand to slap the defiant look from his son's face. Without taking his eyes off his father's face Hollie grabbed the older man's wrist before his open hand connected, and held it, not gently.

"If you ever lay a hand on me again, owd mon, I swear to God I will break your god-damned wrist. Do you understand me?"

"Thee was ever wild, boy, and required discipline –"

"Wild? By Christ, sir –"

"That is enough," Aaron Calthorpe said sternly, pushing his way between the two of them. "This behaviour credits neither of you. Hollie, thee is going too far. And Elijah, thee should be proud of the lad –"

"That painted Whore of Babylon – tricked out like Jezebel? 'She painted her face, and tired her head, and looked out at her window' – to think that any son of mine should be dressed in lace. And ribbons. His mother would turn in her grave. That dissolute wastrel- "

"Is a most respected officer in the Army of Parliament, Elijah, and if I know anything about the lad, is got up like a maypole a-purpose to bait thee. And has succeeded mighty-wise, by the look of it. This is neither the time or the place to have this discussion, gentlemen." Calthorpe scowled at the pair of them. "Thee has not set eyes on the boy in twenty years, Elijah. Can thee not be a little pleased to see him?"

"If the Lord has seen fit to deliver my only son back to my bosom, Master Calthorpe – such poor fare as he is - I must give thanks where it is due. To the Lord, not to thee."

"I'm going nowhere near the old bastard's bosom," Hollie said mutinously.

Elijah Babbitt scratched the back of his neck, squinting at his firstborn. There was little in it for height, but a considerable difference in breadth, and most of the advantage on Elijah's side. "Thee has thy lady mother's stubbornness, Holofernes," he said thoughtfully. "Most surely, thee has a look of her."

"My lady mother must have been one hell of a plain lass," the captain said sulkily, and this time he didn't see the slap coming. Or didn't try to deflect it, one or the other. Nor did Calthorpe look to defend him.

"Asked for that, you did, lad."

"Did I always, Aaron?" he said mildly, and Calthorpe had no answer to that.

# 28 THE SINS OF THE FATHERS

Hollie had said he wouldn't set foot over his father's threshold – had promised himself that, when he'd set his heart on this whole stupid idea – and now here he was not only setting foot over the threshold but agreeing to be quartered there, and the rest of the troop with him.

He'd intended to hate the old bastard with a deep and abiding passion forever and instead all he could think was how old his father looked – how the skin on his neck was loose and dry and patched with dirty silver stubble where the old man had missed a patch when he shaved. How thin his wrists were, like a bundle of sticks under Hollie's hand when he'd grabbed him. And that was the man who'd made his childhood a waking hell. Hollie could snap him like a twig.

And the house. Didn't look like it had seen a broom since Elizabeth's reign. Not that he was overly nice about such things, but the cobwebs in the corners of the old-fashioned painted plaster walls were blacker than the hobs of Hell. "I see thee didn't replace the housekeeper, owd mon," he said drily, and his father muttered something and turned away.

Found himself out in the stable yard watching some of the mares, some with foals at foot, some just barrel-shaped with the expectation of same, and thinking of Het. Who would doubtless not have been flattered. No, he wished, very much, to have her at his right hand. He might fancy himself as in command on the field, but Het was most definitely commanding officer of hearth and home, and he'd have loved to see what she'd make of Drake Height. Other than - when she finished tearing out her hair - to roll her sleeves up and pile in. Much though he hated to admit it, his father's horses were beautiful, and the yard was spotless. There was one long-legged filly with a white star on her nose that he coveted quite shamelessly – and a couple of the sturdier colts would make admirable cavalry mounts, when they'd grown–

He was thinking like he was going to come back here and he wasn't. There was nothing here for him, nothing. If the house burnt to the ground tomorrow with Elijah Babbitt in it, it wouldn't have bothered him. He felt nothing for his father. He watched the mares move slowly across the field, peaceful, calm.

"Jezebel," his father's unwelcome voice came at his elbow.

"What?"

"Jezebel. The filly. Thee can take her, boy. If thee wants her."

"Stooping to bribery, sir?" Hollie said contemptuously. "Take more than a horse to win me –" And he was about to go in search of his men, making themselves comfortable about the barn and outbuildings – thieves, ruffians and Anabaptists, but before God they were faithful to him, straight down the line – when Elijah gripped his elbow, hard enough to hurt.

"Rather she went in the service of Parliament than under some ungodly cavalier, Holofernes. And at least thee will take care of her. I cannot say much in thy favour, but thy horses are well cared-for."

"No, well, you never did have much good to say of me, did you?" And that sounded bitter, and beseeching, and he wished it unsaid as soon as he'd said it. His father's eyebrows rose.

"I barely know thee, boy. I know thee is intemperate, ill-disciplined, proud and wilful."

"I see."

"And I'll own I am disappointed thee is yet only a captain –"

He was about to say something else intemperate and ill-disciplined when he realised that his father was making a joke. The gaunt, uncompromising features never changed

– horribly familiar from his own reflection, and that, Hollie, is how you'll look in twenty years if you don't mend your ways – but there was the very faintest hint of a twitch at the corner of his mouth. He didn't think he'd ever heard the old bastard crack a joke before.

"Come away into supper, boy. I've asked Gatty to make your old room ready."

# 29 GRIEVOUS WORDS

Luce found the whole thing weird and uncomfortable. For one thing, he was appalled to realise that his ruffianly commanding officer had been brought up in unexpectedly privileged surroundings. Drake Height was certainly not the hovel he'd come to expect. Old-fashioned, and most distinctly bachelor's hall, and in need of housekeeping, but still retaining a degree of rough dignity. From what Luce had seen of the rest of Bolton, this was the lap of luxury.

And then there was Elijah Babbitt, who was altogether too much like his son for comfort – either of their comforts – and the pair of them sat across the dirty tablecloth from each other sniping at each other, Hollie uncharacteristically drunk and vicious, and Elijah getting more sober and godly by the minute. Luce had made some thin excuse – putting something on the fire, probably – and as he passed behind Hollie, had surreptitiously removed the captain's sword from its hanger. He didn't really think the big redhead would go for his father. Not really. But he wasn't sure.

"So, boy. Account for the past twenty years, now you've seen fit to returm."

"As you see." Hollie had stripped himself of his borrowed finery and was his customary plain self again. Sprawled in his chair, picking at a greasy mutton stew with the point of his knife and smiling to himself, somewhat worryingly.

"We fought at Edgehill," Luce prompted, thinking it uncivil not to offer any contribution to the conversation. "Most creditably."

Hollie turned his head and looked at his junior officer, unsmiling. "Aye, you did, didn't you?"

"*We*," Luce said sternly, "did."

"You did, brat. I concentrated on getting myself shot.

Which I failed to do. Gone in the wits, apparently. So the Commander of the Army of Parliament tells me. Don't like me, does my lord Essex. With me being mental and that." Hollie looked at his right hand, eyeing the crooked little finger thoughtfully. "Can't imagine how that might be, could you, father?"

"So my son is a coward," Elijah sneered.

"No." Hollie shook his head. "Not a coward. Just didn't care. Don't worry, Luce, I do now." He snickered unpleasantly. "Did I not mention, father, I've got a wife at home. "

Elijah's eyes rested on his son's face. "Then I pray God keep her safe, Holofernes."

"Can do without your God, myself. So – with respect – you can take your prayers and shove them up your most godly arse. We don't need 'em. We don't need *you,* sir. You had me twenty years ago and you damn' near killed me." He pushed his chair back and bowed, steadily. "I bid you good night, father. Luce – if you want me, I'm in wi' Tyburn, for I won't spend another second under his roof."

# 30 THY FAITHFULNESS IN DESTRUCTION

"Thee stands his particular friend," Elijah said, and Luce looked up, startled.

"Er – yes. Yes, I – I am the captain's particular friend," he said , not sure where this conversation was headed, and wondering how quickly he could make his excuses and go to bed.

The old man nodded. "I imagine thee finds it a hard task. He was ever a solitary boy."

"I should prefer not to discuss my commanding officer, Master Babbitt," Luce said, lifting his chin in a manner he hoped was intimidating enough to deflect further question.

"A faithful friend, then."

"And somewhat immune to cajolery."

"He was a stubborn whelp as well. Though I think he is that still, no? Intractable, and wayward, and proud as Lucifer. There has never been any telling my son what he chooses not to hear," Elijah said, and Luce thought he heard pride in his voice. "Would thee care for more wine, Cornet Pettitt – if the lad left any?"

"No, sir, I would not."

There was a pause. "Gets bitter at night, up here on the hills. Boy probably forgets, living so long away, amongst yon soft Southrons. No offence, cornet. If he will spend the night in the stables – wouldn't be the first time, the awkward little bugger – I'd at least take him a blanket –"

It would, Luce thought, be an interesting encounter, but on the whole he thought not. "I think perhaps leaving him to, um, order his thoughts –"

"Calm down, thee means. Aye, lad, tha's right. Go after

him and it'd make matters worse."

"I think I will bid you a good night, sir, and seek my bed." Luce smiled politely, pushing his chair back.

"Thee will be away early, in the morning, I'm thinking." Elijah nodded to himself. "Aye, well, I'll see a decent breakfast for us, at least. Gatty can stop here and keep house – I'm leaving nowt behind that can't be picked up. From what I see of thy troop thee could use decent mounts. Take thy pick. The filly belongs to Holofernes. Leave her be."

A log split on the sullen fire with a sound like a pistol shot. "Er, sir –"

"Plain Trooper Babbitt," Elijah said. "I'll not have it said I was too proud to serve under my own boy. I'm coming with thee on the morrow. I can see thee stands in want of spiritual guidance, the lot of thee. I'll stand as chaplain."

"It will be a - a hard journey, sir, for a man of your years –" Luce said desperately. The thought of sharing quarters with Babbitts plural was grim, but the possibility of being pursued day and night by the pair fighting like cats in a sack, was worse.

"Aye, well. It'll be a test of faith. I'll see thee at dawn, Cornet."

The look on Hollie's face was priceless, as he led his horse out into the yard in the first red light of a cool, misty dawn and saw his father mounted up with the rest of the troop, wearing a breastplate that must have seen service against the Armada and with a most unofficial broadsword slung over his back.

"Get off that horse, and get back in the house, you old bastard," he said, perfectly coolly.

Elijah's head lifted. "Is that how thee normally gives an order, boy?"

"I didn't ask you to come, and I don't want you. There's no room in this troop for worn-out old fools. Now get back in that house."

"I will not."

Hollie grinned, humourlessly. Settled his lobster-tailed helmet on his head and mounted up. Turned in the saddle, still smiling. "Then I'll see you killed, first chance I get, father, for I'll not have you. Am I making myself clear?"

There was a long, embarrassed silence. Cullis scratched his unshaven jaw with a noise like striking matches. "Cornet Pettitt. Colours."

None of the troop looked at Hollie, and no one wanted to speak. Luce lifted the colours, and the silk unrolled with a ripple in the damp air.

Elijah Babbitt straightened himself in the saddle. "Let us pray for guidance in our endeavours. O Lord, show thy favour on this –"

And there was a soft click, as Hollie drew his pistol and cocked it, sighting along the barrel at the point where his father's level brows met.

"Ride," he said.

They rode.

# 31 THE NEW BLADE

The rain had been pattering on the windows and the soft golden light of candles had gentled the worn cloth on the table and the weariness in the eyes of the officers around it, and as Lady Anne Fairfax looked around at the room she could almost have herself believe that this was no more than an ordinary supper of gentlemen. Nothing more. Out in the wet streets of Bradford, the night was still, and warm in spite of the rain. You might almost believe that this was a plain house, in a plain town, with plain, good company, and not a Council of War, with the threat of attack by the Earl of Newcastle and his men an ever-present danger. Thomas looked weary, and the dark Scot Sergeant-Major Gifford looked grim by firelight. Out in the street, hooves clattered, as the patrols crossed and re-crossed – someone singing, softly, as he passed under the window, the tramp of boots fading into the distance.

A peremptory thumping at the front door, and then a brief flurry of barely-heard voices downstairs. Not agitated, and the tension in the room eased a little. Footsteps, on the stairs.

"Sir Thomas - sir." Captain Smith poked his head round the door. "You might want to, er – reinforcements, sir."

And Thomas was scarcely on his feet before the door was shoved open and the reinforcements promised by Essex declared themselves.

"Babbitt's troop of horse, from –"

"Essex," the new arrival interrupted, through gritted teeth. "Eighty of us, and that's your lot. Eighty one. Full strength." The very specific number seemed to raise his hackles, for some reason, and he drew his sword with no ceremony at all and slammed it onto the table. "Captain

Babbitt," he said curtly. "There's my blade. Do wi' it what you want."

And there was a long, awkward pause, in which the captain stood looking from one to another as if he were daring them to comment.

"Well, you are most welcome, sir. My lord Essex did write and tell us of your direction but, ah, we had expected you some little while sooner. Though I see you spared no time in attending us," Thomas said gently, looking meaningfully at the newcomer's muddy boots and travel-stained linen, and the elegant Henry Fowles stroked his moustache to hide a grin. "Your eighty – one – men are most welcome, captain. Please. Be seated. William – make room, please." A scraping of chairs on the rough boards of their temporary accommodation, as Thomas's little brother budged up. "A toast, gentlemen," Thomas said softly, at last, and there was only Nan who heard the slight hesitation as he curbed his stammer. "To our, er, new blade –"

The newcomer looked up, both wary and suddenly oddly shy, as the officers round the table raised their glasses in his direction. "My thanks," he said stiffly, as William passed him a glass of his own. His hand trembled. Nan noticed things like that, while people didn't see her, in her corner by the fire. Not quite so cocksure as he liked to pretend, then, the captain.

"Captain Babbitt is a North Countryman by birth, so my lord Essex tells me – from Bolton," Thomas said, trying to put him at his ease, and William gave a broad grin at that.

"A fellow! Surely not a Bolton Percy man, sir? Then we must be neighbours, for I know Bolton Percy well – not ten miles from York?"

"Not any fellow of yours, sir," the captain said balefully. "Bolton, in Lancashire. Born and bred there. And proud to be so."

William looked quickly into his glass at the abrupt

rebuff, then regrouped and rallied. "We've a troop of musketeers from Lancashire, came over the border not so long back to stand with us. You might know some of 'em? Come down for a chat, if you're that way. Though you won't be longing for a familiar voice, if you've your own Lancashire men about you."

"Captain Babbitt's troop was raised in Essex," Thomas began, and Fowles snapped his fingers.

"I have it. I thought I knew the name, captain. You're one of the career men, no? Bought in from the Low Countries?"

"That is correct. I learned my trade under Wallenstein. And then I learned more of it under Gustavus Adolphus. I have near enough twenty years' field experience, sir. Do you?" Hollie was turning the fragile glass in his fingers, untasted. He looked at it as if he'd just realised it was fragile, and set it down, carefully, at a distance.

Fowles grinned. "What were you, in short coats when you went out? No need to fly out at me, captain. I meant only to commend your – most valuable – experience, to such as might not be aware of it. And my understanding is that your men are equally practised in the arts of war. You've an ill-assorted troop, from what I hear – half the most notorious rebels and Dissenters in the Army, and a junior officer in petticoats: what is he, Sir James Ramsey's boy? –"

The redhead flushed. "I was sixteen when I went out, sir. And my cornet is the Earl of Essex's nephew by marriage, and no relation of Ramsey's." He picked the glass up again, glared over the rim of it. "And if you are referring to the previous reputations of certain of my troop, sir, I can assure you that although my men were taken from which raff and scaff other officers may have found unmanageable or unwanted, there is discipline in my company."

Nan caught Thomas's quick, amused glance, only intended for her, and she looked modestly down at her mending to hide a smile. So much for Essex's promise of stout support – eighty ill-disciplined ruffians and an officer no more broken to bridle than a wild moor pony. The new captain tucked a lock of thick and tangled russet hair behind one ear and straightened his shoulders, looking as fierce and cornered as a fox at bay. "My men were at Reading, Sir Thomas. They were the only troop at Reading innocent of acts of looting and wanton drunkenness." And he met Thomas's eye, square and defiant. "I said they *were* either unmanageable or unwanted. Not, sir, that they remain so."

William applauded softly. "Bravely done, captain."

Hollie sipped guardedly at his canary wine, glowering, and said nothing.

"Well, eighty men is eighty men, be they practised in every depravity and vice in Christendom, as long as they can sit a horse and fire a pistol," Gifford said amicably.

"I'll not sit here and be laughed at." He set his wine down, barely tasted, with an abruptness that spilled a few drops across Nan's precious clean tablecloth. Pushed his chair back and stood up. "I've a troop to settle, my lord, and horses to see to. You will excuse my rough manners, I trust. I'm a plain fighting man, not –" he looked round the table, still neatly laid with the cooling supper, and cocked an eyebrow –"a courtier. I'll bid you a good evening."

And with a bow that bordered in the abrupt, he let himself out, with a whisk of cooling night air, and letting the door bang to behind him.

"Well," Gifford drawled, "I hope his command is better than his manners. So that's the sort of assistance Essex offers, is it? Call it an insult, myself."

"Un-*fair*, sir," Thomas said mildly, and Nan wanted to go to him and put her hand on his arm because she knew her husband, knew how his poor soft heart would fly to the defence of the outsider in his ranks. "You must needs touch the captain on his pride, and that was not kindly done. The Lord knows Captain Babbitt has little enough to sustain his pride, by the look of him, that we must attack what little he has. You ought not to have mocked his troop – and I don't care if it was meant in fun, Henry, before you tell me I've no sense of play and that it was all done in jest. That was unkind. In all of us."

Elegant Henry Fowles looked up from his plate. "Perhaps not, Thomas, but I'm not sure I want to spend my days guarding the walls from Malignants and my tongue lest I offend our new comrade's delicate sensibilities. A bit too touchy for me, sir. I've no wonder Essex sent him down here. I imagine we'll be sending him straight back, if he makes a habit of such behaviour."

Thomas was shaking his head, gently. "Gentlemen, please. Think on. How would you feel, were you sent far from home to a room full of strangers whose first act was to mock that which you hold most dear?"

Fowles rolled his eyes. "Tom, you are too soft-hearted. The man's a ruffian. He admits it. And he said himself his troop were worse –"

"I doubt your temper would be of the sweetest, were you to undertake the ride from Essex to Bradford with such despatch and receive such an unkind reception at the end of it," Thomas said mildly. "Wait and see, Henry, before sitting in judgment."

"What, wait and see if he steals the spoons?"

"Proud, *and* pig-stubborn on his mettle. Are ye *sure* he's not a Fairfax, Thomas?" Gifford said, but his smile as he looked on Thomas was affectionate. They'd forgotten about Nan, and well that it were so, for she could look on her husband from her place beside the fire without his being aware of it. Her gaunt and faintly-scarecrow Thomas, with his dark eyes shadowed with tiredness and his black hair rough and uncombed on his shoulders. Unsurprising that he should see something kindred in a gaunt and faintly-scarecrow officer turned loose in a room full of strangers, knowing Thomas. "Wrong side of the border, sir," William said mildly. "Not been a

Lancastrian in our side of the family since the days of Richard. Has there, brother?"

# 32 WITH PRIDE COMETH CONTENTION

Hollie stood in the rain in the street outside Fairfax's quarters, torn between an almost unbearable desire to go home and hide under the bed, and an equally unbearable suspicion that he ought to go back and apologise. Once again, his temper had got the better of him – and when would he learn to curb his tongue with his betters, even if they did imply that his troop were no better than desperadoes?

He'd worked bloody hard with those men – even Eliot and Ward, though he still wouldn't look to the bastards to cover his back in a fight, they could be relied on. Unless there was profit involved, in which case he wouldn't ask. But every one of them – every last man, since Reading – he knew them like the back of his hand, knew their weaknesses, knew how far he could push them. With the exception of his self-appointed troop chaplain – for Christ's sake, a fighting chaplain – and he knew how far he could push him, even: just preferred not to go within a hundred yards of the old bastard to do it. The hell with it, the next time an invitation came to dine with any of the Army great and the good, he was going to send Lucey and pretend to be taken with the gripes. And if they wanted him that much, he'd be in the stables, which was most clearly where Sir Thomas la-di-da Fairfax and his posh sniggering mate, the one with the nice tailoring and the girl's pretty mouth, thought he ought to be. Fine. Well, he'd bugger off back to the stables, and the lot of them could do without him.

"Back early, sir," Luce observed, comfortably ensconced in front of a fire with a mug of ale at his elbow and a book in his hand, whilst his superiors sloshed about in the rain getting insulted by their betters and not getting offered any supper. Hollie glared at him before slamming the door with a force that rattled the windows and didn't relieve his feelings one bit.

"I didn't care for the company, brat."

"Sorry to hear that." The brat tucked a finger into his book and did his commanding officer the courtesy of finally paying attention. "Surely they didn't invite Prince Rupert?"

"Ha ha, you're not funny. I wouldn't expect you to –" Understand? Really? When Hollie had sat next to Lucifer at more at one dinner and listened to his fellow officers bore on about untried whelps, and green youths, with the lad sat next to him sinking lower and lower into his chair with embarrassment at every word? "Oh, put your boots on, boy, I only come back to get you. They won't be any further on than the first remove. I'll just have to make my excuses."

Luce stopped with one arm in the sleeve of his good doublet. "Er, Hollie. What did you actually *do*, sir?"

Hollie took a deep breath. "You can only take me somewhere twice, brat. Once to go and once to apologise. Anyway, he started it."

"Hollie…."

"Sir Thomas implied that my – our – troop were something of an ill-disciplined rabble, Lucifer. And I won't take that, not from him nor from any other bugger. There is evidently some misapprehension amongst some of this Army's commanders that we might look like a ragged-arsed bunch, and we might ha' been dragged up off t'streets wi' no company manners for the most part – but before God we are a fighting troop I can be proud of, lad, and I won't have him or any other high-nosed whelp do us down."

"Then I suggest that we shame him into reconsidering his opinion, captain." The brat smoothed his hair back and tied it again, neatly, before placing his soft felt hat squarely on his impeccable head. And how the hell he managed to do that without looking in a glass, Hollie would never know. "Perhaps we might make a start by managing to sit through a whole dinner without either sliding under the table drunk or challenging any of the party to trial by combat?"

Hollie bridled – was about to protest, long and furiously – and then caught Luce's resigned expression. "Th'art laughing at me, brat," he said, and the lad nodded.

"Can we keep the heathen vernacular down to a dull roar, as well, sir?"

"I wouldn't fret thi'sen, lad. I only do it wi' t'people I like."

# 33 THE COMMAND OF THE NORTHERN ARMY

Every last man around the table turned and stared at the pair of them, and since neither he nor Luce had two heads last time he'd looked, that set his hackles up again, straight off.

"Captain Babbitt," the Scot said, astonished.

"Hollie," Hollie said, though it galled him to do so – and if the brat gave away the full version of his given name, he'd skin the lad and eat him. Last thing he needed in these dour West Riding wool towns was the reputation of a Puritan. (Let his father have that.) "Didn't take me as long as I thought it would to get sorted out," he muttered. "Thought I'd come back." Luce kicked him in the ankle, hard, and not very surreptitiously. "And make apologies for my abrupt departure," he finished. Grudgingly.

Gifford grinned, as though as he'd won a minor battle.

"Cornet Pettitt, out of Captain Babbitt's troop," - and Luce gave one of his barely-civil bows, because where Hollie was fiery on his mettle the brat went cold as charity. Gifford's grin softened - the lad had that effect on people: he expected to be liked, and so he bloody was - and to Hollie's mortification the little bugger gave one of his sweet smiles, all forgiven. "Lucifer, amongst friends,," he said, and if Hollie hadn't been in company he might have either banged either the lad's head or his own against the nearest wall, as the Scot's dark face lit with wicked glee.

"A troop of Puritans, captain! Ye sought to deceive us, wi' your talk of looting and drunkenness!"

And then Black Tom was on his feet at the head of the table, waving a hand to quell the laughter, with a smile that was oddly shy, as if he were unsure of his own welcome in his own quarters. "Take no notice of my colleagues, sir, they but seek to tease in a friendly and good-humoured manner –“ glaring at Gifford as if he were daring the Scot to argue that one. “I am glad to see you return, captain. I meant no offence to your men, sir. The Lord does not judge by words, but by deeds – outward seeming is of no count –“

Luce took a smart step forwards, appearing to be advancing on the dinner table with intent, and in fact placing a sharp elbow under Hollie’s ribs. He didn’t need the warning. “Will you accept my apology, captain?” Fairfax said, and it wasn’t till Black Tom’s gaze slid sideways, so quick as to be almost imperceptible, that Hollie noticed the little woman sitting in the chair by the fire with her needlework in her lap.

By God, though, she was a plain lass, Lady Fairfax. Plain and brown with a beaky nose and a pair of most ferocious eyebrows - and remarkable eyes that were fixed on him, daring him to cross her man in front of his officers.

“I think I must tender my own, first, sir,” Hollie said stiffly, and  the less scruffy of the Fairfax brothers - judging by the sallow skin and the dark eyes,- which must make him William, nodded his approval. “My temper's - hasty, where the honour of my troop is concerned.”

“I remember you from Edgehill,” William Fairfax said flatly. “You’ve no cause to worry for the honour of that troop, from what I recall."

“Oh, that was all down to him,” Holly muttered, meaning Luce, and Luce scowled back at hiim.

"No it wasn’t. That was your idea.”

“It was a piece of magnificent -"

"Stupidity,” Hollie said, trying to head him off, “and I’m not like to do it again, take note.”

“You prone to random acts of intemperate stupidity, then?” Gifford wanted to know, and Hollie denied it and Luce agreed. The Scot grinned again. “I take it all back, Captain Babbitt. If yours are the troop from Edgehill that charged the Royalist gun placements at the end, then I'm honoured to know ye both, gentlemen."

At which fair-skinned Hollie blushed like a maid, hoping in the forgiving firelight no one would notice that his hair and his cheeks were the same colour, and Luce was blinking as if he might cry. Even the pretty officer with the girlish mouth next to William Fairfax was looking sulkily impressed. "Praise God, Thomas, Essex has sent us a troop with some mettle – 'tis what's wanting, to scour out my lord Newcastle!"

"Because *every* army needs suicidal stupidity," Luce muttered, under cover of the indignant outcry following those words.

Lady Fairfax stood up – although she was so little, you could scarce tell the difference – clapping her hands as if they were so many naughty children. "Gentlemen! Sit to your meat, if you please, and cease teasing one another."

"I believe I neglected to introduce my wife," Black Tom said dyily. "Lady Anne. There is a popular assumption that I hold command of the Army in the North, gentlemen. Be assured, I only sign the orders." He gave his plain little wife a smile that came close to transforming his own forbidding features, and Hollie thought he might take to Fairfax after all.

# 34 HOWLEY HALL, OTHERWISE KNOWN AS MIDIAN

Almost, after that, it was a pleasant enough evening in cheerful company, with Lady Nan by the fire working her way through a heap of mending and keeping a quiet and civilising watch on the conversation. Fowles seemed to be the man as needed the most curbing, always on the edge of some outrageous remark. Luce and Lady Nan's maid were fluttering their eyelashes at each other across the hearth (at which Hollie stifled a mental groan, foreseeing the brat at his most poetic again for a month, though he was damned if he could imagine what any sensible man might see in the stolid blonde Christian – though any port in a storm, and the lad had been on short rations since Windsor) Gifford was looking dour and unpromising across the table, though Hollie suspected the black Scot couldn't help that particular arrangement of his features, the man seemed as amicable as any. The Fairfax brothers sharing some family joke –

"Did you come by Howley Hall, captain?" Black Tom said politely, and Hollie stopped gawping surreptitiously at the company and gave his attention to his new commander.

"Not that I know of, sir. We hacked across country – through the Forest of Rawtenstall, from Bolton. Being such a ragged lot – " he gave Fowles a hard stare, at which the pretty captain raised his glass in mocking salute –"we can get where water wouldn't. String us out a bit and half the time folk don't even notice we're Army."

William raised his eyebrows. "Indeed, sir? How *very* interesting." He exchanged a significant look with his brother that was wholly lost on Hollie.

"Did you happen to pass anything of note on your

travels, captain?" Black Tom asked, and Hollie might be ignorant but he wasn't daft.

"Like what? – Sir?"

"Howley Hall fell to the Malignants not three days since, Captain Babbitt."

"You would have passed within a few miles of the Papist Army, gentlemen," Fowles added. "I did wonder if perhaps you might have some – further- intelligence?" His voice trailed off delicately, and he raised his eyebrows. Hollie returned him stare for stare.

"You think we're with them, don't you?" he said, with dawning outrage. "You reckon me and him are a pair o' bloody spies –"

"Mind your tongue before my wife, sir," Fairfax said coldly.

"Well you do, don't you? That was what all that – nonsense – about Jamie bloody Ramsay's bloody nephew was about -"

"Captain Babbitt, *will* you mind your manners!" Fairfax roared at him, and Hollie was so taken aback he sat down without ever realising he'd got to his feet in the first place, and sat blinking at his new commander. "Yes, Captain Fowles was testing you. He was also using the opportunity to bait you, as is Henry's wont, and I took him to task for it. Do you take us for fools altogether, that you could just walk into our council of war without our seeking to be sure you were who you claimed to be?"

"What with judas-haired cavalry officers my size being ten a penny," Hollie muttered, not quite under his breath, and Fowles glanced up at him and grinned.

"They might have put Prince Rupert in a wig, captain. Though I'm told his manners are better in company."

Luce sipped at his wine politely. "I imagine the manners of the company he keeps are better, too," he said, with a sweet smile, and Black Tom gave a sharp bark of laughter.

"That's you told, Henry. Well, gentlemen. I bid you

welcome to Bradford, though I fear your stay will be a short one, if my lord Newcastle and his men have any say in it."

"Oh aye?"

"They plan to use Howley Hall as a base of operations to besiege us here in Bradford."

There was a long silence. Luce looked at Hollie. Hollie looked at Luce. Then Hollie scratched the back of his neck under his ponytail – a thing he often did when he was just about to say something unhelpful. "Couldn't help but notice on the way in, sir, but – remarkable lack of, uh, defensive fortifications you got in Bradford? Lack of city walls, sort of thing? Did I just miss 'em , or –"

Fowles was grinning again. "Not a one, captain. Not a single one."

"Are you lot out of your bloody minds?" Hollie yelped – glanced, involuntarily, at Nan, and gave her a tiny, sheepish grin. "What the – what are you hoping for, an act of divine Providence or summat? The confident hope of a bloody miracle? How much supplies have we?"

Gifford shrugged, "Twelve days.."

"Powder and shot?"

"Little bit," Fowles said nonchalantly, leaning across the table to annex a somewhat congealed wing of chicken from William Fairfax's plate.

"Bloody hell," Luce said faintly, and Hollie gave him a stern look.

"*Language*, Lucifer." Folded his hands on the tablecloth and tried to look professional. "What's the Malignant numbers, do we know?"

"Oh, couple of thousand? Five? Six?"

"Ten," Black Tom said mildly. "Give or take. According to my information."

"And we are?"

"'Bout four, by my reckoning," Fowles cut in. "Plus another eighty as of this evening." He gave Luce a friendly wink. "That'll make all the difference, lad."

“Doubtless,” Luce said faintly.

“Gentlemen, this is shop talk,” Lady Nan said from the fireplace. “And *that* is supper. Thomas, help our guests to something to eat –“

“Couldn’t possibly,” Hollie said smartly. “We had summat before we came out –“

She stood up. The top of her head would have barely reached his shoulder. He reminded himself not to stand up in Lady Nan’s presence unless she wished to carry on a conversation with his breastbone. “Young man,” she said sternly, and thirty-six year old Hollie looked meekly at his mostly-full glass. “We won't starve for want of a bite of bread and cheese. Now. I insist. The kitchens have gone to some trouble for this supper.”

Luce’s lips were twitching, and Hollie made a mental note to give the lad a clip round the ear later on for his ill-concealed amusement. Fowles dug him surreptitiously in the ribs.

"Don’t argue with Mistress Fairfax,” he whispered. “It don’t pay. She always wins.”

It was a remarkably civilized evening. Anyone would think Hollie had his troop on half-rations, the way Luce was going at his supper, and a couple of times he had cause to give the lad a warning look. Not often they got to be in decent company and he didn’t want this lot looking down on them. He was itching to be on, himself. Had things to do and no matter how much this rather refined council of war might like to pretend they weren’t bothered, Hollie was of a mind to go off and do some serious thinking.

Made his farewells as soon as was politely possible, didn’t quite grab Luce by the scruff of the neck and drag him away but it was touch and go. It had stopped raining, and the night was warm and – it smelt of may blossom and elder, sweet and sickly and almond-fragranced, and of wet earth and the wide moor, and it smelt like home. Not home. It smelt like where his benighted father lived. Ironic that he'd hauled the brat from his dinner as if the hounds of hell were after them and then stood in the street snuffing the wet air like a dog. "I want the lads in," he said briskly to Luce. "Now."

"What? Tonight?"

"Thing is, brat, I don't know that lot back there. None of us do. And I'm not sure how I'd take it meself, if some feller I don't know from Adam pulls me in tomorrow morning and puts it to me that we've just come all this way to land ourselves well and truly in the – er – "

"Excrement," Luce said wryly. "You're getting the hang of it, sir."

"That'd be it, brat. In the brown and sticky stuff. I might, were I a less temperate and reasonable man, be inclined to take it a bit amiss, like, that nobody a bit higher up the chain of command thought to mention it."

"You mean my Uncle Robert, I assume."

"I usually do, Luce. I still reckon he'd be quicker pushing me down t'stairs. Now bugger off and round up the usual suspects."

The troop were somewhat less than impressed to be hauled from warm beds – some of them even in their own – in the small hours after a long day's ride. Even less impressed to find their commanding officer up, dressed, grinning malevolently, and perched on the edge of a table in his quarters instead of sitting on a chair like a Christian. "Pile in, pile in," he called cheerfully, and that was normally a bad sign in itself. "Be a bit of a squeeze, but I'll shout up."

Luce stood at the far end of the table, arms folded, scowling at the troop. "Let's have a bit of hush," he said, and then, "Shut up, the bloody lot of you!"

"Well," Hollie said, into the astonished silence. "That worked. Prob'ly wondering why I've dragged you all in in the middle of t'night. I'll be straight with you, lads. We had a lovely ride over here through t'Forest of Rawtenstall, and it's just as well we did come by Bolton or we'd have probably dropped slap bang into the middle o' Newcastle's bloody Malignants. We must of missed the buggers by a few miles -"

"Praise the Lord for His providence and mercy in our deliverance," a grim voice came from the middle of the troop, and Hollie looked down his nose at the speaker.

"Shut up, you old bastard," he said, and carried on where he'd left off. " – Looks like we got most of the Malignant Army in the North breathing down our necks. Ten thousand of them, I'm led to believe. Trooper Babbitt, if you mention the hosts of bloody Midian, I will take you outside and shoot you myself. We number slightly less than half that. We got supplies for a bit less than two weeks, we're running low on powder and shot, and for anybody who wasn't paying attention when we come in, Bradford is not a fortified town. Nearest fortified town of any size loyal to the Cause is Hull, a day's march away. Anybody got any comments?"

"Aye," an anonymous voice said from the back. "We're fucked."

"We'll try that again. Anybody got any *helpful* comments to make?"

There was a long silence. "Prob'ly be all right for supplies," Brockis said thoughtfully. "Summer, see. We can be a bit, like, self-sufficient."

Ward sniggered. "No thieving," Hollie said automatically.

"Yes, sir, wasn't thinking of it, sir," that most unregenerate of reprobates said innocently, and Hollie gave him a hard stare.

"Make sure you carry on not thinking of it, trooper. Owt starts going missing round here and I'll be looking at you and Eliot first off." He thought about it. "Mind, if you two want to start lifting owt useful off of the Malignants, you fancy a nice little ride out to Howley Hall one moonlit night and I'll make sure I'm facing t'other way when you do it."

He ran his hands through his hair. "So, other than that we're buggered, anybody got any bright ideas?"

# 35 THE CONFIDENT HOPE OF A MIRACLE

It was nothing he hadn't been able to work out. There was no surprise weapon, no magnificent plan. The only strategy was to get out as fast and as hard as they could and meet the Malignants head-on before they massed at Bradford. And after that, the chances were at odds of two to one with no artillery and scant ammunition, they'd mostly be dead anyway.

"Well, aren't *we* happy this morning," Luce said wryly, when he expressed that thought, surreptitiously, around the table.

"Of course I'm not happy, Lucifer, I'm stuck in frigging Yorkshire with half of Newcastle's bloody troop up my arse. What do you want, the Song of fucking Songs?"

"Something will come up, sir. As ever."

"Aye, Prince fucking Rupert, usually. That'd proper put the tin lid on it, wouldn't it?"

"What's that about Rupert, Captain Babbitt?" Gifford called down the table.

"Debating whether to dye my hair black and ask Newcastle for safe passage," Hollie said sourly. "See if I can have him on that I'm Prince Rupert of ze Rhine, havink come hot-footed from the siege of Readink, ja? Me and me personal lifeguard, all four thousand of 'em. And Luce dressed up as my dog."

Black Tom didn't laugh. Luce and Fowles both snorted helplessly, and received a stern look apiece. "This is not a laughing matter, sir."

"I have t' laugh, or I'd bloody well cry," Hollie muttered not quite quietly enough.

"Do you have something to add, captain?" Black Tom

said icily.

"Since you put it like that, my lord, aye, I do. There's ten thousand of them, and there's four thousand of us. You will forgive my plain speaking, sir, but might I ask how many of your horse fight Swedish order?"

"What, like Prince – "

"Is Lady Anne present, sir?" Hollie said sweetly, and on seeing Black Tom's blank shake of the head, went on, "Don't you bloody well dare mention that man's name in my presence, Henry Fowles. Don't you bloody well *dare*. We've got no artillery, and precious light on shot. Fine. Bollocks to firepower. We can't touch 'em for it. Can't even come close. What we have got is eighty madmen on horseback."

"Swedish order," Black Tom was saying, thoughtfully, rubbing his chin. By the sound of it he hadn't shaved that morning either. "D'you say so, captain?"

"Can't do owt else, my lord. You *seen* the size of my horse?"

Which even cracked a smile out of Fairfax. "I have, sir. I see your point."

Gifford propped his elbows on the table. "Care to explain, laddie, or is it a private joke?"

"Ever seen meinherr Rupert and his lovely ladies fight? Frightening, it is. The whole boiling lot of the buggers come on at the charge, the hell with pistols, swords at the point, and while our lads are stood looking at them thinking what the hell is that – or more like, running away, the times I've seen it done – Rupert comes smashing through the middle and chops the poor sods to gobbets." There was a lot of grim nodding round the table. "Aye, well, he didn't invent it, much though he might like to make out he did. Picked it up same place as I did. Swedish Army under Gustavus Adolphus. See, thing is, I've got ten years on our Rupert, and when he was reading about it, muggins here was fighting it. That lad ain't got brakes," Hollie grinned up the table with his hair in his eyes. "I have."

"Well, I never," Black Tom said mildly. "I wonder if my lord Essex knows what a weapon he's surrendered into my hands. Do you know Colonel Cromwell out in the Fen Country, sir?"

Luce didn't think he'd ever seen Hollie actually struck dumb before. Mute, blushing ferociously, and wholly wrong-footed. "Not in person, sir, though we have been on the same patch," he said, before the captain had his head turned any further by unfamiliar praise.

Fairfax nodded. "You'd like him, I think. He seems to think much as you do. I've been writing to the House of Commons requesting his support this way for some time, though I've yet to have a response. Well, it seems Providence has sent you instead, sir. Can you have your troop ready at first light?"

# 36 ADWALTON MOOR

If it was very quiet, it was possible to hear the sound of Newcastle's approaching army on the march, in between the first sleepy whistles and chirrups of birds as they stirred ready for dawn, and the muffled thumps, clatters and curses of four thousand troopers roused untimely from their beds and forming up for battle.

They still weren't a particularly beautiful troop, he thought. Mounts of all shapes and sizes and tempers, troopers in an assortment of armour. It worked. He did what he'd fallen into the habit of doing, this week in Bradford, picking someone out of the troop at random and demanding to inspect their weapons. Having them disciplined if there was a spot of rust on a blade, or a stiff lock on a carbine. The horses were fit and ready. Scruffy – groomed, but scruffy – tack clean, if mended. He narrowed his eyes at the ranks, doing the last-minute observation more for his own comfort than theirs. Swung himself up onto Tyburn's broad back, the big black shifting and dancing a little, eager to go. He found himself tapping his fingers on the rein in rhythm with Newcastle's approaching drums, sounding an absent advance. Still odd, to be forming your men up amongst the shuttered sleeping houses and walled herb-gardens of a town not a day's ride from from the moors where you were born. The air was still cool and moist, though the sun burning off the mist far too quickly.

"All right, brat?"

Luce gave him a big grin. "All right, sir."

"You excited or summat, Lucifer?"

The lad nodded. "We're going to make Fairfax proud of us today, sir. I just know we are. It's going to be a good day."

"It's going to be a hot one, Lucey, so you keep that bloody mare on a tight rein or she'll be foundered by dinnertime. Colours?"

"I *knew* there was something I'd forgotten, sir – " Still grinning, he heeled the mare in a half-circle, showed Hollie the colours rolled up under his left arm. "Do I look daft?"

"I don't think you want me to answer that question, Cornet Pettitt," Hollie said sternly, trying not to laugh. "Behave in a sober manner, sir, befitting a soldier in the Army of Parliament." Out of sheer devilment, though, he leaned out of his saddle and broke off a single rose from a climbing bush overhanging a garden wall as he passed. Stuck it behind his ear. "Red rose," he said. "Lancashire. Just saying. In case any bugger thinks I've gone native, like."

"Very sober," Luce said, trotting the mare up alongside him.

And Fairfax – not Black Tom, but Ferdinando, the senior one, Black Tom's sire – eyeing them as they passed with a sort of mingled amusement and admiration, and Luce brought the colours up in salute and the silk unfurled in the warm breeze with a little liquid rippling sound. "Pardon," Eliot said, not quite inaudibly.

Hollie looked straight ahead. "You're on a bloody charge for that, later," he said out of the corner of his mouth.

"Not me, sir, it was my horse," the trooper said, much louder, and Luce choked at the side of him and Hollie, rolling his eyes heavenwards, decided he couldn't stand much more and gave the order to trot on.

A bare couple of miles, and they could see the sunlight glinting off plate in the distance. "Christ," he said faintly, pulling Tib off the road to look at the massing troops of Newcastle's men. "There's a few of 'em out there, ain't there?"

Luce wasn't grinning any more. "No more than there was at Edgehill, I'm sure."

"Babbitt – flank. Fowles – flank. You two are with me."

It was a different Fairfax from the customary gentle, diffident Black Tom. Looked like him – definitely had the same big white stallion, as Surrey laid his ears flat back and squealed at Tyburn. "On the far right, Babbitt," Black Tom corrected, sounding reassuringly like himself again. "Put some miles between these two. And what the – what *have* you got stuck in your helmet, in the Lord's name?"

"Rose, sir," he said stiffly, wanting the ground to open up and swallow him. Tom's eyebrows rose. "Most – romantic, sir. A keepsake, no doubt. Get off over there, captain. Keep your head down, keep your wits about you, and wait for the order, d'you hear me?"

Gifford on the left. Ferdinando Fairfax in the middle. That was sort of irrelevant. This was the flank that mattered, this, out here amongst the hedges and the enclosures on the edge of the moor, and he had the troop walk on, slow and careful over the whins because not all this lot were moor-bred like he was. Keep going, slow and steady, keep going, past Fowles's men lining up neat and nice and orderly as you like. Musketeers nestling into the hedges – one smartarse admiring his rose, cheeky bastard, which set Luce giggling just behind him. "They're going to come between the gaps in the hedge," he said, turning in his saddle. "Ever seen a cavalier dumped on his arse in a gorse-bush?"

And then they came. And he kept looking at Fairfax – give the order, damn it, give us the order to go – and Fairfax kept shaking his head, no, hold your ground. And by God he wanted to go after them, wanted to be unleashed and thundering over the tussocky grass like the instrument of vengeance the Lord had made him.

"Stand your ground, gentlemen, stand your – " Tyburn was shaking his head restlessly, shifting and pawing the rough ground, wanting to be gone. Hollie gave Luce a sly sidelong glance. "That don't mean you can't fire at will, mind. Keep your heads down, horses on a tight rein, and pick the buggers off. Take your time." Out of the corner of his eye could see the petals of the blood-red rose, ruffled by the warm breeze. Unslung his carbine from his shoulder, laid it across his lap, holding the big horse steady with the pressure of his knees as he loaded the gun.

He could see Luce's hands shaking. Doubted the lad had fired those elegant pistols more than a dozen times. "See that lad with the red feather in his hat? Bet you can't take his hat off," he said, and the brat gave him a wan smile.

"Bloody sure you couldn't, Rosie," Brockis grumbled, behind him.

"Go on, then, smartarse, let's see you do it." Back-reined the black three strides, tucked in beside his troop sharpshooter, and all of a sudden it was a game and not life and death, and the whiteness was fading from round the brat's mouth. "Shilling says you can't," Hollie said casually, and Brockis sniggered.

"You ain't got two pennies to rub together, Rosie-boy, don't be giving me that."

"If what you mean is you can't do it...."

Brockis sniffed. Lifted his carbine to his shoulder. Sighted. All in one smooth, enviably efficient movement. His finger's tightening on the trigger was almost imperceptible, but the brave scarlet feather in the cavalier officer's tall-crowned hat a quarter mile away suddenly shortened. "That'll be a shilling, lad."

"Reckon you might have pissed him off, Brock," Hollie said innocently, as the Malignant's face jerked in their direction, mouthing words probably best left inaudible. He saw Fairfax give them a stern look as short-feather's troop started to pull away from the main body of Newcastle's horse and edge towards the right flank. "Dear me, it looks like we might have caused a bit of trouble."

Short-feather being shouted at by one of his colleagues. Hollie liked Malignants he could wind up to the point of impulsive madness by a bit of judicious poking. He wasn't as keen on plain, professional soldiers in plain blue sashes on workmanlike horses who tried to talk them down. Short-feather was getting proper cross, finger-pointing and occasionally glaring fiercely in their direction. It wasn't going to work twice. He couldn't get the bugger the same way again. Brockis' luck wasn't that good. His own aim wasn't that good. He aimed for a tall tussock of rank grass right under short-feather's horse's tail.

Missed by a country mile, and the ball grazed the horse's backside. Its squeal of pain was audible from this side of the moor, it went straight up on its back legs, and short-feather was dumped unceremoniously on his backside in the sedge. Hollie clapped his hand over his mouth, trying not to giggle, as short-feather hopped with one foot in the stirrup in circles round his fractious mount. Wondering if Fairfax would note his innocent-face from this distance. Saw that most worthy of commanders look over to them, turn to the galloper at his side, point at them. "Christ I've done it this time, haven't I?"

Bracing himself for an official ticking off.

"Captain Babbitt, what the *hell* do you think you're doing?"

Oh good, he'd sent one of the prissy ones. D'Oyley? Darling? Something like that. Middle-aged, leathery, bug-eyed and choleric with righteous indignation, little pointy beard all a-tremble, like the antenna of some buff-coated insect. "Misfire?" Hollie said innocently, and D'Oyley gave him a jaundiced look. "Do I look like I came down with the last shower? You are deliberately baiting the enemy into action –"

"Well if you knew, what d'you ask for?"

"Who's in charge of this wing, captain, you or Thomas Fairfax?"

"Fairfax," Hollie said, " but –"

"No, captain, not "but". I know you are barely broke to bridle, sir, but you do know what an order is, I assume?"

"But –"

"Don't argue with me, Captain Babbitt, or I will have you packed off back from whence you came as a plain trooper. Now. Sort that rabble of yours into shape and do what you're paid to do. There's the enemy, sir. You were very quick to tell Sir Thomas what a fierce fighting unit you command. Let's see you do it."

"What?" Twenty years of knocking around with Shuck and his gun crews had either damaged Hollie's hearing or his comprehension, because he thought he'd just been given a bollocking and ordered to charge in the same breath. D'Oyley – Darling? – glowered at him.

"You heard me. Get stuck in."

He was about to say something – looked at the galloper, and closed his mouth. Jealous. D'Oyley would have given his eye-teeth to be poised on the trembling edge of an attack, and not ferrying abusive messages up and down the lines. It would be tactless to grin, but he couldn't help it. "Luce? You with me?"

Luce brought the colours up with a snap. "Sir."

The black's head came up and Hollie's view of the world was somewhat impaired by two sharply-pricked ears. "Steady as she goes, lads," he called, "minding out for rough ground. Gorse bushes will smart. Don't fall off."

An easy, smooth trot. "Coming, then, lad?" he said over his shoulder to D'Oyley.

"Wish to God I was," that dour individual said gloomily, and wheeled his horse as Hollie's troop advanced at a measured and moderate trot.

For about five yards, till they got the feel of the ground, and then Hollie couldn't bear it a second longer, no matter who was watching to see how disciplined his men may be: tossed his head with a wild yell of delight, smacked the black in the flank with the flat of his sword, and took off like a thunderstorm. Brockis on his tail, probably the only man in the troop who could ride and fire at the same time, methodically picking at Malignants. Percey. He could tell it was Percey stuck to his arse like a burr to a blanket because he could hear the lad wrestling to get his reins in one hand and his sword in the other without turning himself into a galloping cat's-cradle. Luce, white to the lips again and staring straight ahead at the oncoming cavalry.

Pick one, Hollie. The hell with it. Go after short-feather, you know he'll bite. The expression on the little feller's face was priceless as he realised that this particular troop of cavalry did not stop, politely get off and fire, and then obligingly stand around holding their horses while you shot back at them, no matter what the prevailing fashion. This rabble came on at the gallop – oh yes, laddie, even on this ground, because some of us was born and brought up on rough ground – and they slammed into your unsuspecting well-behaved little unit and those of your horse that weren't expecting it took off at a flat panicked run. It was a warm day, and the sun was shining, and Hollie's wrist was feeling particularly limber, so he did a bit of chasing, just for fun. Wheeling Tyburn back from scattering Malignants like chaff on the wind and bringing him back at a smooth collected canter, just in case some of them overbred bastards had thought the horse was uncontrollable – catching short-feather's eye and grinning meaningfully at him. You're next, lad. The little bugger wasn't scared, give him that. Intimidated, and doing his damnedest not to look it in front of his men, which was why Hollie was going after him. Lovely familiar smell of black powder and horse sweat and crushed grass and he sniffed appreciatively – the benighted Malignant who'd thought about taking him on took one look at this snuffing maniac on the frothing black horse and melted abruptly back into the fray.

Lucifer and his red mare doing a sterling job, set on three against one and that wasn't very fair, though the lad was doing well enough. Long cut on the brat's forearm – left hand, wouldn't hinder him, though such cuts stung like hell later on in Hollie's experience – the sleeve of his buffcoat dark stained. Tickled him greatly that none of the lad's assailants paid Hollie much notice, too busy with their easy mark, right up until the point where at about half a length's distance he put his heels to the black and took the lighter of the two Malignant cavalry horses flank on, knocking it and its rider staggering off balance, hooves scrabbling for purchase on the rough ground. Keep barging at the horse, its nerve was beginning to go, eyes rolling wild and white-ringed. "You really ought to train your mounts better," Hollie said sternly, blocking the cavalier's flailing blade with two feet of stout Birmingham steel. "Now fuck off."

Disengaging his own blade and punching it through the man's shoulder, feeling the resistance of solid muscle. Hurt like hell, disabled a man for weeks – but it didn't kill him. Hollie wasn't in the business of killing, not unless he had to. The cavalier dropped like a rock, slithering down his horse's neck in a smear of blood. Luce wasn't particular, and ran the second through whilst his attention was distracted. The third thought about fighting it out and decided discretion was the better part of valour, and fled, pursued enthusiastically by Matthew Percey.

"Shall we, er, bugger off?" Hollie said, surveying the disorganised devastation that his troop had left of short-feather's men. "Luce?"

The lad transferred the drooping colours to his right hand. Sweat was dripping off the end of his nose. "Eh, lad, tha looks a bloody mess," Hollie said critically. "Come on."

"Don't – look – so bloody – trim yourself," Luce wheezed, fixing him with a baleful glare.

"Up your bum, Cornet Pettitt," he said primly, and the lad collapsed in silent giggles over the red mare's neck. "Kindly behave in a sober manner, sir, as befits a – what?"

Luce pointed weakly over Hollie's shoulder. He wheeled Tib in a tight circle, hand on his sword – "Oh, it's you."

D'Oyley looked exhausted, and his horse was drooping.

"You all right?" Hollie asked, and the galloper gave him a jaundiced look.

"Don't ask, Babbitt. Good work. Black Tom's – " he took a deep, rasping breath, "- impressed. Just hope we get out alive to appreciate it."

"What?"

"Lost. The reserves."

"What d'you mean, we -" He took his helmet off and ran a hand through his sweaty hair. "Lost how? Gone missing? What –"

"Need to bring – your men back in, Babbitt. On our own."

"Fuck is he talking about?" Hollie asked Luce.

Luce looked blank, shrugged. Blinked. Stopped looking blank. "Er, sir?"

"Don't you start being enigmatic, Lucifer. I'm not sure I can stand – oh."

"Oh, indeed." D'Oyley had got back sufficient breath to sound his usual sour self. "You didn't think we'd actually won the day,?"

"Chance would be a fine thing," Hollie muttered, settling his unpleasantly-moist helmet back in place with a wince. "Orders?"

D'Oyley jerked his thumb over his shoulder eloquently. "Bradford."

"What – retreat?"

"We lost touch with Gifford, Babbitt. The Lord alone knows where the reserves under Lord Fairfax are. We're on our own out here and if you look round, you will note that the natives don't look friendly," the galloper said drily. "If you want to stand and fight, be my guest."

"Casualties, Luce?"

Luce pulled a resigned face and did a quick head count. "Ten, fifteen?"

"Not Trooper Babbitt?" he said hopefully, and the brat shook his head.

"Sorry, sir. Shall I –"

"No bloody choice, have we? I'll bloody go down fighting, though, see if I don't."

# 37 ON THE BACK FOOT

It was a long, hard fighting retreat, with the sun burning on plate and the horses sweating and lathered, back across the moor and through the hedges they'd fought so bloody hard for. Luce was whimpering with weariness and bitter disappointment as he rode and it was starting to get right on Hollie's nerves because he felt the same himself, felt like he could just put his head on the black's soaked neck and sob like a baby –

"Lucey, pack that in – right now," he said viciously, and the brat looked down at his blood-streaked hand on the bridle and said nothing, though his lip quivered.

Behind him, he could hear his father's stentorian whisper as he prayed for victory, mercy, deliverance, or a bit of all three, and he had neither the breath or the fire left to tell him to shut up.

"Black Tom wants you," D'Oyley said at his shoulder, and it was on the tip of his tongue to tell the man to go to hell, but instead he said nothing, just dipped his head in acknowledgement that he'd heard and turned the black's head. Luce wordlessly tucked into his place. The colours were grey with dust, the red mare dappled with it. There was a tiny corner of Hollie's mind that thought he owed Fairfax more respect than to turn up in all his dirt, streaked with the dust of the road, stinking like a plough-horse, but they were all in like case. Black Tom had done his best by them. They'd done their best by Fairfax. It had been a half-arsed idea at best, to try and take on a force twice their size and hope to surprise them. It had failed, and it wasn't for want of heart.

Fowles still there at Fairfax's shoulder, though not quite so elegant or amused now. That was good. Looked pleased to see him. Fairfax looked too bloody ill to be pleased to see anyone – gaunt and yellow, Christ, what ailed him?

Fairfax shook his head. "An old illness, captain, nothing to concern you." Riding with a hand to his belly when he thought no one was looking, like that was nothing to concern anyone, and Hollie must have looked disbelieving because Fairfax's dirty, sweat-streaked features relaxed into a grim smile. "You have my word, captain, I will not fall off my horse and show you all up. Babbitt."

"Sir?"

"Essex said you were unbreakable, sir, and I took him at first to mean ungovernable." His mouth twitched again in what was either a smile or a grimace of pain. "Though you're that too, I think. Lad, that troop has some mettle."

Not much wit, but plenty balls. That sounded like his lot, all right. He nodded wearily because his mouth was too dry to answer more civilly, and Fairfax looked sorry. "Captain Babbitt, I'd not ask more of you. You've done me proud, this day, already. There's a blockade across the road at Bradford, lad, and we are all but surrounded by Newcastle's men. Can you do it again?"

His first response was no. He couldn't ask it again, not of – seventy? Ish? – weary men and stumbling horses, to charge a block of rested Malignants. It was madness. It was suicide.

No commander had ever been proud of Hollie, before. He wasn't daft enough to be flattered into wanting to throw his life away for the honour of it. He didn't expect to get much more out of this than six and a half feet of Yorkshire soil – oh, Het, Het, who will tell you that your man put his pride above sense, at the last? – and yet how could he resist the mute and desperate appeal of Fairfax's black, red-rimmed eyes?

Well, fuck it. They didn't have to come if they weren't willing. "I'll do it," he said flatly. Fairfax thought he was speaking for his troop. He wasn't.

Probably about half the troop were still fit. Brockis

reeling in the saddle, white with loss of blood, and a blood-soaked rag tied about his thigh. He shouldn't be going anywhere. "Bloody am," the old poacher said grimly. Percey terrified and set-lipped and Hollie didn't even bother asking Percey because it didn't matter what he said, the lad would follow him anyway.

"You're out of your bloody mind, Matthew," he said, and Percey gave him a shaky grin. "Prob'ly, but someone's got to keep an eye on you."

Cullis said nowt, just looked at him like he was soft for even asking.

His own bloody father, meeting his eyes with a challenge like a sword blade, straightening his old bones in the saddle and saying, "The Lord will make them as stubble to our swords, Holofernes, and well thee knows it." Calthorpe – another bloody God-botherer – bringing the patched mare up alongside him and inclining his head in devout agreement. How the hell could you argue with a pair of godly lunatics like them two? They'd mar another couple –

"Luce, will you stay and lead the rest if –"

"There isn't a rest, sir," Luce said, looking straight ahead of him down the road. "Looks like we're all coming."

There was a reply to that, and he would have given it, if his mouth hadn't been so dry that he'd had to swallow, hard, a few times before he was able to say anything.

"Well, will you look at that," Ward's familiar sarcastic voice from the back. "Bugger me if there's not a tear in our Rosie's eye."

Which meant that his reply was a much more characteristic, "Fuck off, Ward."

"Other troops tend to lead with prayer," Luce said, sounding slightly hysterical.

"Brat, other troops don't have to put up with Ward. On my command, gentlemen."

# 38 SET ON LIKE A TERRIER

As charges went, it was a shambles. He couldn't get Tib out of a canter, and even that was reluctant. The back marker must have been a hundred yards behind and blowing like a bellows. He thought it was the horse and not the rider, but he couldn't be sure.

Bloody short-feather, unscathed, damn him, from the moor, latched on like a fly on a scab, and without speed and without momentum all Hollie could do was keep hacking at the man, hoping to make the bugger go away by sheer concentrated venom. Brockis at his shoulder, the rag round his thigh turning wet and red again, loading and firing increasingly slowly and clumsily. Doing a little damage, but not enough, not nearly enough, and as he turned to tell the old poacher to get the hell out of the scuffle Brockis slithered slowly down his horse's neck.

Hollie swore – lashed the buckle end of his reins left-handed across the cavalier's face, most ungentlemanly, bloody well worked though and the bastard flinched aside just long enough for Hollie to go barging through and grab his troop sharpshooter by the strap of his carbine as he fell, and hope to God Tyburn wasn't as weary as he felt.

Something hit him in the back, high up on the shoulder, with a surprisingly musical ping: hard enough to make the world briefly lose its edges. Brockis was no bloody help. Brockis was as limp as the rag round his leg. Hollie's numb and tingling left arm wasn't much bloody use, either, but he wasn't letting go of Brockis, not for Charles Stuart and the whole of his bloody army.

Luce, looking comically cross, bright red in the face and laying about him with the butt end of the colours, which would have made Hollie laugh if he'd been able to breathe for the pain between his shoulders. And some hard-bit middle-aged professional – he was almost sure he knew the man's face from his younger days in the Low Countries, another career man like himself, clearly, though God knows that didn't entitle him to any quarter – circling him now like he could smell blood, which he probably could: Brockis's, like as not. Cold eyes, assessing every weakness – the lather on Tyburn's heaving flanks, the dent in Hollie's breastplate, the fact that he had one hand full of Brockis and the other full of reins –

And then while Hollie was staring into the dispassionate eyes of impending death feeling like a snared rabbit, the point of a sword suddenly punched through the cavalier's throat from behind and he dropped, choking blood and clawing at the blade with his gloved hand.

Elijah Babbitt withdrew his sword and wiped it on the skirts of his buffcoat. "What is thee waiting for, boy? Ride."

Turned his horse to face Newcastle's next wave of men. "Go on. I'll hold them for thee."

Aye, he would as well. Twenty of them, and one sixty-odd year old, dried-up, God-bothering rebel who Hollie would have willingly shot in the head twenty years ago.

"Will thee buggery, owd mon. You come wi' me, or I stop here wi' thee. I'll not leave none o' this troop behind."

"'Less they're dead," his father said. "He is. Leave him, Holofernes. Tha can do nowt for him."

"I don't know that –" He did. He had his hand on Brockis's shoulder. He knew it very well. Hollie, you're a professional soldier. You're used to men being killed. You shouldn't take it personally. Brockis wasn't a professional soldier. He was a fucking poacher. He should never have been on a battlefield. He'd been one of Hollie's first ruffians, the big countryman with the black and white badger-streaked hair that had given him his nickname. Hollie didn't even know what the man had been christened, by what name to bury him – he'd just always been Brockis. He'd been one of Hollie's lads. Now *that* was personal.

There was nothing else he could do. He let the poacher's body slide to the dust.

"Thee comes with me, Trooper Babbitt. That is an order."

He wouldn't lose another in his care this day, not if he could help it. Not even his appalling sire. Elijah's gaunt, blood-spattered face broke into a grim smile of approval.

"Thee is as mard as thy mother, boy."

# 39 UNBREAKABLE

They reached Halifax, a couple of miles distant, by the Providence of a lane from the field where they'd broken through. God knows how, but they did. And Fairfax looked as ragged as his men, and a feeble cheer went up as the last of them came limping in, and then Fairfax told them they were still marching back to Bradford and it was a sign of just how much affection they held that scruffy scarecrow of a commander that they didn't fall on him in a body and murder him.

"Yes, now," he said wearily, before anybody asked. "It's only eight miles. Once we reach the rest of Lord Fairfax's men –"

"Whatever's left of 'em," someone muttered, and Black Tom managed a grin.

"Indeed, whatever's left of them. The Lord has seen us safe so far, and I see no reason why he should desert us at this late hour."

Hollie, for one, was past caring. He'd slid off his horse – sat down rather more suddenly than he'd meant to on a flight of steps leading up to a cottage door, to the consternation of the householder – and yanked his helmet off one-handed, because his back was stiffening up appallingly. Tried to unbuckle his plate one-handed, couldn't do it. Called Luce. Luce nowhere to be found. (Turned out to be on a bucket-stealing mission, as he returned from the banks of the Calder dripping wet and blissful, probably the coolest man in the troop, if not the whole of Fairfax's men. The red mare was pleased to see him, if no one else, as she stuck her muzzle into his ill-gotten bucket with every sign of evident relief.)

He was eventually released from his plate by his father, which he hated, and which gave Elijah grim pleasure.

"Some ne'er-do-well has shot thee in the back, boy," the old man said with grisly relish. "Look at this dent in thy plate –"

"I could not give a toss about dents in my plate," Hollie muttered, head on his knees, muffled by half a yard of sweaty russet hair. "I am not putting that fucking thing back on. It's killing me."

"Boy –"

"If you call me that again, owd mon –" but Elijah wasn't talking to him, he was talking to Luce.

"Holofernes. Drink." Being offered the red mare's second-hand water out of his father's sweaty helmet somehow didn't turn his stomach the way it might have another day. "Gently, boy, or thee will make thyself sick," the old man warned. "And thee did that many a time –"

Ward – the man was unstoppable – snorted with delight, and Hollie looked up with a mouthful of lukewarm water, glared at him, and then downed the rest in one gulp. Hadn't had a drink since – Christ, last night, must have been.

"More?" Luce said, and he shook his head.

"You."

"Had some," Luce said dryly, indicating his drenched linen. "Straight out of the river. Very nice it was, too."

"Get stuffed, brat."

"Wash thy face, Holofernes," Elijah cut in, and that was a step too far for Hollie. In his head, he wanted to surge to his feet, yelling abuse at the old man. His bloody stiff, weary, battered body wouldn't do it. Instead he sat meekly while his father used the cuff of his shirt to clean a long, shallow slash across Hollie/s cheek that he hadn't realised he had. It hurt. "Might take bad ways, if you leave it to fester," the old man said sourly. "Wouldn't put nowt past them Cavaliers."

One foot in front of the other, taking Tib down to the river to drink, and then it was going to be back on the march again. Even the weight of his buffcoat was painful on his bruised shoulder. No plate. No helmet. He didn't care. If every bloody Malignant in Christendom fired on him between here and Bradford, he couldn't do it. The wind ruffled his tangled wet hair and he didn't think he'd ever felt anything so sweet in all his life.

# 40 ...IF A LITTLE CHIPPED

They'd made Bradford, just before moonrise on that hot June evening, and Luce had never been so relieved to see four walls as he was to see the little house in Kirkgate where they'd been quartered less than two days ago. The troop, though – the troop were spent, and yet still strutting with pride: personally commended by Black Tom Fairfax, with a captain who'd not only been called unbreakable, but was still tough enough to be one of the last men mounted.

Luce looked at Hollie, bone-white in the moonlight on his big black horse, and realised that the only thing keeping the big redhead from slumping over the stallion's neck was that every time he swayed forwards the pain in his back would jar him back to alertness. Not pride, not obstinacy, but mute agony.

"Not long, sir," Luce said reassuringly, and Hollie – possessed of a sense of the absurd, even in extremis – gave him a wry sidelong glance, without turning his head.

"Till what, brat?"

"Well – till we get you off the horse –"

"I like the idea that it's a two-man job, Lucey."

"I imagine it will take three of us. And a block and tackle," he said thoughtfully, and Hollie snorted, then caught his breath.

"Don't make me laugh, brat. It bloody hurts."

There were any number of unhelpful suggestions from the troop. Calthorpe reckoned the only thing to do with a bad back was the application of a hot flat-iron – to which Hollie's response was short and to the point. Ward – unexpectedly – handed over three inches of murky liquid in the bottom of an anonymous bottle which he claimed to have been brandy, which was appreciated, but just about anaesthetic enough to get Hollie off the horse.

"It's fine," the captain said, shoulders braced against

the warmth of the kitchen chimney breast trying to look nonchalant. “Stop fussing.”

“Boy, the last time I saw thee walking like that, thee was in skirts and thee had a full –“

“You’re not helping, Elijah,” Luce said softly, before the troop were treated to further tales of the captain’s incontinent babyhood. A brief whip-round produced nothing more alcoholic than a fermented apple core in the bottom of Luce’s snapsack.

Davies helpfully heated an old saddle-blanket to scalding over the fire-dogs and then offered it to Hollie. “Better than your old flat-irons, so my old granny used to say, sir –“

"Davies, you can take your granny, and –“

“I think the captain is tired,” Luce said briskly, and if Hollie had been able to turn his head more than a few inches before the abused muscles of his back locked up again, Luce suspected he’d have been on the receiving end of a very hard stare. As it was, it was remarkably easy to ignore a commanding officer who could only address the area directly in front of him. “I think you’d do well to rest, sir.”

“I think I’d do better to have you strangled,” the redhead said through gritted teeth.

“Doubtless, sir. Percey, would you be so good –“ And for once Luce and Percey, those two self-appointed guardians of Hollie’s welfare, were in perfect accord. Twenty minutes later, Percey reappeared with a tiny, precious black bottle of tincture of poppy, begged from Lady Fairfax. “Well, he’s been bad all day with his belly, poor old cove,” Percey said by way of explanation, “so I reckoned she’d have it by .“

Hollie protested, but no one was having any of it.

“Right as rain in the morning, Rosie,” Cullis said with grim relish. “Me mother was a martyr to lumbago, good night’s sleep set her straightt.“

“And thee is big, boy, but thee is not yet so big that I

can't dose thee like a puppy," Elijah said flatly, leaving the rest of the troop with the uncomfortable mental image of their unbreakable, commended personally by Fairfax, captain, being held by the scruff of the neck and spoon-fed his physic by his father.

"No," Hollie said defiantly.

"Oh yes," Luce said, and Hollie looked at him and muttered, "Judas."

Put to bed with half the troop hanging over him – he hadn't had this many attendants on his wedding night, for Christ's sake – all agog to be indispensable, and he absolutely couldn't bear it. The brat closed the door with a firm, "Good night," and Hollie liked his cornet a good deal, at times. When the lad wasn't trying to poison him.

"Luce."

"I'm here," the brat said, from a roll of blankets under the window. "Rest easy."

"Why should England tremble, indeed."

"Hollie. Shut up. And go to sleep."

He couldn't. Too bloody scared. Scared that he might not wake up – scared of what dreams he might have, slithering out of memories of twenty years soldiering in the Low Countries, while his guard was down – scared of what Luce might think of him, if he knew the half of what the young Hollie had seen and done. He lay still, watching the cold white moonlight creep across the bare floor, fighting sleep with all the strength and will in him. "*Luce.*"

"Still here. Go to sleep."

"You don't make a bad lil' apothecary. Trust you better than bloody Witless, that's for sure."

"Witcombe is perfectly competent, Hollie. Hush."

"Witless is a fat tub of guts. *And* he's got cold hands."

"If your objections to Trooper Witcombe are purely aesthetic, sir –"

A long silence. He could hear the lad breathing, slow and steady across the room. Only Hollie awake in the world, then. "*Luce.*" Sounding frightened, even in his own ears, and hating it.

"Still here," the brat said eventually, with resignation. "Look, d'you want me to get the men to sit up with you by shifts –"

"I bloody well do not, Lucifer. You're stuck wi' me. You want to take this up professionally, brat, if that poeting lark don't pay."

"I have yet to meet a rich poet, Hollie."

"I've yet to meet one at all, thank God, present company excepted. Can't see me having much to say to a poet –"

"*This* poet," Luce said sternly, "would like to hear only one thing from you, captain. To wit, good night."

"Thee is starting to sound like Thankful Russell, brat. Do you two practice, or summat?"

"That is *absolutely* my last word, Captain Babbitt. Good night. *Sleep well*," the brat said menacingly, making it sound less of a courteous wish and more like a direction.

# 41 UPRIGHT, WITH BREECHES ON

"Then we are all settled, gentlemen," Black Tom was just saying, when the door to the council of war thumped open and the ghastly vision that was Hollie Babbitt this morning limped into view.

The big redhead looked round the table. His eyes rested on Luce – narrowed – with a look that promised vengeance later. "Are we?" he said grimly. "Anyone like to tell me what *my* lads are doing?"

"Going with my father, to Hull," Fairfax said. And then, "Sit down, Captain Babbitt, before you fall down –"

"I'll not," Hollie said.

Fowles stood up, dragged a chair from round the table, and hauled it in front of Hollie. "You will, sir, if I have to put you in it bodily."

"I am not a cripple, sir. I do not stand in want of your pity."

"No, well, from what I heard, sir, you're doing well to be standing at all," Fowles said drily. "Your cornet says you stopped a ball in the back yesterday afternoon –"

He shrugged – regretted it, as the protesting muscles in his back went into spasm again – "It was nothing," he said irritably. "As you see."

"Upright. With breeches on," Luce said, looking studiously at his fingernails and quoting one of Hollie's politer precepts. "Yes, sir, we will be going to Hull with the main body of the army."

"*Will* we, Lucifer."

"*You* will, captain, if I have to order you knocked on the head and taken thence on a hurdle," Fairfax cut in. "I asked much of you yesterday. Too much, I suspect. I would not –"

"*I* would," Hollie said flatly, trying to look grim and

martial at the same time as he eased himself onto Fowles' chair without bending in the middle.

"Oh, give over, Babbitt! Look at the state of you," Fowles snapped. "The intent is that we – us lot, that's going to Leeds – that we travel light and we move swift. You reckon you're up to it?"

"And Lady Fairfax?" Hollie said.

"Is my concern, and not yours," Black Tom said. "Captain, I am giving you an order."

"But I thought you would *need* me –"

Fairfax looked surprised. Might well he. Hollie *felt* surprised. Desperate, and plaintive, and betrayed, all in the one sentence, and that particular tone of voice hadn't come out of him since he was  about six years old. When he'd finally worked out it did no good.

"Captain Babbitt, were you – intact, were your troop rested, then indeed, I should make use of you. As you are, it would be little short of murder were I to require such service of you tomorrow. I should prefer not to have that on my conscience, sir. I am not so short of men that I must needs take –"

"I am not a cripple," Hollie said again. He would have folded his arms, but he wasn't sure it wouldn't hurt. Luce was eyeing him across the table with a distinctly sceptical air. Bloody brat, let him have his head in one matter, and he appointed himself physician-in-chief to the troop.

He glared back at the lad. Luce raised one eyebrow in amused challenge. Hollie folded his arms, damned if he was going to be beaten by anything so bloody stupid as a locked shoulder. Swore under his breath - evidently not quietly enough, as Fairfax rejoined the attack.

"No. No, well, I see not. Obviously, you're perfectly able to sit a horse, and your troop is sufficiently refreshed this morning that you'll be able to pull off a stunt like yesterday's with the greatest of ease, should I have need of it. Give over, Captain Babbitt. In your present state, the lot of you are more of a liability than an asset. Now go with my father – stand at his shoulder as you have stood at mine." The corner of Black Tom's mouth twitched. "And don't, in all charity, tell him I said it would be an easier ride with him than with me, or he'll take offence and we'll never hear the last of it."

# 42 AN INCIDENT ON THE ROAD

There were a number of things you could say about Hollie Babbitt, Luce thought ruefully, and some of them were even good. He was stubborn, bloody-minded, and he didn't know how to give up. He also sulked like a spoiled child unless he got his own way. He had not had his own way over the insignificant matter of getting his damn fool head shot off chasing Black Tom round Yorkshire, and had consequently sulked publicly for the best part of twenty hours. Had been funny, to start off with, watching the big redhead tie himself in knots , riding up and down the troop every ten minutes trying to give orders without addressing his junior officer directly. Stopped being funny about noon when most of the troop were dry with dust and their mounts were stumbling with weariness, and Hollie wouldn't give the order to halt.

"We push on," he said flatly, not even looking at Luce.

Luce blinked at him. "But if nothing else, let the men water their horses – "

"No."

And that was it – no negotiation, no rational discussion. Just no, because Hollie bloody Babbitt hadn't been allowed to have his head. Despite the fact that he'd have got himself killed, and probably took half the troop with him – was still, even after a better night's sleep than most, hobbling like an old beldame and wearing his plate on a very loose buckle so it didn't press against the bruises on his back. "Captain Babbitt, sir –"

"Don't take that tone with me, Pettitt. Keep the men moving. Walk on."

And even the indefatigable Tyburn was balky, switching his tail and tossing his head up and down as the big redhead tried to keep him moving. "Get *on*, you black bastard," Hollie cursed, and even that was unlike him, because of all creatures that horse got away with murder – literally, on occasion, they said.

Luce turned his mare, patted her soaked and sweating neck, nudged her into a walk. Met Matthew Percey's dark and reproachful eye, and shrugged. "I tried, Mattie –"

Percey nodded, too dry to speak in the blazing July heat.

"'S not a bad day for a ride out," Ward suggested sarcastically, scratching absently at the wet, red patch on his bristly jaw where the cheekpiece of his lobster-pot had rubbed him raw. "Hot enough for you, Rosie, you mental bastard?"

Hollie's stiff shoulders twitched. He'd heard that. "Orders of the commander in chief, no swearing in the troops," he said without turning round. "Twelvepence, you foul-mouthed scut."

Ward groaned and muttered something.

"Happy to keep fining you twelvepence till either you stop swearing, Ward, or you end up owing the Army half your wages. I'm not feeling particularly fucking temperate this morning –" there was a quickly stifled snigger from the middle of the troop as someone realized the captain wasn't intending to be humorous.

Luce glanced sideways at Percey. "I think he must be up to about a pound," he whispered, and Percey's drooping mouth twitched.

For once though Ward was right and it was - it would have been, in different circumstances - not a bad day for a ride out, as hot, brilliant July days went, if you didn't mind the choking dust and the fat flies that buzzed around sweaty skin and the myriad little scuffs and wounds of an active troop.

"'Bout quarter of a mile nearer, sir, I reckon," Davies said, appearing suddenly at Hollie's elbow, and the big redhead looked up, squinting in the glare of late afternoon sun reflecting off plate.

"Be on us by sunset, the bastards," he said - looked at

Luce's blank expression and raised an eyebrow. "Did you not notice our little escort, cornet?"

"Sir?"

"About four troop of horse," Davies said smugly, pointing to the smudge of glittering dust coming on between the hedges on the far horizon. Luce's road-dry mouth went slightly drier, and he licked his lips. "That's what I can see, mind," Davies went on, with an inappropriately cheerful desire to be helpful. "Might be infantry coming behind 'em, but I can't see them for dust."

"Them lot's been making time on us since noon, while this lot of bloody girls was complaining about the state of their fingernails." He gave Luce a thoughtful look. "Any chance you might have give me a bit of back-up earlier, Lucifer, when we could have put a bit of miles between us - instead of assuming it's just bloody Rosie sulking again?"

He looked down - not at his fingernails, which were in an admittedly appalling condition, but in embarrassment. "You could have said -"

"It's my bloody troop, Luce. I shouldn't have to."

"Sir."

"Well then. Best get back to your mates and tell 'em we're being tailed, Lucifer. Options currently, stand and fight it out or run like shit off a shovel. Not my favourite set of options, but that's what we got. Seems from your intercession on behalf of your mates that you're all feeling a little bit too hot to do any running, so we're going to have to stop till you lot catch your breath and fight it out. Do tell me if any of your mates back there have got any objections, won't you?"

The big redhead was clearly furious, and Luce was ashamed. "Sorry, sir. Hollie."

"Don't you bloody Hollie me, Cornet bloody Pettitt. No, tell you what, I wouldn't like to make you any less popular with the men, since I appear to be persona non fucking grata with my own troop I'll do it."

And he pulled the black horse on to the shady grass at

the side of the road. "Fall out, ladies, Cornet Pettitt has appealed to my better nature. Those who hadn't been paying attention at the back, there's about four troop of horse coming up behind us at a hell of a rate. I know some of you might struggle with the maths so that's one of us to four of them. Been lovely making your acquaintance, girls, now fuck off and do something useful." He took his helmet off and shook his sweaty hair loose on his shoulders. "Half an hour. Then I want the bloody lot of you ready for action."

"Make thy peace with the Lord," that customary grim voice from Trooper Babbitt.

"In half an hour? Need more 'n that," Ward muttered.

Hollie had loosened the black's girth and was rubbing the worst of the sweat from the horse's coat with a wisp of grass - which the black was trying to eat, being in unhelpful mood. Luce cleared his throat.

"Fuck off, Lucifer."

"Oh, for - I'm *sorry*. I didn't realise -"

"No. You didn't. You were too busy being one of the lads to remember you're supposed to be an officer." The black snorted and shoved his head under Hollie's arm. "Don't do that, horse, it bloody well hurts," he said absently, trying to glare at Luce at the same time as he pulled the horse's ears through his hand. "You're supposed to be on my side, Luce. I know you don't like upsetting anyone - apart from bloody me, for some reason - but you're an officer. Making shitty calls is your job." He twitched his hurt shoulder irritably and winced again. "It'd be lovely to be bosom friends with the lads, but to be honest, I'd rather they was still alive and hating my guts."

"I'm sorry -"

"I know you're sorry." He looked away, finally. "Well. Don't water that mare, she's too hot. Walk her about a bit till she cools down."

"I might be a useless officer but I can take care of my own horse. I might not be permitted to have a concern for the welfare of my men –"

"No, well, neither will the four troops of god-damned cavalry right on your neck, Lucifer, and to be honest I'd rather be a bit thirsty and a bit footsore but still breathing. Your choice."

"Hollie –"

"Captain Babbitt."

"Fine. *Captain Babbitt.* This has got nothing to do with whether or not I am currying favour with the men –"

"And everything to do with you making me look stupid in front of my troop. Aye. I know what you're after, lad. You must think I'm daft -"

"Hollie, will you get it into your thick head - I do not want to command your bloody troop!" Being on horseback gave Luce the advantage of height, for once, and he was able to lean out of his saddle and make his point most forcefully. So forcefully, in fact, that a good half of the troop straggled down the grass resting their horses looked up, grinning. "If you're going to go off half-cocked – *again* – sir – at least get your bloody facts right. Captain Babbitt. *Sir.*"

The redhead blinked. Then, unexpectedly, grinned. "Thee is a stroppy little bugger at times, Lucifer."

"And thee can be a very childish big one. Sir." He was quite proud of his approximation of a Lancashire accent.

"Aye. Well. It's the company I keep."

"Here they come, sir. Well -" sharp-eyed little Davies pointed down the lane. "Here one of 'em comes, any rate - "

Luce, still walking the mare up and down, squinted into the dust. And then laughed, as the troop started to scramble to mount. "That's not a bloody Malignant, Hollie. That's Fowles."

Hollie - hopping round a black stallion who was not eager to resume his work - made a noise somewhere between a yelp and a snarl. "What d'you mean, that's bloody Fowles?"

"I mean, it's bloody Fowles. Unless there's some cavalier type impersonating him, in which case he's doing a remarkably good job - "

"Stand down!" the captain roared, just before one of his troop took a pot-shot at one of Black Tom's most trusted officers, and then, "Fowles, what the hell d'you think you're doing?"

Definitely Fowles. Still neat and elegant and slightly supercilious, even filthy and streaked with sunburn. "And a good evening to you too, Rosie. Been trying to catch up with you all afternoon, sir. What're you up to this evening?"

The expression of blank surprise on the redhead's face was priceless. "Why, Sir Henry, I never knew you cared," Luce muttered wickedly, and Hollie glared at him.

"Just because I'm talking to you, brat, don't mean I've forgiven you. I don't believe I have any engagements this evening, Fowles. Why d'you ask?"

"Oh, you know, the usual. Information received that there's a nest of Malignants from out of Cawood Castle waiting for us in Selby... wondered if you might be in the market for a bit of cleaning up?"

"Cawood Castle?"

"Just the other side of Selby, couple of miles to the north of here. Lovely place. If you're interested, sounds like exactly your line of work. Poor things, there they are, rubbing their hands with glee at the prospect of catching Sir Thomas and the chaps on the hop after we get off the ferry, and what do they get?"

There was a pause. "What'?" Hollie said suspiciously. "No one mentioned a ferry."

"Only from one side of the Ouse to the other, Rosie. You could probably spit that far, if you'd a mind. Nowt a pound, as some of your charming compatriots would put it - I believe William told you we have some musketeers rom your side of the border - couple of hours to cross, if that. Depending on the tide, but it's flat as a millpond out there

- "

And Luce, still with one wary eye on his unpredictable commander, saw the big redhead blanch under his fierce sunburn, saw his throat work as if he was trying to swallow dry bread. "Stop trying to tease Sir Henry, captain," Luce said sternly. "The only water you hold in any kind of aversion is any kind that dilutes your wine, and well you know it."

At which Fowles guffawed and slapped his thigh and said that was it, that was fighting talk, and that if Hollie would care to bring his lads up at their own pace they'd be sure of a warm welcome in Selby.

And then after Fowles had ridden back to his own troop Hollie stopped holding his breath and blew his limp hair out of his eyes.

Luce had finally walked the mare cool and was presently sprawled in a most nonchalant and graceful manner under a tree, working his way industriously through an apple from his snapsack, core and all. "Didn't know you didn't like boats, sir," he said cheerfully.

"That obvious?"

"I thought you were going to faint when he said that about the ferry."

Hollie took a deep breath. "It crossed me mind." The lad blinked at him – well, it was something of an admission, from unbreakable Hollie – "Don't know what I'd have done, lad, if you hadn't said that. Um. Thanks."

"Looked like a fine and upstanding member of this particular bunch of fairies, probably," Luce said. "I owed you that, I guess."

"Aye. Quits?"

The brat rummaged in his snapsack and came up with a wizened yellow apple. Handed it over with the air of a man delivering a precious gift. Wasn't the sweetest or the juiciest apple in the world, but Hollie treasured it like it was gold.

Then, not having eaten since they'd left Bradford, he

ate it down to the stalk.

# 43 A CLOSE THING

He left Luce in charge - just to see what the lad would do - and stood leaning on Tyburn's backside as the brat started officiously directing the men to water the horses in strict order. He had his eye on the brat, and the brat knew it, and the lads were playing him up gloriously. He could have stepped in and sorted it out, but instead he thought he'd just stand there grinning and passing unhelpful remarks. Luce shot him a look full of loathing as he passed, ambling up the Gowthorp leading the black horse, the pair of them as relaxed as if they'd been for a walk round the lanes while Luce was knee-deep in argumentative troopers and malodorous horses. "You rotten bastard," the brat said, but he said it affectionately, and Hollie gave him a wry salute.

"Won't need that horse for an hour or so, Rosie," Fowles said, eyeing them suspiciously. Tyburn's reputation for tricksiness had spread.

"No? Here you go, Lucey...." and he handed the reins over, smirking.

Fairfax's quarters were almost unbelievably undistinguished - a plain little house, leaning perilously out over the street, plain and scrubbed spotless. "Up there."

Hollie was just about to set foot on the stairs when Fowles gripped his elbow, hard enough to hurt. "Before you go in, Rosie, better tell you. We lost Mistress Fairfax. He's not taking it well."

"What - *lost*-lost? Christ, that was careless! Where'd you last have her?"

"Ha ha, very funny, that's exactly the kind of crack I'd prefer you not come out with in there. Fell into Newcastle's hands on the run up to Leeds. It was a bloody close thing, Rosie, it was touch and go. There was about fifty of us in Bradford after you lot headed off. There was six of us left - me, Giff, Sir Thomas and three troopers. Rest of us - dead, or taken. Glad you wasn't there. Would have broke your heart."

It was on the tip of Hollie's tongue to say it wouldn't have happened if he'd been there, because he wouldn't have let it. Looked at the puzzled shock on Fowles's eyes - still - the look of a man who couldn't believe his own good fortune at the same time as he was wondering how he could have failed someone so badly. "I should have stopped with you," he said awkwardly. "I might have -"

"Might have, could have, should have. Saddest words in the English language, Rosie." Fowles let go of his arm and then gave him a little push. "Right. Come on."

Black Tom was sitting by the window, looking out into the still, golden evening, out across the little walled garden behind the house, across the tops of the little apple tree up against the garden wall and then across to the abbey, the river, the streets of Selby. Looking at all this light and life and warmth and, Hollie suspected, not seeing any of it.

"Captain Babbitt's here, sir." Fowles cleared his throat. "Sir?"

And Fairfax's lightless black eyes turned from the window and rested on Hollie as if he didn't quite know who he was, and didn't care much. The man had aged ten years in a few days. Looked old, and sick, and frightening.

"Christ, sir, is thee all right?" Hollie said, startled by being eyed by an animated corpse.

"No, Babbitt, of course I'm not all right," he said, and there was enough humour and asperity in that dry voice that you knew Black Tom was still in there. "Some bloody fool let my wife be captured. Of course I'm not all right."

"Which, er, bloody fool would that be, sir?" Fowles said warily.

"Me," Fairfax said, and the light went out of his eyes again. "She is in the hands of men of honour, no harm will come to her, I know all that. Even so. She should not have been in harm's way. Her place is here, captain, not - not -"

"Well, it's quiet, at least," Hollie said, wanting to be helpful, and Fowles choked, and apparently tripped on a nonexistent bit of fluff, saving himself from falling with a resounding thump against Hollie's back-plate.

The big redhead sat down with a yelp of pain, and Fowles trod, heavily, on his foot for good measure, just in case he'd thought the thump in the back was in any way accidental.

"Ever so sorry, captain," that most hard-faced of reprobates said demurely.

Hollie, with his teeth firmly planted in his lip to keep from any more girlish squealing, gave him a look which promised later vengeance.

"When we - left you," Fairfax said, as if none of that had taken place, "- before - it seemed to me that - that - that if I had need of you -"

"No need. To ask." He had to stop for breath in the middle, but other than that he sounded fine.

Fairfax nodded - frowned. "Your back -"

"Will be fine, if the rest of your bloody - sorry - officers can leave it alone. What does tha - sorry - what do you need me to do?"

First time he'd ever forgot himself with one of his superiors that far, as to slip into his own good plain North Country speech, and not his proper, professional officer's tone. Black Tom blinked at him, and then a slow, hesitant smile started to spread across his face. "What tha does best, Rosie," he said, in an astonishingly broad accent of his own. "Give 'em hell."

It was simple revenge. Men of honour or not, Lady Nan wasn't theirs to take – and nothing but blood was going to wash out that particular failure on Black Tom's part. She was his wife, and he'd not took care of her. No matter how much he couldn't have done it any other way - he'd failed in an undertaking he'd stood up in front of a parson and promised before the Lord.

Leastways, that was how Hollie would see it, if some

bastard had stolen his girl.

# 44 MAKING MOLL'S ACQUAINTANCE

Little Moll sat gloomily on the stairs, listening to the raised voices from inside the room. Mama was gone, her father was distracted, and Christian was fussing and impatient by turns.

If she'd been tall enough to reach the kitchen door latch, she'd have let herself into the garden, but she wasn't, so she'd taken 'Lethea and a bowl of frumenty and gone to sit on the shadowy stairs where her father was closeted with all his soldiers. The frumenty wasn't very nice, and she couldn't hear papa that well through the door; all she could hear was someone's footsteps, thumping up and down the bare boards, sounding heavy as a cart horse. There wasn't any laughing today. Sometimes there was laughing, but not today, not yesterday, not since mama had gone.

The thumping stopped, the door jerked open, and someone said, " - In the garden, then."

Moll pressed herself and 'Lethea and the bowl of frumenty against the wall, but not far enough.

The soldier came stamping down the stairs. stood on 'Lethea, and lost his footing with a yelp. "*What* the bloody hell –"

"You stood on 'Lethea," Moll said crossly. "You might have hurted her." And she held up the little rag doll, in her best dress made of scraps of tawny worsted from one of Moll's worn baby gowns, for inspection. "Say sorry."

He looked down at her – at 'Lethea – and he managed to look sad and cross and a bit puzzled all at the same time. Like papa did, a lot, these days. He reminded her a bit of papa – tall and bony and just a little bit ragged at the edges – but he was reddy-brown instead of black, and he wasn't so handsome. Then he gave her and the doll an awkward, stiff bow. "My apologies, Mistress 'Lethea," he said, very solemnly.

Moll nodded in satisfaction. "That's good. All friends again. Are you going in the garden?"

"It would appear so."

She tucked her hand into his, 'Lethea under her arm and the bowl of frumenty in her free hand. "Then you can open the door for me. I'm not big enough. I'm nearly four."

"Indeed."

"I'm Moll Fairfax. That's my papa. And this is Alethea. She's not real, you know. She's only pretend."

He stopped with the door ajar. "I see."

"Did they send you to get something?"

"No."

"Did you need a wee?"

He looked down at her. He looked a lot nicer when he smiled, even when he was trying to look scary and serious. "Er, no."

"Why did they send you out?" A thought struck her. "You weren't naughty, were you?"

No, but he had been hurted, and her papa had sent him out into the garden because he couldn't sit still for long and they were talking about soldiery things and they couldn't think while he was walking up and down. He was Hollie and his friend was the pretty soldier with the fair hair that Christian went out walking with.

"Christian's my nurse, but she's cross today, so I sneaked."

"She's like to be crosser still, if she finds you sat out here with me, lass."

Moll pressed herself closer against his knee and propped the little cherrywood bowl containing her supper squarely in his lap. "Spoon it in," she said firmly. "Christian helps, 'cause I'm not very neat. But she's not here, so you have to. It's not nice," she admitted. "Do you make *your* little girl eat all her supper if it's not nice?"

He admitted he didn't, but it was because he didn't

have a little girl, so if he did she would have to eat up all her supper. Moll made him try her frumenty, and he agreed it needed honey. "And more raisins," she said, and he agreed with that too. "Mama makes it nicer," she said, and she didn't want to cry about mama because *everyone* was sad about mama, and it wasn't as if she'd gone away forever, and father said she would be looked after, but even so she wasn't here, and Moll's grubby small hands clenched into fists in the folds of her skirt and she felt her chin wobble.

Hollie took a big breath. "Don't cry, lass," he said, sounding like he didn't know quite what to do. "I haven't got a clean handkerchief –"

"I wasn't crying," she said with dignity, and he nodded.

"Aye, well, didn't think you were for one minute. Got summat in your eye?"

"'Zackly so." Which was what her father always said.

"Wouldn't worry about your mam, lass. I've met her. She won't stand any nonsense."

Moll folded her hands. "What did she say when you met her?"

"To me? Sit down and eat your supper after I've gone to all the trouble of getting it, as I recall. Reckon she might have told me off a bit for being rude as well."

Hollie and Moll exchanged a look of mutual sympathy. "She tells me off if I don't let Christian brush my hair prop'ly–"

"I've avoided that one so far, lass. You reckon I should keep my head down next time I see your mam, in case she notices?"

Moll nodded, seriously. "She'd be cross."

Not as cross as Christian was, mind, when she came into the garden. If it hadn't been for her friend, she thought Christian might have gone as far as to spank her for running away. As it was she shook her by the shoulders and called her a froward little baggage to leave her nurse worriting, with soldiers everywhere you turned and the house packed and ready to go –

"They're done, then, mistress?" Hollie stood up, looking towards the house. She thought he'd forgotten her already.

"Are you all going to rescue my mama?" she said quickly, and he looked at her and gave that sudden smile that changed him from looking cross and dislikeable into someone quite nice.

"You reckon I should? Put her over the back of my saddle? D'you think she'd mind?"

She bit her finger, thoughtfully. "I think she might, you know. She'd be all rumpled."

He didn't chuck her under the chin. She hated it when grown-ups did that. He looked like he was thinking about it, though. Christian shook her arm. "Say thank you to Captain Babbitt for taking care of you and –" she looked at the frumenty on his breeches –"helping with your supper. Make your curtsey like a good girl –"

"Thank you, Captain Babbitt," she said, spreading her skirts like a fine lady as she wobbled to the ground.

"The pleasure was mine, Mistress Fairfax," he said, equally seriously, bowing over her small, dirty hand.

She put her hand shyly on his shoulder. "You won't forget - about the frumenty?"

"Moll Fairfax, will you *cease* teasing the captain!" Christian snapped, and started to pull her towards the house. The last she saw of her friend, he was still smiling.

"I won't forget, lass," he called. "More honey, plenty raisins, and I'm not to be cross if she don't eat it all. I won't forget."

And neither did Moll.

# 45 BLOOD AND FIRE

It was oddly dreamlike, walking back through the deserted dusky streets of Selby with Fowles at his elbow, talking of this thing and that, as though they were nothing more than two comfortable middle-aged burghers, on their way home to a good dinner and a dry bed, rather than a rather elegant baronet and a scruffy mercenary on their way to collect a troop of horse apiece and go tearing through this sleepy little town calling down bloody vengeance on a pack of unsuspecting Malignants.

"Luce."

"What? - sir?"

"You got a pen and paper, brat?"

Luce looked at him as if he'd started speaking in a foreign language. "What?"

"Thing that you write with, you know, that thing that leaks ink all over the inside of your snapsack?" He wasn't larking about any more. "Brat, it's an order. Give it here."

Fumbling with a pen, holding a crumpled sheet of paper up against a wall to write on whilst the brat held the ink for him - "Look the other way, Lucifer, I can't -"

Not much to say, really. He had to tell her he loved her. Not fashionable, not poetic, probably not even of a great deal of interest to the lass, but there it was, he had to say it. Thinking of plain, grim, pious Thomas Fairfax, half distracted without his little wife's firm hand on his reins. Thinking of that bunchy, brown little mite on the stairs with her doll, and the solid weight of her leaning against his knee, and her sticky, grubby little paw confidingly in his. He'd never had a child sit in his lap before, let alone shovelled the supper into one. They were - she was - heavier than he'd expected, and more - alive, and fragile, and warm - and the thought of how frail little Moll Fairfax's bones were frightened the wits out of him. How could you bear it, that they were that dear and that breakable, all at the same time? But then how could he not bear it, if the Lord so willed - see, he was starting to sound like his father - a solid, sticky, trusting little person of his own - with Het's calm, unafraid grey eyes. Wouldn't wish anything from his own side of the family on an innocent babe.

"God almighty, Rosie, have you took to poetry as well?"

He went about three feet into the air, and Cullis sniggered evilly behind him. "Sorry, lad. Didn't mean to make you jump. Made a right bloody mess of your verse,that has. When youse two's finished making rhymes, Fowles says the naughty little buggers are stirring, and would the pair of you like to get a shift on?"

Deliberately coming up behind Fowles, on his predictably-elegant dark bay horse, at a rattling gallop, and sliding Tyburn into a skidding halt on the cobbles that struck sparks from the big black's shod hooves and sent Fowles's unsuspecting mount straight up on its hind legs in a brief squealing panic.

"Now then," Hollie said coolly, feeling that he'd extracted some small revenge for the wallop in the back.

"Twat," Fowles said, grinning back at him.

Black Tom, considerably happier now that he was on a horse and doing something, giving the pair of them dirty looks, and then out of the corner of his eye Hollie saw an old dun mare, and a grey-cloaked, square-set figure, with wisps of thick fair hair escaping from under her hood, and sat in front of her on the saddle bow a small, taut figure in a plain green worsted gown -

Little Moll with her little pointed brown face set in anxiety, looking straight at him, but she didn't recognise him. Too frightened. Fairfax spoke to the nurse briefly and the dun mare turned, started to plod away, to a place of safety - was there such a thing, in this place? -

And Tib collecting under him like a bent bow, still

now, ears pricked and alert. Hollie raised a hand - walk on, nice and slow, keep it steady - hoofbeats echoing between the houses. The sun dropping red behind the abbey, and black Tyburn half-mad with excitement as Hollie sat the stallion in front of his men and – well, his intention was to keep them calm, both the troop and his frothing horse, and a remarkably bad job he'd made of it on both counts.

"Brace yourself, brat. They're on us."

And Luce hadn't had chance to do much more than look blank before the first shot came from behind the hedges and one of Fowles's horses went squealing up on its back legs, unhurt, sound, and spooked, and then they were in the middle of an exchange of fire in a colourless grey dusk with no idea who was where and with whom. Which was, to be fair, business as usual in Hollie's line of work and he grinned at Fowles and Fowles had grinned at him and the pair of them had whistled up the troops and gone hammering through the middle of the Royalist party like the wrath of God, scattering Malignants like chaff on the wind. Lucey's red mare coming up on his shoulder and the lad shouting something at him and he didn't have a clue what it was so he just agreed with it, and the brat going tear-arsing off with Calthorpe's pied mare and the Westons lumbering after him, firing as fast as load could they at a particularly vexatious knot of cavalry troopers with more sense than their panicking comrades.

Starting to get stifling as the sun dropped, one of those airless nights when the milk turns as fast as you look at it, and Hollie finding that the only way to keep the sweat out of his eyes was to keep jerking his head like a fly-bothered horse – Fowles alongside him frowning, mouthing, "You all right, Rosie?" and he'd took his helmet off and shoved his sweat-soaked mane off his face, wondering what Het would say if he came home with a practical Roundhead crop.

And Fowles gone, storming the Malignant rearguard as Black Tom had so drily put it afterwards,: by Christ it was a storm, the crack of musket fire so close together that it sounded like tearing linen, like the rending sound of summer thunder, and the gold and white flare of the gun muzzles sparking in the deepening shadows. Tib flinging his head up and down snuffing at the scent of black powder, and Hollie with the reins in one hand and his sword drawn in the other, the leather of one slick with sweat and the grip of the other as sure as the touch of his girl's hand –

And then forgetting all about Fowles and the droop of disapproval to his ladylike mouth as Luce and Calthorpe and the Weston boys came racketing back up, sweating and blown but not a mark on any of 'em, God be thanked, and Hollie setting his blade at point against his shoulder and wheeling the black to face his sweaty and disreputable troop, closing one eye against the glare of the last of the setting sun glinting off arms and plate. "Right, lads, time to earn us keep. Form up, close order, reckon we're in the market for prisoners so if it's got decent kit, knock it on the head and fetch it home."

"God love 'em, I've seen better organised rat's nests," Cullis sniggered. "There must be close on a hundred of them buggers, and –"

"More the merrier, owd lad, the more the merrier." Hollie sheathed his sword and hefted a pistol instead – stood up in his stirrups and squinted down the barrel.

"Christ, Rosie, don't bother aiming, they'm thicker than lice on a whore's –" Luke Weston broke off with a yelp as Cullis barged the old cob's quarters into his stolid plough-horse.

"Act like you're civilised, will you, you heathen bastard."

Hollie, shaking his head, fired into the disorder of Cavaliers: scattered a few, possibly winged one

"Bastards are swearing in French," the indefatigable Luke shouted. "What the bloody hell have they *got* in there?"

"Bought and paid for by Her Royal Majesty," Hollie shouted back, grinning now, reloading his pistol. "Welcome to England, *messieurs,* and I hope it rains every day of your fucking visit."

"Your aim's been crap since Radway field, laddie," Cullis said, shoving his commanding officer rudely aside. "Stand back and let the dog see the bleeding rabbit, come on."

Luce peered over the sergeant's shoulder, as elegant and composed as ever despite his honey-blonde hair sticking to his forehead in great sweaty hanks. It always cheered Hollie up when his impeccable cornet looked as ragged as he did himself. "Sergeant Cullis, what's –"

And there was a flat crack, echoing in the narrow street leading to the barricade, and Luce fell back with a yelp and his hand to his bleeding cheek where a splinter of good Yorkshire granite had nicked him, kicked up by the ball of a beady-eyed Royalist sharpshooter.

"Little bastard," Hollie said amiably. "Let's have a look – dear me, brat, you're going to look like Thankful Russell." He grinned – aimed – "Missed the bugger. Ah, Christ, I miss Brockis - I want that bastard dead or ali – nah, sod it, nobody's going to pay for his shabby arse. Davies. Take him out."

"Right you are, sir," the little Welshman said cheerfully and the beady-eyed Malignant went down gurgling, shot through the throat.

"Right, lads, I reckon His Nibs is getting bored," Cullis cut in, and turned his elderly cob towards the main street, where the fighting seemed to be centring. "See where your man there's dropped? Get stuck in where the gap is."

"Show 'em a bit of good North Country steel," Hollie added over his shoulder, giving the black horse a most undignified boot in the ribs and heading at a racketing gallop for the gap.

One of the Royalist horses down, shrieking most horribly and trying to rise on the cobbles, and the beast's master lunging with his sword as the black launched himself over the fallen horse and thank God Tib had been something of a hunter in his youth and corkscrewed like a cat to land on all four feet with Holly halfway down his neck, cursing, rather than the pair of them gutted. And the red mare popping over the gap right behind him so that Holly had to go forward, hacking at the swordsman back-handed – by, the boy was pissed off though, not often you heard Lucey swear but some of the language he was coming out with fair put Hollie to the blush –the brat clearly didn't like the thought of his looks spoiled by a Malignant bullet.

Hooves kicking up sparks from the cobbles as more and more of the troop came across and there were too many of them now for pistols to be any use, it was bloody hand to hand fighting, that smart bastard with the sword gone down under Tib's feet with his face smashed in by the raging stallion – won't be exchanging that one, sir, sorry about that - and his weapon kicked sparking across the cobbles. Fowles' men coming back through, milling briefly in a rather pointless melee between the houses.

"Who is in command here?" Fowles said, and Hollie cut round behind the twitchiest of the Malignant officers as they all went sullen-mute – overbred and high-strung idiots to a man, proper death or glory boys – and gently applied sword point to the base of skull. "Don't be smart," he said softly.

The man jerked. "I am. *Sir.* And I demand to know on whose authority –"

"Sir Henry Fowles, officer to Sir Thomas Fairfax, and – " Fowles glanced at Hollie and opened his mouth to make a courteous introduction.

"Don't you bloody *dare*, Fowles," Hollie said, before the bugger gave him away. "Captain Hollie Babbitt, as is the same." Like he'd ever be able to face the Royalist Army again if they had him marked down as a Puritan's whelp. "And you are?"

"Colonel Peter Nesbit, sir –" he snarled, quivering with outrage. "Under the Articles of War, sir, I demand -"

"We got a colonel, Fowles." Hollie put a hand to his breastplate in exaggerated awe. "What d'you reckon? Worth more, or less, than a lady?"

Fowles was nodding. "You have a point, sir, you have a point."

Hollie grinned. "Well, since we're all friends together now, lads, my young colleague here is going to collect weapons. Hand 'em over or drop 'em if your honour prefers, I'm sure I don't mind."

Luce – bloody and deceptively ruffianly – started to collect weapons, murmuring thanks and carrying a dozen blades that had probably cost a year of a weaver's wages apiece, rolled up in a torn silk sash he'd took off the dead swordsman. Like carrying a faggot of firewood, Hollie thought with amusement.

Then there was another sudden flurry of shot – shouting –

"Fairfax," Fowles said, and Hollie said something slightly more explicit, and there was a horse screaming – "*Now*," and he left Luce standing with his bundle of swords, he took what men he could get, took off at a flat gallop down the narrow lane to Cawood, following the sounds. This particular happy band of Malignants had assumed that the dozen or so men with Black Tom were their easy meat and they did not expect to find another twenty violently assaulting them from the rear. White Surrey on his hind legs, his white mane and shoulder running with blood. The blood was Fairfax's. The reins were loose on the white stallion's neck, Black Tom's left hand limp and useless and streaming blood.

"Excuse me," Hollie said, perfectly civilly, to the cavalier blocking his way. "Would you mind?"

Beggars couldn't be choosers, so while the cavalier was endeavouring to indulge himself in a little light swordplay, Hollie shot him. Left-handed, so his aim wasn't great, but there it was. Fairfax was still bleeding and it wasn't slowing. There must have been four horses abreast in this narrow lane and not one of them was intending to give an inch. Hollie's knee was pressed painfully hard into the black's flank by White Surrey's backside – Black Tom swaying in the saddle, face the colour of parchment. "It's all right, I've got your back," Hollie said, and those black eyes focussed on him with difficulty.

"The little wench," Fairfax said, very clearly, and started to slip from the saddle.

"Fowles!" Hollie roared. "Here!"

Things got a little confused, after that. So many men jostling around, and Hollie trying to hold the white stallion's bridle in one hand and his sword in the other, whilst keeping the two battle-crazed horses from turning on each other, not being shot himself, and keeping Fairfax in the saddle. He was swearing a lot. He knew Black Tom was still alive because he'd get the occasional faint reprimand from behind his shoulder. Wanted to laugh. Didn't like having another man's blood on him, made him as squeamish as the brat, drying sticky across his cheek, across his wrist - best not think about that, Hollie, you might puke, which would do your reputation no good at all.

"Captain Babbitt!"

Christ, it was D'Oyley. Fowles. He recognised pretty much everybody – upright, intact, unhurt - even Luce at the back, wide-eyed and shaking even from this distance - and his appalling father - couldn't some Malignant have done Hollie the kindness of shooting the old bastard? – peering from under his eyebrows and giving directions to get Fairfax down off the horse gently, gently -

"They're gone, Tom." Fowles, kneeling in the wet grass besides Fairfax. "Seen them off. Rosie's cornet brought you a present –"

What was that high keening noise, like a little trapped rabbit, behind the hedge?

The dun mare, lifting her head to whicker a greeting to Tyburn. Square, stolid Christian, her eyes enormous in her grey-white face. Little Moll, her fists beating a feeble drumbeat on the nurse's solid chest.

"Lass," Hollie said, and all that shouting and swearing had worn his voice to a raspy thread and the child didn't hear him over her own hoarse screams. "*Mistress Fairfax.*"

The child was a pitiable and unlovely sight, running with snot and tears, and Hollie slid off the black's back – stumbled, because he hadn't realised till now that his legs were shaking under him – held out his hands to the girl. Realised he was still sticky with her father's drying blood. Put that hand behind his back. "Lass, listen to me. *Listen* to me. He will be fine." Hoping it were true, that his father's prodding God might come good.

"All will be well, and all manner of things shall be well," a voice said at his shoulder, and Luce gave him a shaky smile. "Mistress, if you make all that noise, your father will be sad, because he thinks you're a very brave girl –"

Moll drew herself up to her full height. "Don't want *you*," she said, with a hiccupping breath. "I want mama. Want my father." Looked at handsome, fair-haired, elegant Lucifer with absolute contempt: whimpered, and buried her face in the unlovely skirts of Hollie's buffcoat.

"Rosie." Fowles looked exhausted. "Seems we owe your father a debt of gratitude. It's a clean wound – a ball straight through his wrist, bled a lot, but it's cleaned it out, so how lucky is that? You appear to be making yourself indispensable to the Fairfax household –"

The child was still sobbing, and Hollie put the cleaner of his hands on her hair, somewhat awkwardly. He wasn't sure if Luce was comforting the stolid Christian – in a very dignified and respectable public fashion – or if she was comforting him, but certainly, there was comforting going on.

"The trooper of yours, er, slightly grubby looking

gentleman, Babbitt? Seemed to suggest that you have been known to carry a flask of, er, medicinal brandy about your person?"

"About a frog's eyelash full, but aye, I do. Reckon you might have to get it yourself, mind." He tipped his head towards his snapsack, slung over Tyburn's saddle. "How does he fare?"

"Thomas? Sat up – weak as water, but not listening to any of us – in need of sleep, food, and Lady Nan, in reverse order –"

"I've been sick," Moll said sorrowfully, and she had, too.

"Do you have children, Captain Babbitt?" Fowles said wryly, and he shook his head.

"Not – yet."

Fowles reached down to ruffle the girl's hair affectionately. "You should, sir. I find the bodily emissions so much easier to deal with, when they're your own."

# 46 ENTREAT ME NOT TO LEAVE THEE

"Come, child." Fowles held out his hand to Moll. "Your father is fine. See."

Didn't convince Moll, who took one look at the greyish, blood-soaked figure sitting propped up against Elijah Babbitt, and started to scream. Hollie just stood there like a great useless streak of nowt looking down at the lass hanging off his buffcoat and yelling herself scarlet in the face. Christian couldn't do anything with her. Luce took one look and shied off. Fowles tried bribery, tried pleading, got nowhere.

"Mary."

The child had a point: that faint, stern voice coming from the apparently bloodied remains of Thomas Fairfax put the wind up Hollie, too. "Child," Fairfax said, "Come here. You must be brave -"

"No!" she howled. "Want to go home!"

Fowles took a deep breath and lifted the little girl into her father's arms. Which must have hurt Fairfax like hell, and started his wrist off bleeding again, to the disgust of Elijah, who muttered something about grizzling brats and tightened the rag about Fairfax's arm.

"Mary, you must be a big brave girl, now, and go with Christian with all speed -"

"Not on that horse she won't," Fowles said, eyeing the elderly mare with disfavour.

The little girl's mouth was trembling, and she buried her head in Fairfax's blood-soaked sash. "Don't go, papa," she said wildly - threw her arms round his neck and clung, all the more alarming for the silence of her intensity.

"Moll, now, lass, I have to, you know that, you've been ever such a good girl -"

"Give the lass to me, sir," Christian said grimly. "I'll put such fancies out of her head, you may be sure -"

Moll wouldn't go. Moll had had enough, this day. That independent little miss from the garden was quite unrecognisable in the screaming, red-faced mite clinging to her father. Fairfax staggered to his feet. "Mary, we don't have time for this. Christian - put her on that horse."

"No! No! I won't go!" The child's stoutly-shod feet were drumming Christian's hips as the nurse put her over her shoulder by main force.

"Still want one of them?" Fowles muttered into Hollie's ear.

He thought that scarlet, swollen little face, crumpled with misery, would haunt his dreams. The one thing he was sure of was that none of his were going to end up haunting battlefields before they were out of leading strings.

Fairfax raised his bandaged wrist. "Moll, be a sensible child. Gentlemen. We ride. No, Fowles, not in half an hour. I'm not in my grave yet. I want some men to go with Lord Fairfax -"

Fowles looked at Hollie. Hollie looked, quite expressionlessly, back. Fowles nodded. "I'm on it, sir. See you in Hull, Rosie."

Fairfax's eyebrows rose. "*Deo volens.*"

"Aye, that an' all," Hollie said, swinging himself into his saddle. The black horse's head came up - wearily, even Tibs got tired, but still willing - and Hollie wheeled the horse to face his bedraggled troop. Sunburnt, sweaty, grinning, knackered, and absolutely still game. Christian planted the sniffing, wretched child on the dun mare's saddle and then scrambled up beind her. Turned the mare's head to go with Fowles -

The little girl's scream was so anguished that even that fat, placid old dun mare startled, and Fairfax's bloodless grey face looked as if he'd been shot for the second time. Luce made a involuntary little noise of protest beside Hollie –

"No, Christian, not with Sir Henry," Fairfax said, sounding like every word was dragged out of him. "With me – " he took a deep shaky breath –"it's all right, Mary. Tha comes with me."

"*Entreat me not to leave thee, or to return from following after thee, for whither thou goest, I will go, and where thou lodgest, I will lodge.*" It was probably the most sentimental sentence ever heard from Elijah Babbitt, and even then it was a straight quote from the Bible. Hollie turned and gave his father a long, thoughtful look.

"You would as well, you old bastard," he said. Elijah gave a fractional shrug.

They rode.

# 47 THROUGH THE DARK

Darkness falling fast, and a hazy midsummer moon bright enough to ride by. A brief moment, as Tyburn stumbled over his own feet with weariness, when Hollie thought it would have been easier to go to Hull with Lord Fairfax – be in bed by now, no doubt, all tucked up in his blankets, after a stiff drink and a hot supper. Rather than a stiff back and a hot horse, which was what he had. Mustn't grumble, Babbitt, mustn't grumble. Could be worse. They were slowing. Almost imperceptibly, but definitely slowing, and that wasn't good, because Hollie doubted for one minute that their Malignant tail would have took one look at that shabby, staggering shower with their commander leaking blood across half of Yorkshire and decided to let them go unscathed, in the spirit of decency and fair play.

Both his own and Fairfax's horses were so spent they did no more than lay their ears back at each other. "We can't stop, sir."

"The child can't keep up this pace," Black Tom said. It wasn't a plea for understanding, but a statement of fact. "We're going as fast as she can keep up with. I'll not leave my daughter, Babbitt."

"Nowt to do with the little maid, sir. It's the mare. She's done in. I wouldn't leave the lass, either."

"Then you take her up, captain."

It wasn't meant as a serious suggestion, it was Black Tom at the end of his tether, laying about him in a most uncharacteristic desire to hurt, like any other wounded animal. Hollie shrugged. "If you want. Sir."

And then pulled the black back into the file, holding him in till he was alongside Luce –

"Got a job for you, brat, if you're up for it. Take the Rabbit – that bloody lightweight thing o' yours won't stand the weight – we're going to take the child up -"

Luce gave him a jaundiced look. "And the colours, and I'll stick a brush up my arse and sweep the floor while I'm at it, shall I?"

"Thought you'd welcome the opportunity for a bit o' time alone with your girl, Lucifer."

To which the brat had no response but the beginnings of a sheepish grin.

The nurse wasn't quite so willing, for a few minutes. Talked sternly of baggage, and dignity, and feminine necessities, to which Hollie's only response was, "Aye, and a Royalist patrol, coming up on our – uh – behind us, no doubt. Get on."

"And what of the child's things, captain? Is she expected to come into Hull dressed like some weaver's brat –"

He could see Luce, out of the corner of his eye, making the final adjustments to the Rabbit's girth. The red mare stripped – sweaty, but already perkier without the brat's weight, though God knows Luce was no Colossus – "Mistress, you've got till Cornet Pettitt gets here to take what you want out of that mare's saddlebags, and then you are going in front of Lucey, and the child goes wi' me."

"The child is asleep, you can't just –"

And then Moll's tousled head poking from the folds of Christian's cloak like some nestling under her mother's wings. "Who's that man, Christian?"

"That's Captain Babbitt, maid," she said, "you remember him–"

Didn't recognise him in plate, in the dark, in the shadows of his helmet. Her strained little face was tight with fear and weariness. "Hand her over," he said, feeling little better than a murderer, and the child hid her face in Christian's cloak and whimpered again. And then he had one of his rare moments of inspiration. "I reckon 'Lethea might like a ride. lass. I still have to make up for standing on her, don't I?"

Settling the child in front of him, Tyburn not happy at all but standing his ground even though his ears were flat back and his tail clamped between his legs, Moll's little back still rigid with sobs against him and her grubby small hands buried in the horse's mane. "Now then, Moll. Lucey is going to turn the mare loose – no harm will become of her, she's much happier without the weight of two great girls like you and Christian – and then we'll be away."

"It's a long way up," she said, still wary.

"Aye, lass, it is, but then you're not going to fall off, are you?" And God knows what he'd do in the event of a skirmish, apart from – what? Drop the child in the ditch and come back for her? Fairfax would never forgive him – he wasn't sure Het would, either, if he had the care of the lass and he cocked it up. "Is thee settled?"

A very small, very stiff nod. Christ, but that little lass had backbone. She sat very upright, head up, looking between the big black horse's ears as stern as any trooper he'd set eyes on. "Can we ride with papa, Captain Babbitt?"

He looked quickly over his shoulder. The nurse was mounted, now, and Luce giving her stern looks as he picked over the baggage for absolute essentials. And the nurse giving Luce distinctly melting looks in return, being clearly one of those females who liked a man to be in charge. The lad was incorrigible. "Hold on tight, then, flittermouse."

# 48 A DOLL IN THE ROAD

It was a long night's ride, alternately walking and cantering to rest the horses, with the constant fear of running across the Royalist patrols sniffing at their heels like hounds on the scent of a fox. Bitter cold after the sun had gone down, and the lass fretfully drowsing and waking against his shoulder – his bad one, though no blame to her, she wasn't to know that – shivering and muttering in her sleep.

He'd lost the doll. There'd been exchanges of fire – little ones, nowt to break a sweat over, just a brief flurry of abuse and shot on either side – all the way from Selby. Sometimes they were right off in the rear, sometimes some of the livelier troopers went tottering off into the darkness in pursuit, and sometimes they came back. Sometimes they didn't. There were a few loose riderless horses running with the troop that hadn't been there before. He wasn't sure what was real and what was a dream-fight at the moment, drifting in and out of sleep still mounted. "Upright, wi' breeches on," he said to Luce, who jerked awake and blinked at him as if he'd started speaking foreign. All right for Luce, he had that sturdy wench in front of him, at least one of them could hold on to the other for warmth. He had poor little Moll – how the hell was he going to tell her he'd lost 'Lethea about fifteen miles back, when a bloody Malignant had come out of the hedge almost under Tyburn's hooves and it had been a choice between letting go of Moll or getting shot by the enterprising cavalier bastard. Wrestling with reins and child at once, the girl had started to scream blue murder, Tyburn had started to panic, and Hollie had been near as damn-it paralysed with fear, torn two ways as to where his loyalties should lie. Moll was half off the black horse screaming for Christian and her father, in that order, and

Hollie – fighting left-handed at arm's length while he tried to hold the child down by the back of her gown – would have been dead meat if it hadn't been for Calthorpe, cantering ponderously out of the dark with a primed pistol.

Aye, well, that was where the doll was, and it had taken her till something like midnight to forgive him that sudden lapse into temper – and he'd only given her a shake by the scruff and told her he'd tan her arse if she pulled another stunt like that again, which was mild by Babbitt standards – and then she'd been so worn out she'd fallen asleep in the crook of his arm: he was familiar and he was all she had to hand. She was limp, and comfortingly warm, and the heat of her against his arm was putting him to sleep. There was something wrong about that. In his brief experience of Mistress Mary Fairfax she'd always had hot, sticky little hands, but surely to God he shouldn't be able to feel her warmth through buffcoat and plate.

"Lucey. Lucey you've got a sister, does she look all right to you?"

"What, m'sister?" the lad said blearily.

"No, you lackwit, the child!"

There was a long pause, and then Luce shook Christian awake. "Mistress – I think the little girl is poorly- "

She came awake at the magic words "poorly" and "child". Shook her head once, and then was alert. "She's done up, poor coo-dove."

The sun was rising. "She can't keep on," Christian said, and there was that in her tone which was not open to negotiation. "Sir Thomas will have to stop –"

Sir Thomas would not stop. Sir Thomas looked at his whimpering little daughter and there were tears in his eyes – "not though it cost me all I hold most dear in this world can I set aside my duty," he said. And then, in a small, all too human voice, "Give the lass to me."

They settled her in his arms, in front of him. Her eyes were half-open, bright as a little bird's under drooping lashes. One small hand was curled in his stiff, bloodstained sash. "It will be all right, Moll," he said softly.

And then he rode away, the big white stallion's harness glinting rose and gold in the dawn, with D'Oyley at his side because they didn't want Hollie, Christ, who would want Hollie, after what he'd done this night – the little lass would die, he'd pushed her like she was one of his own rough troopers, and not a gently born fragile girl-child – he could taste blood in his mouth, realised he'd bitten through his lip –

Luce was looking at him with sympathy. "Sir Thomas wants you, Hollie."

Recollected to the here and now, he looked up at the lad, who jerked his head, almost imperceptibly, at their commander.

"My daughter wishes to thank you," Fairfax said. Black Tom worn and filthy and bloody as any of them, black eyes sunk in his head with weariness and pain, and looking back at Hollie as if he hadn't just nearly killed the man's only daughter, but as if he'd done something priceless. Moll's restless head turned on her father's shoulder.

"Thank you, Hollie," she whispered.

"Captain Babbitt," Christian corrected automatically.

"Look after 'Lethea for me?" the child said, and then turned her face away, and Fairfax smoothed her hair. "Indeed. Thank you, Hollie," he said, and he sounded awkward, and like a man with too many things going on in his heart to find the right words. "For preserving my daughter."

To which there was no answer, other than to look on that fragile form and pray for her preservation with a fervour he'd thought had been lost a long time ago. Fairfax gave him a weary smile. "As the Lord wills it, Hollie," he said, with a sigh. "I shall see you in Hull."

The glitter of the rising sun off White Surrey's harness made his eyes water. Or at least that was what he told Luce it was.

# 49 GOING DOWN TO THE SEA IN SHIPS

He'd been that tired he hadn't even minded the whisper of the word "boat". Hadn't even minded the ferry itself, which Luce had nervously told him was a good four hour crossing. No, Hollie had taken one look at that rackety wooden edifice the Swallow, and found himself wholly unmoved. Gone down into the hold with Tyburn, lay down on the planks next to the horse, and next thing he knew it was mid-morning, they were half way across the Humber estuary, and the sun was glittering off the grey open sea.

Luce had been sitting on the deck looking out at that heaving grey mass with his eyes sparkling and his lips parted, the wind tossing his loose hair this way and that. Having a lovely time, the little sod.

"'*They that go down to the sea in ships, that do business in great waters; these see the works of the Lord, and his wonders in the deep*,'" Elijah Babbitt muttered. He couldn't do anything so inconspicuous as sit on a coil of rope and mutely admire the wonders of the deep: no, he had to stand at the rail looking like some maniac Old Testament prophet, quoting great chunks of the Psalms, and attracting every eye on the boat.

Hollie finished the quote for him. With feeling. "*For he commandeth, and raiseth the stormy wind, which lifteth up the waves thereof. They mount up to the heavens, they go down again to the depths: their soul is melted because of trouble. They reel to and fro, and stagger like a drunken man, and are at their wits' end.*"

"Hollie, we're crossing a river," Luce pointed out, gently. "If you want to really see the sea at its worst, you need to go out to Venning country – they get some wild old weather out there in the Fens. It's flat as a mill pond here. Get a couple of pints into Drew and he'll tell you some right tales – waves thirty feet high –"

"Good. For. Venning."

The *Swallow*'s captain came over and leaned comfortably on the rail next to Elijah. He was a long-legged, rangy, sunburned specimen, with long, straggling fair hair over his shoulders, and a seaman's far-seeing pale blue eyes. "Any o' you lot want some breakfast?" he said cheerfully. "We got a lovely bit o' fat bacon, fry up lovely it will with a bit of biscuit –"

"I don't think we've got time," Hollie said, eyes firmly closed, in the hope that if he didn't look at the ship it might go away. "Be in Hull in a minute… won't we?"

"Couple of hours yet, with this wind – what's up with him?"

"I think the captain's gone to see to his horse," Luce said staunchly.

"Taking the long way round, then, ain't he? Oh – no – ah. I see." The captain took his hat off and ran a hand over his freckled, balding head. "Never understood it, meself. Been on the sea since I was at me mother's tit and I don't think I've ever been took bad. Rainbow."

"Where?" Luce sprang to his feet.

"'S my name, sir. Tom Rainbow. Says Rains-burrow on the papers, but who's got the time to write all that out?"

"Lucifer – Luce. Luce Pettitt. Cornet Luce Pettitt." Luce shook Rainbow – Rainsborough's hand, then checked, surreptitiously, to make sure he still had all his fingers. The man had a grip like a horse-bite.

"That 'un?" He jerked his thumb towards Hollie, currently curled up against a coil of rope with one hand over his mouth, the colour of new cheese. "Better tell him, an' all, he pukes on my clean deck and he cleans it up hisself."

"That's Captain Babbitt."

"And related to –" he glanced at Elijah, who was studiously avoiding the lot of them –"that 'un, by the look of him?"

"Father and son."

"Ahhh…." Rainsborough nodded. "Makes sense. Me brother's in the navy, and the old man, God rest his soul, he died last year, he was a Navy man as well. In the blood, ain't it? So let's have this straight – son, the sicky one – he's officer over the, er, the godly one?"

"That'd be it," Luce said, with a sigh. "It's complicated."

Rainsborough's eyebrows twitched. "You're not wrong. Ah well. Give him biscuit, that'll sort him out. The sicky one, that is. Don't fancy giving the other one nothing. Looks like he'd snap your hand off. I seen seagulls with nicer beaks than that 'un."

"If you want to go and offer Hollie – er, Captain Babbitt – ship's biscuit, sir, I imagine you are likely to receive a similar response."

"Bit bitey-bitey, is he? Don't look it, poor whelk."

Hollie's considered response, to being presented with a dried-out husk of mouldy bread by a smug complete stranger, was to keep his mouth firmly closed, and look resolutely at the deck. Which smelt of melting tar, and rotting fish, and dirty water, and – oh, God, why would the bugger not go away?

"Be a good couple of hours yet till we land, and the tide's on the turn," the smart-arse said, still shoving that weevilly crust at Hollie. "Carry on like this and you'll be no good to man nor beast."

Hollie shut his eyes and turned his face into the cool, salty breeze, straight off the – no, he wasn't going to think about that. That Rosie Babbitt had a deep and abiding aversion to all matters maritime was a bit of a joke amongst those who'd known him for any length of time. He let 'em think it was because the motion of the ocean made his delicate sensibilities a bit queasy. It wasn't. To a sixteen-year-old boy who'd never seen a body of water bigger than the Ribble, the North Sea in March had been the most frightening, cold, implacable thing he'd ever seen. There was no reasoning with the sea, no fighting with it. *Rackhay* had known that. Rackhay had got him incoherently drunk, for the passage home at the beginning of the war, and left him passed out below decks for the duration. To be fair, Rackhay hadn't even told him they were getting on a boat that day, knowing Hollie's considered response would have been to go and hide under the bed. All very friendly and free with the geneva and next thing Hollie knew he was waking up with a raging headache just off Harwich, dumped on board with the rest of the baggage. Christ, there were times he missed Rackhay.

And what did he have instead, now? Bloody Luce. Bloody Luce, looking at him across the deck with the corner of his mouth quirked up, like an indulgent parent with an awkward child.

“Wind's getting up, then,” the persistent pest said, still wielding his crust.

"Good,” Hollie said through gritted teeth. "Give us that bloody thing here."

# 50 PULLING THE DOG'S TAIL

Luce's girl had been packed off with her little charge and Lady Fairfax as soon as Black Tom's lady was returned by Newcastle, exchanged for a mortified and fulminating Colonel of Horse. There were the usual rumours that Lady Nan had started organising Newcastle to within an inch of his life, and that he had less taste for being under the cat's foot than Fairfax. Regardless - Newcastle's point was made, and the lady returned, and Black Tom was happier. Luce hadn't been worth talking to for most of a week, though.

No, once Lady Nan was safely out of the way, Fairfax decided - with his usual grim common sense - that the last thing they needed in a fortified town was four troops of cavalry sat round scratching themselves and eating their heads off. Which was meat and drink to Hollie, who'd put his hand up straight off -"I'm in."

"In what?" Fairfax had eyed him coldly, and he'd tried to look stern and military, whilst hiding a spreading grin behind his hand.

"Right good at self-sufficiency, us. You'd never know we were there. No trouble at all."

And the brat had frowned, and then caught on. "Unless you were a Malignant. You'd know we were there then, I'm sure."

"Oh, you little rascal," Fowles said admiringly. "I'll have a bit of that, then."

"Gentlemen, there will be no thievery in my ranks," Fairfax snapped, and Hollie had given his best innocent look, thought of Ward and Eliot and crossed his fingers behind his back.

"Nowt to do with thieving," he said innocently. "Just being a bit independent, you might say. More than capable of paying our way. Just A bit o' light disruption here and there."

"You are suggesting, sir, raiding parties?"

"Precious little else for us to do, Thomas. Might as well get the use of us," Fowles had added hopefully.

Fairfax hadn't been absolutely happy about it, but they'd been at it for the best part of a month and nobody had complained. Apart from the Royalist troops. They'd complained mighty-wise. And Hollie had meant it about the disruption - thank God Fairfax didn't know the half of what they'd got up to.

There'd been one night, under a bright, buttery harvest moon, when he'd called in some volunteers and they'd gone and relieved a good dozen of Newcastle's horses from their outpost half a day's ride up the line. Luce had expressed disappointment and disapproval at this larceny in direct contradiction of orders, so - after Hollie had given the horses a once-over, and a more spavined, swaybacked bunch of sorry nags he'd not set eyes on in a long day's march - he'd taken them back and turned them loose again. He didn't say he'd returned them quite to where he found them, and he imagined that a dozen panicked horses squealing and blundering about in Newcastle's pickets, especially if some of the horses happened to have lanterns tied to their halters or their tails , might have given the sentries the impression, say, of an attack by a troop of armed men, and have caused alarm and confusion and not a little embarrassment to my lord Newcastle's finest. But that'd be nowt to do with them, Hollie being the best part of three miles away by then with his hands in his pockets, whistling.

You had to feel sorry for poor old Black Tom, who had to toe the line and give his officers a bloody good carpeting for such ungentlemanly carryings-on, whilst trying not to laugh. There were them as thought Hollie was three parts daft, and to be fair, it was the most fun he'd ever had on campaign. Fowles was game, but didn't take it seriously, thought it was just larking about –

"Pulling the dog's tail," Hollie said cheerfully, sat on a bench outside an inn near Wetherby in the blistering sun.

"Doubtless." Fowles none the wiser.

"Newcastle, up in Lincolnshire, seeking for whom he may devour, and good luck to him. Front end of the dog, yes? The bitey bit."

"I am aware of the physiognomy of a dog, Holofernes. It's too hot to get metaphysical, sir. I thought better of you."

"So did I, at one point," Luce murmured, shoving a jug of ale towards Fowles. "He doesn't improve with acquaintance."

"If all I'm going to get is abuse off you two –" Hollie leaned against the wall in the sun and watched swallows in the eaves above his head until Fowles gave him a kick.

"The bitey end's in Lincolnshire. Gobbled up Lincoln – gobbled up Gainsborough –"

"Hell of a big dog, this," Fowles said, quickly moving his apple pasty before Hollie, the notorious starveling, could demonstrate the gobbling up process.

"Got his eye on London, next, I'm told."

Fowles blinked. "Well, well. Who's quite the little intelligencer, then?"

"Got mates, Henry - friends in high places, Lucifer and I." Hollie closed one eye in what was either a knowing wink or a sun-dazzled squint. "You'd be amazed what we hear."

"I didn't know you were that close to your uncle, Lucifer?"

"I'm not," Luce said, with a resigned sigh. "I happen to be on good terms with his secretary, that's all. Not *me* that indulges in scurrilous correspondence with the Earl of Essex's officers."

"Captain Venning does not gossip, cornet," Hollie said smugly.

"Captain Venning is worse than a girl – sir. If he doesn't gossip, how come you know Henry Ireton's keen on Bridget Cromwell, probably before either her father or his commanding officer know it?"

"Old news, brat –"

"When you two have quite finished brawling amongst yourselves," Fowles said patiently, and Luce contented himself with tipping his commanding officer's hat into his eyes in a most insubordinate manner.

"Pull the dog's tail sufficiently in Yorkshire, and the bugger will turn round from London to have a go at us," Hollie said, and Fowles looked at him with his mouth open.

There was a long pause. The birds sang, and the sun shone, and somewhere in the inn someone dropped a dish with a clatter. "And there I was thinking you were just a malign influence," Fowles said faintly. "God help us all if there's not thought going on under that mop."

Hollie shrugged. "Nobody's getting hurt. Not like we're wasting any of *our* resources."

# 51 STAMFORD BRIDGE

They'd settled quite comfortably into the East Riding. Got themselves a forward base at Beverley - or at least that was what they were telling Fairfax, because Luce seemed to spend every hour God sent of his free time at a farm two miles outside that town moonng over the farmer's daughter. Hollie spent most of *his* spare time lay in the garden of their quarters in Beverley –he was getting quite accustomed to writing from a horizontal position. He didn't think he'd be able to smell the sweet spice of gillyflowers again without thinking of those afternoons, long and hot and lazy, with the sun on the back of his neck and the bitter smell of ink on his hands.

No, he didn't think he'd ever been happier, on campaign. You'd hardly notice they were at war, out here in the flat green wilds of Yorkshire. It wasn't going to last, he knew that. This was the calm before the storm, a storm he was admittedly bringing on himself, with this insistence on baiting Newcastle, but, like he'd said to Fowles, no one got hurt. Raiding Royalist positions – feeding them casual misinformation, disrupting their supply lines, exchanging some of their more decent-looking cavalry horses for some of his own invalids – there was no harm done. Eliot and Ward were in their light-fingered element, and if they weren't card-sharping across half the inns in the county they were robbing the local Royalist sympathisers blind. Luce had even enlisted in the troop of one unfortunate Captain Betterton, for something under a day – disappeared off into the wilds of Stamford Bridge, up near York, with Betterton, from whence he was recaptured by his own troop, a sadder and wiser man.

"Know where you're better off, do you?" Hollie said, and Luce looked reproachful.

"It was horrible, captain. I had no idea - they're badly-provisioned – badly trained – terrified, mostly. Some of them are no age at all – and they're nearly all hungry –"

"Not what you expect from the dashing Cavaliers, then?" Hollie stopped grinning, partly because Luce looked like he might belt him if he didn't, and scratched the back of his neck thoughtfully. "What d'you reckon, Luce? Go back and take a few prisoners?"

"Don't be ridiculous, sir."

"We could feed 'em." He leaned back and shouted for Cullis. "Hoi! Sergeant! Can we stretch the provisions for another half-dozen?"

"Get stuffed," Cullis's voice floated back. "Not unless you want Davies doing the cooking."

"Fair point," Hollie said quickly, "fair point. No feeding the Malignants."

"Thee is being absurd, Holofernes. Thy duty is to smite the enemy –"

"Shut up, you old bastard. If I was addressing you you'd know about it. Brat. You feel that sorry for Betterton's lads?"

Luce shrugged. "I shouldn't. I know. I can't help it."

"Mard as clarts," Elijah Babbitt muttered disapprovingly. "Thee is a pernicious influence, boy."

"Trooper Babbitt," Hollie said, eyeing his father coldly, "any more o' that kind o' talk to a superior officer and I'll have your arse up on a charge. Now shut up."

Nothing they could do, of course. It wasn't as if it would be reasonable, or sensible, or rational, to mount an attack on Betterton's position at Stamford Bridge. It wasn't as if once Hollie had an idea in his head he'd carry it through, no matter how daft, because no sensible officer would go out of their way to offer an enemy outpost aid. Any right-minded commanding officer would sit tight and look to starve the bastards into submission – light on shot, light on powder, nowt but weevilly biscuit and dried-out salt beef, salt horse more like, for rations. Surrounded on all sides by hostile troops, with God knows how many miles of river between you and the rest of your Army. Poor old Betterton had a shitty deal, in Hollie's opinion.

It was a side of Yorkshire he hadn't seen. Hollie's experience of that county had always been somewhat coloured by a perfectly natural prejudice towards God's own country, on the other side of the Pennines. Stamford Bridge was bare and bleak and barren, the fields full of bitter yellowing grass, the Derwent barely ankle-deep at the ford. The only thing this country seemed to possess in abundance was stones. A few thin, malevolent cattle, herded by a thin, slinking malevolent black and white dog and a thin, furtive child of indeterminate gender who flinched at their passing. A picket of thin, ungroomed horses, one big bay with a great raw open gash on its shoulder, clotted with flies.

"Captain Babbitt, what did Fairfax say about thieving?" Luce said, only half in jest, and Hollie – just about dismounted, with his own fit, happy horse's reins in one hand – stopped, and gave his junior officer one grim glance over his shoulder. "If Betterton's leaving his horses in this state, that fucker wants shooting," he said. The black horse stood where he'd been left, nosing resignedly at the grass.

"You over there!"

That short on powder, the bloody sentries were reduced to shouting at you across half an acre of rank tussocks. "State your business, sir!"

"Aye, bloody right, me here!" The bay sidled nervously away from Hollie's hand. "Look at the state of this beast, you bloody heathen. Get Betterton out here now. *Now*, I said –"

You had to feel sorry for that poor sentry. He and his comrades had come pounding across the parched grass, swords drawn, facing God knows what they thought Hollie's troop were, because Hollie's troop did not behave like any other troop in the Army of Parliament. They hadn't trudged in singing psalms, and nor had they come thundering in at the charge. For once.

"And before I get Captain Betterton, who might you be, sir?"

Decent lad, for a Malignant. Kept his head, didn't try to start anything, just looked at Hollie quite coolly. Hollie grinned. "Sorry, mate. It's not an official visit, and we ain't the King's men." He had to stifle an urge to giggle. "Babbitt's Troop of Horse. Um. Under Fairfax. Put the sword down, there's a good lad. I understand you've made the acquaintance of my cornet here already –" Luce took his helmet off and gave a courteous little bow from the waist – "- and he tells me you're a bit light in the powder and shot department. So, we won't play silly buggers, lads, because I'm neither. Davies?"

Davies obligingly drew his pistol.

"Are we under attack?" the sentry said, sounding bemused, and Hollie gave in to the laugh.

"Not unless you push it, lad, no. I want to see Betterton. Now." The Royalist blinked at him, and he gave the man a stern look. "I'm the senior officer here, mate. Do it."

"Well, I'm Betterton," the sentry admitted. "Simon Betterton. I'm afraid you have the advantage of me?"

"Sorry, sir," Luce muttered. "I thought you'd worked it out –"

"Oh, for - ! Hollie Babbitt."

"Christ, *you're* Babbitt!" Betterton yelped, and Hollie jerked his head at his father, looming up behind him like some vengeful spectre. "So's he. Confusing, ain't it?"

"What – what – what –"

"- the hell d'you mean by leaving that horse in that state?" Hollie finished for him, and Betterton flushed scarlet and stammered something. Which Luce interpreted, kindly, as the horse was in a better state than some of the troop.

"Witless."

Poor Betterton took that as a term of abuse until Hollie's chubby troop bonesetter slithered off his horse and presented himself. "Sir?"

"This is Witless, Captain Betterton – damn, sorry, Witcombe, when will I ever get it right? You wouldn't think to look at him, but he's competent, for a stammering bag of guts –"

"And Captain B-babbitt can be quite –" Witcombe's lips pursed silently for a minute –"polite," he forced out eventually, "though you'd n-not know to look at him."

"Up your bum, Witless. Go and grope some Royalists - be a nice change for you. Go on, Captain Betterton, get the bugger out of my sight."

The locals were surly, the soil was half an inch thick over solid rock and as dry as a bone. "hrist, Betterton, what possessed you to dig in *here*?"

"The Earl of Newcastle," Betterton said ruefully.

"He must be out of his fucking *mind*," Hollie said. "Has he *been* round these parts?"

Betterton had shorter hair than crop-headed Elijah. So much for Cavalier lovelocks. Poor Simon Betterton was, at a guess, not quite thirty and half-bald, and his thinning dark hair was cropped close as a bowling-green. He did, however, affect an elegant little moustaches, which, given the darkness of his hair, gave the appearance of a third eyebrow having slipped down for a drink. Nice lad. The whole bloody lot of them – half-strength, if Hollie had any guess, probably something less than forty men, those that weren't laid up sick or hurt – were decent, nervous, uncomprehending farm lads pulled in from half across the North East of England.

"Not at liberty to disclose," Betterton said primly, and Hollie shrugged, and passed him an oatcake. Wasn't exactly festival fare, but it was amazing what a difference a bit of coin made to how well you got treated. If you didn't mind going as far as York to get your provisioning, and if you considered leathery oatcakes and cheese to be the height of civilisation, which Luce – pulling hairs out of his cheese with an expression of polite distaste – clearly did not.

"Don't mind me asking, but – why?" Betterton said, with his mouth full.

"Mmm?" Hollie, at thirty-six, still with a wary eye on his father's heavy right hand where company manners were concerned. Licked crumbly cheese off his wrist with a sigh of pleasure. (Hairs and all, Lucifer.) "Why what?"

"We're s'posed to be fighting each other," one of the Royalist lads said, sounding awkward.

"Can be arranged, sir, if tha doesn't leave that last bit o'cheese where it is," Hollie said, and the unfortunate soldier's hand jumped back from the platter, to a burst of laughter. "I was only having thee on. Finish it up. I keep eating like this and my missis is going to have to move all t'buttons on my coat."

Well, what could you say? Because your cornet's conscience was that tender he came away from less than a day in this company miserable and guilty? Because you hoped to God if you were ever stuck out in some barren outpost like Stamford Bridge starving and beleaguered, some bugger might take pity on you? Because there was more likeness between Hollie and Simon Betterton, than there was between Hollie and Black Tom Fairfax?

Not without offending Betterton, you couldn't. A good man, with a shitty job, doing the best he could with the poor raw materials he had at hand. Hollie picked a husk of oat from between his teeth – shifted abruptly to one side to avoid the disapproving poke in the small of the back from Elijah at his son's shameful manners - and shrugged. "Not today we're not. Too bloody hot for fighting."

"Don't rightly know what Newcastle will have t'say about it," Betterton said sadly. "Won't take it personal, will you, Hollie?"

"Won't have to know, will he? If he's not got the common sense to see you rightly provisioned, the bugger deserves all he gets."

"Not that we'm trying to get you to come over," Luke

Weston said comfortably, "but be a cold day in hell afore Black Tom'd see us left out like this. Botty owd bugger, that Newcastle –"

Hollie belted him round the back of the head, flat-handed and not particularly gently. "That's the man's commanding officer you're talking about. Show a bit o' bloody respect."

"Kettle," Luce murmured, "meet pot."

"I can say what I like to junior officers, Lucifer. Including, get on your horse and pop back to York for more ale, there's a good lad."

"You wouldn't."

"Push me and see?"

It didn't make Betterton smile. He ran a hand over his bristly head, looking worried. "See, thing is, man, I'd feel that badly, if we end up facing each other across the field, after we've broke bread wi' you."

"Wouldn't bother," Hollie said. There was an indignant intake of breath from one of his troop – he raised his head and eyed the miscreant. "It's not a fucking bribe, Eliot. Might have known it be you. That's not how it works, you mercenary bastard."

"Says you!" Eliot squawked.

Hollie shrugged. "Says me. Self-confessed mercenary bastard, gentlemen. Very fond of Black Tom, I am, but he's not one of us. He can afford his principles. Me, I got a lass back along trying to keep the bloody farm from dropping to bits round her ears and all on a soldier's pay – Parliament stops paying me, I'm off home. Anybody here in it for love?"

Luce shyly raised his hand, and there was a groan from both sides.

"*No*, really?" Cullis sniggered.

"You see my point," Hollie said, and it had at least brought a smile to Betterton's forlorn features. "If I happen across you lot on a battlefield in the commission of my duties, lads, all bets are off. I don't believe we got much to fight over, today." He gave the meagre waters of the Derwent ford a hard stare. "I ain't arguing the toss over that, gentlemen. You're welcome to it."

"Thee is either a fool or a saint, Holofernes," Elijah said grimly.

"And you a good Christian, Trooper Babbitt. Luke, chapter six. And as ye would that men should do to you, do ye also to them likewise. Fancy not knowing that. Get that bay's shoulder seen to, Betterton." He shook his head. "*Simon.* I'll not stand on ceremony with a mate."

"I'll write thee a receipt for a good salve I know of," Elijah muttered ungraciously –"elder leaves in hog's grease, though I can't say it won't leave a scar, thee has left it too long –"

Hollie looked at his father, then back at Betterton. "Bloody hell. That's the best you're likely to get for an apology, out of him."

Betterton's moustache was wriggling, by which Hollie assumed the Royalist captain was trying not to laugh. "Aye, I know that feeling, man. You ever come by Monkseaton, I'll stand you a drink for this day's work."

"If I ever end up in – where the hell *is* Monkseaton? – I imagine I'll need a bloody drink," Hollie said. "Likewise. Lancashire by way of Essex, me, so if tha's ever passing through White Notley –"

"God willing," Betterton said wryly. "Gan on, the lot of you. 'Fore I think better of it and decide I'm coming over to you lot. Hollie –"

"'S short for Holofernes," Hollie said, and it was about the highest compliment he could pay a friend to disclose that piece of information, and Betterton nodded sagely.

"Best not call you that, eh? I'm going to write up to Newcastle and tell him –"

"Tell him we attacked you," Hollie said promptly. "Come out of nowhere, we did – bloody vicious little buggers, them Roundheads."

"Thicker 'n lice on a whore's –"

"Weston," Cullis said warningly, and Luke Weston looked mildly ashamed. "Only trying to be helpful."

"You want me to say you came on to us?"

"Been trying to poke the bugger up all summer. Christ knows I have no desire to be stuck out here when winter comes on."

"I hear you," Betterton said with feeling, eyeing the flat, barren fields with disfavour.

Not being daft, Hollie had made a tactful withdrawal from Beverley after that. It had been a good summer. He knew it was coming to an end: any day now Percey would come galloping in and tell him Newcastle was on the turn. Cracking little scout, Percey had turned out to be, and even he was brown and fit and lean rather than skinny and white like he'd been since Hollie had set eyes on him. Even the horses were sleek and fat as butter. They'd had six weeks of it – a bloody good run – but it was over.

Back to bloody Hull. Still, there was one thing to be said for Hull. Het could write to him again there. Only one letter had come through in all that long hot summer, although his cup of happiness had run over at that one, for there hadn't only been an irreverent and badly-spelled epistle from Drew Venning, but a stiff note from Russell enclosing a much longer note from Het, the contents of which were most satisfyingly affectionate. He only hoped Russell hadn't read it before she sealed it, not wishing to be responsible for that young man's blushes.

He wondered, idly, if there were gillyflowers in the garden at White Notley. He'd only seen it black and frozen bare. He already had a recipe for honey cakes from Luce's young lady's mother's cook. Luce claimed to have no appetite with his girl – made up for lost time when he got home, mind, it was like trying to provision a young wolf. Would have been rude to leave all those fresh-baked cakes going cold, untasted. Hollie reckoned he was the only man in history to go on campaign and come back with more meat on his bones than when he'd set off.

"Pack up your traps, brat."

"Hm?" Luce looked up absently from his scribbling. "What?"

"Recalled to our duty. Spent enough time flirting and sunning ourselves. Look at the state of thee, Lucifer, freckled like a custard, tha looks like a labourer, not a gentleman."

Luce was about to protest, realised he was being teased, and gave Hollie a sceptical look. "And I assume scarlet and peeling is the fashionable look for gentlemen this year, is it?"

# 52 BLOODY RAINBOW

*Hull*
*September, 1643*

Hollie was restless, and bored, and irritable, and near-perpetually starved. Rattling like a loose board in a gale, as the siege lengthened, but mercifully gifted with sufficient reputation for intemperacy for the troop to assume that any erratic behaviour was just Captain Babbitt's usual hot-headed manner, and not a shameful inability to think straight when he was trapped between four city walls.

Fairfax knew, he suspected. Black Tom knew a lot more than he let on for. He had a habit of keeping Hollie close at hand and running him ragged. It helped, to a degree. Most nights he was back in his quarters after midnight, dismissed at the point when he was too stupid with weariness to be any help to anyone. Sometimes he was too tired to dream. Sometimes he wasn't, and then he'd end up sat up the rest of the night with Luce, with the pair of them indulging in a shared fiction that the brat hadn't been asleep anyway. Of all things, the dreams had been worse, since he married again, because it was Het's face he saw now, white and mad and wasted in a ditch in a ruined city, with his own child dead and starved in her arms. Het choking on black bile as she died of fever in her cold bed. Those were the good ones. Wakeful, Hollie didn't care to remember some of the things he'd seen in his youthful campaigning days in the Thirty Years' War. (Might have done himself. Wasn't thinking about.) In his dreams, he remembered every last detail.

And he worried for the brat - for most of his troop, though he'd rather cut off his own foot that admit it. Percey was thin enough already, without adding scant rations to his woes. Luce had a boil on the back of his neck, which he joked about, and which everyone knew damn well was an absolute agony under the weight of a buff coat. Sounded comical, boils. Hurt appallingly, and everyone who'd ever been under siege knew damn well that first your men started out with such things, and next thing you knew it was scurvy, and all the other ailments of too many men and no fresh food - and then it was starvation, and black disease.

"Rosie."

He started back to alertness, hand going automatically to his sword as it did these days, and Fowles – thin, faintly disreputable Fowles these days, not quite so elegant as he had been – grinned at him. "Busy, are you, lad?"

"Christ, I wish I was," Hollie said ruefully, and Fowles nodded. "I know what you mean. Might have a bit o' work for Davies, if he's free?"

"Something involving the ability to shoot straight?"

"That would be it, captain. Sorry."

Hollie's aim had never been great, and since Edgehill if he had any weight at all on that badly-healed right wrist his hand started to shake. Witless had offered to break it and set it again, with a little more relish than Hollie thought was strictly called for. The offer had been politely declined. "Can have Lucey as well, if you like. Little bugger's turning into a hell of a marksman."

"Is he, so? I imagine it's all the practice he's getting."

"Aye, well, he still rides like my maiden aunt–"

"-Doubtless some small consolation, sir."

"Anyway, I thought we were getting low on powder. Again."

"Ah, well, you see." Fowles tapped the side of his nose, grinning. "That's where I come in. Since my lord Newcastle has got the hell out of Lincolnshire, largely due to the good offices of a certain gentleman who is too modest to expose himself to public acclaim – isn't he, Hollie? – it would appear that our stout friend in the Fens is finally being allowed off the leash."

"You what?"

"Cromwell's coming."

"*No.*"

The name of Oliver Cromwell was acquiring near-mythic proportions in besieged Hull. If you believed half of what you heard, the great day when Noll Cromwell arrived would be heralded with bronze trumpets and the ranks of the King's Army would part and run as stubble before his sword. That, or he'd be bringing reinforcements thousands strong, half a hundred field guns, gilded muskets, pearls of the Indies – not that Hollie was cynical, much. "Who's he supposed to be bringing this time?"

"Ye of little faith, Holofernes. On his way over from the Lincolnshire side as we speak, sir. With powder. Barrels of the stuff."

"Walking across the bloody river, is he?" Hollie sniffed – realised there were limits to even Fowles' toleration, and awaited the reproof that came in short order. It was understood that sixteen years with Elijah Babbitt would make even the most devout into the next best thing to an atheist, but even so.

"No, you miserable heathen, he's coming in on the Lion, with Rainsborough."

"Ah, Christ, not him asgain!" The one consolation he had was that Rainsborough was unlikely to recognise his face. Hollie had spent most of the crossing over the Humber head-down over the rail puking his guts up, while Rainsborough stood at his elbow making helpful remarks.

"Met Old Noll, have you?" Fowles said, correctly interpreting Hollie's expression and changing the subject neatly.

"No."

"You'll like him." Fowles was nodding, with a smile of anticipation on his refined features. "You will have much in common, I think, provided you can keep off the matter of religion. I doubt he'll have much time for your atheism."

"I'm not a bloody atheist, Fowles. Pack it in, telling

people I am. I am a perfectly respectable, upright, godly man who just happens to think that my beliefs are none o'your fucking business."

"And a bit sweary."

"And a bit sweary," he agreed grudgingly

"Well, I wouldn't be doing that in front of Old Noll, either. He'll have the swear-box out."

"Twelvepence per curse," Hollie said ruefully. "I know."

"Been stung already, have you?"

"Put it this way, I've been threatened with having my mouth washed out wi' soap."

"By your troop chaplain, no doubt. A most ferocious individual."

"Oh aye, he's right took to the idea of Army discipline, that one. Likes a bit of discipline, does my father. The old –" Fowles was looking embarrassed, so Hollie shut up. Anyone who'd seen Hollie with his shirt off tended to be embarrassed when the subject of Elijah Babbitt came up.

"Yes. Well. I don't think the Army would approve of that kind of – well, I'm sure it's all water under the bridge now, isn't it? All forgiven and forgotten – "

The other popular assumption that was because Elijah had attached himself like a leech to his son's troop, all must be sweetness and light between them, with the old man displaying a most Christian display of paternal admiration . Most touching that Elijah was so determined to fight with his boy that he'd appoint himself as a lowly trooper. Presumably Hollie's habit of referring to his father as "the old bastard" was evidence of a sentimental filial affection, as well. Hollie gave Fowles a look of deep suspicion. "Oh aye, it's all over and done with. If I haven't shot him yet, I'm not likely to."

Four days of fasting and prayer later, and Old Noll went back across the Humber. About a day after that, Fairfax's cavalry went after him – for the most part, having prayed most devoutly for strength and deliverance, though in the case of at least one member of the troop, praying that a bridge would be suddenly built across that river, or peace suddenly declared, so that he wouldn't have to present himself at the dockside. In front of Rainsborough. Oh Christ, not Rainsborough. Please God, the Malignants would put a hole in the bugger's ship before Hollie had to set foot on that floating deathtrap and its smirking captain.

Anybody.

*Anybody* but fucking Rainsborough.

# 53 SALTFLEET, GOD WILLING

Luce looked up as the door banged shut and a gust of warm night-scented air wafted in. It was a beautiful late summer night, warm and still and heavy, with a great full moon hanging low in the sky. It was a night for walking hand in hand in the fields with your girl, for whispering sweet words and poetry, for garlanding your lady with the sweetbriar and the honeysuckle –

It was not a night for your commanding officer to be glowering at you across the table with that particularly ferocious look that normally did not bode well. Luce closed his book politely. "News, sir?"

"Bloody bad news, brat. About as bad as it gets. Anything to drink in this place?"

"I believe there may be some small beer in the kitchen –"

"That's *not* what I had in mind," Hollie said grimly.

Luce closed his book politely. "A problem, sir? Can I help at all?"

Hollie - thwarted of anything more alcoholic than slightly stale and lukewarm beer - sat down with a thump at the table and dropped his head onto his folded arms. "Oh aye," he said, in a muffled voice. "Can you arrange to have me knocked on the head before Thursday?"

"Eh?"

"Thursday. We're out."

"Out?"

"Lucey, are you being more than normally thick, or am I just not speaking English? Out. Gone. Shaking the dust of Hull off of our boots."

"But that's - *good*, isn't it? Sir?" Given that the big redhead had been as unpredictable as an autumn wasp for weeks, Luce would have thought that anything that put some miles between Hollie and a city under siege would have been like manna from heaven. Luce had seen Hollie under siege on several occasions: once he'd been stark mad, and the last time he'd tried to get himself killed just to relieve the tedium. This time he was just scared, and that was probably the worst of it. Not guaranteed to fill you with confidence, although this further evidence of their unbreakable captain's humanity was oddly endearing, at times.

"No," Hollie said, without looking up. "It's bloody not. We're getting shipped off to Saltfleet with Black Tom, on one o' Rainsborough's ships."

"But that's good, surely?"

"By *sea*," he said, with grim clarity. "I hate the sea, brat. I *hate* it. It don't like me much, either, or it wouldn't keep trying to kill me."

Thursday came, and after a day listening to seamen talking incomprehensibly about winds backing and lee shores, Fairfax had his cavalry brought down to embark troop by troop. The air smelt of tar and salt. Luce sniffed appreciatively.

"What," Hollie coldly said, appearing suddenly at his elbow, "are you snuffing at?"

Luce waved a vague hand. "This. It smells of - excitement."

"It smells of dead fish." The big redhead glared at him. "Yes, brat, I *am* sober. And I ain't enjoying it. Now, if you'll excuse me, there's eighty lads need direction in how to walk up a god-damn plank, as it seems there's not a one of you bastards with the common sense to work it out for yourselves."

He swung on his heel and shoved his way through the melee at the bottom of the gangplank, barking orders and cursing and periodically cuffing anyone who didn't get out of his way quickly enough. It was possible to track his progress through the troop by the ripple of men jumping back out of his path. Sergeant Cullis stumped across the cobbles, smirking. "Look at him go," he said. "Like the parting of the Red Sea, God love him."

"What on earth did you say to him -"

"Me? Don't be daft, nothing to do wi' me. He's just not being shown up in front of his old man."

Both of them looked at the spare figure of Trooper Babbitt, propped up against a bollard sitting on a coil of rope with the Good Book in one hand and an apple in the other, silently seeking consolation. The late afternoon sun turned the old man's sandy-grey hair to a ruddy gold. "The old feller looks well on it, don't he?" Cullis said unhelpfully. "Smiting the heathen seems to be agreeing with him."

"Winding his son up seems to be agreeing with him," Luce said, thinking of the number of times in the last week he'd had to intervene before the commanding officer of a most reformed and well-behaved troop of horse had dragged their reputation back into the gutter. Hollie had a permanent blood-blister square in the middle of his lower lip, where he seemed to have his teeth perpetually set these days. There was a sudden commotion, a hollow thumping of hooves as the horses started to embark - Calthorpe's Delilah going up as meek as milk, with the Rabbit's nose at her tail because the Rabbit never went anywhere Delilah didn't go. The red mare Rosa -

"Back in a minute," Luce said apologetically, watching his mare balk and dance at the strange ground beneath her hooves. Other horses started to pick up her fractiousness, and there was a moment of brief panic as it looked as if Wilder's big gelding might go over the side of the ship in his squealing distress. Luce wasn't sure what was the more embarrassing, that his mare was doing her level best to kick a hole in the side of the *Lion*, that half Fairfax's cavalry were watching her with disapproval, or that deliverance might come all too publicly in the disreputable guise of the captain himself, stripped to his shirt sleeves, yanking the mare by the headcollar and then eyeballing her furiously. The mare kicked out, and Hollie smacked her across the shoulder with the end of the rope. "Come *up*, you missish bitch!"

Then the mare was disappearing into the darkness of the hold, and Luce was hot with embarrassment and trying not to hear the comments on the lamentable want of discipline in his troop. Another brief flurry of subterranean squealing, thumping and swearing, and then the last few horses were going down. There was a long silence as Tyburn came stepping across the cobbles as nice as ninepence. The big black was blindfolded, but it didn't seem to bother him. Hollie appeared on the deck at the same time as his horse. Elijah Babbitt considerately removed the stallion's blindfold. "I thought you could do wi' a hand bringing your big lad on," he said into the silence. The black, feeling the rope slacken, pricked his ears and took a dainty step across the deck, picking his way across coils of rope to push his nose hopefully into his master's shirt, nosing for titbits. Hollie - scarlet, sweaty, and furious - pulled the horse's ears absently through his hand. It was so quiet it was possible to hear the sound of the water slapping, gently, against the hull of the *Lion*.

Who knows what would have been said if the ship's captain hadn't chosen that moment to come up from the hold where he was supervising the horses' safe stowage. Stopped, blinking in the setting sun , and took his hat off, running a hand through his thinning mousy hair. "There's a horse on my deck," he said in some surprise. Tyburn threw his head up and snorted. The surprise was mutual. "What bugger owns *tha*t?" Captain Rainsborough said, scowling at the idle hands on deck.

"'S mine," Hollie said in a muffled voice, both hands clasped to his bloody nose where the horse's tossing head had caught him a thoroughgoing smack. Leading rein slack, Tyburn took a step towards the rail, head up and ears pricked in fascination at this new world of moving land opening up before him.

Rainsborough looked at the filthy, ragged, sweaty object in the bloodstained shirt, dripping gore onto the deck through his clasped hands. Unsurprisingly, didn't recognise him, given that Hollie was neither hanging head-down off the rail retching his guts up nor dressed in anything resembling befitting his station. "*Who* is your commanding officer?" he said, in an awful voice.

"Fairfax, prob'ly," Hollie snuffled, and Elijah went and caught up the horse and stood behind Rainsborough, glowering. "*My lad* is in charge," he said, narrowing his eyes.

Rainsborough turned on his heel. "Not on this ship, he ain't. Get that bloody horse below decks."

Tyburn went. Elijah went.

Hollie stood dabbing his nose with the back of his wrist glaring at Rainsborough, who looked him up and down and flicked a contemptuous eyebrow. "Oh it's *you*! Might ha' bloody *known* it be you."

# 54 SAFE DELIVERY

Tyburn was remarkably - unnaturally - placid, as they led the horses up out of the hold. Hollie just sat on the quayside with his head on his knees, waiting for the ground to stop moving. "If God had meant me to swim, he'd have give me fucking fins, Ward, so shut the fuck up!"

"Aw now come on, Captain Babbitt, Ward were just made to be a sailor," Cullis said. "Long sea voyages, him and Eliot'd be right at home - taking turns in the barrel, like."

Ward grunted indignantly, and there was a ripple of uncharitable laughter from the men. "Miss Captain Venning, I do. Web-footed lil' bugger 'ud tell us how to go on," one of the Weston lads said reflectively, and Hollie - mutely - agreed. Personally, if he never clapped eyes on water again he'd be content. Rainsborough thumped him familiarly between the shoulders. "Proper landlubber, this one, ain't he? Never make a Navy man, you wouldn't! Only come up the river and the lad's as white as a sheet!"

"Aye, well, this time tomorrow I might care," Holly said, and as it was near enough the first words he'd spoken since he'd set foot off dry land – if you could call Hull dry land - half a day ago, there was an almost audible sigh of relief from the rest of his troop. He sat up cautiously. The river was still there, and he looked away from it. It didn't help, he could still smell it, that combination of stinking mud and stagnant water.

"By, lad, tha's gone a funny colour," Calthorpe said admiringly. "Reckon 'ee can stay looking so? Tha'd fritten t'Malignants t'death!"

Lucifer was hovering, intently, with a dried out husk that the lad had been claiming all the way from Hull was ship's biscuit. Luce, mind, had never shut up. "Here you go, captain, it'll do you the world of good," he said brightly, shoving the desiccated crust under Hollie's nose.

Hollie waved it limply away. "Keep it, lad. We might run short of shot later."

All the horses were off the ship now, the last of them being led up from the hold to stand in a drooping huddle on the quayside. "Anybody hungry?" Isaac Weston asked, shading his eyes as he looked out at the boats rocking at anchor. "Reckon we could get a decent bit o' fish, hereabouts. Belly thinks me throat's been cut -"

"*Stop*," Hollie muttered, "talking about food."

"Aye, now, have a bit of consideration, for one as made the crossing to the Low Countries when he was a nipper and hated it that much it was ten year before he could face trying it again," Cullis added unhelpfully.

Hollie made it to his feet - chose not to look at the sleeve of his doublet, which was a harsh reminder of the last meal he'd eaten before they left Hull. "Give me the fucking biscuit, brat," he said to Luce. Stuffed it in his mouth, whole, and glowered at his grinning troop. "Right. Happy now?"

"Never 'ee fret, lad, I'll not tell anyone you're feared of a bit o' water -" Rainsborough chuckled.

Rainsborough had Hollie marked down as queasy from the minute they set off, and he'd not let up for a minute, taking the piss. The man was a bloody menace. What with Luce and his infernal bloody biscuit, Elijah preaching all over the deck, and bloody Rainsborough poking him, he'd hardly had time to dwell on feeling anxious. Sick - repeatedly - but not scared. "*Feared* of it? Not me that's frit, by the smell of it, you squalid bugger!"

"He'll do," Cullis said comfortably. "When you start getting sweary, you're on the mend, lad. Right, you shower. Let's go and investigate the fleshpots of Saltfleet."

There was herring. There was very, very fresh herring. It was broiling, in a griddle, in a crisp, golden, oatmeal coat, and just about every man in the troop gave an involuntary whimper of longing at the rich, oily scent as they passed the inn door. "Course, with you being off your feed and that," Isaac Weston said happily, "that be more for the rest of us, won't it?"

"In your dreams, Trooper Weston," Hollie said primly. "Reckon you just got yourself a duty seeing the horses stabled. We might save you a fishbone, if you're lucky. And if anybody wants me, I'll be down there -" he glanced at the quayside – "thanking God for my safe preservation."

# 55 CRY HAVOC

Not that Hollie took to herring particularly, but three weeks later, standing on a hill somewhere up near Spilsby, twenty miles inland, under the beady eye of both Black Tom Fairfax and that shadowy mythical figure of Noll Cromwell - unable to so much as scratch his arse without getting a narrow-eyed glare of disapproval from one or other of the godly factions – on the whole, he looked back on those couple of days in Saltfleet as his last moments of blissful liberty. Breakfast this morning had been a handful of blackberries, the ones the Devil hadn't managed to spit on yet, and even that was surreptitious while he was stood in front of a bramble bush with his eyes devoutly downcast listening to his bloody father rant on. He sucked his pricked and purple-stained thumb reminiscently. A man could get very sick of prayer and fasting.

"Reserve. For Christ's sake. Left in the *reserve.*"

He ducked a shoulder in ingrained reflex even as he said it, still half-expecting to feel the buckle end of his father's reins flick across his face for the casual blasphemy. As ever, Luce's face remained impassive, his eyes modestly downcast on the red mare's neck, and as ever, Hollie knew damn' well the lad was mentally astonished that even after twenty years he still gave a toss what his father thought.

"I doubt it'll be quiet, mind." The red mare shifted restlessly, her hindquarters barging into Tyburn, and the big black threw up his head with a chink of harness. Always seemed so very quiet, just before a fight. As if the world was still and waiting, even the birds in the trees silent with anticipation. Someone in the troop was muttering. Hollie closed his eyes and gritted his teeth. His father, doubtless, bothering the Almighty. Why was it always one of *his* bloody men that had to draw every disapproving eye in the cavalry lines?

Wasn't as if, for once, it had been Hollie's lads that had buggered it up this time. Black Tom had described it, charitably, as an outpost that had fallen into Royalist hands. In a manner of speaking. Horncastle had been an outpost, right enough, and a more meek and pious troop of bloody simpletons Hollie had yet to cast an eye over, and predictably enough the daft buggers had been mostly on their knees and rolling their eyes heavenwards when the King's men had come howling down like the proverbial wolf on the fold. To which report, when the simpletons had come yammering back up to Spilsby with the news of their rout, Hollie had very pointedly said nothing. Not a word passed his lips about posting godly lackwits out on the peripheries when you had blood and fire to your hand. He'd not even looked at Fairfax, though he was aware of Fairfax looking at *him*. Luce had been looking downright bloody shifty, which was his customary approximation of an expression of maligned innocence. Fairfax had continued to say nowt, and it had been starting to get on Hollie's nerves when eventually his commander had nodded. "That'll do," he said, "that'll do."

What he meant was, it was time to take things into their own hands. If the King - in the shape of Sir John Henderson - was getting his lads mobile in the hope of relieving the garrison at nearby Bolingbroke Castle, it was maybe time to encourage him to have second thoughts.

Black Tib tossed his head again, and the mare pirouetted again – Luce blushing, visibly, between the bars of his helmet as he tried to make her stand, without success.

"See missy's on the rag again," Ward sniggered loudly, and Hollie turned and glared at him over his shoulder. Then someone moved –

"Forlorn hope," Cullis said, like Hollie couldn't see perfectly well for himself it was them dragoons in the front starting to trot down the ridge towards the Royalist troops, but the sergeant was talking for the sake of it because he couldn't bear the silence of waiting any longer.

Hollie took his right hand off the reins and flexed his stiff wrist – the hell with it, he knew his wrist wasn't up to close work in this damp autumn weather, he drew his sword left-handed and withdrew the black to the far left of the troop, out of anybody's way. Held up his right hand to Luce, who nodded in reply, and tucked the mare into the gap.

Expecting the first shot and the echo of musket fire off the hillside still made him jump, even though he knew it was coming. Bloody stupid way of operating anyway, dragoons: ride your horses to within thirty feet of each other and then get off to fire, silly buggers deserved all they got. He stood up in his stirrups, quickly looking for Fairfax – that was why Tib was restless, Fairfax's big white stallion on his mettle – and then an eye to the other one, the one Fairfax had been demanding for weeks, now that he could finally see the bugger. Nowt to look at, Colonel Oliver Cromwell, on his solid chestnut horse. Scruffy, big nose, straggly red-brown hair over the shoulders of his worn buffcoat. Which thought caused Hollie – scruffy, big nosed Hollie, with his tangled red-brown hair caught back in a loose tail down the back of his worn buffcoat – to grin to himself. He could have been stood next to Cromwell a hundred times this last couple of weeks and never given him a second look. The way they went on about the man, he'd expected at the least a white robe and a shining halo.

And then he saw Cromwell give the order to advance –

"Trot on, you buggers," Hollie called, "- and I said *trot*, not go tear-arsing off to bloody Bolingbroke, Lucifer!"

And then they were moving, the black's muscles rippling like silk under him and the big horse's ears flicking back and forth, wondering, like his rider, what was with the slow and disciplined trot and why they weren't going in at a flat gallop like they normally did. Down the slope of the ridge, the black settling to his work now as he scented powder-smoke, and then as the ground levelled out lengthening his stride - still trotting, Colonel Cromwell, no need to look at me like that, head up and tail up in proper elegant parade style. Then they were in it, in the thick of it, loose horses and dragoons struggling to remount and dragoons firing. He saw his own colours ripple out of the corner of his eye, and then there was a Malignant on him and he brought his sword up with a clash that jarred his arm, recalled sharply to his business. Been caught that way before, Babbitt. Hollie didn't do dainty swordplay. He was too big and his horse was too big and he hadn't the temperament for it. He let the Malignant play with him for a few heartbeats, letting the cavalier's lovely, expensive blade slide down his own Birmingham steel standard-issue sword, just for long enough for the man to think he had him, a grin of anticipation on his wet red lips – and then Hollie dug his heels into Tyburn, disengaged his blade, and drove through the Malignant's breastplate with the weight of his horse's charge behind him.

*Now* who's grinning, you Cavalier bastard?

Flicked his hair out of his eyes with a nod of satisfaction, wheeled the horse, and happened to be facing in the right direction when he saw Cromwell's chestnut go straight up on its hind legs, shot in the throat, and then totter backwards, crashing into the melee.

Cromwell unharmed, staggering to his feet, spattered with his horse's blood, roaring something incomprehensible but looking distinctly sweary – looks like more than twelvepence worth, Noll – some smart-arse on an expensive horse in a beautiful blue silk sash crashing in with his sword at point, thinking the colonel was easy meat.

Thinking not Hollie's strong point, in battle. Laying about him with the buckle end of his reins – like father, like son – and the flat of his sword, the big black horse tense and collected under him, and a gap, a horse's length, opening up before him in the fray. Hollie leaning over the horse's neck, sudden homely smell of wet leather and horse sweat, and the stallion put in a neat three strides at a full gallop, and took the Royalist officer broadside-on. The Cavalier horse staggered, and as the two mounts went shoulder to shoulder for the briefest of heartbeats Hollie kicked his feet out of the stirrups, and hurled himself bodily across the blue-sashed rider.

Being knocked flying by self-destructive cavalry officers was not one of the contingencies they taught you, at posh officer school. Hollie hit the ground with most of the breath knocked out of him, and the officer underneath him – who stopped braying his complaints after Hollie had punched him in the head with his bridle-gauntleted hand. "Get on the fucking horse," he wheezed at the stunned Cromwell, who nodded, put a hand out to the pretty Cavalier mount – "the *black* one –"

Because the pretty Cavalier horse had had enough of this lark, and he was rearing and backing in the fray like he was going to turn his well-bred tail and bolt first chance as he got, and it didn't matter if one shabby captain of horse took a bullet in the ear but by Christ it would make a difference if a colonel copped it. Cromwell got a hand in the black's mane and hauled himself into the saddle - the last Hollie saw of his stallion was the colonel and Tib having a brief tussle of wills as Cromwell rejoined his troop, while Hollie and the pretty Cavalier horse had an equally brief tussle of wills on the matter of staying where they were. Stupid creature with more hair than wit, and he wrenched its elegant head up and dug his heels into its heaving flanks. The witless horse went in circles and he fended off an annoying young Cavalier, who must have been younger than Mattie Percey and had one of those ridiculous waxed moustaches that Hollie loathed. He ought to kill the boy just for being able to grow a better set of whiskers than Hollie had ever managed.

"Stop arsing around, child," he said irritably, smacking the boy's wavering sword out of his hand. "There – thee is disarmed. Now piss off home to thy mother."

"I have nothing to offer but my honour," the boy said stiffly, and Hollie thought it would be unkind to laugh, but –

"Aye, well, I'm a married man, so your, er, honour's perfectly safe." He struck a chivalric pose to make the lad smile, instead of looking at him like he was AntiChrist. Not in the business of slaughtering children, no matter what the rumours said. "Sir, you are now my prisoner, till such time as you are exchanged. Do you give your word of honour not to raise arms further against the cause of Parliament?"

The young cavalier nodded warily.

"See, I can talk proper, when I set my mind to it. Now bugger off to the back – ask for Sergeant Cullis, tell him Hollie – er, Captain Babbitt – sent thee, and get him to feed you."

He saw the young man off the field – gave him an amicable salute as the lad surrendered himself, in a dazed way, to a gang of equally bemused troopers, and then belted the pretty Cavalier horse into a canter and rejoined his men. All whole, not a scratch amongst them, except the luckless Wilder, who'd got a bloody nose when his horse had reared in the melee

Tucked in back with Fairfax's men on the flank, tidying up stunned and unresisting Royalists like so many sheep being safely gathered in by a couple of very wise, very experienced sheepdogs. Barely a shot being fired, now. He almost felt sorry for them. Routed, foot and horse, didn't come close – mostly because the foot part on the Parliamentarian side hadn't turned up yet, still slogging their way up from Bolingbroke. He'd never done anything like it. It was hard work – a damn' sight harder than the wild joy of a thundering charge, this clearing out of nests of rats. Hard, disciplined work, demanding concentration and unrelenting effort - which Hollie did not excel at, and which was giving him a headache.

He was getting sick of the pretty horse, and he

suspected the horse was equally tired of him. He was too tall for the beast, and it clearly wasn't accustomed to anything that didn't involve prancing. He missed Tyburn, who knew his business, and didn't leap about like some kind of demented flea every time someone shot off a musket within half a mile. That wasn't musket fire. Musket fire sounded different – sharper, less widely-spaced. That was the thunderous rumble of artillery, bang, bang, bang like a blacksmith's forge. Hollie realised he was staring stupidly towards the sound of heavy gunfire.

"What are you looking at?" Luce said, bringing the lathered mare up beside him.

"Hope," Hollie said enigmatically.

"What?"

He nodded towards the sound of the guns. "Lifting up mine eyes to the hills, from whence cometh my hope. Or at least, lifting up mine eyes to the siege at Hull, if I'm not losing my wits altogether. Summat's shifting over yonder, and let's hope it's in our favour."

# 56 A LAMENTABLE WANT OF DISCIPLINE

He'd never been so relieved in all his life than when they were called off the hunt, and he wasn't sure which had tired him the worse, the constant well-drilled obedience or the constant fighting with the pretty horse, but when he finally slipped out of the saddle his knees nearly gave way under him and he stood for a minute holding the stirrup and feeling most peculiar.

"You all right?" Luce said at his ear, and he nodded mutely, tugging his helmet off and letting the chill wind ruffle his sweat-soaked hair. The pretty horse stood with its head hanging, patches of lather darkening its glossy neck, and he patted its nose awkwardly. Looked at the expensive tack – at the curb bit pulled tight enough to bruise the beast's mouth: no surprise the animal was arsy. Well, he had neither the time nor the inclination to spend on making the animal amenable. God willing, he'd get his mount back shortly. He thought it was an exaggeration that they called Colonel Cromwell's own troop a pack of horse thieves and Anabaptists, but if the colonel thought Tyburn was a gift, he had another think coming.

"You look worse than I feel," he said to Luce, with a faint smile that was all he could manage at the moment. Luce – ruffled, dirty, his fair hair stuck raggedly to his forehead and a red weal just above his eyebrows where his helmet had chafed – gave him a shaky grin in return.

"Hard work, isn't it?"

"Not sure I'm up to it. I can spend all day hacking at the buggers and feel fresh as a daisy, but keeping up with the godly doesn't half take it out of me." He pulled his hair loose and ran his free hand through the tangled mass. "Christ, Luce, we won the day."

"Was that in the nature of a prayer, boy?" Elijah said, looming up out of the dusk, and Hollie was so knackered he didn't even twitch.

"Aye, that's right, that was me at my devotions. What?"

"I was assuring myself of thy continued well-being, Holofernes. There has been a Malignant in this camp, asking for thee. I was feared for thy safety."

"Was there. Did he have a big dog with him –" Hollie gave Luce a sly grin, "- strong German accent and a bad wig?"

Elijah looked blank.

"Not the Palatinate Ponce, then. Not Rupert," Hollie said with mock resignation. "Damn." And then raised an eyebrow as Elijah's hand jerked instinctively. "*Not* a good idea to belt thy commanding officer, Trooper Babbitt. He might take it badly and, oh, I don't know – have thee hanged for insubordination, striking a senior officer, summat like."

"A young man," Elijah continued, stiffly. The older of the Babbitts was not blessed with a sense of humour. "Somewhat vain about his person, before I took it on myself to correct the error of his ways."

Hollie stopped smirking. "What?"

"A most vainglorious young popinjay, boy, with a moustache of a form never intended by the Lord –"

"What," Hollie said, shoving his hair out of his eyes with a hand that shook with rigidly-controlled fury, "did you do with him?" Because tempting as it was to give the witless old bastard two feet of Birmingham steel in the belly, it wouldn't leave Hollie any the wiser as to what his father had done with the young Cavalier he'd captured earlier on.

"I handled him as roughly as he deserved, Holofernes, and left him stripped of his weapons and bound behind the horse lines." Luce had seen that glint in his commanding officer's eyes before and he grabbed Hollie's arm, quickly, and hard enough to hurt, before the captain hauled off and belted his father with the nearest heavy object.

"You *stupid* old –" Speechless with fury, Hollie turned on his heel and stalked away into the darkness. Elijah looked at Luce, likewise lost for words.

"What did I do? Should I not –"

"That young officer had given his parole, I believe," Luce said delicately. "I understood him to be Hollie – er, Captain Babbitt's prisoner of war."

"But he is a Malignant, Lucifer. Is he not the enemy, and is it not then my duty to smite him?"

"Er, no, Trooper Babbitt, not if he's surrendered, no. I think you'll find that's contrary to the Articles of War. I think that's why Hollie – er, Captain Babbitt is so angry."

Elijah was shaking his head. "When is he not?"

"Fair point, trooper, fair point, the captain does seem to be on a remarkably short fuse of late –" He stopped himself abruptly because it seemed like a very quick way to get himself shot, to start siding with Elijah Babbitt against his son. "Which is of course his prerogative as a senior officer," he finished, fixing the trooper with as stern a glare as he could muster.

# 57 DECENT LADS, FOR THE MOST PART

Age hadn't made the vicious old bastard any less heavy-handed, Hollie thought, hacking at the rope binding the unfortunate young officer's wrists. The lad was black and blue, one eye swollen almost shut, and dried blood black in his draggled moustache.

"*That*," he said through gritted teeth, "was my estimable sire. I could apologise on his behalf, but I am more inclined to fetch the old bastard down here on a rope halter and get him to make his own God-damned apologies."

The prisoner was shivering. Unsurprisingly, as Trooper bloody Babbitt had not only stripped him of his weapons, but stripped him of his coat as well. "I am going to kill him," Hollie said, with a bright smile in the lad's vague direction. "First I'm going to kill him, and then I'm going to skin him, and then I'm going to feed the pieces to my dog. And I don't even *have* a bloody dog.."

"I get the idea," the prisoner said through chattering teeth, and Hollie snarled and yanked his own coat off and wrapped it round the young Royalist's shoulders.

"Fine impression you must have of the Babbitt household," he said irritably, "one's mad and the other's rough as rats."

"B-both mad, I think. But in a good way."

"If you look in the pockets of that thing, there's a flask of brandy. I use it for cleaning muskets." The prisoner looked up at him sharply, realised Hollie was joking, and his thin, bruised face relaxed into a wary smile. "You worth owt, young man, or are we just keeping you out of trouble?"

"Edmund P-parkinson, sir, as is cornet to Sir John

Henderson... who m-might value my return, or might not." He put out his hand to Hollie. "A person of little im-port, I f-fear."

"Captain Babbitt," Hollie said stiffly, looking at the prisoner's hand – a well-bred young man's hand, long-fingered and clean and with no fingernails at all to speak of. Sighed. Too young, and too nice, by half. Somebody else's Luce Pettitt. It was a depressing thought, that the Royalist Army was made up of decent lads, for the most, like his own. Not slavering Papists and mad-eyed tyrants all desperate to grind the faces of the poor, but plain, ordinary, slightly confused lads like Luce and Simon Betterton, wherever the hell he was now – or disillusioned professionals, like himself – or men doing the best they could for what they thought was the best possible reasons, like Fairfax and Cromwell, and them latter types were the ones that got you into trouble. He took a deep breath. "I should like to say my friends call me Hollie, but they, er, don't, for the most part. Bastards aren't that respectful. Just plain Rosie will find me."

"Rosie Babbitt. I have – heard of you, sir." By the way the lad's prominent adam's apple was wobbling up and down, it hadn't made good hearing.

"Not roasted a baby or buggered an alderman since breakfast, I can assure you."

Parkinson laughed, quite unwillingly, and Hollie gave him a sly sidelong glance. "Don't worry, we say much the same about you lot on this side. There must be someone going around roasting all these babies – and I hope it's not the same bloody alderman who keeps copping for it, or his arse is going to be red raw – but if it's not my lot and it's not thine,  damned if I know who it is. You must be starving, Parkinson, 'cos I bloody know I am, and one of the things they do have right about my troop is that the buggers are like one of the plagues of Egypt when there's food around, If thee can cope with the sight of my estimable sire glaring at you across the fire, come and sit down to meat with us."

He sat Parkinson next to Pettitt. They'd probably talk about poetry, or something lofty, and the rest of the troop probably wouldn't get a word in edgewise, but that was fine. After an initial wariness they seemed to take to each other, and Hollie sat down to the scrapings of what was left in the pot, and a wedge of bread and cheese.

His back was aching. His wrist was aching. Still had the headache, though a drink went a long way to seeing that off. He probably should feel happy about being a part of this most glorious victory, though he didn't – Ward and Elliot were very merry indeed, and he gave the pair of them a stern glance, keep the bloody noise down, or we'll have Fairfax, Cromwell, and probably both over here to see what all the jollerfication's about. The Lincolnshire clay under his backside was cold, an autumn chill rising up from the earth, and he could well do without a night in a ditch, this time of year. Wanted his bed, and his wife in it. Would have given his immortal soul at that moment, for his own bed, and his own girl in it.

"Babbitt, tha's getting too old for this," he said to himself, then glanced, quite involuntarily, up at his father – sitting bolt upright and apparently perfectly comfortable, scowling intently at his Bible. Hollie straightened his aching shoulders and glared across the fire. In the firelight the old man's hair looked as russet as his own. The way Hollie felt at the moment, he probably looked the older of the two.

# 58 AN UNLIKELY FRIENDSHIP

"Somebody after you, captain," Percey said primly, suddenly touching Hollie on the shoulder and causing him to nearly choke on his breakfast. He glanced up, cocking an eyebrow, and said something indistinct round a mouthful of dry bread. Swallowed.

"What's he after?"

Percey shrugged. "Dunno. Sir. Well, not after you by name. He's down the horse lines. Brought Tyburn back, see, and he wants a word."

There was a ripple of badly-stifled amusement round the fire, and Hollie handed the remains of his breakfast to Percey with a sigh of resignation. "Oh, Christ, what's the benighted animal done *now*?"

So far this year Tib had struck up an unlikely friendship with his wife's elderly riding horse - resulting in Yaffingale's current interesting and expansive condition - lamed someone's incredibly well-bred chestnut gelding in a most undignified brawl in the horse-lines, and done more damage to the Army of Parliament than most of Charles Stuart's campaigns together. Not to mention his continual public feud with the other most distinctive horse in the Army, who just happened to belong to Hollie's commander. Percey - who kept a wary and respectful distance from both unpredictable ends, despite his great affection for the big horse - just shrugged. "Dunno, sir."

"*Bloody* horse," Hollie muttered. He always kept the black picketed separate, and there was always some well-meaning pillock who thought the stallion was lonely and neglected. The worst of it was that Hollie was sure that the horse had more of a sense of humour than many of the Army's high command, and acted according. He fully expected to find a further call for the black's castration or summary destruction.

Instead, he found the man inspecting his horse lines in the grey dawn like he owned the place - not like he'd find anything wrong with Hollie's troop, since Hollie had knocked it into his men, with the butt-end of a carbine if need be, that the first thing you did when your feet touched the floor when you dismounted was you looked to your horse. And once you'd looked it over for hurts, you groomed the beast till it was cool and comfortable and as you were brushing you let your hands do the inspecting, you checked for heat and swelling and bruising that you couldn't see, and once you were happy that your horse was sound then and not before did you look to your own comfort. Some of his equipment was a bit ramshackle, but it tended to be bodged for the beasts' comfort, and if it looked scruffy and it kept the horses happy, then Hollie didn't care that Wilding's chestnut had a wad of sheepskin under its noseband where it rubbed at an old scar else, or that Pettitt's Rosa had the better part of an old soldier's coat under her saddle to keep it from rubbing sores on her delicate thoroughbred skin. He took exception to this uninvited appraisal.

The man was bent under Calthorpe's mare's neck, and the mare did what she always did when anyone poked about under her belly, she lifted one shaggy foot like a dog offering a paw. And the cheeky sod actually took it, squatting down on his haunches to check her feet. Nodding with approval the while, like he expected something different.

Tyburn pricked his ears at Hollie and whickered a perfectly amiable greeting - which was more than the bugger underneath Delilah was like to get, the unmannerly swine. "Did you want summat particular?" Hollie inquired, just to make the stranger jump.

Delilah knocked the man's hat off and whuffled her nose over his rumpled hair. That mare was entirely indiscriminate in her affections. He straightened up, and the mare dropped her head on his shoulder as if they'd known each other for years, and the pair of them stood there with the man scratching her whiskery jaw and the patched mare leaning on him with a sleepy, silly look on her face.

Hollie raised his eyebrows. "Owt you wanted? Or just nosing around?" he prompted.

"Dear owd mawther, ent she?" the stranger said, and his Fenland drawl was even thicker than Drew Venning's. A good head shorter than Hollie, and about twice as wide through the shoulders even without the buff coat. Which looked as if he'd slept in it. And eaten his dinner in it, by the crumbs and the gravy stains on his linen. Oh Christ. He'd just cheeked Colonel Cromwell. He hadn't recognised him out of plate, off a horse, in the uncertain light – well, he hadn't expected the man to bring Tyburn back himself, not the bloody commander of the God-damned regiment running his own errands -

"Eep," Hollie said faintly, then gave himself a mental shake. "Calthorpe."

"Eh?"

"His mare." Because the less he actually said, the less likely he was to get himself into any more trouble. Even if it did make him sound slightly simple. Which, to be fair, Het said he was anyway. So all he had to do was -

Cromwell nodded, rubbing the mare's inquiring nose. "You want to sell that black?"

And he forgot he was trying to be tactful and respectful, because Lieutenant-General of Horse or not or not the bugger had just offered to buy Hollie's black horse, casually, like he was asking how much a tart charged – and there were a number of replies to mind, and he had enough sense of self-preservation to dismiss at least one out of hand, as a punch in the head often offends. "I hadn't considered it," Hollie said carefully. "But no, he isn't." And then his temper slipped, just a little bit, because that was Tyburn they were talking about, not just any old horse, but his Tib, and he added, "Not to you, not to anybody, and not at any price - do I make myself understood?"

Cromwell was nodding again. "Thought not, meself. If I had him I wouldn't think to sell him, either. Eh, lad, I have it in my heart to envy you that beast, though I pride myself on a lack of jealousy - " and then he grinned suddenly, "Two deadly sins in the one thought, lad, how's that for putting a godly man to the blush?"

He was still rubbing the mare's nose, whilst shamelessly eyeing Tyburn. Hollie was perilously close to pointing out that lust was a third one of the deadly sins, and that the way the man was eyeing that horse went beyond idle admiration and into a most unseemly desire.

"Does he breed true?"

"Never seen any of his siring, so I couldn't tell you," Hollie said truthfully. "First foal of his that I know if is due in the spring. I've had him since a two-year-old, but we never stopped in the same place long enough to put him to a mare." And then realised he was standing here in the mizzling dawn before most sane men were out of their blankets, talking to the rising star of the Parliamentarian cavalry like the pair of them were two horse-copers at a fair, with Percey a length behind him collapsed with laughter.

The colonel gave a deep sigh of heartfelt longing. "Before the Lord, lad, give me a dozen like him and I'd give you a troop of horse fit to give that tyrant a bloody nose." And then, suddenly, his grey-green eyes flashed - about the only handsome thing about him - "Let me try his paces, sir. Yesterday afternoon – sir, I tell you true, I have never known his like. Let me keep him – for the day, sir, only for the day, to try his paces in the light, on good ground –"

Hollie couldn't have been more astonished if the man had asked him to pimp his daughter - if he had one. "I - what - hardly, sir! No! Absolutely not!"

"I've a Barb mare of my own. Let me try your black's paces and the first foal's yours."

"You're out of your mind," Hollie said flatly, and prepared to turn away. Cromwell grabbed his wrist in a grip like a horse-bite.

"No, lad, but I've a dream. Imagine a company of horse with that blood in 'em, sir. Hast thou given the horse strength - hast thou clothed his neck with thunder? Give me my mare's desert fire and thy black's endurance -" he pushed his hair from his eyes with a grubby hand. "Let me take him, sir. For an hour, no more."

Hollie looked at his black. At the fact that the stallion was groomed, and rested, and sound, and had a tell-tale tidemark of apple around his muzzle where someone who was perhaps not as disciplinarian as the rumours suggested had been slipping him titbits. Looked at Colonel Cromwell, who they said was stern and upright and who was looking at the black stallion with an expression more usually seen on a lad eyeing up his best girl.

"Thee means to breed from my horse?" he said, leaning his elbow on the stallion's back in a proprietorial manner, while Tyburn investigated his pockets. "Tha reckons Friesland blood, for a cavalry mount?"

Cromwell joined him on the other side of the horse, picking up one of Tib's hooves and running an admiring hand down the length of the black's foreleg. "Friesland for his strength and for his nature –"

Percey had his fist in his mouth at this point and Hollie shot him a filthy look,

" - desert blood for speed and fire, and good stout English breeding for courage. What d'ee make of that, captain?"

"Reckon you'd get summat worth the having," he said thoughtfully. "He's big, though. I ent short, and he's – well."

Cromwell shrugged. "The Barb's not. She's hardly shoulder-high to him." The perverse horse submitted willingly to the colonel's attentions and didn't even try to bite him once. Those grey eyes didn't miss a trick. "You always ride him in a bitless bridle, sir?"

"Had his mouth tore to ribbons as a colt out in the Low Countries, before I had the keeping of him. He won't take a bit in his mouth." Hollie stood at the black's head and slipped a finger under the black's noseband, checking the fit, because he didn't care if the man had command of the whole of the cavalry, and he didn't care how offended Cromwell might be by his mistrust, Tyburn was his horse and there wasn't another soul living he'd have confidence in to tack the horse up. Then he straightened up and glared at the colonel. "I am not Tyburn's master, Colonel Cromwell. He don't own any man his master. And you try and put your spurs to him and he'll dump you on your arse. With all due respect. Sir. You can either work with him, and he'll do you proud, or you can try and force him to do summat he doesn't want to and he'll make a fool of you."

Cromwell's mouth twitched with unwilling humour. "Sounds like someone else I know, sir. Well, they did tell me you was touchy on your troop's honour, Captain, but I never thought to see you so tender for your horse's."

Hollie winced, as the heavy-set colonel heaved himself into the saddle.

"Big lad, ent he?" Cromwell said, beaming like a child on a holiday treat as he shortened the stirrups and took the reins in one hand. "I do reckon as how this is what it's like to ride a thunderstorm, lad." Slapped the black's arched neck, and Tyburn shook his mane in evident affront. "Now, my dark one, yesterday was business, now let's see what 'ee does for pleasure!"

Give the colonel credit, though, on the ground he looked like a bag of dirty laundry but on horseback he knew his business. Grinning all over his face as Tyburn bounced and shied and tossed his head and then settled to his work and stepped out like a parade horse. Hollie was torn between an unreasoning jealousy at seeing his horse handle so well under a stranger, and near-bursting with pride as he realized that there were others now stopping their work, drifting down to the lines to watch the black go through his paces. Watching Tib in his glory, and half-wondering if perhaps he should sell the horse to Cromwell after all, for there was no hope of the stallion ever using the half of these elegant paces in his work as a rough cavalry mount -

And then the black got bored with his elevation in the world, and with immense dignity and consideration dumped the colonel slithering down his shoulder and came back down the field at a most elegant trot, head up and tail high, stepping out like a heraldic beast to stand with his nose resting companionably on Hollie's shoulder. Cromwell heaved himself to his feet and stamped after the black, liberally spattered with mud and shaking with laughter. "Got bored wi' me, then?"

There wasn't an answer to that, so Hollie stood biting his lip and looking at the floor and trying not to laugh out loud. Tyburn flicked an ear at the colonel, politely acknowledging him, and edged just out of his reach.

"That's insubordination, horse," Cromwell said. "Never get promoted with that kind of attitude."

# 59 IN WHICH LUCE MEETS THE LORD'S ELECTED ERRAND-BOY

They'd done a little more of their scouring out, the next day, hunting Malignants in a leisurely fashion half across Lincolnshire, and Hollie was filthy, his creaky wrist aching like fire as he rubbed the black down. And he wasn't sure which of the two of them smelt the worse, him or Tib, but certainly neither was fit for company. There was a long, shallow cut across the horse's quarters, and he wasn't sure if it was a slash from a blade from yesterday or from a branch today: he touched the cut, carefully, and Tib flinched and side-stepped. Job for Het's marigold salve, then, though he wasn't sure she'd approve of her potions being used on his horse.

And while he was standing there looking at his horse's arse with a silly grin on his face, one of Cromwell's pet God-botherers had crept up on him. He had no idea why the colonel described his lot as a lovely company - he'd heard 'em described as a pack of horse-thieves and Anabaptists, himself. What they were, more's the pity, were well-disciplined, self-righteous, and superior. This one must have been all of the age of Luce Pettitt, with none of the charm. "What?" he said, without turning round.

"I seek Captain Babbitt," the young man said frigidly.

He remembered a very similar conversation on his first acquaintance with Luce, which had culminated in him smacking the lad briskly in the head. At two yards high, with cinnamon-brown hair worn halfway down his back and a conspicuous nose, Hollie Babbitt wasn't what you'd call the easiest man to mistake. "That be me, then," he said mildly, propping his other elbow on Tib's backside and swinging round to face the spotty youth with a half ton of solid Friesland stallion between them, and wondering if this one was a horse-thief or an Anabaptist. What he wasn't, clearly, was bright.

"Colonel Cromwell requests your attendance, captain."

"Oh, does he, now. Fair enough. I'll be along in a bit."

The young man – fat lad, for someone who'd presumably been on campaign rations for the best part of six months - stiffened with outrage. "Sir, Colonel Cromwell is not accustomed to being kept waiting -"

"And I'm not Colonel Cromwell's dog, mate. Now cut along and tell him I'll be up when I'm finished, seeing as you've appointed yourself as the Lord's elected errand boy for the day."

"This is sheer insolence, sir -"

"Oh, will you bugger off, sir. I've a horse to see to. After which Colonel Cromwell can have my undivided attention. Happy?" He rubbed briskly with his shirt sleeve at a spot on Tyburn's saddle, deliberately ignoring the lad. Who was refusing to go away. His rotund shadow was still lying resolutely across the ground at Hollie's feet. The black dropped his head with a blubbering snort and started to crop the grass. Holly could hear the lad's indignant breathing above the moist crunching of his horse's grazing.

"Is there a problem, Hollie?"

Luce ambled across from the rest of the troop's mounts, as elegant and amiable as if he was passing the salt at a dinner party. Even in somewhat worn shirt sleeves the brat managed to look neat and personable. Cromwell's errand boy stared at Luce as though he was the fiend incarnate, flushed scarlet, and turned on his heel. Fled back across the field, not quite running, but definitely going at a fast mince.

"What the hell was all that about?" Hollie said, shaking his head. "Funny little bugger -"

"Who," Luce said delicately, "was that?"

"Damned if I know. Feed 'em well in the Lovely Company, though, don't they - by, yon mon was in fine flesh, for a - Lucey, what is the matter with you?"

Luce swallowed visibly. "Nothing, captain, no, nothing is the matter. Would you like me to - to come with you -" he glanced up at the tubby little figure fleeing up the field - "to see the Colonel?"

"Er - no. You know what, Luce, no offence, mind, but if you're going to be as mental as his lot are, no, I don't reckon I do."

And dismissing the lot of them with a flip of his tangled ponytail, Hollie turned his attention to Tyburn. And when he'd satisfied himself that the black was mostly unharmed, bit bedraggled, but sound, then he thought he might have a little stroll over to the Lovely Company and see if they was as all as well-fed as Noll's tame errand boy. And if so, if they might have a bit left over. Having witnessed Colonel Cromwell's lack of attendance to personal grooming first hand, Hollie had every intention of going as he was, and if the bugger didn't like it - well, he could take his Barbary mare and find some other stud horse to stand her to, couldn't he?

He didn't take to Cromwell's horse lines, though, not one bit. Though, to be fair, each and every one of the beasts was well-maintained, happy, fit, sound. The bit that bothered him, somehow, was the tidiness of the whole operation. The way there weren't any troopers lurking about the place with their own mounts and a pocketful of purloined apples, or sitting about in untidy heaps mending bits of tack. As far as Holly could tell, there was no tack needed mending. Everything was neat, and square, each horse picketed the same distance apart. Wouldn't do for Hollie's lot, where the big grey Rabbit had hell on if he wasn't picketed next to Pettitt's Rosa, and you couldn't put Wilding's chestnut next to Eliot's white-faced bay or they fought like cats in a sack. And there wasn't a place here for loose cannon like Tyburn, he reckoned Tib would have to be broke or gelded before they could leave him tethered like this. Still. He put a hand out to the nearest horse.

"Step away from that beast!"

Oh, Christ, another of Noll's self-righteous minions. At least the ladylike fat one had the grace to blush. This one managed to look well-bred and contemptuous and Holly hated well-bred and contemptuous. It brought out the worst in him and God knows he didn't need any encouragement to act up. "What business have you here?"

Hollie turned round with his best bravo swagger, tossed his hair over his shoulder like the veriest street ruffian, and grinned. "Well now. Depends who's asking, don't it?"

And it always tickled him how touchy the sanctimonious were, if you questioned their authority. This one looked like someone had just kicked a poker up his arse, rearing back onto his heels and giving Hollie an outraged stare. Since he had to look up a good four inches to do it, the impact was somewhat diminished.

"Captain Margery," he hissed, his little moustaches trembling with fury.

"Margery?" Hollie echoed faintly. You couldn't make it up. "Some rotten bugger had you christened Margery? Christ, man, tell me who it was and I'll get 'em for you -"

"*Ralph* Margery," he said, bug-eyed with righteous fury, and it really didn't help Hollie's efforts to keep a straight face. Captain Margery took another step closer, his fists clenching. Hollie took a step backwards, partly because he didn't care for the smell of onions emanating from Captain Margery's breath, but mostly because if Margery wanted a fight he was going to bloody well get one. And if he thought Hollie was gentlemanly enough not to hit him with the water bucket that Providence had placed right under his nose, Margery was going to get a nasty surprise. He was also, probably, going to get wet.

"Delighted to make your acquaintance, Margery," Hollie said happily, edging against the bucket.

"Oh, in the name of all - Rosie, will you pack that in!" And that was a familiar voice, by God - cheerful and nasal and afflicted with the kind of Midland accent that made the speaker sound incurably stupid. Even when the speaker was Henry Ireton, who was assuredly not. He was grinning hugely. It was, just, possible he was both surprised and delighted to see Hollie Babbitt about to start a brawl in his horse lines.

"Captain Ireton, this is none of your affair!" - Margery was evidently seeing his prey escaping him. "Do you know this - this -"

"Know Rosie Babbitt? I should say! Captain Babbitt and I were with Essex in Windsor, were we not?" In case Margery didn't realize the long-standing nature of his comrade's acquaintance, Ireton draped a casual arm round Hollie's shoulders. "He's daft, Ralph," he added. "You don't want to get on the wrong side of our Rosie. You remember the lunatic what charged the guns at Edgehill - well, this is him. You gone respectable, then - long overdue, if you ask me?"

"Get stuffed," Hollie sniffed. To be fair, he had a soft spot for Ireton, who'd not only stood up for him in front of the Earl of Essex on more than one occasion, but who had a deceptively dry sense of humour and didn't mind who he used it on. There was a popular assumption that Henry Ireton was dour, humourless, godly, and stern. He was. Sometimes. Ireton was dutiful and conservative, that was right enough, but he was also, at core, a straight down the line decent lad. "One o' Fairfax's lads, me. And proud to be so, so don't start getting ideas in your head, for I find I don't much care for t'company hereabouts."

"If you're an officer - which I doubt, myself - why did you not make yourself known, instead of sneaking about our lines like a horse-thief? Answer me that!"

"Best ask the colonel, Margery, he's got form for sneaking round other folks' horse-lines himself. As it happens, I been asked special, so if you want to take exception to my presence, best take it up with Old Noll." He winked brazenly. "Personal invite, if you take my drift."

"Leave it, Madge," Ireton said warningly. "Come on, Rosie. Let's be having you." He didn't quite, drag Hollie away. The arm across his shoulders was deceptively powerful, though. Ireton gave him a sidelong look of utter despair. "I don't know what gets into you, at all. What's Madge ever done that you needs bait him -"

Hollie shrugged. "I *hate* people like that."

"I imagine he feels much the same about you! Truthfully – what are you up to, over here?"

"What I said. Colonel was poking round my troop before the fight, he had his eye on Tibs, I didn't have a clue who he was and I told him to pi - get lost. Reckons he's got a mare would benefit from Tibby's closer acquaintance - I do apologise, Captain Ireton, am I boring you?"

"Yes," Ireton said, honestly. "Enough horse talk. There are those in this company reckon Colonel Cromwell's wife probably has four legs and a tail. Although," he added primly, "I won't hear such talk in my presence."

"Oh, yes?" Hollie raised an eyebrow. "Heard about you and Mistress Cromwell, sir. Vision of womanly loveliness, is she?"

Ireton scowled at him. Unconvincingly, with a foolish grin lurking in his neatly-pointed beard. "I'll not countenance idle gossip, captain. My intentions towards Bridget are purely honourable."

"She doesn't look like her sire, I hope?"

"Er, no. Not a wen to be seen. That I know of. She might have dozens of the things, mind, under her shift -" he gave a rueful little shrug. "Wouldn't make no odds to me if she was warty like a toad, mind."

Hollie shook his head. "That is a *horrible* image."

# 60 LEAVEN TO GOOD WHEATEN DOUGH

Of course, now Ireton had put the thought in his head, he couldn't stop himself from looking at Colonel Cromwell's wens. The colonel was eating an apple and writing a letter simultaneously, to the detriment of both.

He waved a grubby hand at Hollie, in the vague direction of what was probably a stool underneath a shirt that was more darn than linen. "Sit down, sit down," he said indistinctly. "Have an apple. There's plenty -" he moved more papers around on his cluttered table-top - "Somewhere under here. I think."

He located one and tossed it across the tent. "Got to finish this letter to my wife before we tend to business," he said firmly. "Worries, if she don't hear from me at least every day."

Hollie took a bite of apple. Thought about it. "Haven't got a spare pen, have you?"

Unexpectedly, the colonel chuckled. "A proper trial, the fair sex, ent they? But get the right one and she is a comfort in thy adversity -"

"Wouldn't want to be the adversity that'd take on my wife, sir."

"Where is she, then?" Cromwell said conversationally, without looking up. His pen scratched across the paper.

"Essex. White Notley, near to Witham."

"But you're not an Essex man?"

"Er, no." Not with this accent. "No, I'm North Country born. Never guess, would thee?" He hadn't written much. Just enough to let her know he was alive. He'd be home before the winter set in, God willing. Well, he hadn't said all that - stick a piece of paper and a pen under his nose at that short notice and he'd just about time to limber up his rackety wrist, never mind think of all that

- but she was a bright lass, she'd work it out. The important thing was that he missed her, and that she still had him, whole and sane. Cromwell was eyeing him speculatively.

"Finished already, then? Good lad. Pass it here and it can go in with mine. That'll make the lil' mawther stare, when her letter comes in with an official seal?" He grinned, patted Holly's letter with a meaty paw. "Glad you're an Essex lad, then, even if only by marriage and not birth. Got family in Essex myself, 'bout twenty miles from you at Hatfield Broad Oak. Makes my job a sight easier, see. Give any thought to the Eastern Association, have you?"

There was a long silence. Carefully, Hollie looked down at his hands in his lap - tucked his crooked little finger back straight with the rest of his hand, momentarily stunned. "Eastern Association? Me? You mean -" he glanced warily at the open tent flap. "Me?"

"Well, not on your own, Captain Babbitt, no. Yes, you. And your men. Would you come?"

"Me?" Hollie said again. The words made sense - definitely in English - but the actual sense was evidently escaping him. The Colonel was beginning to look amused.

"No, lad, him sat behind you. I'll be straight with you, captain. I'd not care for your reputation, myself. All very well for them young bloods careering about the countryside raising all hell but you're getting too old for that sort of wildness now, sir. You're a respectable officer - "

Hollie looked down at his bloodstained cuff and back up at Cromwell, raising an eyebrow without so much as a flicker of a smile.

"Aye, man, I said respectable, and it's about time you started acting like it! You're no green youth to keep letting your temper get the better of you - you've a wife at home - hang it, you're a man of property! It's about time you faced up to your responsibilities, Captain Babbitt!"

"I'll not meddle with politics, sir," Hollie said stiffly.

"I think you'll find, captain, that politics is going to meddle with you. Whether you like it or no. And you can either fight alongside o' me, and be in the shaping of this war, or you can lie down and let His Majesty trample all over you and say thank 'ee for it like a good boy, afterwards. Now sit down, cos I ent finished with 'ee, not by a long chalk."

And it almost smoothed Hollie's bristling hackles that while his own voice had been freezing from its natural North Country burr into the glacial, professional, officerly tones that only came easy when he was on his mettle, Cromwell's accent was rapidly veering somewhere east of Ely and getting boggier by the minute. Just like Drew Venning's did when he was strongly moved - or pissed. It was oddly reassuring, like having the imperturbable Venning at his side. He straightened his shoulders and folded his hands neatly in his lap just like the old days, being disciplined as a boy - and he hated himself for doing it, too, but it was a natural response under the glare of those fierce grey eyes.

The colonel took a deep breath, shaking his head. "Eh, Hollie, Hollie, what to do with 'ee? Thee is a byword in the troops for recklessness and intemperacy - thee is arrogant, ungovernable, and willful. Thee cannot take a direct order without questioning - 'tis your way or no way, with you." He gave Hollie a rueful smile. "Were that all I had to say to 'ee, I'd box your ears and send you home. Above all creatures on this earth, sir, thee is faithful, from what I hear. Thee sees thy duty clear and will hold to it in the face of all, and that is most commendable - if," he added dryly, "not the most comforting company. No, Hollie, thee has thy faults, the Lord knows, but I cannot fault thy steadfastness. I have heard - from my lord Fairfax, as well as, somewhat more grudgingly, from my lord Essex - of thy conduct in battle , and seen it for my own eyes, that what thee wants in sense thee makes up for in fire. Well, I've put thee to the blush sufficient, captain, and I'll say no more. My own company is a good and respectable one, as you've seen for yourself, I think. A solid and most dependable band. Ireton thee knows already, I think, and he speaks well of you - and my own boy, Young Noll - he is, much as myself, you may take as you find. Nonetheless, even good wheaten dough needs its leaven."

Cromwell looked down his legendary nose, fixing Hollie with those piercing eyes. "Thy troop should not sit comfortably with my company, captain, yet could I take those ruffians of yours and make good plain fighting men with such spirits in them. And yet may such spirits give fire to my own troops, if the Lord wills it so, to the benefit of both. Thee is a good man, Captain Babbitt, but not, I think, a godly one, and yet I think thy poor restless soul seeks grace. Now. What is thy answer? Will thee join me, or no?"

# 61 COMFORT IN THY ADVERSITY

Hollie sat there blinking at that most scruffy and inspiring of commanders, periodically opening his mouth like some kind of benighted fish, and eventually came out with a feeble croak. It wasn't intended to be humorous, but it was tickling Old Noll, who was grinning behind his apple.

"First time I've heard of 'ee lost for words, lad!"

"It's a – kind – offer," he said eventually, warily.

"Nothing kind about it, captain. I ent so daft as to turn away a good weapon when the Lord puts it into my hand."

"What – *me*?"

Cromwell's grin broadened. "Not used to flattery, I take it. Good. That's what I like to hear. It was no coincidence that your lads stood alongside mine, Holofernes - it was the Lord's will –"

That unhelpful bit of Hollie that engaged temper and disengaged common sense flared into brief life – "It was nowt to do with God, and everything to do with Black Tom Fairfax. Sir."

"Ah, I forget thee is Fairfax's man."

"So far as I am anyone's but my own – aye, I am Fairfax's man." And realised with a very odd feeling that was half pride and half panic that it was true, and he was. "I – sir, I'd be honoured to fight with your men, don't think I'm not most sensible of the honour you do me, but – I could do wi' a bit of time to think it through."

"Sensible."

"Summat else they don't say about me very often, then." Something else they didn't say very often about Hollie Babbitt was that he was shy in company but he felt it now, awkward and shy and like a green lad set down in a room full of grown men and expected to hold his own. No Rackhay to hide behind. No Essex to blame. Cromwell didn't laugh. He carried on looking at Hollie, straight and serious, and then nodded.

"Can't wait that long for your answer, captain. I can give you a week to make your mind up." And then his undistinguished, homely face lit into a smile. "No more talking business, lad. Got a packet o' letters for your lot here – I been carrying 'em round o' me for about a week."

Hollie put his hand out for the bundle, feeling like a man who'd walked into a dream. Luce's mother – he recognised the neat, upright handwriting. One in Venning's badly-spelt scrawl. Two from Russell, both significantly stout and well-sealed. He didn't care about the rest. Opened one absently –

"Christ."

Cromwell scowled at him, and Hollie shook his head.

"Mistake. I shouldn't – it's not addressed to me – my – " he shook his head again, and the words still said the same thing. "Wrong Babbitt, sir. That's – he's – it was meant for my father. For the – for our – " he folded the page again. "Sons of bitches have got an eye to Bolton. Sorry. Begging your pardon. They – I don't know what he's going to say, colonel. I don't –"

"Bad news," Cromwell said, and it wasn't a question, and Hollie just looked at him stupidly.

"Aye, you could say that. Tha knows I'm Bolton-bred? Won't mean owt to thee but – " He ran a hand through his hair, tugged most of it loose from its loose ponytail, tossed it out of his face absently – "How the hell am I supposed to tell him? I were born there – mother died in that house – it's his bloody life. Up to the ars- earholes in bloody Malignants? It'll kill him."

"The Lord will comfort him in his adversity," Cromwell said consolingly, and for once Hollie never said a word, he just nodded. Only half listening, because half a year ago he'd confidently thought he couldn't care less if Drake Height burned to the ground and his father with it, and now he found that the thought of the home of his boyhood filled with a Royalist garrison – filthy bloody godless cavaliers, drinking and wenching and cursing in his bloody house – it felt like a violation, like one of them had laid ungentle hands on some part of his own hidden self.

# 62 NOTHING HID WHICH SHALL NOT BE MANIFESTED

“Trooper Babbitt.”

The old man’s head came up and Hollie still couldn’t quite stifle a shiver as those mad hawk-yellow eyes fixed on his face. “Thee would speak to me, boy?” Elijah said wonderingly, and he had a point, it wasn’t often Hollie went out of his way to find the old bastard, let alone engage him in conversation.

"Aye. *Privately*, Calthorpe, bugger off.”

Aaron Calthorpe inclined his head gravely and got up, closing the Bible that both men had been poring over as he went.

“Tha can leave that here, Aaron,” Hollie said wryly, and Elijah frowned at him. “I reckon I need to have a quick read of the Book of Job.”

“Is this your idea of wit, Holofernes –“

He handed over the letter. “Opened in error. I wasn’t thinking –“

“Thee often did not.”

Which he accepted. And then he sat with his eyes downcast as his father scanned the letter – more of it than Hollie had done, right to the end, his eyes travelling slowly over every word.

Then Elijah tossed the page to the ground. “Well, boy, at least Gatty has a roof over her head. For which small evidence of God’s mercy we must be grateful. And thee brought the filly away with thee.”

“Well, bugger me if I'm not grateful. Thy bloody housekeeper is become a Royalist whore and we managed to keep one horse out of forty. Truly we are fucking well blessed.”

“Two horses,” Elijah said absently. “Jezebel and my

own Asher –"

"Fucking marvellous. Turned out of thy own home by the Earl of fucking Derby –"

"Moderate thy language, Holofernes."

"Do you not care?"

"Care?" Elijah raised his eyes to Hollie's face again. "Care for what? That one of Derby's officers sees fit to quarter his troop in my –"

"*Our*," Hollie corrected him through his teeth.

"Our house? I'll not see Bolton again in this life, boy. They're welcome to it. And thee has thy own life to lead. I can't see thee coming back to live at Drake Height any time soon."

"Well, where the hell do *you* plan to go? When thee gets too bloody old and decrepit to tag after me?"

The old man shrugged. "The Lord will provide, Holofernes. By His grace I may yet die in the service of Parliament and save thee the trouble of concerning thisself any further."

"You are out of your fucking *mind*."

"No, boy, I am, as thee points out so regularly and with such affection, a worn-out owd man, and neither use nor ornament."

Hollie took a deep breath, to save himself from punching the obstinate old bastard in the head. Stood up. Looked back at the old man, sitting staring at that crumpled letter on the ground. "Want to take the lads back up north and scour the bastards out?" he said without thinking, and Elijah looked up – blinked – went to speak, and then stopped.

"What should thee care, boy?"

He was asking himself the same question. "I don't," he said. "Couldn't care less."

"But thee would lead the men back up north with no other end but to relieve Drake Height –"

"Of its unwelcome guests? I'll do owt for a scrap, father, you know that. Nothing to do with you personally.

Anyway, if I can get your house back, you might piss off and stop following me around."

Elijah was smiling his grim smile, and it was on the tip of Hollie's tongue to ask just what pleasure the old bastard was getting out of tagging up and down the countryside behind a son he couldn't stand the sight of, twenty years ago. And he wasn't sure he wanted an answer to that, not today, not with two stout packages addressed in Thankful Russell's hand tucked inside his shirt, not with his head and his heart and most of the bits between in a state of turmoil.

"I need to talk to you," Luce said, materialising out of thin air by the look of it no sooner Hollie had turned his back on his father. Seemed like everyone wanted to talk to Hollie today, the one day he couldn't wait to go and hole up somewhere and tear into his letters from home.

"Good. Is it necessary to do it now, or will it keep?"

"Now. I think."

"Bloody would be, wouldn't it?"

The brat flushed, the corners of his mouth turning down sulkily, and then as ever with Lucey Pettitt, he forgot he was supposed to be sulking two minutes later –"Are you all right, sir?"

"Aye. Probably. Get on with it, Luce. What?"

"It's that – that – that young man in the Lovely Company. The little one with the, the, the er – the plump one - she - he's not a man, sir -"

"Brat, if you've dragged me over here to indulge in idle tittle-tattle about a trooper in Cromwell's care that I neither know of nor give a bugger about – don't. I'm not in the mood. Is it important?"

"Not as such –"

"Fine. It will keep. Go and poke some bloody Malignants or something, Lucifer. I'm obviously not giving you enough to do."

Hollie stalked off, muttering to himself, cracking the seal – seals, plural, Russell had got a bit excited - first letter. Didn't bother reading Russell's scribble, wasn't interested in the Earl of Essex's gossip, he only cared what his girl was doing. "Lucey. *Lucey.* Lucifer come here. Now."

The brat was no more than ten yards away looking dejected, and turned on his heel and came back at a lolloping trot, all bright-eyed and eager like a good dog. "Read that," Hollie said, and Luce looked blank.

"What?"

"I think I'm going mental. I keep reading that and thinking my wife's told me she's - "

Luce looked, and gave Hollie one of his sweet, absolutely uncomprehending smiles. "In an interesting condition, sir. That is what she says. You, er, you sound surprised?"

"Surprised. Aye. You could say surprised. Brat – you're having me on, right? My lass – my Het – she's – she's expecting my –"

"That is the customary expectation of marriage, sir, the begetting of children. Er – congratulations, sir?"

"Aye, but – brat, she – me and her –" he hadn't got any more words, so he just grinned helplessly at his cornet. "I'm going to be a father, Lucey. God help the poor little whelp. Bloody hell."

"I am delighted, sir, of course, but –"

Hollie giggled. "Me. Rackhay would turn in his grave if he knew – Christ, me with a brood of my own, Luce, can you imagine? What d'you reckon – red hair or dark? Not bothered if it's a lass or a lad, so long as it don't take after me in the looks department and it's healthy – She'll hardly be showing yet, bless her. June to October – not long, is it? D'you think I ought to go home, Luce? Will she be all right if –"

"Sir. *Hollie.* Be at *peace*, sir – "

"Peace, Luce? Probably last I'll bloody know of it, with a babe at home –"

"Sir," Luce said, with a note of malicious relish in his

voice, "we are still at war, unless you think we should write to His Majesty and ask him to suspend hostilities until the safe arrival of your son." And then the lad grinned at his commander's outraged expression. "D'you remember saying that to me?"

"Not the same thing, Lucifer, not the same thing at all. You were just after getting your leg over –" the brat flushed, clearly still touchy on the subject of his lusty widow at Edgehill – "anyway, it might not be a lad. Not sure I want to read the other letter, brat. Might be Het saying it was a mistake. Bloody hell, lad, I don't know if I'm coming, going or been – "

"Let's hope my lord Newcastle stays put, then," Luce said drily.

"Got to tell Fairfax. Bugger. Got to tell Cromwell as well – ah, Christ, Luce, talk about serendipity, that's got me out of a bit of a fix. We'll be going with the Eastern in the spring. Don't mind, do you? Good lad." Patting Luce absently on the shoulder, Hollie wheeled about – unfolded his letter again –and wandered off whistling, narrowly avoiding a collision with Aaron Calthorpe.

# 63 OUR FRIENDS IN THE NORTH

"I thought it was bad news from ho – from up North," Calthorpe said, eyebrows raised.

"It depends on your point of view," Luce said. "There are some might say that news of a new Babbitt on the way is very bad tidings indeed."

Calthorpe said nothing. He only smiled.

Elijah Babbitt, on the other hand, did have a contribution to make. "The boy did not tell me?" he said, and there was a note in his voice that made both men look awkwardly away. "Lucifer, thee knew of this – and my son said nowt to me? To his father?"

"To a fellow officer," Luce said stiffly. "He – the captain – he spoke to me as a fellow officer. No more."

"He'd only just heard the news, 'Lijah. Give him time, man."

Elijah shoved rudely past the pair of them, following his son, and then changed direction and veered off towards the horse lines.

"That was not well done," Calthorpe said absently, his eyes on the captain's distinctive russet hair as the big redhead made his way back towards Fairfax's encampment.

Luce let his breath out in a great sigh, blowing the loose hair out of his eyes. "No. Well. You know how he is."

"Aye, and I thought he'd learned kindness in your company, Lucifer." Luce flushed and looked at his boots. "Did he tell thee that the Earl of Derby's garrisoned a troop at his father's house?"

"What?"

"He didn't, then. Aye. Well. There's them as might say the property of a most notorious rebel should be forfeit when he takes up arms against his rightful king, especially when t'rebel's boy is a senior officer in the Army of Parliament. Me, I reckon that any Malignant who can sleep easy of a night up at Drake Height, is a man wi' no conscience."

"I'm sorry, Trooper Calthorpe, I don't –"

Calthorpe sighed. "Lad, there are times when I think thee might be nobbut ninepence in the pound. What d'you reckon the Earl of Derby's lads are going to' leave of that house, when they're done wi' it? You reckon they're going to be mindful that 'Lije has got nowheres else to go, no family but that awkert addle-yedded gret crayter –"

"That awkward great creature is your commanding officer, trooper," Luce murmured, biting his lip.

"Aye. Well. No doubt. All I can say, then, is if he can see the owd mon turned out to starve by them naughty Malignants, he ought to be ashamed. And I'll not say I've always seen eye to eye with 'Lije, but he done the best he could, and – will you speak to him, Luce? Thee wouldn't see the owd mon left without a roof over his head, at his time of life – he might listen to thee."

# 64 THE ROAD HOME

It just never seemed like the right time, what with Hollie ambling about in a happy daze for half the time and as edgy as a cat for the rest. Freely admitting that he was currently less than useless as a commanding officer, but since they were presently in that happy state of waiting for something to happen as the days shortened and the autumn died into winter, Hollie distracted wasn't the worst thing in the world - and Luce in charge was better than it was last time

Black Tom - that good-hearted, deceptively dour-looking commander - had said Hollie could take leave as soon as the Army moved to winter quarters. Fairfax been thrilled at the prospect of a new infant in the ranks, to the extent where he'd written to Lady Nan at home asking her if any of little Moll's tiny baby caps and gowns were still fit for service.

Luce thought the whole thing was no doubt thrilling and sweet and all the rest of it, but - really, one babe was much the same as another. He had one nephew already. And he still thought the idea of Auntie Het and that scruffy, distracted object sitting opposite him with one elbow on the table, peering at dispatches and eating a doorstep of bread and honey - breeding - it was nothing short of indecent. A little more attention to his military duty, and a little less to his marital ones, might not come amiss, Luce thought primly: looked up from his supper, and met Hollie's eye. Was reminded, not for the first time, that Hollie was neither so old nor so malevolent as he liked to pretend to be.

"Hollie?"

"Mm?" Not distracted - just not listening.

"What are you going to do about your - uh, about Trooper Babbitt?"

"Knock him on the head and bury him in a ditch." Not

even that distracted, either.

"No, seriously. When we go to winter quarters. Where's he going to go?"

"How the hell should I know? To hell in a handcart, for all I care."

"But he's your -"

"I like you, Lucey. I've got a deal of respect for you as a fellow officer and as a man. On the other hand, if you don't keep your long nose out of my business, you may rapidly find yourself transferred to one of the Scots regiments. In Scotland. Bloody cold in Scotland, Lucey, and full of bare-arsed barbarians. And if you think I don't speak proper English, brat, you want to try keeping your end of the conversation up with them buggers. They'd like you, our Luce. Most o't' Scotsmen I've met think I'm a great mard southern bastard. They'd like you a lot." He grinned at Luce, not particularly amicably. "Make a man of you, mind. Now. The old bastard is big enough and ugly enough to make his own arrangements. Not my problem."

But Elijah wasn't making any arrangements at all, that was what bothered Luce. Elijah was doing nothing. Elijah rarely left his quarters, not even to sit with Calthorpe, that other old Dissenter, arguing the finer points of the Old Testament. He just sat, staring at nothing, or at his son, until as often as not Hollie would get up and slam out of the room, and then Elijah would go back to looking at nothing.

October dragged on into the grey ember-days of November, and then finally, it was official, they were at winter quarters: Hull was going to be their home until the spring, those who had nowhere else to go. Long, dreary days looking out over the slaty dark waters of the Humber, watching the mist creep up the river - "Drinking yourselves insensible with bloody Rainsborough, no doubt," Hollie said, yanking the black horse's girth tight with what Luce thought was unnecessary vigour. Judging by Tyburn's affronted snort, he thought it was unnecessary, too.

"*Me*? Hardly. He's your mate, not mine," Luce sniffed.

"Oh aye, bosom companions, me and Rainsborough - every time I see him I end up puking my guts up."

"I did warn you about the ale in the Golden Lion!"

"Aye, well, it was the pie that did it, brat. It was not a bad pint."

"No, I believe it was several bad pints, captain. And if that's your idea of wetting the baby's head then the Lord help us all when the poor child is born - they'll be fetching you home in a wheelbarrow."

Hollie grinned, and then tried to look dignified and sober. Which he had assuredly not been after what had started out as a quiet celebratory drink in a quiet, respectable inn with Thomas Rainsborough, and had ended with Hollie not worth talking to for three days, Rainsborough's seaman's bonnet hanging at half-mast underneath the troop colours, and Black Tom Fairfax giving the pair of them the dressing-down of their lives for such raucous public behaviour, unbefitting of two senior officers in the Army of Parliament. On balance, Hollie agreed that trying to ride his horse into the tap-room of the Golden Lion had been an ill-conceived idea. However - Rainsborough had bet Tyburn wouldn't do it. Hence the seaman's bonnet on the troop colours, because by that point in the evening neither of them had had a penny to bless themselves with.

Luce had no room to talk, anyway. Hollie had been called out more than once in his time to whisk the brat home in some rare states. Just that Luce didn't get caught trying to get a sixteen-hand battle-trained warhorse under the low beams of a busy tavern.

"I'm a respectable family man, Lucifer," he said primly.

"Of course you are, sir. In White Notley."

"Shut up, brat. Right. Good to go. You ready? - oh, Christ, what does *he* want?"

Elijah was standing in the doorway. Despite the fact

that the sun was barely a streak of scarlet over the horizon, and the stable yard was wet and black with the thin rain of another grey mizzling dawn, he was fully dressed, shaved, combed.

"Thee is going - to Essex, boy?"

"I am going home," Hollie corrected, and Luce flinched at the coldness in his voice.

Elijah nodded. And held out his hand. Hollie shied off as though his father had offered him a burning brand. "What's that?"

"Thee was a fretful child, Holofernes. I thought - I wondered - if the child is owt like thee, he - might save thee a few sleepless nights, boy."

"Trying to buy me again, sir? Thee is beyond contempt. Lucifer. Mount up. I don't care for the company round here."

Luce gave his commanding officer a disgusted look, left the mare's reins hanging and took the little parcel from Elijah's outstretched hand. "A string of corals," he said. "Hardly the gold of the Indies, Captain Babbitt."

Luce glanced up at Elijah and was astonished to see a flicker of humour on the trooper's dour face. "I reckon even thee sets thy worth higher than that, boy."

"I still don't want it," Hollie said flatly, pulled the black horse's I head up, and set off out of the stable yard at a fast trot.

Luce sighed. "I'm sorry," he said.

"Best get after him." Elijah nodded. "Bid thee Godspeed, Luce, and - " his scraggy throat worked, "have an eye to the lad, will tha? And when tha comes back - tell me about the child."

Luce put the soft parcel inside his doublet. "I'll do better than that, trooper. His wife is my aunt, remember. I will see to it myself that the child has his corals. Auntie Het won't put up with his -" and then stopped, blushing, and quickly mounted his mare. "Sergeant Cullis is a most experienced officer, if you need - I'll make sure I write - "

he took a hand off the reins, tucked his hair awkwardly behind one ear. "What - what will you do, till the spring, trooper?"

"Pray," Elijah said, with a shrug. "Pray for the lass's safe delivery."

And Luce swallowed hard, remembering the absence of a mother in that bleak farm on the edge of the Lancashire moors. Yes, he imagined that Elijah would pray for Het Babbitt. "God bless you and keep you, Trooper Babbitt," he said, with more fervour than was customary. And then he set the mare cantering after his commanding officer.

"What kept you? Talking to that poisonous old bastard?" Hollie said irritably.

"Making last-minute arrangements."

"Oh aye. Don't play silly buggers with me, Lucey." They rode in silence for a few minutes. "He must think I'm bloody simple. Oh, here's your corals, lad, what I have sentimentally kept for the last thirty years, with me being such a doting father –" he spat, with more venom than accuracy, into the dry yellow grass that rustled at the side of the road. "Christ, he makes me sick."

Luce fished inside his doublet and pulled out the parcel. "I believe these are new, sir. They do not appear to have been – chewed."

"So he's gone out and bought me some pathetic little trinket. Ha. Like he thinks he can buy my favour. *Ha*." Hollie wheeled his horse. "I suppose I'm supposed to feel sorry for the old bastard, am I? Spending the wettest winter since the Flood wi' the damp playing hell with his rheumatics, neither chick nor child within a week's ride and not a friendly face for miles. Well, I hope the old bastard starves – we left Davies behind, didn't we? He can cook -"

"Moggy? No, Moggy left for Herefordshire last week."

"Might have to do his own cooking, then, and I hope it chokes him. Calthorpe's around –"

"Gone to spend the winter at his daughter's in

Burnley."

"Christ, brat, who've we left?"

Luce shrugged. "Witless – Witcombe, you've got me at it – gone up to his parents in London. I think he was talking about going back to his master's practice for a month or so. The lad's not a bad surgeon, for a –"

"Fat lad, aye. Who else?"

"Eliot and Ward, God knows. Up to no good, wherever it is. They'll turn up. More's the pity. The Lord does not favour us that far. Um – Percey, you know about Percey –"

"Probably in Essex by now," Hollie grumbled. "Sat in the kitchen with my wife making a fuss of him, the little –"

"You sent him on ahead, sir!"

"Aye, well, I wanted to give her a bit o' notice, people keep telling me breeding women get these fancies. Them lollopin' Westons have gone back to Bristol, I know that. Christ. It's just bloody Cullis, isn't it?"

"And one or two others. Yes."

"Be hell of a lonely, stuck out here for the next few months, wouldn't it?" Hollie said musingly. "I'd go mental. I would – I'd go stark staring mad, stuck in this bloody hole."

Luce sighed. "Shall I go back and fetch him, sir? I should not like to have Trooper Babbitt's – sanity on my conscience."

Hollie glared at him. "Give us them bloody beads." Looked critically at the string of coral and silver beads in his hand. "Must have cost him a few bob. You'd have thought the old bastard might have been better served spending it on taking care of himself, the stupid old sod. I've seen better cared-for dogs in the street. I'll not have him showing me up, Lucifer, I'd not put it past the old bastard to starve himself to death or summat just to shame me. Fetch him. And tell him it's a god-damned order."

# ABOUT THE AUTHOR

M J Logue is a trained archivist and literature graduate who lived in York overlooking the Ouse for five years, studying in the archives of York Minster by day and cleaning the school by night. Her interest in the seventeenth century began when she lived next door to a ruined manor on the edge of the Peak National Park, as a result of which she wrote her first novel aged 15. She now lives with her husband, son and three cats in West Cornwall.

Follow the adventures of Hollie, Luce, Cullis, Russell and the rest of the rebel rabble in
Red Horse: An Uncivil War 1 (1642)
A Wilderness of Sin: An Uncivil War 3 (1645)
and coming soon
The Smoke of Her Burning: An Uncivil War 4 (1644)
Stay in touch with the author for news, giveaways, previews, Luce's bad poetry and the occasional 17th century recipe at

www.uncivilwars.blogspot.co.uk

or on Twitter

http://twitter.com/Hollie_Babbitt

Printed in Great Britain
by Amazon